W9-CRV-617

NEW YORK TIMES BESTSELLING AUTHOR

LINDSAY McKENNA

USA TODAY BESTSELLING AUTHOR

MERLINE LOVELACE

THE ROGUE
&
A MAN OF HIS WORD

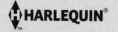

ISBN-13: 978-1-335-00691-2

The Rogue & A Man of His Word

Copyright © 2019 by Harlequin Books S.A.

The publisher acknowledges the copyright holders of the individual works as follows:

The Rogue
Copyright © 1993 by Lindsay McKenna

A Man of His Word
Copyright © 1999 by Merline Lovelace

Recycling programs for this product may not exist in your area.

Printed in U.S.A.

www.Harlequin.com

CONTENTS

Lindsay McKenna is proud to have served her country in the US Navy as an aerographer's mate third class—also known as a weather forecaster. She was a pioneer in the military romance subgenre and loves to combine heart-pounding action with soulful and poignant romance. True to her military roots, she is the originator of the long-running and reader-favorite Morgan's Mercenaries series. She does extensive hands-on research, including flying in aircraft such as a P3-B Orion sub-hunter and a B-52 bomber. She was the first romance writer to sign her books in the Pentagon bookstore. Visit her online at lindsaymckenna.com.

Visit the Author Profile page
at Harlequin.com for more titles.

THE ROGUE

Lindsay McKenna

Prologue

"Killian, your next assignment is a personal favor to me."

Morgan Trayhern was sitting with his friend and employee in a small Philipsburg, Montana, restaurant. The situation with Wolf Harding and Sarah Thatcher had been successfully wrapped up, and now it was time to pack up and go home. Morgan grimaced apologetically, as Killian's features remained completely closed, only a glitter in his hard, intelligent blue eyes suggesting possible interest.

Morgan picked up a fork and absently rotated it between his fingers and thumb. They'd already ordered their meals, so now was as good a time as any to broach the topic. "Look," he began with an effort, purposely keeping his voice low, "whether I want to or not, I'm going to have to put you on an assignment involving a woman, Killian."

Killian sat relaxed, his long, spare hands draped casually on his thighs as he leaned back in the poorly padded metal chair. But anyone who knew him knew he was never truly relaxed; he only gave that appearance. He stared guardedly at Morgan. "I can't."

Morgan stared back, the silence tightening between them. "You're going to have to."

Killian eased the chair down and placed his hands on the table. "I told you—I don't deal with women," he said flatly.

"At least hear me out," Morgan pleaded.

"It won't do any good."

Exhaustion shadowed Morgan's gray eyes. "Just sit there and listen."

Killian wrestled with an unexpected surge of panic that left a bitter taste in his mouth. He held Morgan's gaze warningly, feeling suddenly as if this man who had been his friend since their days in the French Foreign Legion had become an adversary.

Morgan rubbed his face tiredly. "The assignment deals with Laura's cousin from her mother's side of the family," he began, referring to his wife, who'd managed to befriend Killian—at least as much as Morgan had ever seen him allow. "This is important to me—and to Laura—and we want to know that you're the one handling the situation. It's personal, Killian."

Killian's scowl deepened, and his mouth thinned.

"Laura's cousin, Susannah Anderson, came to visit us in D.C." Morgan's eyes grew dark and bleak. "From what we've been able to piece together, on the way home, Susannah was at the bus station in Lexington, Kentucky, when a man came up and started a conversation with her. Moments later, he was shot right in front of her eyes. We think Susannah saw the murderer, Killian—and he shot her, too, because she was a witness. The bullet hit her skull, cracked it and exited. By some miracle, she doesn't have brain damage, thank God. But the injury's swelling left her in a coma for two months. She regained consciousness a month ago, and I was hoping she could give us a lead on her attacker, but she can't remember what he looked like. And another thing, Killian—she can't talk."

Morgan rubbed his hands together wearily, his voice heavy with worry. "The psychiatrists are telling me that the horror of the experience is behind her inability to speak, not brain damage. She's suppressed the whole incident—that's why she can't describe the killer. Laura went down and stayed with Susannah and her family in Kentucky for a week after Susannah was brought home from the hospital, in hopes that she'd find her voice again." Morgan shrugged. "It's been a month now, and she's still mute."

Killian shifted slightly, resting his hands on the knees of his faded jeans. "I've seen that mute condition," he said quietly, "in some of the children and women of Northern Ireland."

Morgan opened his hands in a silent plea to Killian to take the assignment. "That's not the whole story, Killian. I need you to guard Susannah. There's evidence to indicate that the killer will go after Susannah once he finds out she survived. I think Susannah was an innocent bystander in a drug deal gone bad, but so far we don't know enough to point any fingers. Susannah's memory is the key, and they can't risk her remembering the incident.

"Susannah was under local police guard at the Lexington hospital while she was there, and I had one of my female employees there, too. Since her release, I've told Susannah to stay on her parents' fruit farm in the Kentucky hills. Normally she lives and works down in the small nearby town of Glen, where she teaches handicapped children."

Morgan grasped the edge of the table, and his knuckles were white as he made his final plea. "She's family, Killian. Laura is very upset about this, because she and Susannah are like sisters. I want to entrust this mission to my very best man, and that's you."

Glancing sharply at his boss, Killian asked, "I'd be a bodyguard?"

"Yes. But Susannah and her parents aren't aware of the possible continued threat to her, so I don't want them to know your true capacity there. They're upset enough after nearly losing their daughter. I don't want to stress them more. Relaxation and peace are crucial to Susannah's recovery. I've contacted her father, Sam Anderson, and told him you're a friend of mine who needs some convalescence. Sam knows the type of company I run, and has an inkling of some of the things we do. I told him you were exhausted after coming in off a long-term mission and needed to hole up and rest."

Killian shrugged. The story wasn't too far from the truth. He hardened his heart. "I never take assignments involving women, Morgan."

"I know that. But I need you for this, Killian. On the surface, this assignment may look easy and quiet, but it's not. Stay on guard. I'm trying to track the drug deal right now. All our contacts in South America are checking it out, and I'm working closely with the Lexington police department. There's a possibility it could involve Santiago's cartel."

Killian's jaw clenched at the name of José Santiago,

the violent Peruvian drug kingpin they'd finally managed to extradite and get behind bars.

Morgan gave Killian a pleading look. "Susannah's already been hurt enough in this ordeal. I don't want her hurt further. I worry that her family could become a target, too."

Cold anger wound through Killian as he thought about the mission. "Picking on a defenseless woman tells you the kind of slime we're dealing with."

Morgan gave Killian a probing look. "So will you take this assignment?"

Morgan knew that Killian's weakness, his Achilles' heel, was the underdog in any situation.

"One more thing," Morgan warned as he saw Killian's eyes thaw slightly. "Susannah isn't very emotionally stable right now. Her parents are Kentucky hill people. They're simple, hardworking folks. Sam owns a two-hundred-acre fruit farm, and that's their livelihood. Susannah ought to be in therapy to help her cope with what happened to her. I've offered to pay for it, but she's refusing all help."

"Frightened of her own shadow?" Killian asked, the face of his sister, Meg, floating into his memory.

Morgan nodded. "I want you to take care of Susannah. I know it's against your guidelines for a job, but my instincts say you're the right person to handle this situation—and her."

His own haunted past resurfacing, tugging at his emotions, Killian felt his heart bleed silently for this woman and her trauma. Avoiding Morgan's searching gaze, he sat silently for a long time, mulling over his options. Finally he heaved a sigh and muttered, "I just can't do it."

"Dammit!" Morgan leaned forward, fighting to keep

his voice under tight control. "I *need* you, Killian. I'm not *asking* you to take this assignment, I'm *ordering* you to take it."

Anger leaped into Killian's narrowed eyes, and his fist clenched on the table's Formica top as he stared at Morgan. "And if I don't take this assignment?"

"Then, whether I like it or not, I'll release you from any obligation to Perseus. I'm sorry, Killian. I didn't want the mission to come down to this. You're the best at what we do. But Susannah is part of my family." His voice grew emotional with pleading. "Whatever your problem with women is, put it aside. I'm begging you to help Susannah."

Killian glared at Morgan, tension radiating from him, every joint in his usually relaxed body stiff with denial. He *couldn't* protect a woman! Yet, as he stared at Morgan, he knew that if he didn't take the assignment his boss would release him from his duties with Perseus, and the money he made was enough to keep Meg reasonably well-off. If he hadn't come to work for Perseus, he'd never have been able to free her from the financial obligations brought on by her tragedy.

His need to help his sister outweighed the risk of his own pain. The words came out harshly, bitten off: "I'll do the best I can."

Relief showed on Morgan's taut features. "Good. My conscience is eating me alive on this situation, Killian. But this is the only way I can make amends to Susannah for what's happened. She was innocent—in the wrong place at the wrong time."

"I'll leave right away," Killian rasped as he took the voucher and airline ticket Morgan proffered. No use putting off the inevitable. He'd pick up his luggage at the motel across from the restaurant and get under way. No longer hungry, he rose from the booth. Morgan appeared grateful, but that didn't do anything for him. Still angry over Morgan's threat to fire him, Killian made his way outside without a word. Walking quickly, he crossed the street to the motel, his senses as always hyperalert to everything around him.

What kind of person was this Susannah Anderson? Killian wondered. He'd noticed Morgan's voice lower with feeling when he'd spoken about her. Was she young? Old? Married? Apparently not, if she was staying with her parents. A large part of him, the part that suffered and grieved over Meg, still warned him not to go to Kentucky. His soft spot for a woman in trouble was the one chink in his carefully tended armor against the pain this world inflicted on the unwary.

Yet, as he approached the motel on this hot Montana summer morning, Killian felt an oblique spark of interest that he hated to admit. Susannah was a melodic name, suggestive of someone with sensitivity. Was she? What color was her hair? What color were her eyes? Killian could read a person's soul through the eyes. That ability to delve into people, to know them inside out, was his greatest strength. On the flip side, he allowed no one to know him. Even Morgan Trayhern, who had one of the most sophisticated security companies in America, had only a very thin background dossier on him. And Killian wanted it kept that way. He wanted no one to know the extent of the pain he carried within him—or what he'd done about it. That kind of information could be ammunition for his enemies—and could mean danger to anyone close to him. Still, his mind dwelled on the enigmatic Susannah Anderson. She could be in more danger with

Killian around than from any potential hit man. Why couldn't Morgan understand that? Killian hadn't wanted to tell Morgan his reasons for refusing to take assignments involving women; he'd never told anyone. A frown worked its way across his brow. Susannah had been a victim of violence, just like Meg. More than likely, she was afraid of everything.

Arriving at his motel room, Killian methodically packed the essentials he traveled with: a long, wicked-looking hunting knife, the nine-millimeter Beretta that he wore beneath his left armpit in a shoulder holster, and his dark brown leather coat.

When he'd placed a few other necessary items in a beat-up leather satchel, Killian was ready for his next assignment. He'd never been to Kentucky, so he'd have a new area to explore. But whether he wanted to or not, he had to meet Susannah Anderson. The thought tied his gut into painful knots. Damn Morgan's stubbornness! The woman was better off without Killian around. How in the hell was he going to handle his highly volatile emotions, not to mention her?

Chapter 1

"We're so glad you've come," Pansy Anderson gushed as she handed Killian a cup of coffee and sat down at the kitchen table across from him.

Killian gave the woman a curt nod. The trip to Glen, Kentucky, and from there to the fruit farm, had passed all too quickly. However, the Andersons' warm welcome had dulled some of his apprehension. Ordinarily, Killian spoke little, but this woman's kindness made his natural reticence seem rude. Leathery-looking Sam Anderson sat at his elbow, work-worn hands clutching a chipped ceramic mug of hot black coffee. Pansy, who appeared to be in her sixties, was thin, with a face that spoke of a harsh outdoor life.

As much as Killian wanted to be angry at everyone, he knew these people didn't deserve his personal frustration. Struggling with emotions he didn't dare explore,

Killian whispered tautly, "I'm glad to be here, Mrs. Anderson." It was an utter lie, but still, when he looked into Pansy's worn features he saw relief and hope in her eyes. He scowled inwardly at her reaction. He couldn't offer hope to them or to their daughter. More likely, he presented a danger equal to the possibility of the murderer's coming after Susannah. Oh, God, what was he going to do? Killian's gut clenched with anxiety.

"Call me Pansy." She got up, wiping her hands on her red apron. "I think it's so nice of Morgan to send you here for a rest. To tell you the truth, we could sure use company like yours after what happened to our Susannah." She went to the kitchen counter and began peeling potatoes for the evening meal. "Pa, you think Susannah might like the company?"

"Dunno, Ma. Maybe." Sam's eyes became hooded, and he stared down at his coffee, pondering her question. "My boy, Dennis, served with Morgan. Did he tell you that?"

"No, he didn't."

"That's right—in Vietnam. Dennis died up there on that hill with everyone else. My son sent glowing letters back about Captain Trayhern." Sam looked up. "To this day, I've kept those letters. It helps ease the pain I feel when I miss Denny."

Pansy sighed. "We call Susannah our love baby, Killian. She was born shortly after Denny was killed. She sure plugged up a hole in our hearts. She was such a beautiful baby…"

"Now, Ma," Sam warned gruffly, "don't go getting teary-eyed on us. Susannah's here and, thank the good Lord above, she's alive." Sam turned his attention to Killian. "We need to warn you about our daughter. Since she came back to us from the coma, she's been actin' awful strange."

"Before the tragedy," Pansy added, "Susannah was always such a lively, outgoing young woman. She's a teacher over at the local grade school in Glen. The mentally and physically handicapped children are her first love. She used to laugh, dance, and play beautiful music." Pansy gestured toward the living room of the large farmhouse. "There's a piano in there, and Susannah can play well. Now she never touches it. If she hears music, she runs out of the house crying."

"And she don't want anything to do with anyone. Not even us, much of the time," Sam whispered. He gripped the cup hard, his voice low with feeling. "Susannah is the kindest, most loving daughter on the face of this earth, Killian. She wouldn't harm a fly. She cries if one of Ma's baby chicks dies. When you meet her, you'll see what we're saying."

"The violence has left her disfigured in a kind of invisible way," Pansy said. "She has nasty headaches, the kind that make her throw up. They come on when she's under stress. She hasn't gone back to teach, because she hasn't found her voice yet. The doctors say the loss of her voice isn't due to the blow on her head."

"It's mental," Sam added sadly.

"Yes… I suppose it is…" Pansy admitted softly.

"It's emotional," Killian rasped, "not mental." He was instantly sorry he'd spoken, as both of them gave him a strange look. Shifting in his chair, Killian muttered, "I know someone who experienced something similar." Meg had never lost her voice, but he'd suffered with her, learning plenty about emotional wounds. He saw the relief in their faces, and the shared hope. Dammit, they shouldn't hope! Killian clamped his mouth shut and scowled deeply, refusing to meet their eyes.

Pansy rattled on, blotting tears from her eyes. "You understand, then."

Pansy gave him a wobbly smile and wiped her hands off on the towel hanging up on a hook next to the sink. "We just don't know, Killian. Susannah writes us notes so we can talk with her that way. But if we try and ask her about the shooting she runs away, and we don't see her for a day or two."

"She's out in the old dilapidated farmhouse on the other side of the orchard—but not by our choice," Sam offered unhappily. "That was the old family homestead for over a hundred years 'fore my daddy built this place. When Susannah came home from the hospital last month, she insisted on moving into that old, broken-down house. No one's lived there for twenty years or more! It's about half a mile across the hill from where we live now. We had to move her bed and fetch stuff out to her. Sometimes, on a good day, she'll come join us for supper. Otherwise, she makes her own meals and stays alone over there. It's as if she wants to hide from the world—even from us…"

Killian nodded, feeling the pain that Pansy and Sam carried for their daughter. As the silence in the kitchen became stilted, Killian forced himself to ask a few preliminary questions. "How old is Susannah?"

Sam roused himself. "Going on twenty-seven."

"And you say she's a teacher?"

A proud smile wreathed Pansy's features as she washed dishes in the sink. "Yes, she's a wonderful teacher! Do you know, she's the only member of either of our families that got a college degree? The handi-

capped children love her so much. She taught art class."
With a sigh, Pansy added, "Lordy, she won't paint or
draw anymore, either."

"Nope," Sam said. "All she does is work in the orchard, garden and tend the animals—mostly the sick
ones. That's what seems to make her feel safe."

"And she goes for long walks alone," Pansy added. "I
worry. She knows these hills well, but there's this glassy
look that comes into her eyes, Killian, and I sometimes
wonder if she realizes where she's at."

"Have there been any strangers around, asking about
Susannah?" Killian asked offhandedly. Now he understood why Morgan didn't want to tell these gentle, simple people the truth of the situation. But how the hell
was he going to balance everything and keep a professional attitude?

"Oh," Pansy said with a laugh, "we get lots of folks
up here to buy our fruits, nuts and fresh garden vegeta-
bles. And I'm known for my healin' abilities, so we always have folks stoppin' by. That's somethin' Susannah
took to—using herbs to heal people with. She's a good
healer, and the hill folk, if they can't get to me because
I'm busy, they'll go to Susannah. We have a huge herb
garden over by the old homestead, and she's making our
medicines for this year as the herbs are ready for pickin'."

"That and using white lightning to make tinctures
from those herbs." Sam chuckled. And then he raised his
bushy eyebrows. "I make a little corn liquor on the side.
Strictly for medicinal purposes." He grinned.

Killian nodded, reading between the lines. Although
the Andersons were farm people, they were well-off by
hill standards. When he'd driven up earlier in the brown
Land Cruiser he'd rented at the airport, he'd noted that

the rolling green hills surrounding the large two-story white farmhouse were covered with orchards. He'd also seen a large chicken coop, and at least two hundred chickens roaming the hundred acres, ridding the land of insect pests. He'd seen a couple of milking cows, a flock of noisy gray geese, some wild mallards that made their home in a nearby pond, and a great blue heron walking along the edge of the water, probably hunting frogs. In Killian's mind, this place was perfect for someone like him, someone who was world-weary and in need of some genuine rest.

"Why don't you go out and meet Susannah?" Pansy asked hopefully. "You should introduce yourself. Maybe what she needs is someone her own age to get on with. That might help her heal."

White-hot anger clashed with gut-wrenching fear within Killian. Anger at Morgan for forcing him to take this mission. Fear of what he might do around Susannah if he didn't maintain tight control over his emotions. Killian kept his expression passive. Struggling to keep his voice noncommittal, he said, "Yes, I'll meet your daughter. But don't get your hopes up about anything happening." His tone came out harder than he'd anticipated. "I'm here for a rest, Mrs. Anderson. I'm a man of few words, and I like to be left alone."

Pansy's face fell a little, but she quickly summoned up a soft smile. "Why, of course, Mr. Killian. You are our guest, and we want you to feel free to come and go as you please."

Kindness was something Killian had *never* been able to deal with. He stood abruptly, the scraping of the wooden chair against the yellowed linoleum floor an irritant to his taut nerves. "I don't intend to be lazy. I'll help do some work around the place while I'm here."

"I can always use a pair of extra hands," Sam said, "and I'd be beholden to you for that."

Relief swept through Killian, at least momentarily. Work would help keep him away from Susannah. Yet, as a bodyguard, he'd have to remain alert and nearby—even if it was the last thing he wanted to do. But work would also help him get to know the farm and its layout, to anticipate where a threat to Susannah might come from.

Sam rose to his full six-foot-five-inch height. He was as thin as a spring sapling. "Come meet our daughter, Mr. Killian. Usually, this time of day, she's out in the herb garden. It's best I go with you. Otherwise, she's liable to start 'cause you're a stranger."

"Of course," Killian said. Everything about the Anderson home spoke of stark simplicity, he noted as he followed Sam. The floors were covered with linoleum, worn but clean, and lovingly polished. The handmade furniture looked antique, no doubt crafted by Anderson men over the generations. A green crocheted afghan covered the back of the sofa. Pansy had mentioned when he arrived that it had been made by her mother, who had recently passed away at the age of ninety-eight. Evidently, a long-lived family, Killian mused as he followed Sam out the creaky screen door onto the large wooden porch, where a swing hung.

"Now," Sam warned him, "don't take offense if Susannah sees you and takes off for her house. Sometimes when folks come to buy our produce they mistakenly stop at the old house. She locks herself in and won't go near the door."

Not a bad idea, Killian thought, with her assailant still

on the prowl. Sometimes paranoia could serve a person
well, he ruminated. He looked at himself. He was paranoid, too, but with good cause. As they walked down a
well-trodden path lined with fruit trees he wondered how
much Susannah knew of her own situation.

"Now," Sam was saying as he took long, slow strides,
"this here's the apple orchard. We got mostly Gravestein
and Jonathan varieties, 'cause folks are always lookin' for
good pie apples." He gestured to the right. "Over there
is the Bartlett pears and Bing cherries and sour cherries.
To the left, we got Alberta and freestone peaches. Ma
loves figs, so we got her a row of them, too. Susannah
likes the nut trees, so I ended up planting about twenty
acres of black walnuts. Darn good taste to the things, but
they come in this thick outer shell, and you have to wait
till it dries before you can even get to the nut. It's a lot
of work, but Susannah, as a kid, used to sit around for
hours, shelling those things by the bucketful. The black
are the best-tasting of all walnuts."

Killian nodded, his gaze never still. The surrounding rolling hills, their trees bearing nearly mature fruit,
looked idyllic. A variety of birds flew through the many
branches and he heard babies cheeping loudly for their
parents to bring them food. Still, the serene orchard was
forestlike, offering easy cover for a hit man.

After about a fifteen-minute walk up a gentle slope,
Killian halted beside Sam where the orchard opened up
into an oblong meadow of grass. In the center of the
open area stood an old shanty with a rusted tin roof. The
sides of the ramshackle house were grayed from years of
weathering, and several windows needed to be repaired,
their screens torn or rusted or missing altogether. Killian
glanced over at Sam in surprise.

"I told you before—Susannah insists upon living in this place. Why, I don't know," Sam muttered. "It needs a heap of fixin' to be livable, if you ask me." He stuffed his hands into the pockets of his coveralls. "Come on. The herb garden is on the other side of the house."

Susannah sank her long fingers into the welcoming black warmth of the fertile soil. Then, taking a clump of chives, she placed it in the hole she'd dug. The inconstant breeze was dying down now that dusk had arrived. She heard the singing of the birds, a peaceful reminder that no one was nearby. A red-breasted robin flew to the white picket fence that enclosed the large herb garden. Almost immediately he began to chirp excitedly, fluttering his wings.

It was a warning. Susannah quickly looked around, feeling vulnerable with her back turned toward whoever was approaching. Her father rounded the corner of the house, then her heart began beating harder. There was a stranger—a man—with him.

Ordinarily Susannah would have run, but in an instant the man's steely blue gaze met and held her own, and something told her to stay where she was. Remaining on her knees in the soil, Susannah watched their progress toward her.

The man's catlike eyes held on hers, but instead of the naked fear she usually felt at a stranger's approach since coming out of the coma, Susannah felt an odd sizzle of apprehension. But what kind? His face was hard-looking, revealing no hint of emotion in his eyes or the set of his mouth. His hair was black and military-short, and his skin was deeply bronzed by the sun. Her heart started to hammer in warning.

Her father greeted her with a smile. "Susannah, I've brought a friend to introduce to you. Come on, honey, come over and meet him."

The stranger's oddly opaque gaze held her suspended. Susannah gulped convulsively and set the chives aside. Her fingers were stained dark from the soil, and the jeans she wore were thick with dust. Slowly, beneath his continued inspection, Susannah forced herself to her bare feet. The power of the stranger's gaze, the anger she saw in the depths of his eyes, held her captive.

"Susannah?" Sam prodded gently as he halted at the gate and opened it. "Honey, he won't hurt you. Come on over…"

"No," Killian said, his voice hoarse. "Let her be. Let her get used to me."

Sam gave him a quizzical look, but said nothing.

Killian wasn't breathing. Air seemed to have jammed in his chest. Susannah was more than beautiful; she was ethereal. Her straight sable-colored hair flowed around her slender form, almost touching her breasts. Her simple white cotton blouse and jeans enhanced her figure. Killian could see no outward signs of the violence she'd endured, although at some point in her life her nose had been broken. The bump was prominent, and he wondered about the story behind it. Her lips were full, and slightly parted now. But it was her eyes—large, expressive, dove gray—that entranced him the most.

Who is he? Why is he looking at me like that? Susannah looked down at herself. Sure, her jeans were dirty, but she had been gardening all day. Her feet, too, were covered with soil. Automatically she raised a hand to touch the front of her blouse. Was one of her buttons undone? No. Again she raised her head and met those eyes that, though emotionless, nonetheless drew her. There was a sense of armor around him that startled her. A hard, impervious shell of self-protection. She'd often sensed the same quality around her handicapped children when they first started school—a need to protect themselves against the all-too-common hurts they were subjected to. But there was more than that to this man's bearing, Susannah realized as she allowed her intuition to take over. She also sensed a darkness, a sadness, around this tall, lean man, who was probably in his mid-thirties. He felt edgy to her, and it set her on edge, too. Who was he? Another police detective from Lexington, come to grill her? To try to jar loose her frozen memory? Susannah's hands grew damp with apprehension. This man frightened her in a new and unknown way. Maybe it was that unexpected anger banked in his eyes.

Killian used all his senses, finely honed over years of dangerous work, to take in Susannah. He saw her fine nostrils quiver and flare, as if she were a wary young deer ready for flight. He felt the fear rise around her, broadcast in every line of her tension-held body. Meg's once-beautiful face floated in front of him. The terror he'd felt as he stood at her hospital bedside as she became conscious for the first time since the blast slammed back into him. Smiling didn't come easily to him, but he'd forced one then for Meg's benefit, and it had made all the difference in the world. She'd reached out and weakly gripped his hand and begun to cry, but to Killian it had been a good sign, a sign that she wanted to live.

Now, for Susannah's benefit, Killian forced the corners of his mouth upward as he saw terror come to her widening eyes. Although he was angry at Morgan, he didn't need to take it out on her. Almost instantly he saw the tension on her face dissipate.

Fighting the screaming awareness of his emotional response to Susannah, Killian said to Sam in a low voice, "Go ahead and make the introduction, and then leave us. I don't think she's going to run."

Scratching his head, Sam nodded. "Darned if I don't believe you. For some reason, she ain't as afraid of you as all the rest."

Killian barely nodded as he continued to hold Susannah's assessing stare. Her arms were held tightly at her sides. Her fingers were long and artistic-looking. She seemed more like a girl in her teens—barefoot and in touch with the magic of the Earth—than a schoolteacher of twenty-seven.

"Honey, this is Mr. Killian," Sam said gently to his daughter. "He's a friend of Morgan's, come to stay with us and rest up for a month or so. Ma and I said he could stay. He's a friend, honey. Not a stranger. Do you understand?"

Susannah nodded slowly, never taking her eyes off Killian.

What is your first name? The words were there, on the tip of her tongue, but they refused to be given voice. Frustration thrummed through Susannah. How she ached to speak again—but some invisible hand held her tongue-tied. Killian's mouth had curved into the barest of smiles, sending an odd heat sheeting through her. Shaken by his presence, Susannah could only nod, her hands laced shyly together in front of her. Still, she was wary. It wasn't something she could just automatically turn off.

Killian was excruciatingly uncomfortable, and he

wanted to get the social amenities over with. "Thanks, Sam," he said brusquely.

Sam's gaze moved from his daughter to Killian and back to her. "Honey, supper's in a hour. Ma would like you to join us. Will you?"

Susannah felt her heartbeat picking up again, beating wildly with apprehension over this man named Killian—a male stranger who had come to disrupt the silent world where she'd retreated to be healed. She glanced down at her feet and then lifted her chin.

I don't know. I don't know, Pa. Let me see how I feel. Susannah was disappointed with herself. All she could do was shrug delicately. Ordinarily she carried a pen and paper with her in order to communicate with her folks, or friends of the family who stopped to visit. But today, not expecting visitors, she'd left her pad and pen back at the house.

"Good enough," Sam told her gruffly. "Maybe you'll let Killian walk you back afterward."

Killian stood very still after Sam disappeared. He saw the nervousness and curiosity reflected in Susannah's wide eyes—and suddenly he almost grinned at the irony of their situation. He was normally a person of few words, and for the first time in his life he was going to have to carry the conversation. He spread his hand out in a gesture of peace.

"I hope I didn't stop you from planting."

No, you didn't. Susannah glanced sharply down at the chives. She knelt and began to cover the roots before they dried out. As she worked, she keyed her hearing to where the man stood, outside the gate. Every once in a while, she glanced up. Each time she did, he was still standing there, motionless, hands in the pockets of his jeans, an old, beat-up leather jacket hanging loosely on his lean frame. His serious features were set, and she sensed an unhappiness radiating from him. About what? Being here? Meeting her? So many things didn't make sense to her. If he was one of Morgan's friends, why would he be unhappy about being here? If he was here for a vacation, he should be relaxed.

Killian caught Susannah's inquiring gaze. Then, dusting off her hands, she continued down the row, pulling weeds. The breeze gently blew strands of her thick hair across her shoulders, framing her face.

Although he hadn't moved, Killian's eyes were active, sizing up the immediate vicinity—the possible entrances to the shanty and the layout of the surrounding meadow. His gaze moved back to Susannah, who continued acting guarded, nearly ignoring him. She was probably hoping he'd go away and leave her alone, he thought wryly. God knew, he'd like to do exactly that. His anger toward Morgan grew in volume.

"I haven't seen a woman in bare feet since I left Ireland," he finally offered in a low, clipped tone. No, conversation wasn't his forte.

Susannah stopped weeding and jerked a look in his direction. Killian crossed to sit on the grassy bank, his arms around his knees, his gaze still on her.

As if women can't go with their shoes off!

Killian saw the disgust in her eyes. Desperately he cast about for some way to lessen the tension between them. As long as she distrusted him, he wouldn't be able to get close enough to protect her. Inwardly Killian cursed Morgan.

Forcing himself to try again, he muttered, "That wasn't an insult. Just an observation. My sister, Meg, who's about your age, always goes barefoot in the garden, too." He gestured toward the well-kept plants. "Looks like you give them a lot of attention. Meg always said plants grew best when you gave them love." Just talking about Meg, even to this wary, silent audience of one, eased some of his pain for his sister.

You know how I feel! Weeds in her hands, Susannah straightened, surprised by the discovery. Killian had seen her facial expression and read it accurately. Hope rushed through her. Her mother and father, as dearly as they loved her, couldn't seem to read her feelings at all since she'd come out of the coma. But suddenly this lanky, tightly coiled stranger with the sky-blue eyes, black hair and soft, hesitant smile could.

Are you a psychiatrist? I hope not. Susannah figured she'd been through enough testing to last her a lifetime. Older men with glasses and beards had pronounced her hysterical due to her trauma and said it was the reason she couldn't speak. Her fingers tightened around the weeds as she stood beneath Killian's cool, expressionless inspection.

Killian saw the tension in Susannah's features dissolve for just an instant. He'd touched her, and he knew it. Frustrated and unsure of her reaction to him, he tried again, but his voice came out cold. "Weeds make good compost. Do you have a compost pile around here?"

Susannah looked intensely at this unusual man, feeling him instead of listening to his words, which he seemed to have mouthed in desperation. Ordinarily, if she'd met Killian on a busy street, he would have frightened her. His face was lean, like the rest of him, and his nose was large and straight, with a good space between his slightly arched eyebrows. There was an intense alertness in those eyes that reminded her of a cougar. And although he had offered that scant smile initially, his eyes contained a hardness that Susannah had never seen in her life. Since the incident that had changed her life, she had come to rely heavily on her intuitive abilities to ferret out people's possible ulterior motives toward her. The hospital therapist had called it paranoia. But in this case, Susannah sensed that a great sadness had settled around Killian like a cloak. And danger.

Why danger? And is it danger to me? He did *look* dangerous, there was no doubt. Susannah couldn't find one telltale sign in his features of humanity or emotion. But her fear warred with an image she couldn't shake, the image of the sad but crooked smile that had made him appear vulnerable for one split second out of time.

Chapter 2

Killian watched Susannah walk slowly and cautiously through the garden gate. She was about three feet away from him now, and he probed her for signs of wariness. He had no wish to minimize her guardedness toward him—if he could keep her at arm's length and do his job, this assignment might actually work out. If he couldn't...

Just the way Susannah moved snagged a sharp stab of longing deep within him. She had the grace of a ballet dancer, her hips swaying slightly as she stepped delicately across the rows of healthy plants. He decided not to follow her, wanting to allow her more time to adjust to his presence. Just then a robin, sitting on the fence near Killian, took off and landed in the top of an old, gnarled apple tree standing alone just outside the garden. Instantly there was a fierce cheeping, and Killian cocked his head to one side. A half-grown baby robin was

perched precariously on the limb near the nest, fluttering his wings demandingly as the parent hovered nearby
with food in his beak.

Killian sensed Susannah's presence and slowly turned
his head. She was standing six feet away, watching him
pointedly. There was such beauty in her shadowed gray
eyes. Killian recognized that shadow—Meg's eyes were
marred by the same look.

"That baby robin is going to fall off that limb if he
isn't careful."

*Yes, he is. Yesterday he did, and I had to pick him up
and put him back in the tree.* Frustrated by her inability to
speak the words, Susannah nodded and wiped her hands
against her thighs. Once again she found herself wanting
her notepad and pen. He was a stranger and couldn't be
trusted, a voice told her. Still, he was watching the awkward progress of the baby robin with concern.

Unexpectedly the baby robin shrieked. Susannah
opened her mouth to cry out, but only a harsh, strangu-
lated sound came forth as the small bird fluttered helplessly down through the branches of the apple tree and
hit the ground roughly, tumbling end over end. When
the baby regained his composure, he began to scream
for help, and both parents flew around and around him.

Without thinking, Susannah rushed past Killian to
rescue the bird, as she had yesterday.

"No," Killian whispered, reaching out to stop Susannah. "I'll do it." Her skin was smooth and sun-warmed
beneath his fingers, and instantly Killian released her,
the shock of the touch startling not only him, but her, too.

Susannah gasped, jerking back, her mouth opened in
shock. Her skin seemed to tingle where his fingers had
briefly, carefully grasped her wrist.

Taken aback by her reaction, Killian glared at her, then immediately chastised himself. After all, didn't he want her to remain fearful of him? Inside, though, his heart winced at the terror he saw in her gaze, at the contorted shape of her lips as she stared up at him—as if he was her assailant. His action had been rash, he thought angrily. Somehow Susannah's presence had caught him off guard. Infuriated by his own blind reactions, Killian stood there at a loss for words.

Susannah saw disgust in Killian's eyes, and then, on its heels, a gut-wrenching sadness. Still stunned by his swift touch, she backed even farther away from him. Finally the robin's plaintive cheeping impinged on her shocked senses, and she tore her attention from Killian, pointing at the baby robin now hopping around on the ground.

"Yeah. Okay, I'll get the bird," Killian muttered crossly. He was furious with himself, at the unexpected emotions that brief touch had aroused. For the most fleeting moment, his heart jumped at the thought of what it would feel like to kiss Susannah until she was breathless with need of him. Thoroughly disgusted that the thought had even entered his head, Killian moved rapidly to rescue the baby bird. What woman would be interested in him? He was a dark introvert of a man, given to very little communication. A man haunted by a past that at any moment could avalanche into his present and effectively destroy a woman who thought she might care for him. No, he was dangerous—a bomb ready to explode—and he was damned if he was going to put any woman in the line of fire.

As he leaned down and trapped the robin carefully between his hands, the two parents flew overhead, shriek-

ing, trying to protect their baby. Gently Killian cupped
the captured baby, lifting the feathered tyke and staring
into his shiny black eyes.

"Next time some cat might find you first and think
you're a tasty supper," he warned sternly as he turned
toward the apple tree. Placing the bird in his shirt pocket,
he grabbed a low branch and began to climb.

Susannah stood below, watching Killian's lithe progress. Everything about the man was methodical. He never
stepped on a weak limb; he studied the situation thoroughly before placing each foot to push himself upward
toward the nest. Yet, far from plodding, he had an easy
masculine grace.

Killian settled the robin in its nest and quickly made
his way down to avoid the irate parents. Leaping the last
few feet, he landed with the grace of a large cat. "Well,
our good deed is done for the day," he said gruffly, dusting off his hands.

His voice was as icy as his unrelenting features, and
Susannah took another step away from him.

*Thank you for rescuing the baby. But how can such a
hard man perform such a gentle feat? What's your story,
Killian?* His eyes turned impatient under her inspection,
and Susannah tore her gaze away from him. The man
had something to hide, it seemed.

*How much more do you know about me? What did
my folks tell you?* Susannah felt an odd sort of shame at
the thought of Killian knowing what had happened to
her. Humiliation, too, coupled with anger and fear—the
entire gamut of feelings she'd lived with daily since the
shooting. Out of nervousness, she raised a hand to her
cheek, which felt hot and flushed.

Killian noted the hurt in Susannah's eyes as she self-consciously brushed her cheek with her fingertips. And in that moment he saw the violence's lasting damage: loss of self-esteem. She was afraid of him, and part of him ached at the unfairness of it, but he accepted his fate bitterly. Let Susannah think him untrustworthy—dangerous. Those instincts might save her life, should her assailant show up for another try at killing her.

"I need to wash my hands," he said brusquely, desperate to break the tension between them. He had to snap out of it. He couldn't afford to allow her to affect him— and possibly compromise his ability to protect her from a killer.

Unexpectedly Susannah felt tears jam into her eyes. She stood there in abject surprise as they rolled down her cheeks, unbidden, seemingly tapped from some deep source within her. Why was she crying? She hadn't cried since coming out of the coma! Embarrassed that Killian was watching her, a disgruntled look on his face, Susannah raised trembling hands to her cheeks.

Killian swayed—and caught himself. Every fiber of his being wanted to reach out and comfort Susannah. The tears, small, sun-touched crystals, streamed down her flushed cheeks. The one thing he couldn't bear was to see a woman cry. A weeping child he could handle, but somehow, when a woman cried, it was different. Different, and gut-wrenchingly disturbing. Meg's tears had torn him apart, her cries shredding what was left of his feelings.

Looking down at Susannah now, Killian felt frustration and disgust at his inability to comfort her. But that edge, that distrust, had to stay in place if he was to do his job.

Turning away abruptly, he looked around for a garden

hose, for anything, really, that would give him an excuse
to escape her nearness. Spying a hose leading from the
side of the house, he turned on his heel and strode toward
the faucet. Relief flowed through him as he put distance
between them, the tightened muscles in his shoulders
and back loosening. Trying to shake pangs of guilt for
abandoning her, Killian leaned down and turned on the
faucet. He washed his hands rapidly, then wiped them
on the thighs of his jeans as he straightened.

He glanced back toward Susannah who still stood near
the garden, looking alone and unprotected. As he slowly
walked back to where she stood, he thrust his hands into
the pockets of his jeans. "It's almost time for dinner," he
said gruffly. "I'm hungry. Are you coming?"

Susannah felt hollow inside. The tears had left her
terribly vulnerable, and right now she needed human
company more than usual. Killian's harsh company felt
abrasive to her in her fragile emotional state, and she
knew she'd have to endure walking through the orchard
to her folks' house with him. She forced herself to look
into his dark, angry features. This mute life of pad and
pencil was unbelievably frustrating. Normally she believed mightily in communicating and confronting problems, and without a voice, it was nearly impossible to be
herself. The old Susannah would have asked Killian what
his problem with her was. Instead she merely gestured
for him to follow her.

Killian maintained a discreet distance from Susannah as they wound their way through the orchard on the
well-trodden path. He wanted to ask Susannah's forgive-
ness for having abandoned her earlier—to explain why
he had to keep her at arm's length. But then he laughed
derisively at himself. Susannah would never understand.

No woman would. He noticed that as they walked Susannah's gaze was never still, constantly searching the area, as if she were expecting to be attacked. It hurt him to see her in that mode. The haunted look in her eyes tore at him. Her beautiful mouth was pursed, the corners drawn taut, as if she expected a blow at any moment.

Not while I'm alive will another person ever *harm you,* he promised grimly. Killian slowed his pace, baffled at the intensity of the feeling that came with the thought. The sun shimmered through the leaves of the fruit trees, scattering light across the green grass in a patchwork-quilt effect, touching Susannah's hair and bringing red highlights to life, intermixed with threads of gold. Killian wondered obliquely if she had some Irish blood in her.

In the Andersons' kitchen, Killian noted the way Susannah gratefully absorbed her mother's obvious care and genuine concern. He watched the sparkle come back to her lovely gray eyes as Pansy doted over her. Susannah had withdrawn into herself on their walk to the farmhouse. Now Killian watched her reemerge from that private, silent world, coaxed out by touches and hugs from her parents.

He'd made her retreat, and he felt like hell about it. But there could be no ambiguity about his function here at the farm. Sitting at the table now, his hand around a mug of steaming coffee, Killian tried to protect himself against the emotional warmth that pervaded the kitchen. The odors of home-cooked food, fresh and lovingly prepared, reminded him of a far gentler time in his life, the time when he was growing up in Ireland. There hadn't been many happy times in Killian's life, but that had been one—his mother doting over him and Meg, the lighthearted lilt of her laughter, the smell of fresh bread baking in the oven, her occasional touch upon his shoulder or playful ruffling of his hair. Groaning, he blindly gulped his coffee, and nearly burned his mouth in the process.

Susannah washed her hands at the kitchen sink, slowly dried them, and glanced apprehensively over at Killian. He sat at the table like a dark, unhappy shadow, his hand gripping the coffee mug. She was trying to understand him, but it was impossible. Her mother smiled at him, and tried to cajole a hint of a reaction from Killian, but he seemed impervious to human interaction.

As Pansy served the dinner, Killian tried to ignore the fact that he was seated opposite Susannah. She had an incredible ability to communicate with just a glance from those haunting eyes. Killian held on tightly to his anger at the thought that she had almost died.

"Why, you're lookin' so much better," Pansy gushed to her daughter as she placed mashed potatoes, spareribs and a fresh garden salad on the table.

Susannah nodded and smiled for her mother's sake. Just sitting across from Killian was unnerving. But because she loved her mother and father fiercely she was trying to ignore Killian's cold, icy presence and act normally.

Sam smiled and passed his daughter the platter of ribs. "Do you think you'll get along with Killian hereabouts for a while?"

Susannah felt Killian's eyes on her and refused to look up, knowing that he was probably studying her with the icy gaze of a predator for his intended victim. She glanced over at her father, whose face was open and readable, and found the strength somewhere within herself to lie. A white lie, Susannah told herself as she forced a smile and nodded.

Killian ate slowly, allowing his senses to take in the cheerful kitchen and happy family setting. The scents of barbecued meat and thick brown gravy and the tart smell of apples baking in the oven were sweeter than any perfume.

"I don't know what you did," Pansy told Killian, "but whatever it is, Susannah looks so much better! Doesn't she, Sam?"

Spooning gravy onto a heaping portion of mashed potatoes, Sam glanced up. "Ma, you know how uncomfortable Susannah gets when we talk as if she's not here."

Chastened, Pansy smiled. "I'm sorry, dear," she said, giving her daughter a fond look and a pat on the arm in apology.

Susannah wondered glumly how she could possibly look better with Killian around. Without a doubt, the man made her uncomfortable. She decided it was just that her mother wanted to see her looking better. Aching inwardly, Susannah thought how terribly the past three months had worn down her folks. They had both aged noticeably, and it hurt her to realize that her stupid, failed foray into the "big" world outside Kentucky had cost them, too. If only she hadn't been so naive about the world, it might not have happened, and her parents might not have had to suffer this way. Luckily, her school insurance had covered the massive medical bills; Susannah knew her folks would have sold the farm, if necessary, to help her cover expenses.

"Let's talk about you, Killian," Pansy said brightly, turning the conversation to him.

Killian saw Susannah's eyes suddenly narrow upon

him, filled with curiosity—and some indefinable emotion that set his pulse to racing. He hesitated, not wanting to sound rude. "Ordinarily, Pansy, I don't open up to anyone."

"Whatever for?"

Sam groaned. "Honey, the man's got a right to some privacy, don't he?"

Pansy laughed. "Now, Pa…"

Clearing his throat, Killian moved the mashed potatoes around on his blue-and-white plate. He realized he wasn't going to be able to get around Pansy's good-natured probing. "I work in the area of high security." The explanation came out gruffly—a warning, he hoped, for her to stop asking questions.

"Surely," Pansy said, with a gentle laugh, "you can tell me if you're married or not. Or about your family?"

Tension hung in the air. Killian put down his fork, keeping a tight rein on his reaction to what he knew was a well-intentioned question. Sam shot him an apologetic look that spoke volumes, but Killian also saw Susannah's open interest. She'd stopped eating, and was waiting to hear his answer.

Killian felt heat creeping up his neck and into his cheeks. Pain at the memory of his family sheared through him. He dropped his gaze to the uneaten food on his plate and felt an avalanche of unexpected grief that seemed to suck the life out of him momentarily. Unwillingly he looked up—and met Susannah's compassionate gaze.

Killian shoved his chair back, and the scraping sound shattered the tension. "Excuse me," he rasped, "I'm done eating."

Susannah saw pain in Killian's eyes and heard the roughness of emotion in his voice as he moved abruptly to his feet. The chair nearly tipped over backward, but he caught it in time. Without a sound, Killian stalked from the kitchen.

"Oh, dear," Pansy whispered, her fingers against her lips. "I didn't mean to upset him…"

Susannah reached out and gripped her mother's hand. She might not be able to talk, but she could at least offer the reassurance of touch.

Sam cleared his throat. "Ma, he's a closed kind of man. Didn't you see that?"

Pansy shrugged weakly and patted her daughter's hand. "Oh, I guess I did, Sam, but you know me—I'm such a busybody. Maybe I should go after him and apologize."

"Just let him be, Ma, and he'll come around," Sam counseled gently.

"I don't know," Pansy whispered, upset. "When I asked him about his family, did you see his face?"

Susannah nodded and released her mother's hand. As she continued to finish her meal, she ruminated on that very point. Killian had reacted violently to the question, anguished pain momentarily shadowing his eyes. Susannah had found herself wanting to reach out and reassure him that all would be well. But would it?

Morosely Susannah forced herself to finish eating her dinner. Somehow she wanted to let her mother know that there had been nothing wrong with her questions to Killian. As she had so many times these past months, she wished she could talk. Pansy was just a warm, chatty person by nature, but Susannah understood Killian's discomfort over such questions. Still, she wanted to try to communicate with Killian. She would use the excuse that he could walk her home, since it would be nearly dark. Her father never allowed her to walk home alone at night. At the same time, Susannah felt fear at being alone with him.

What was there about him that made her want to know him? He was a stranger who'd walked into her life only a few hours ago. The fact that he was Morgan's friend meant something, of course. From what her cousin Laura had told her, she knew that Morgan Trayhern drew only loyal, responsible people to him. Still, they were hard men, mercenaries. Susannah had no experience with mercenaries. In fact, she had very little experience with men in general, and especially with men her own age. She felt she wasn't equal to the task of healing the rift between her mother and Killian, but she knew she had to try. Otherwise, her mother would be a nervous wreck every time Killian sat down to eat. No, something had to be done to calm the troubled waters.

Killian was sitting in the living room, pretending to watch television, when he saw Susannah come out of the kitchen. He barely met her gaze as she walked determinedly toward him with a piece of paper in her hand. He saw uncertainty in her eyes—and something else that he couldn't have defined. Knowing that his abruptness had already caused bad feelings, he tensed as she drew close enough to hand him the note.

Walk me home. Please?

Killian lifted his head and studied her darkly. There was such vulnerability to Susannah—and that was what had nearly gotten her killed. Killian couldn't help but re-

spond to the silent plea in her eyes as she stood waiting
for his answer.

Without a word, he crushed the note in his hand, got
to his feet and headed toward the door. He would use
this excuse to check out her house and the surrounding
area. When he opened the door for her, she brushed by
him, and he felt himself tense. The sweet, fragrant scent
of her perfume momentarily encircled him, and he unconsciously inhaled the subtle scent.

It was dusk, the inky stains across the early-autumn
sky telling Killian it would soon be dark. As he slowly
walked Susannah back to her house, his ears were tuned
in to the twilight for any out-of-the-ordinary sounds. He
needed to adjust his senses to the normal sounds of this
countryside, anyway. Until then, he would have to be
even more alert than normal. There were no unusual
odors on the fragrant air, and he couldn't ferret out anything unusual visually as he restlessly scanned the orchard.

When they reached her home, Killian realized that
it had no electricity. He stood just inside the door and
watched as Susannah lit a hurricane lamp filled with kerosene. She placed one lamp on the wooden table, another
on the mantel over the fireplace, and a third in the living
room. The floorboards, old and gray, creaked beneath
her bare feet as she moved about. Uneasy at how little
protection the house afforded against a possible intruder,
Killian watched her pull open a drawer of an oak hutch.

Susannah located a notebook and pen and gestured
for Killian to come and sit down with her at the table.
Mystified, Killian sat down tensely at Susannah's elbow
while she wrote on the notepad.

When she'd finished writing, she turned the notepad around so that Killian could read her question. The light from the kerosene lamp cast a soft glow around the deeply shadowed kitchen.

Killian eyed the note. "Is Killian my first or last name?" he read aloud. He grimaced and reared back on two legs of the chair. "It's my last name. Everyone calls me by my last name."

Susannah made a frustrated sound and penned another note.

What is your first name?

Killian scowled heavily and considered her request. Morgan's orders sounded demandingly in his brain. He was to try to get Susannah to remember what her assailant looked like. If he remained too cool and unresponsive to her, she wouldn't want to try to cooperate with him. Yet to reveal himself would be as good as opening up his horrifying past once again. That had happened once before, with terrible results, and he'd vowed it would never happen again. Dammit, anyway! He rubbed his mouth with his hand, feeling trapped. He had to gain Susannah's cooperation. Her trust.

"Sean," he snarled.

Susannah winced, but determinedly wrote another note.

Who do you allow to call you Sean?

Killian stared at the note. Despite Susannah's obvious softness and vulnerability, for the first time he noticed a look of stubbornness in her eyes. He frowned.

"My mother and sister called me by my first name. Just them," he muttered.

Susannah digested his admission. Maybe he used his last name to prevent people getting close to him. But evidently there were at least two women in his life who could reach inside those armored walls and get to him. There was hope, Susannah decided, if Killian allowed his family to use his first name. But she'd heard the warning in his voice when he'd spoken to her mother. She might be a hill woman, and not as worldly as he was, but surely it wasn't unreasonable to expect good manners—even from a mercenary. She held his blunt stare and felt the fear and anger seething around him. That cold armored cloak was firmly in place.

Grimly Susannah penned another note.

My mother didn't mean to make you uncomfortable. If you can find some way to say something to her to defuse the situation, I'd be grateful. She meant well. She didn't mean to chase you from the dinner table.

Killian stared at her printed note for a long time. The silence thickened. Susannah was right; he'd been wrong in his reaction to the situation. He wished he had the words, a way to explain himself. Frustration overwhelmed him. Looking up, he thought for a moment that he might drown in her compassionate gray gaze. Quirking his mouth, he muttered, "When I go back down tonight, I'll tell her I'm sorry."

Susannah smiled slightly and nodded her head.

Thank you. I know so little of Morgan's men. None

of us know anything about mercenaries. I hope you can forgive us, too?

Steeling himself against Susannah's attempt to smooth things over, Killian nodded. "Don't worry about it. There's nothing to forgive." He started to get up, but she made an inarticulate sound and reached out, her hand closing around his arm. Killian froze.

Susannah's lips parted when she saw anguish replace the coldness in Killian's eyes as she touched him. She hadn't meant to reach out like that; it had been instinctive. Somewhere in her heart, she knew that Killian needed touching—a lot of it. She knew all too well through her work the value of touching, the healing quality of a hand upon a shoulder to give necessary support and courage. Hard as he appeared to be, was Killian really any different? Gazing up through the dim light in the kitchen, she saw the tortured look in his eyes.

Thinking that he was repulsed by her touch, she quickly released him.

Killian slowly sat back, his heart hammering in his chest. It was hell trying to keep his feelings at bay. Whether he liked it or not, he could almost read what Susannah was thinking in her expressive eyes. Their soft gray reminded him of a mourning dove—and she was as gentle and delicate as one.

My folks are simple people, Killian. Pa said you were here for a rest. Is that true? If so, for how long?

Killian felt utterly trapped, and he longed to escape. Morgan was expecting the impossible of him. He didn't have the damnable ability to walk with one foot as a protector and the other foot emotionally far enough away from Susannah to do his job. The patient look on her face only aggravated him.

"I'm between missions," he bit out savagely. "And I want to rest somewhere quiet. I'll try to be a better house guest, okay?"

I know you're uncomfortable around me. I don't expect anything from you. I'll be staying up here most of the time, so you'll have the space to rest.

Absolute frustration thrummed through Killian. This was exactly what he *didn't* want! "Look," he growled, "you don't make me uncomfortable, okay? I know what happened to you, and I'm sorry it happened. I have a sister who—"

Susannah tilted her head as he snapped his mouth shut and glared at her. He wanted to run. It was in every line of his body, and it was in his eyes. The tension in the kitchen had become a tangible thing.

Who? What?

Agitated, Killian shot to his feet. He roamed around the kitchen in the semidarkness, seesawing back and forth about what—if anything—he should tell her. She sat quietly, watching him, without any outward sign of impatience. Running his fingers through his hair, he turned suddenly and pinned her with an angry look.

"My sister, Meg, was nearly killed in a situation not unlike yours," he ground out finally. "She's disfigured for life, and she's scared. She lives alone, like a recluse. I've seen what violence has done to her, so I can imagine what it's done to you." He'd said enough. More than enough, judging from the tears that suddenly were shimmering in Susannah's eyes.

Breathing hard, Killian continued to glare at her, hoping she would give up. He didn't want her asking him any more personal questions. Hell, he hadn't intended to bring up Meg! But something about this woman kept tugging at him, pulling him out of his isolation.

I'm sorry for Meg. For you. I've seen what the violence to me has done to my folks. It's awful. It's forever.

As Killian read the note, standing near the table, his shoulders sagged, and all the anger went out of him. "Yes," he whispered wearily, "violence is wrong. All it does is tear people's lives apart." How well he knew that—in more ways than he ever wanted to admit.

If you're a mercenary, then you're always fighting a war, aren't you?

The truth was like a knife in Killian's clenched gut. He stood, arms at his sides, and hung his head as he pondered her simple question. "Mercenaries work in many capacities," he said slowly. "Some of them are very safe and low-risk. But they do deal with violent situations, too." He lifted his head and threw her a warning look. "The more you do it, the more you become it."

Are you always in dangerous situations?

He picked up the note, then slowly crushed it in his

hand. Susannah was getting too close. That just couldn't happen. For her sake, it couldn't. Killian arranged his face into the deadliest look he could muster. "More than anything," he told her in a soft rasp, "you should understand that I'm dangerous to you."

It was all the warning Killian could give her short of telling what had happened when one woman *had* gotten to him, touched his heart, made him feel love. He'd sworn he'd never tell anyone that—not even Meg. And he'd vowed never to let it happen again. Susannah was too special, too vulnerable, for him to allow her to get close to him. But she had a kind of courage that frightened Killian; she had the guts to approach someone like him— someone so wounded that he could never be healed.

"I'll see you tomorrow morning," he said abruptly. He scanned the room closely with one sweeping gaze, then glanced down at her. "Because I'm a mercenary, I'm going to check out your house and the surrounding area. I'll be outside after I make a sweep of the house, and then I'll be staying at your folks' place, in the guest bedroom." He rubbed his jaw as he took in the poor condition of the window, which had no screen and no lock. "If you hear anything, come and get me."

I've been living here the last month and nothing has happened. I'll be okay.

Naiveté at best, Killian thought as he read her note. But he couldn't tell her she was in danger—good old Morgan's orders again. His mouth flattening, he stared across the table into her weary eyes. "If you need help, come and get me. Understand?" As much as he wanted to stay nearby to protect Susannah, Killian knew he couldn't possibly move in with her without a darn good explanation for her and her parents. He was hamstrung. And he didn't want to have to live under Susannah's roof, anyway, for very different reasons. As much as he hated to leave her unprotected at the homestead, for now he had no choice.

At least Susannah would remain safe from him, Killian thought as he studied her darkly. His mind shouted that he'd be absolutely useless sleeping down at the Anderson house if the killer tried to reach her here. But what could he do? Torn, he decided that for tonight, he would sleep at the Andersons' and ponder the problem.

With a bare nod, Susannah took in Killian's vibrating warning. He had told her he was a violent man. She sensed the lethal quality about him, and yet those brief flashes she'd had of him without his defenses in place made her believe that deep down he longed for peace, not war.

Chapter 3

As she bathed and prepared to go to bed, Susannah tried to sift through her jumbled feelings. Killian disturbed her, she decided, more than he frightened her. Somehow she was invisibly drawn to him—to the inner man, not the cold exterior he held up like a shield. She pulled her light knee-length cotton gown over her head and tamed her tangled hair with her fingers. The lamplight cast dancing shadows across the opposite wall of the small bathroom. Ordinarily, catching sight of moving silhouettes caused her to start, but tonight it didn't.

Why? Picking up her clothes, Susannah walked thoughtfully through the silent house, the old planks beneath the thin linoleum floor creaking occasionally. Could Killian's unsettling presence somehow have given her a sense of safety? Even if it was an edgy kind of safety? Despite his glowering and his snappish words,

Susannah sensed he would help her if she ever found herself in trouble.

With a shake of her head, Susannah dumped her clothes into a hamper in the small side room and made her way toward the central portion of the two-story house. At least four generations of Andersons had lived here, and that in itself gave her a sense of safety. There was something about the old and the familiar that had always meant tranquility to Susannah, and right now she needed that sense as never before.

She went into the kitchen, where the hurricane lamp still threw its meager light. Pictures drawn in crayon wreathed the walls of the area—fond reminders of her most recent class of children. Last year's class. The pictures suggested hope, and Susannah could vividly recall each child's face as she surveyed the individual drawings. They gave her a sense that maybe her life hadn't been completely shattered after all.

Leaning down, Susannah blew out the flame in the lamp, and darkness cloaked the room, making her suddenly edgy. It had been shadowy the night she'd walked from her bus toward the brightly lit central station—she could remember that clearly. She could recall, too, flashbacks of the man who had been killed in front of her. He'd been sharply dressed, with an engaging smile, and he'd approached her as if she were a longtime friend. She'd trusted him—found him attractive, to be honest. She'd smiled and allowed him to take the large carry-on bag that hung from her shoulder. With a shudder, Susannah tried to block the horrifying end to his brief contact with her. Pressing her fingers against her closed eyes, she felt the first signs of one of the massive migraines that seemed to come and go without much warning begin to stalk her.

As she made her way to her bedroom, at the rear of the house—moving around familiar shapes in the dark—Susannah vaguely wondered why Killian's unexpected presence hadn't triggered one of her crippling headaches. He was dangerous, her mind warned her sharply. He'd told her so himself, in the sort of warning growl a cougar might give an approaching hunter. As she pulled back the crisp white sheet and the worn quilt that served as her bedspread, Susannah's heart argued with her practical mind. Killian must have lived through some terrible, traumatic events to project that kind of iciness. As Susannah slid into bed, fluffed her pillow and closed her eyes, she released a long, ragged sigh. Luckily, sleep always cured her headaches, and she was more tired than usual tonight.

Despite her physical weariness, Susannah saw Killian's hard, emotionless face waver before her closed eyes. There wasn't an iota of gentleness anywhere in his features. Yet, as she searched his stormy dark blue eyes, eyes that shouted to everyone to leave him alone, Susannah felt such sadness around him that tears stung her own eyes. Sniffing, she laughed to herself. How easily touched she was! And how much she missed her children. School had started without her, and she was missing a new class of frightened, unsure charges she knew would slowly come out of their protective shells and begin to reach out and touch life.

Unhappily Susannah thought of the doctors' warnings that it would be at least two months before she could possibly go back to teaching. Her world, as she had known it, no longer existed. Where once she'd been trusting of people, now she was not. Darkness had always been her friend—but now it disturbed her. Forcing herself to shut off her rambling thoughts, Susannah concentrated on sleep. Her last images were of Killian, and the sadness that permeated him.

A distinct click awakened Susannah. She froze beneath the sheet and blanket, listening. Her heart rate tripled, and her mouth grew dry. The light of a first-quarter moon spilled in the open window at the head of her old brass bed. The window's screen had been torn loose years ago and never repaired, Susannah knew. Terror coursed through her as she lay still, her muscles aching with fear.

Another click. Carefully, trying not to make a sound, Susannah lifted her head and looked toward the window opposite her bed. A scream jammed in her throat. The profile of a man was silhouetted against the screen. A cry, rooted deep in her lungs, started up through her. Vignettes of the murderer who had nearly taken her life, a man with a narrow face, small eyes and a crooked mouth, smashed into her. If she hadn't been so frightened, Susannah would have rejoiced at finally recalling his face. But now sweat bathed her, and her nightgown grew damp and clung to her as she gripped the sheet, her knuckles whitening.

Breathing raggedly, she watched with widening eyes as the silhouette moved. It wasn't her imagination! The shriek that had lodged in her chest exploded upward. A sound, a mewling cry fraught with desperation, escaped her contorted lips. *Run!* She had to run! She had to get to her parents' home, where she'd be safe.

Susannah scrambled out of bed, and her bare feet hit the wooden floorboards hard. Frantically she tore at the bedroom door, which she always locked behind her. Several of her nails broke as she yanked the chain guard off and jerked the door open. Blindly she raced through the living room and the kitchen and charged wildly out the back door. Her bare feet sank into the dew-laden grass as she raced through the meadow. Her breath coming in ragged gulps, she ran with abandon.

The shadows of the trees loomed everywhere about her as she sped onward. As she sobbed for breath, she thought she heard heavy footsteps coming up behind her. Oh, God! No! *Not again!*

Killian jerked awake as someone crashed into the back door of the farmhouse. At the sound of frantic pounding he leaped out of the bed. Wearing only light blue pajama bottoms, he reached for his Beretta. In one smooth, unbroken motion he slid the weapon out of its holster and opened the door. Swiftly he raced from the first-floor guest room, through the gloomy depths of the house, to the rear door, where the pounding continued unabated.

The curtains blocked his view, but Killian knew in his gut it was Susannah. Unlocking the door, he pulled it open.

Susannah stood there, her face twisted in terror, tears coursing down her taut cheeks and her gray eyes huge with fear. Without thinking, he opened his arms to her.

She fell sobbing into his arms, her nightdress damp with perspiration. Killian held her sagging form against him with one hand; in the other was his pistol, safety off, held in position, ready to fire. Susannah's sobs were a mixture of rasps and cries as she clung to him. Killian's eyes narrowed to slits as he dragged her away from the open door, pressing her up against the wall, out of view of any potential attacker. Rapidly he searched the darkened porch beyond the open door, and the nearby orchard. His heart was racing wildly. He was aware of Susannah's soft, convulsing form trapped between him and the wall as he remained a protective barrier for her, in case the killer was nearby. But only moonlight showed in the quiet orchard and the countryside beyond.

Seconds passed, and Killian still could detect no movement. Susannah's sobs and gasps drowned out any chance of hearing a possible assailant. "Easy, colleen," he whispered raggedly, easing away from her. The feel of her trembling body beneath him was playing havoc with his carefully controlled emotions so much so, he'd called her colleen, an Irish endearment. Fighting his need to absorb the softness of her womanly form against him, Killian forced himself away from her. Shaken, he drew her into the kitchen and nudged the door closed with his foot. "Come on, sit down." He coaxed Susannah over to the table and pulled the chair out for her. She collapsed into it, her face filled with terror as she stared apprehensively at the back door. Killian placed a hand on her shoulder, feeling the terrible tension in her.

"It's all right," he told her huskily, standing behind her chair, alert and waiting. The kitchen had only two small windows, just above the counter and sinks, and the table was in a corner, where a shooter wouldn't be able to draw a bead on them. They were safe—for the moment. Killian's mind ranged over the options a gunman would have. He could barge into the kitchen after her, or leave and wait back at her house. Or he could leave altogether and wait for another opportunity to kill Susannah.

Susannah shook her head violently and jabbed her finger repeatedly toward the door. She glanced up at

Killian's hard, shadowy features. Her eyes widened even more when she spotted the pistol that he held with such casual ease. He was naked from the waist up, she realized, the moonlight accentuating his deep chest and his taut, leanly muscled body. Gulping, Susannah tore her attention back to the door, waiting to hear those heavy footsteps that had been pursuing her like hounds from hell. Her breathing was still harsh, but Killian's hand on her shoulder made her feel safer.

Killian looked around, his hearing keyed to any strange noises. Surprised that the Andersons hadn't awakened with the amount of noise Susannah had made, he glanced down at her. Undiminished panic still showed in her eyes. One hand was pressed against her heaving breast. She looked as if every nerve in her body were raw from whatever she'd just experienced.

Leaning down, he met and held her wide, searching gray eyes. "Susannah, what happened? Was someone after you?"

She nodded her head violently. Her mother always had a pencil and paper on the kitchen table for her. She grabbed them and hastily scrawled a message.

A man! A man tried to get in the window of my bedroom!

Killian's eyes narrowed.

Susannah gasped raggedly as she held his burning, intense gaze.

He patted her shoulder, hoping the gesture would offer her some sense of security. "You stay put, understand? I'm going to try and find him. I'll go back to your house and have a look around."

Susannah gave a low cry, and the meaning of the sound was clear as she gripped Killian's arm and shook her head. *No! No, don't go! He's out there! He'll kill you! Oh, please, don't go! He's after me, not you!*

Killian understood her silent plea for him to remain with her. But it was impossible under the circumstances. "Shh… I'll be all right," he said soothingly. "I want you to stay here. You'll be safer."

Gulping unsteadily, Susannah nodded, unwillingly releasing him.

With a look meant to give her solace, Killian rasped, "I'll be right back. I promise."

Shaking badly in the aftermath of her terrified run, Susannah sat huddled in the chair, feeling suddenly chilled in her damp cotton gown. Killian moved soundlessly, like a cougar, toward the door. But as he opened it and moved out into the night, Susannah felt a new wave of anguish and fear. Killian could be murdered! Weaving in and around the fruit trees, the dew-laden grass soaking his bare feet and pajama legs, Killian quickly circled the Anderson house. If the killer was around, he wasn't here. Moving with the soundlessness of a shadow, he avoided the regular path and headed for Susannah's house. As he ran silently through the orchard, a slice of moon and the resulting silvery light allowed him to penetrate the night. Reaching the old homestead, his pistol held upward, Killian advanced toward the rear of the house, every sense screamingly alert. His nostrils flared, he inhaled, trying to get a whiff of any odor other than the sweet orchard fragrances.

Locating Susannah's bedroom at the rear, Killian saw nothing unusual. Remaining near a small grove of lilac bushes that were at least twenty feet tall, he waited. Patience was the name of the game. His original plan to remain at the Anderson house obviously wasn't a good one, he thought grimly as he waited. Frustration ate at him. He'd have to find a way to stay at Susannah's home in order to protect her. The chill of the predawn air surrounded him, but he was impervious to it.

His gaze scouted the surrounding area, his ears tuned in to pick up any sound. *Nothing.* Killian waited another ten minutes before moving toward the house. The killer could be inside, waiting for Susannah to return. His mouth dry, he compressed his lips into a thin line and quietly stole toward the homestead. His heart set up a sledgehammer pounding in his chest as he eased toward the open back door, the only entrance to the house. Wrapping both hands around the butt of his gun, Killian froze near the door frame. Susannah had left so quickly that the screen door was ajar, as well.

Still, there was no sound that was out of place. But Killian wasn't about to trust the potentially volatile situation. Moving quickly, he dived inside, his pistol aimed. Silence. His eyes mere slits, he remained crouched and tense as he passed through the gloomy kitchen, his head swiveling from side to side, missing nothing, absorbing everything. The living room was next. Nothing.

Finally, after ending the search in Susannah's bedroom, Killian checked the windows. Both were open to allow the fresh early-fall coolness to circulate. One window's screen was in place; the other screen, on the window behind her brass bed, was ripped and in need of repair. Going outside, Killian checked carefully for footprints around either of the bedroom windows, but the grass next to the house was tall and undisturbed. He noticed that as he walked distinct footprints appeared in the heavily dew-laden grass. There were no previous footprints to indicate the presence of an intruder.

Grimly Killian headed back toward the Anderson house, still staying away from the path, still alert, but convinced now that Susannah had experienced a nightmare about her assailant. Relief showered over him at the realization. Still, the incident had put him on notice not to allow the idyllic setting to relax him too much. Dawn was barely crawling onto the horizon, a pale lavender beneath the dark, retreating mantle of the night sky. A rooster was already crowing near the chicken coop as Killian stepped lightly onto the wooden porch.

Susannah met him at the screen door, her eyes huge with silent questions.

"There wasn't anyone," Killian told her as he entered the quiet kitchen. He noticed that Susannah had put a teakettle on the stove and lit the burner beneath it. He saw her eyes go wider with shock at his terse statement. Her gaze traveled to the pistol that was still in his hand, and he realized that it was upsetting her.

"Let me put this away and get decent. I'll be out in a moment. Your folks awake yet?"

Susannah shook her head. Despite her fear, she felt herself respond to the male beauty of Killian's tall, taut body. Black hair covered his chest in abundance, a dark strip trailing down across his flat, hard belly and disappearing beneath the drawstring of the pajamas that hung low on his hips. Susannah gulped, avoiding his narrowed, burning gaze.

In his bedroom, Killian quickly changed into jeans and a white short-sleeved shirt. He pulled on dark blue socks and slipped into a pair of comfortable brown loafers, then ran his fingers through his mussed hair, taming the short strands back into place. Then he strapped on his shoulder holster and slid the pistol into place.

Rubbing his hand across his stubbled jaw, Killian moved back to the kitchen, still amazed that the Andersons had slept through all the commotion. All the more reason, he warned himself, to stay alert for Susannah's sake.

When he entered the kitchen, he saw that she had poured him a cup of tea in a flowery china cup. She was sitting at the table, her hand gripping the notepad and pencil, as if she had been waiting for his return. Killian sat down next to her.

"You had a nightmare," he told her. "That was all."

Susannah rapidly wrote a note on the pad and turned it around for Killian to read.

Impossible! I saw his shadow!

Killian picked up the tea and sipped it, enjoying the clean, minty taste. "There was no trace of footprints around either of your bedroom windows," he explained apologetically. "I searched your house carefully and found nothing. It was a dream, Susannah."

No! Susannah sat back, her arms folded across her breasts, and stared at his darkly etched features while he drank the tea. After a moment, she scribbled on the pad again.

I saw him! I saw the face of the man who nearly killed me!

Killian saw the bleak frustration, and fear in her gray eyes. Without thinking, he placed his hand over hers.

"You remember what he looks like?" Before, she'd been unable to identify her assailant.

She nodded.

"Good. The police need an identification." Realizing he was gently cupping her cool hand, Killian pulled his back and quickly picked up his teacup. What the hell was going on? Couldn't he control his own actions? The idea frightened him. Susannah seemed unconsciously to bring out his softer side. But along with that softer side lurked the monstrous danger that could hurt her. He took a sip from the cup and set it down. His words came out clipped—almost angry.

"When you settle down over this, I want you to draw a picture of his face. I can take it to the police—it might give them a lead."

Hurt by his sudden gruffness, Susannah sat there, still taking in Killian's surprising words. *A nightmare?* How could it have been? It had been so *real!* Touching her forehead, which was now beginning to ache in earnest, Susannah closed her eyes and tried to get a grip on her rampant emotions. Killian's warm, unexpected touch had momentarily soothed her apprehension and settled her pounding heart—but just as quickly he'd withdrawn.

Opening her eyes, she wrote:

I'll draw a picture of him later, when I feel up to it.

Killian nodded, still edgy. One part of him was keyed to Susannah, the other to the door, the windows, and any errant sound. He knew his shoulder holster disturbed her. She kept glancing at him, then at the holster, a question in her eyes. How much could he tell her? How much *should* he tell her? He sensed her curiosity about him and his reasons for being here.

Feeling utterly trapped, Killian tried to think clearly. Being around Susannah seemed to scramble his emotions. He'd been too long without softness in his life. *And,* Killian lectured himself, *it would have to remain that way.* Still, he couldn't let go of the memory of the wonderful sensation of her pressed against him. He should have thrown her to the floor instead of using himself as a human shield to protect her, he thought in disgust. That way he wouldn't have had to touch her, to be reminded of all that he ached to have and never could. But he hadn't been thinking clearly; he'd reacted instinctively.

Grimly he held her gaze. "From now on, Susannah, you need to stay here, in your folks' home, where it's safer."

I will not stay here! I can't! If it was just a dream, then I'll be okay out there. I don't want to stay here.

He studied her in the silence, noting the set of her delicate jaw and the flash of stubbornness in her eyes. With a sigh, he set the cup down on the saucer.

"No. You'll stay here. In *this* house."

Susannah shook her head.

You don't understand! I tried to stay here when I got home from the hospital. I had awful dreams! If I stay in my room, I can't sleep. At the other house I feel safer. I don't have as many nightmares. I don't know why. I can't explain it, but I will not come and stay here.

Killian studied the scribbled note, utterly thwarted.
No one knew better than he did about the night and the
terrible dreams that could stalk it. He understood Susannah's pleading request, probably better than anyone else
could. His heart squeezed at the pain in her admission,
because he'd too long lived a similar life. With a sigh, he
muttered, "All right, but then I'm staying at your place
with you until we can get this settled. I need to know for
sure whether this guy is real or just a dream."

Shocked, Susannah stared at him, her mouth dropping
open. She felt the brutal hardness around him again and
saw anger, touched with anxiety in his eyes. Her mind
reeled with questions as the adrenaline left her bloodstream and left her shaky in its aftermath. With a trembling hand, she wrote:

Who are you? You carry a gun. I don't think you
are who you say you are. Morgan suspects something, doesn't he? Please, tell me the truth, even if
you don't tell my parents. I deserve to know.

Killian fingered the note, refusing to meet her chal-
lenging gaze. Stunned by Susannah's intuitive grasp of
the situation, he realized he had to tell her. Otherwise,
she'd never allow him to stay at her house.

"All right," he growled, "here's the truth. Morgan suspects that the man who tried to kill you will come and
hunt you down once he knows you survived. You can ID
him, and he's going to try to kill you before you can do
it." He saw Susannah's eyes grow dark with shock. Angry
that he had to hurt her with the truth, Killian snapped,
"I'm here on assignment. I'm to protect you. Please don't
tell your parents my real reason for being here. Mor-

gan feels they've been through enough. I wasn't going to tell you, dammit, but you're so stubborn, you didn't leave me any recourse. I can't have you staying alone at the other house."

Susannah felt Killian's anger buffet her. Despite her fear and shock, she felt anger toward him even more.

How dare you! How dare Morgan! You should have told me this in the first place!

Killian didn't like being put in the middle, and he glared at her. "Look, I do as I'm ordered. I'm breaking my word in telling you this, and I'll probably catch hell from my boss for doing it. I don't like this any more than you do. If you want all of the truth, I don't even want to be here—I don't take assignments that involve women. But Morgan threatened to fire me if I didn't take this mission, so you and I are in the same boat. You don't want me here, and I damn well don't want to be here!"

Stunned, Susannah blinked at the powerful wave of feeling behind his harsh words. She sensed a desperation in Killian's anger, and it was that desperation that defused her own righteous anger.

I'm sorry, Killian. I shouldn't be angry with you.

He shook his head and refused to meet her eyes. The frightening truth was, every time he did, he wanted simply to find his way into her arms and be held. "Don't apologize," he muttered. "It isn't your fault, either. We're both caught between a rock and a hard place."

Without thinking, Susannah slowly raised her hand and placed it across Killian's clenched one on the table.

His head snapped up as her fingers wrapped around his. The anger dissolved in his eyes, and for just a moment Susannah could have sworn she saw longing in his stormy gaze. But, just as quickly, it was gone, leaving only an icy coldness. She removed her hand from his, all too aware that he was rejecting her touch.

All she had wanted to do was comfort Killian. From her work, Susannah knew the healing nature of human touch firsthand. Killian had looked positively torn by the fact that he had to be here with her. Susannah had wanted to let him know somehow that she understood his dilemma. He didn't want anything to do with her because she was a woman. Her curiosity was piqued, but she knew better than to ask. Right now, Killian was edgy, turning the cup around and around in his long, spare hands.

You don't have to stay out there with me.

Killian made a muffled sound and stood up suddenly. He moved away from the table, automatically checking the window with his gaze. "Yes," he said irritably, "I do. I don't like it any more than you do, but it has to be done."

But it was a nightmare! You said so yourself. You can stay here with my folks.

Killian savagely spun on his heel, and when he spoke his voice was hoarse. "There's nothing you can say that will change my mind. You need protection, Susannah."

With a trembling hand, Susannah touched her brow. It was nerve-racking enough to stay by herself at the abandoned farmhouse. She was desperately afraid of the dark, of the terrors that came nightly when she lay down as

her overactive imagination fueled the fires of her many
fears. But Killian staying with her? He was so blatantly
male—so quiet, yet so capable. Fighting her own feelings toward him, she sat for a good minute before writing on the notepad again.

Please tell my folks the truth about this. I don't want
to lie to them about the reason you're staying out
at the house with me. It would seem funny to them
if you suddenly started living out there with me.

Killian couldn't disagree with her. He paced the room
quietly, trying to come up with a better plan. He stopped
and looked down at her exhausted features.
"I'll talk to them this morning."
Relief flowed through Susannah, and she nodded.

Morgan was trying to protect us, but this is one
time when we should know the whole truth.

"I tried to tell him that," Killian said bitterly. He stood
by the table, thinking. "That's all water under the bridge
now," he said. "You saw the killer's face in your nightmare. I need you to draw a picture of him this morning
so that I can take it to the police station. They'll fax it to
Lexington and to Morgan."
Trying to combat the automatic reactions of fear, rage
and humiliation that came with remembering, Susannah nodded. Her hand still pressed against her brow, she
tried to control the cold-bladed anxiety triggered by
the discussion.
It was impossible for Killian to steel himself against
the clarity of the emotions he read in Susannah's pale

face. "Easy," he said soothingly. "Take some deep breaths, Susannah, and the panic will start to go away." He watched her breasts rise and fall sharply beneath her wrinkled cotton gown, and he couldn't help thinking how pretty she looked in the thin garment with lace sewn around its oval neckline. She was like that lace, fragile and easily crushed, he realized as he stood watching her wrestle with her fear.

Miraculously, Susannah felt much of her panic dissolve beneath his husky-voiced instructions. She wasn't sure if it was because of the deep breaths or merely Killian's quiet presence. How did he know what she was experiencing? He must have experienced the very same thing, otherwise he wouldn't know how to help her. And he was helping her—even if he'd made it clear that he didn't want to be here.

"Good," Killian said gruffly as she became calm. He poured them more tea and took his chair again. "I'll sleep in the bedroom down the hall from yours. I'm a restless sleeper," he warned her sharply. "I have nightmares myself..." His voice trailed off.

Susannah stared at him, swayed by the sincerity in his dark blue eyes. There was such torment in them. Toward her? Toward the assignment? She just wasn't sure. Morning light was stealing through the ruffled curtains at the window now, softening his harsh features.

Nervously fingering the rectangular notepad, Susannah frowned, uncertain of her own feelings as she was every time he was with her.

"I won't bother you, if that's what you're worried about," he added when he saw the confusion on her face. He prayed he could keep his word—hoped against hope that he wouldn't have one of the terrible, wrenching nightmares that haunted him.

Agitated, Susannah got to her feet and moved to the window. The pale lavender of dawn reminded her of the color of her favorite flowers—the lilacs. Pressing and releasing her fingers against the porcelain sink, she thought about Killian's statement.

Killian studied Susannah in the quiet of the kitchen. Her dark hair lay mussed against her tense shoulders, a sable cloak against the pristine white of her nightgown. Killian ached to touch her hair, to tunnel his fingers through it and find out what it felt like. Would it be as soft as her body had been against his? Or more coarse, in keeping with the ramrod-straight spine that showed her courage despite the circumstances?

"Look," he said, breaking the tense silence, "maybe this will end sooner than I expect. I'll work on the house over there to stay close in case something happens. I'll paint and fix up the windows, the doors." *Anything to keep my mind off you.*

Turning, Susannah looked at him. He sat at the table, his long fingers wrapped around the dainty china cup on the yellow oilcloth. His body was hunched forward, and he had an unhappy expression on his face. She would never forget the look in his eyes, his alertness, or the sense of safety she'd felt when she'd fallen sobbing into his arms at the back door. Why was she hedging now about allowing him to be near her?

Licking her lips, she nodded. Suddenly more tired than she could remember ever being, she left the counter. It was time to go home. When she got to the screen door, Killian moved quickly out of his chair.

"I'll walk you back," Killian said, his tone brooking no argument. Opening the screen door, she walked out.

Although he wanted Susannah to believe he was relaxed, Killian remained on high alert as they trod the damp path through the orchard back to her home. The sky had turned a pale pink. It wouldn't be long before the sun came up.

Killian felt Susannah's worry as she looked around, her arms wrapped tightly around herself. He wanted to step close—to place a protective arm around her shoulders and give her the sense of security she so desperately needed and so richly deserved. Yet he knew that touching her would melt his defenses. That couldn't happen—ever. Killian swore never to allow Susannah to reach inside him; but she had that ability, and he knew it. Somehow, he had to strengthen his resolve and keep her at arm's length. At all costs. For her own sake.

"Maybe if I patch that torn screen in your bedroom and put some locks on the windows, you'll feel better about being there." He saw her flash him a grateful look. "I'll tell your folks what happened when they get up. Then I'll contact Morgan."

Susannah nodded her agreement. She longed simply to step closer to Killian, to be in his protective embrace again. She couldn't forget the lean power of his body against hers, the way he'd used himself as a barrier to protect her.

She wrestled with conflicting feelings. Why was Killian so unhappy about having to stay out at the house with her? She couldn't help how she felt. She knew that right now, if she went back to her old room at her folks' house, the nightmares would return. Her life had begun to stabilize—until tonight. If only Killian could understand why she had to be at the old homestead.

"I'll make sure your house is safe. Then I want you to get some sleep. When you get up, you can draw me the face you saw in the nightmare."

Killian saw Susannah's eyes darken.

"Don't worry, I'll be around. You may not know it, but I'll be there. Like a shadow."

Shivering, Susannah nodded. Her life had turned into nothing but a series of shadows. Killian's body against hers had been real, and never had she needed that more. But Killian didn't like her, didn't want to be with her. She swallowed her need to be held, still grateful that Killian would be nearby. Perhaps her mind was finally ready to give up the information it had seen, and that should help in the long run.

Touching her throat, she fervently wished her voice would come back. At least now she could make some noise, and that seemed a hopeful sign. She stole a glance up into Killian's grim, alert features. She'd welcome his company, even though he didn't want hers. Right now, she needed the human contact. Thinking back, she realized that the anger she'd sensed in Killian had been due to his not wanting to take the assignment. It hadn't really been aimed directly at her. Sometimes it was lonely out there at the homestead. He wasn't a willing guest, Susannah reminded herself. Still, if her attacker was really out there, she would feel a measure of safety knowing that Killian was nearby.

After thoroughly checking Susannah's home again, Killian allowed her into the farmhouse. He'd double-check around the house and quietly search the acreage around it just to make sure no one was hiding in wait.

At the bedroom door, Susannah shyly turned and gave him a soft, hesitant smile. A thank-you showed clearly in her eyes, and it took everything Killian had for him to turn away from her. "I'll be over about noon," he rasped, more gruffly than he'd intended.

Susannah waited for Killian's promised noon arrival as she sat at her kitchen table. She questioned herself. Her real home was in town, near the school where she taught. Why didn't she have the courage to move back there? Glumly she admitted it was because she was afraid of being completely alone. At least this broken-down homestead was close to her parents.

Killian deliberately made noise as he stepped up on Susannah's porch, carrying art supplies under one arm. He knew all about being jumpy. He'd decked more than one man who had inadvertently come up behind him without warning. Wolf had been one of those men, on assignment down in Peru. The others on the team had learned from his mistake and had always let Killian know they were coming.

Susannah was waiting for him at the screen door. She looked beautiful, clothed in a long, lightweight denim skirt and a fuchsia short-sleeved blouse. She'd tied her hair back with a pink ribbon, and soft tendrils brushed her temples. Killian tensed himself against the tempting sight of her.

Stepping into the kitchen, Killian sniffed. "You've got coffee on?" He found himself wanting to ease the seriousness out of her wary eyes. The dark shadows beneath them told him she hadn't slept well since the nightmare.

Placing sketch pad, colored pencils and eraser on the

table, Killian eased into a chair. Susannah went to the cupboard, retrieved a white ceramic mug and poured him some coffee. He nodded his thanks as she came over and handed it to him.

"Sit down," he urged her. "We've got some work to do."

Looking over the art supplies, Susannah sat down at his elbow. Somehow Killian looked heart-stoppingly handsome and dangerous all at once. His dress was casual, but she always sensed the inner tension in him, and could see some undefinable emotion in his blue eyes when he looked at her. But the anger was no longer there, she noted with relief.

"I'd like you to sketch for me the man you saw in your nightmare," Killian said.

Hesitant, Susannah fingered the box of colored pencils. Her throat constricted, and she closed her eyes for a moment. How could she make Killian understand that since the attack her love of drawing and painting had gone away?

"It doesn't have to be fancy, Susannah. Draw me something. Anything. I have a way to check what you sketch for me against police mug shots." He saw pain in her eyes, and her lower lip trembled as she withdrew her hand from the box of pencils. He cocked his head. "What is it?" He recalled his sister's pain, and the hours he'd spent holding her while she cried after realizing her once-beautiful face was gone forever. A powerful urge to reach out and give Susannah that same kind of help nearly overwhelmed him, but he reared back inwardly. He couldn't.

With a helpless shrug, Susannah swallowed against

the lump and shakily opened up the sketch pad. She had
to try. She believed in Killian, and she believed he could
help her. Suddenly embarrassed, she took her pad and
pencil and wrote:

> I'm rusty at this. I haven't drawn since being
> wounded.

He grimaced. "I'm no art critic, Susannah. I can't draw
a straight line. Anything you can do will look great to
me. Give it your best try."

Susannah picked up a pencil and began to sketch. She
tried to concentrate on the task at hand, but she found her
senses revolving back to Killian's overwhelming presence. All morning she'd thought about him staying here
with her. It wasn't him she couldn't trust, she realized—it
was herself! The discovery left her feeling shaken. Never
had a man influenced her on all levels, as Killian did.
What was it about him? For the thousandth time, Susannah ached to have her voice back. If only she could talk!

Quiet descended upon them. Killian gazed around
the kitchen, keenly aware of Susannah's presence. It was
like a rainbow in his dismal life. There were at least
forty colorful drawings tacked to the kitchen walls, obviously done by very young children. Probably her class.
Peace, a feeling that didn't come often to Killian, descended gently around him. Was it the old-fashioned
house? Being out in the country away from the mad-
ding crowd? Or—he swung his gaze back to Susannah
and saw her brows drawn together in total concentration,
her mouth pursed—was it her?

Unconsciously Killian's shoulders dropped, and he
eased the chair back off its two front legs, loosely holding

the mug of coffee against his belly. Birds, mostly robins, were singing and calling to one another. The sweet scents of grass, ripening fruit and clean mountain air wafted through the kitchen window. Susannah had a small radio on in the corner, and FM music flowed softly across the room, like an invisible caress.

His gaze settled on Susannah's ponytail, and he noted the gold and red glints between the sable strands. Her hair was thick and luxurious. A man could drive himself crazy wondering what the texture of it was like, Killian decided unhappily. Right now, he knew his focus had to be on keeping her protected, not his own personal longings.

The sketch of the man took shape beneath Susannah's slender fingers over the next hour. Frequently she struggled, erasing and beginning again. Killian marveled at her skill as an artist. She might consider herself rusty, but she was definitely a professional. Finally her mouth quirked and she glanced up. Slowly she turned the sketch toward him.

"Unsavory-looking bastard," Killian whispered as he put the coffee aside and held the sketch up to examine it. "Brown eyes, blond hair and crooked front teeth?"

Susannah nodded. She saw the change in Killian's assessing blue eyes. A fierce anger emanated from him, and she sensed his hatred of her attacker.

He reminds me of a weasel, with close-set eyes that are small and beady-looking.

Killian nodded and put the sketch aside. "I'll take this to the police department today. I called Morgan. He knows you've remembered what your attacker looked like, so he's anxious to get this, too. He'll know what to do with it. If this bastard has a police record, we'll be on the way to catching him."

Chilled, Susannah slowly rubbed her arms with her hands.

Killian felt her raw fear. But he stopped himself from reaching out to give her a touch of reassurance. Gathering up the sketch, he rose. "I'll be back as soon as I can. In the meantime, you stay alert."

The warning made another chill move through her as she looked up at him. Somehow, some of the tension around him was gone. The peace that naturally inhabited the farmhouse had always worked wonders on her own nervousness, and Susannah realized that it might be doing the same for him. She nodded in agreement to his orders.

"It would be best if you went down to your parents' house while I'm gone. They know the truth now, and they'll be more watchful for you. In the long run, it's best this way."

Susannah couldn't disagree with him. The more people who were on guard and watchful, the less chance of the killer's finding her. Rising, she left with him.

"Maybe," Killian told her as they walked across the top of the hill, "this will be over soon."

At his words, Susannah's eyes sparkled with such fierce hope, combined with gratitude, that Killian had to force himself to keep from reaching out to caress her flushed cheek.

He'd give his life for her, if necessary, he realized suddenly. Susannah was worth dying for.

Chapter 4

Susannah was helping her mother can ripe figs in the kitchen when she saw Killian return from Glen. She stood at the counter and watched him emerge from the four-wheel-drive Land Cruiser. The vehicle seeming fitting for a man like Killian, she thought, a man who was rugged, a loner, iconoclastic. Though his face remained emotionless, his roving blue gaze held her, made her feel an inherent safety as he looked around the property. Her heart took a skipping beat as he turned and headed into the house.

"Killian's home," Pansy said. She shook her head as she transferred the recently boiled figs to the jars awaiting on the counter. "I'm so nervous now." With a little laugh, she noted, "My hands haven't stopped shaking since he told us the truth this morning."

Wanting somehow to reassure her, Susannah put her arms around her mother and gave her a hug.

Killian walked into the kitchen and saw Susannah embracing her mother. He halted, a strange, twisting feeling moving through him. Mother and daughter held each other, and he remained motionless. It was Susannah who sensed his presence first. She loosened the hug and smiled shyly in his direction.

Pansy tittered nervously when she realized he was standing in the doorway. "I didn't hear you come in, Mr. Killian."

"I should have said something," he said abruptly. Killian felt bad for the woman. Ever since he'd told the Andersons the truth, it had been as if a shock wave had struck the farm. Sam Anderson had promptly gone out to the barn to fix a piece of machinery. Pansy had suddenly gotten busy with canning duties. Staying occupied was one way to deal with tension, Killian realized. His gaze moved to Susannah, whose cheeks were flushed. Her hair was still in a ponytail, the tendrils sticking to her dampened temples with the heat of the day and the lack of breeze through the kitchen. She looked beautiful.

"Did you tell the police?" Pansy asked, nervously wiping her hands on her checked apron.

"Yes. Everyone has a copy of the picture Susannah sketched. Morgan will call me here if they find out who it is. The FBI's in on it, so maybe we'll turn up something a little sooner."

Susannah heard her mother give a little moan, and she reached over and touched her shoulder and gave her a look she hoped she could decipher.

"Oh, I'm okay, honey," Pansy said in response, patting her hand in a consoling way.

Killian absorbed the soft look Susannah gave her worried mother. She had such sensitivity. How he wished he could have that in his life. A sadness moved through him, and he turned away, unable to stand the compassion on Susannah's features.

"Is Sam still out at the barn?" he demanded.

"Yes."

"I'll go help him," Killian said, and left without another word.

An odd ache had filled Susannah as she watched Killian's carefully arranged face give way to his real feelings. There had been such naked hunger in his eyes that it left her feeling in touch with herself as a woman as never before. She tried to help her mother, unable to get Killian's expression out of her mind—or her heart.

"That Mr. Killian's a strange one," Pansy said, to no one in particular, as she spooned the figs into a jar, their fragrant steam rising around her. "He's so gruff. Almost rude. But he cares. I can feel it around him. I wonder why he's so standoffish? It's hard to get close to him, to let him know how grateful we are for him being here."

Susannah nodded. Killian *was* gruff—like a cranky old bear. It was part of what he used to keep people at bay, she thought. Yet, just a few minutes ago, she'd seen the real Sean Killian—a man who had wants—and desires. And her heart wouldn't settle down over that discovery.

Around four o'clock, Pansy sent Susannah out with a gallon of iced tea and two glasses for the men, who were still laboring in the barn. The sunlight was bright and hot for an early-September day, and Susannah reveled in it. Chickens scattered out of her path as she crossed the dirt driveway to the barn, which sat off to one side of the green-and-white farmhouse.

As she entered the huge, airy structure, the familiar smell of hay and straw filled her nostrils. At one end of the barn, where the machinery was kept, Susannah spotted her father working intently on his tractor. The engine had been pulled up and out of the tractor itself and hung suspended by two chains looped around one of the barn's huge upper beams. She saw Killian down on his knees, working beneath the engine while her father stood above him. They were trying to thread a hose from above the engine to somewhere down below, where Killian leaned beneath it, his hand outstretched for it.

Killian had clearly shed his shirt long before, and his skin glistened with sweat from the hot barn air, accentuating his muscular chest and arms. A lock of black hair stuck damply to his forehead as he frowned in concentration, intent on capturing the errant hose.

Susannah slowed her step halfway to them. Her father turned away from the tractor, going to the drawer where he kept many of his tools. Just then, she heard a vague snap. Her eyes rose to the beam that held the heavy engine. Instantly her gaze shifted to Killian, who seemed oblivious of the sound, his concentration centered on threading the hose through the engine.

Sam Anderson was still bent over a drawer, rummaging for a tool.

Susannah realized that the chain was slowly coming undone. At any second it would snap free and that heavy tractor engine would fall on Killian! Without thinking, she cried out a warning. *"Look out, Killian!"*

Her scream shattered the barn's musty stillness.

Killian jerked his hand back and heard a cracking, metallic sound. He glanced to his left and saw Susannah, her finger pointing toward the beam above him. Sam had whirled around at the cry. In one motion, Killian leaped away from the engine.

Susannah clutched the jar of iced tea to her as she saw the chain give way. She screamed as the tractor engine slammed heavily down on the barn floor. But Killian was leaping away as the engine fell, rolling through the straw and dust on the floor.

Setting the iced tea aside, Susannah ran toward him, unsure whether he was hurt or not. He lay on his side, his back to her, as she raced up to him.

"Killian?" she sobbed. "Killian? Are you hurt?" She fell to her knees, reaching out to touch him.

"Good God!" Sam Anderson hurried to Killian's side. "Son? You all right?"

Breathing raggedly, Susannah touched Killian's hard, damp shoulder. He rolled over onto his back, his eyes narrowed and intense.

"Are—are you all right?" she stammered, quickly glancing down his body, checking for blood or a sign of injury.

"I'm fine," Killian rasped, sitting up. Then he grew very still. He saw the look in Susannah's huge eyes, saw her expressive fingers resting against her swanlike throat. Her face was pale. He blinked. Susannah had spoken. Her eyes still mirrored her fear for him, and he felt the coolness of her fingers resting on his dirty arm.

"You're sure?" Susannah demanded breathlessly, trading a look with her father, who knelt on the other side of Killian. "You could have been killed!" Badly shaken, she stared down into his taut face and held his burning gaze. Killian was like a lean, bronzed statue, his gleaming muscles taut from the hard physical labor.

Sam gasped and stared at his daughter. "Honey, you're talking!"

Gasping herself, Susannah reared back on her heels,

her hands flying to her mouth. She saw Killian grin slightly. It was true! She had spoken! With a little cry, Susannah touched her throat, almost unbelieving. "Pa, I got my voice back…"

Killian felt Susannah's joy radiating from her like sunlight itself. He felt embraced and lifted by her joy at her discovery. And what a beautiful voice she had—low and husky. A tremor of warning fled through him as he drowned in her shining eyes. This was just one more thing to like about Susannah, to want from her.

Susannah's gaze moved from her father to Killian and back again. "I can speak! I can talk again!" Susannah choked, and tears streamed down her cheeks.

"Oh," Sam whispered unsteadily, "that's wonderful, honey!" He got to his feet and came around to where his daughter knelt. Leaning over, he helped her stand, then threw his arms around her and held her tight for a long, long time.

Touched, Killian remained quietly on the floor. The closeness of Sam with his daughter brought back good, poignant memories of his early home life, of his mother's strength and love. Slowly he eased himself to his feet and began to brush off the straw that clung to his damp skin. Sam and Susannah were laughing and crying, their brows touching. Tears jammed unexpectedly into Killian's eyes, and he quickly blinked them away. What the hell was happening to him?

Turning away from the happy scene, Killian went to retrieve his shirt. Disgruntled and shaken at his own emotional response, he tried to avoid looking at Susannah. It was *her*. Whatever magic it was that she wielded as a woman, it had a decided effect on him, whether he wanted it to or not. Agitated, Killian buttoned his shirt, stuffed the tail into his jeans and gathered up the broken chain, which lay across the floor and around the engine.

"Come on, honey, let's go tell Ma," Sam quavered, his arm around his daughter's shoulders. He gave Killian a grateful look. "You, too. You deserve to be a part of the celebration."

Killian shrugged. "No…you folks go ahead…"

Susannah eased out of her father's embrace and slowly approached Killian. How beautifully and dangerously male he was. Her senses were heightened to almost a painful degree, giving her an excruciating awareness of his smoldering, hooded look as she approached. His chiseled mouth was drawn in at the corners.

"You're okay?" Susannah breathed softly. Then she stepped back, blushing.

Shocked by her unexpected concern for him despite what had happened to her, Killian was at a loss for words. He gripped the chain in his hands. "I'm okay," he managed in a strangled tone. "Go share the news with your mother…" he ordered unsteadily. What a beautiful voice she had, Killian thought dazedly, reeling from the feelings her voice stirred within him.

Trapped beneath his sensual, scorching gaze, Susannah's lips parted. What would it be like to explore that mouth endlessly, that wonderful mouth that was now pursed into a dangerous, thin line of warning? Every nerve in her body responded to his look of hunger. It was the kind of look that made Susannah wildly aware that she was a woman, in all ways. It was not an insulting look, it was a look of desire—for her alone.

"Come on, honey," Sam said happily as he came up and patted her shoulder, "let's go share the good news with Ma. She's gonna cry a bucket of tears over this."

Killian remained still, nearly overwhelmed by his need to reach out and touch Susannah's mussed hair or caress her flushed cheek. He watched as father and daughter left the barn together. Their happiness surrounded him like a long-lost memory. Taking a deep, steadying breath, Killian began to unhook the ends of the chain from the engine. His mind was waging war with his clamoring heart and his aching body. Susannah could now tell them what had happened to her. His emotions were in utter disarray. Her voice was soft and husky, like a well-aged Irish whiskey.

Angrily Killian cleaned up the mess in the barn and put the chains aside. In a way, he felt chained to the situation at the farm, he thought—chained to Susannah in a connection he could neither fight nor flee. Never had a woman gotten to him as Susannah had. His relationships with women had been few and brief—one-night stands that allowed him to leave before darkness came and made an enemy out of anyone who dared get close to him. What was it about Susannah that was different? The need to explore her drove him out of the barn. He slowly walked toward the farmhouse, savagely jamming down his fiery needs. Maybe now he could talk to Susannah about the assault, he reasoned.

Pansy was serving up lemonade in tall purple glasses in celebration. Susannah felt Killian's approach at the screen door before he appeared. What was this synchronicity the two of them seemed to share? Puzzled, but far too joyous over her voice returning to spend time worrying, she gave him a brilliant, welcoming smile as he walked into the kitchen.

"Sit down, son," Sam thundered. "You've earned yourself a glass of Ma's special hand-squeezed lemonade."

Killian hesitated. He'd hoped to come into the house, go to his room, take a cold shower and settle his roiling emotions. But the looks on their faces made him decide differently. With a curt nod, he took a seat opposite Susannah. Her eyes sparkled like diamonds caught in sunlight. He felt himself becoming helplessly ensnared in the joy that radiated around her like a rainbow of colors.

Pansy gave him the lemonade, gratitude visible in every line of her worn face.

"Killian, we're glad you're all right," she said. "Thank goodness you weren't hurt." She reached over and patted Susannah's hand warmly. "Just hearin' Susannah's voice again is like hearin' the angels speakin'."

Killian sipped the icy lemonade, hotly aware of the fire within him, captive to Susannah's thankful gaze. "Your daughter saved me from a few broken bones," he muttered.

Sam hooted and said, "A few? Son, you would've had your back broken if my Susannah hadn't found her voice in time."

Killian nodded and stared down at the glass. If there was such a thing as an angelic woman, it was Susannah. Her skin glowed with renewed color, and her lips were stretched into a happy curve as she gripped her father's leathery brown hand. Killian absorbed the love and warmth among the family members. Nothing could be stronger or better than that, in his opinion. Except maybe the fevered love of a man who loved his woman with a blind passion that overrode the fear of death in him.

"I can't believe it! This is like a dream—I can talk again!" Susannah told him, her hand automatically moving to her throat.

Killian ruminated over the events. He was perfectly

at ease with saving other people's lives—but no one, with the exception of his teammates in Peru, had ever saved him from certain death. And he had to admit to himself that Sam was correct: If not for Susannah he'd have a broken back at best—and at worst, he'd be dead. Killian was unsure how to feel about having a woman save his worthless hide. He had a blinding loyalty to those he fought beside, to those who saved him. He lifted his head and stared at Susannah. Things had changed subtly but irrevocably because of this event. No longer was Morgan's edict that he stay here and protect her hanging over his head like a threat.

Moving his fingers across the beaded coolness of the glass, Killian pondered the web of circumstances tightening around him. Perhaps his sense of honor was skewed. On one hand, Susannah deserved his best efforts to protect her. On the other hand, he saw himself as a danger to her each night he stayed at her home. What was he going to do? He could no longer treat her as a mere assignment—an object to be protected. Not that he'd been particularly successful with that tack before.

"Getting your voice back is going to be a big help," Killian offered lamely.

With a slight laugh, Susannah said, "I don't know if you'll feel that way or not, Sean. Pa says I talk too much." Susannah felt heat rise in her neck and into her face when his head snapped up, his eyes pinning her. She suddenly realized she'd slipped and used his first name. Vividly recalling that Killian had said that only his mother and sister used his first name, she groped for an apology. "I'm sorry, I forgot—you like to be called by your last name."

Killian shrugged, not wanting to make a big deal out of it. "You saved my life. I think that gives you the right to call me anything you want." His heart contracted at her husky, quavering words, and he retreated into silence, feeling that words were useless. Her voice, calling him Sean, had released a Pandora's box of deeply held emotions from his dark, haunted past. When she'd said his name, it had come out like a prayer. A beautiful, clean prayer of thanks. How little in his world was clean or beautiful. But somehow this woman giving him her lustrous look made him feel as if he were both. His head argued differently, but for once Killian ignored it.

With a happy smile, Pansy came over and rested her hands on her daughter's shoulders. "You two young'ns will stay for dinner, won't you? We have to celebrate!"

Killian wanted the safety of isolation. He shook his head. "I've got things to do, Mrs. Anderson." When he saw the regret in the woman's face, he got to his feet. He felt Susannah's eyes on him, as if she knew what he was doing and why he was doing it. "Thanks anyway," he mumbled, and quickly left the kitchen. His job was to protect this family, not to join it. Killian was relieved to escape, not sure how long he could continue to hold his emotions in check. As he stalked through the living room and down the hall to his bedroom, all he wanted was a cold shower to shock him back to the harsh reality he'd lived with since leaving Ireland so many years before. And somehow, he was going to have to dredge up enough control to be able to sleep under the same roof with Susannah. Somehow...

Early-evening light shed a subdued glow around the kitchen of Susannah's small house. Killian sat at the kitchen table and watched as she made coffee at the counter. He had insisted he wasn't hungry, but Pansy had sent a plate of food with him when he'd escorted Susannah back to her homestead. The meal had been simple but filling. Tonight he was more tense than he could recall ever being. He felt as if his emotions were caught in a desperate tug-of-war.

Was it because of Susannah's whiskey laughter, that husky resonance that made him feel as if she were reaching out and caressing him? Killian sourly tried to ignore what her breathy voice did to him.

"You sure ate your share of Ma's cherry pie, Sean," she said with a teasing look over her shoulder. Killian sat at the table, his chin resting forward on his chest, his chair tipped back on its rear legs. His narrow face was dark and thoughtful.

"It was good."

Chortling, Susannah retrieved the lovely flowered china cups and saucers from the oak cabinet. "You ate like a man who hasn't had too many home-cooked meals in his life."

Killian grudgingly looked at her as she came over and set the cups and saucers on the oilcloth. Her insight, as always, was unsettling to him. "I haven't," he admitted slowly.

Susannah hesitated. There was so much she wanted to say to him. She slid her fingers across the back of the wooden chair opposite him. "Sean, I need to talk to you. I mean really talk to you." Heat rushed up her neck and into her cheeks, and Susannah groaned, touching her flushed face. "I wish I didn't turn beet red all the time!"

Killian absorbed her discomfort. "In Ireland we'd call you a primrose—a woman with moonlight skin and red primroses for cheeks," he said quietly.

The utter beauty of his whispered words made Susannah stand in shocked silence. "You're a poet."

Uncomfortable, he muttered, "I don't think of myself in those terms."

She saw the wariness in his eyes and sensed that her boldness was making him edgy. "Is it a crime to say that a man possesses a soul that can see the world in terms of beauty?"

Relieved that Susannah had turned and walked back to the counter, Killian frowned. He studied her as he tried to formulate an answer to her probing question. Each movement of her hands was graceful—and each time she touched something, he felt as if she were touching him instead. Shaking his head, he wondered what the hell had gotten into him. He was acting like a man who'd been without a woman far too long. Well, hadn't he?

Clearing his throat, Killian said, "I'd rather talk about you than myself."

Susannah sat down, drying her hands on a green-and-white checked towel. "I know you would, but I'm not going to let you." She kept her voice light, because she sensed that if she pushed him too hard he'd close up. She opened her hands to him. "I need to clear the air on some things between us."

Killian's stomach knotted painfully. The fragrant smell of coffee filled the kitchen. "Go on," he said in a warning growl.

Susannah nervously touched her brow. "I'm actually afraid to talk to you. Maybe it's because of what happened, getting shot by that man. I don't know…"

"The hurt part, the wounded side of you, feels that fear," Killian told her, his tone less gruff now. "It was a man who nearly killed you. Why shouldn't you be afraid of men in general?" He had to stop himself from reaching out to touch her tightly clasped hands on the tabletop. Her knuckles were white.

"You seem to know so much about me—about what I'm feeling." She gave him a long, scrutinizing look. "How?"

Shifting uncomfortably, Killian shrugged. "Experience, maybe."

"Whose? Your own?" After all, he was a mercenary, Susannah reminded herself. A world-traveled and world-weary man who had placed his life on the line time and again.

"No...not exactly... My sister, Meg, was—" His mouth quirked at the corners. "She was beautiful, and had a promising career as a stage actress. Meg met and fell in love with an Irish-American guy, and they were planning on getting married." He cleared his throat and forced himself to finish. "She flew back to Ireland to be in a play—and at her stopover at Heathrow Airport a terrorist bomb went off."

"Oh, no..." Susannah whispered. "Is she...alive?"

The horror of that day came rushing back to Killian, and he closed his eyes, his voice low with feeling. "Yes, she's alive. But the bomb... She's badly disfigured. She's no longer beautiful. Her career ended, and I've seen her through fifteen operations to restore her face." Killian shrugged hopelessly. "Meg cut off her engagement to Ian, too, even though he wanted to stay with her. She couldn't believe that any man could love her like that."

"How awful," Susannah whispered. Reaching out, she slid her hand across his tightly clenched fist. "It must have been hard on you, too."

Wildly aware of Susannah's touch, Killian warned

himself that she'd done it only out of compassion. Her fingers were cool and soft against his sun-toughened skin. His mouth went dry, and his heart rate skyrocketed. Torn between emotions from the past and the boiling heat scalding up through him, Killian rasped, "Meg has been a shadow of herself since then. She's fearful, always looking over her shoulder, has terrible nightmares, and doesn't trust anyone." Bitterly he added, "She's even wary of me, her own brother." It hurt to admit that, but Killian sensed that Susannah had the emotional strength to deal with his first-time admission to anyone about his sister.

Tightening her hand around his, Susannah ached for Killian. She saw the hurt and confusion in his eyes. "Everyone suffers when someone is hurt like that." Forcing herself to release Killian's hand, Susannah whispered, "Look what I've put my parents through since I awakened from the coma. Look how I distrusted you at first."

He gave her a hooded look. "You're better off if you do."

"No," Susannah said fervently, her voice quavering with feeling. "I don't believe that anymore, Sean. You put on a tough act, and I'm sure you're very tough emotionally, but I can read your eyes. I can see the trauma that Meg went through, and how it has affected you." She smiled slightly. "I may come from hill folk, but I've got two good eyes in my head, and a heart that's never led me wrong."

Killian struggled with himself. He'd never spoken to anyone about his sister—not even to Morgan. And now he was spilling his guts to Susannah. He said nothing, for fear of divulging even more.

"I'm really sorry about your sister. Is she living in America?"

"No. She lives near the Irish Sea, in a thatched hut that used to belong to a fisherman and his wife. They died and left her the place. Old Dun and his wife Em were like grandparents to Meg. They took care of her when I had to be on assignment. Meg can't stand being around people."

"It's hard for most people to understand how it feels to be a victim of violence," Susannah mused. She looked over at the coffeepot. The coffee was ready to be served. Rising, she added, "I know that since I woke up from the coma I've been jumpy and paranoid. If someone comes up behind me, I scream. If I catch sight of my own shadow unexpectedly I break out in a sweat and my heart starts hammering." She poured coffee into the cups. "Stupid, isn't it?"

Putting a teaspoon of sugar into the dark, fragrant coffee, Killian shook his head. "Not at all. I call it a survival reflex."

Coming back to the table and sitting down, Susannah gave him a weak smile. "Even now, I dread talking about what happened to me." She turned her hands over. "My palms are damp, and my heart is running like a rabbit's."

"Adrenaline," Killian explained gently, "the flight-or-fight hormone." He stirred the coffee slowly with the spoon, holding her searching gaze.

"Morgan only gave me a brief overview of what happened to you," he probed gently. "Why don't you fill me in on your version? It might help me do my job better."

Susannah squirmed. "This is really going to sound stupid, Sean. It was my idea to go visit Morgan and Laura." She looked around the old farmhouse. "I've never gone much of anywhere, except to Lexington to get my teaching degree. A lot of my friends teased me that I wasn't very worldly and all that. After graduating and coming back here, I bought myself a small house in Glen, near where I work at the local grade school. Laura had been begging me to come for a visit, and I thought taking a plane to Washington, D.C., would expand my horizons."

Killian nodded. In many ways, Susannah's country ways had served to protect her from the world at large. Kentucky was a mountainous state with a small population, in some ways insulated from the harsher realities that plague big cities. "Your first flight?"

She smiled. "Yes, my first. It was really exciting." With an embarrassed laugh, she added, "I know, where else would you find someone who hasn't flown on a plane in this day and age. I had such a wonderful time with Laura, with her children. Morgan took me to the Smithsonian Institution for the whole day, and I was in heaven. I love learning, and that is the most wonderful museum I've ever seen. On my way home I landed at Lexington and was on my way to the bus station to get back here to Glen." Her smile faded. "That's when all this happened."

"Were you in the bus station itself?"

Susannah shook her head. "No. I'd just stepped off the bus. There was a row of ten buses parked under this huge roof, and my bus was farthest away from the building. I was the last one off the bus. It was very dark that night, and it was raining. A thunderstorm. The rain was whipping in under the roof, and I had my head down and was hurrying to get inside.

"This man came out of nowhere and began talking real fast to me. At the same time, he was reaching for my shoulder bag and pulling it off my arm. He was smiling and saying he'd like to help me."

"Was he acting nervous?" Killian asked, noticing that Susannah had gone pale recounting the event.

"I didn't realize it at the time, but yes, he was. How did you know that?"

"Because no doubt he spotted you as a patsy, someone gullible enough to approach, lie to, and then use your luggage—probably to hide drugs or money for a later pickup. But go on. What happened next?" Killian leaned forward, his hands around the hot mug of coffee.

Susannah took in a ragged breath. She was amazed by Killian's knowledge. She was so naive, and it had nearly gotten her killed. "He said he'd take my bag into the station for me. I didn't know what to do. He seemed so nice—he was smiling all the time. I was getting wet from the rain, and I was wearing a new outfit I'd bought, and I didn't want it ruined, so I let him have the bag." She flushed and looked down. "You know the worst part?" she whispered. "I was flattered. I thought he was interested in me..." Her voice trailed off.

Susannah rubbed her brow and was silent for a long moment. When she spoke again, her voice came out hoarse. "He'd no sooner put the piece of luggage over his shoulder than I saw this other man step out of the dark and shoot at him. I screamed, but it was too late. The man fell, and I saw the killer move toward me. No one else was around. No one else saw it happen." Susannah shuddered and wrapped her arms around herself. "The next thing I knew, the killer was after me. I ran into a nearby alley. I remember thinking I was going to die. I heard shots—I heard bullets hitting the sides of the building and whining around me."

Closing her eyes, she whispered, "I was running hard,

choking for air. I slipped on the wet street, and it was so dark, so dark…" Susannah opened her eyes. "I remember thinking I had to try to scream for help. But no one came. The next thing I knew, something hit me in the head—a hot sensation. That's it."

Glancing over at Killian, Susannah saw anger flash in his narrowed eyes. Her voice went off-key. "I woke up two months later. My ma was at my side when I came around, and I remember her crying."

"It was probably a drug deal gone wrong," Killian growled. He stared down at his hands. He'd like to wrap them around that bastard and give him back what he'd done to Susannah. "You were at the wrong place at the wrong time. There may have been drugs left in a nearby locker that the man who talked to you was supposed to pick up. Or the guy may have been on the run, using you as a decoy, hoping the killer wouldn't spot him if he was part of a couple." He looked at her sadly. "I'm sorry it happened, Susannah."

"At least I'm alive. I survived." She shrugged, embarrassed. "So much for my trying to become more worldly. I was so stupid."

"No," Killian rasped, "not stupid. Just not as alert as you might have been."

Shivering, Susannah slowly rubbed her arms with her hands. "Sean…the other night when I woke up?"

"Yes?"

"Please believe me. There *was* a man outside my bedroom window. I heard him. I saw his shadow against the opposite wall of my bedroom."

With a sigh, Killian shook his head. "There was no

evidence—no footprints outside either window, Susannah. The grass wasn't disturbed."

Rubbing her head with her hands, Susannah sat there, confused. "I could have sworn he was there."

Killian wanted to reach out and comfort her, but he knew he didn't dare. Just her sharing the tragedy with him had drawn her uncomfortably close to him. "Let me do the worrying about it," he said. "All I need you to do is continue to get well."

Susannah felt latent power swirling around him as he sat tautly at the table. Anger shone in his eyes, but this time she knew it wasn't aimed at her; it was aimed at her unidentified assailant.

"I never thought about the killer coming to finish me off," she told him lamely. "That's stupid, too."

"Naive."

"Whatever you want to call it, it still can get me killed." She gave him a long look. "Would this man kill my parents, too?"

"I don't know," Killian said, trying to soothe her worry. "Most of these men go strictly for the target. In a way, you're protecting your parents by not being in their house right now."

"But if the killer got my address, he might think I was at my home in Glen, right?"

"That would be the first place he'd look," Killian agreed, impressed with her insight.

"And then he'd do what?"

"Probably discreetly try to nose around some of your neighbors and find out where you are," he guessed.

"It's no secret I'm here," Susannah said unhappily. "And if the killer didn't know I was out here at the homestead, he might break into my folks' home to find me."

"Usually," he told her, trying to assuage her growing fear, "a contract killer will do a good deal of research to locate his target. That means he probably will show up here sooner or later. My hunch is that he'll stake out the place, sit with a field scope on a rifle, or a pair of binoculars, and try to figure out the comings and goings of everyone here. Once he knew for sure where you were and when to get you alone, he'd come for you."

A chill ran up her spine, and she stared over at Killian. His blue eyes glittered with a feral light that frightened her. "All the trouble I'm causing…"

"I'm here to protect all of you," Killian said. "I'm going to try to get to the bottom of this mess as soon as possible."

With a sigh, Susannah nodded. "I felt it. The moment you were introduced to me, I felt safe."

"Well," Killian growled, rising to his feet, "I'd still stay alert. Paranoia's a healthy reaction to have until I can figure out if you're really safe or not," he said, setting the cup and saucer in the sink.

Grimly Killian placed his hands on the counter and stared out the window. The blue-and-white checked curtains at the window made it homey, and it was tempting to relax and absorb the feeling. He'd been so long without home and family, and he was rarely able to go back to Ireland to visit what was left of his family—Meg. Sadness moved through him, deep and cutting. Being here with Susannah and her family had been a reprieve of sorts from his loneliness.

"Sean, I really don't feel good about going back to town, back to my house, knowing all this." Susannah stared at his long, lean back. He was silhouetted against the dusk, his mouth a tight line holding back unknown emotions, perhaps pain. Overcoming her shyness, she whispered, "Now that I know the real reason you're here, I'll take you up on that offer to stay with me at night. If you want…"

Slowly Killian turned around. He groaned internally as he met her hope-filled gaze, saw her lips part. The driving urge to kiss her, to explore those wonderful lips, was nearly his undoing.

Susannah took his silence as a refusal. A strange light burned in his intense gaze. "Well… I mean, you don't have to. I don't want you to feel like a—"

"I'll stay," he muttered abruptly.

Nervously Susannah stood and wiped her damp hands down her thighs. "Are you sure?" He looked almost angry. With her? Since the assault, she'd lost so much of her self-esteem. Susannah found herself quivering like jelly inside; it was a feeling she'd never experienced before that fateful night at the bus station.

"Yes," Killian snapped, moving toward the back door. "I'll get my gear down at your folks' place and bring it up here."

Feeling as if she'd done something wrong, Susannah watched him leave. And then she upbraided herself for that feeling. It was a victim's response, according to the woman therapist who had counseled her a number of times when she'd come out of the coma but was still at the hospital.

"Stop it," Susannah sternly told herself. "If he's angry, ask him why. Don't assume it's because of something you said." As she moved to the bedroom next to her own, separated by the only bathroom in the house, Susannah felt a gamut of insecurities. When Sean returned, she was determined to find out the truth of why he'd been so abrupt with her.

Chapter 5

"Are you angry with me?" Susannah asked Killian, the words coming out more breathless than forceful, to her dismay. He'd just dropped his leather bag in the spare bedroom.

Turning, he scowled. "No. Why?"

"You acted upset earlier. I just wanted to know if it was aimed at me."

Straightening, Killian moved to where Susannah stood, at the entrance to his bedroom. Twilight had invaded the depths of the old house, and her sober features were strained. It hurt to think that she thought he was angry with her. Roughly he said, "My being upset has nothing to do with you, Susannah."

"What does it have to do with, then?"

He grimaced, unwilling to comment.

"I know you didn't want this assignment from Morgan…"

Exasperated, he muttered, "Not at first." Killian refused to acknowledge that Susannah appealed to him on some primal level of himself. Furthermore, he couldn't allow himself to get involved emotionally with the person he had to protect. And that was why he had never before accepted an assignment involving a woman; his weakness centered around those who were least able to protect themselves—the women of the world. Emotions touched him deeply, and there was little he could do to parry them, because they always hit him hard, no matter what he tried to do to avoid them. Men were far easier to protect; they were just as closed up as he was, lessening the emotional price tag.

Susannah wasn't about to let Killian squirm out of the confrontation. "I learned a long time ago to talk out problems. Maybe that's a woman's way, but men can profit from it, too." She lifted her hands and held his scrutinizing gaze, gaining confidence. "I don't want you here if you don't want to be, Sean. I hate thinking I'm a burden to anyone."

The ache to reach out and tame a strand of hair away from her flushed features was excruciatingly tempting. Killian exhaled loudly. "I wish you weren't so sensitive to other people's moods."

She smiled a little. "Maybe it's because I work with handicapped children who often either can't speak or have trouble communicating in general. I can't help it. What's bothering you, Sean?"

He shoved his hands into the pockets of his jeans and studied her tautly. "It's my nature not to talk," he warned.

"It does take courage to talk," Susannah agreed, gathering her own courage, determined to get to the root of his problem with her. "It's easier to button up and retreat into silence," she said more firmly.

His mouth had become nothing more than a slash. "Let's drop this conversation."

Susannah stood in the doorway, feeling the tension radiating from him. He not only looked dangerous, he felt dangerous. Her mouth grew dry. "No."

The one word, softly spoken, struck him solidly. "I learned a long time ago to say nothing. I'm a man with a lot of ugly secrets, Susannah. Secrets I'm not proud of. They're best left unsaid."

"I don't agree," Susannah replied gently. She saw the terror lurking in the depths of Killian's eyes as he avoided her searching gaze. "My folks helped me through the worst of my reactions after I came out of the coma. They understood my need to talk about my fears by writing them down on a piece of paper when I couldn't speak." She blinked uncertainly. "I couldn't even cry, Sean. The tears just wouldn't come. The horrible humiliation I felt—still feel even now—was lessened because they cared enough to listen, to hold me when I was so scared. At least I had someone who cared how I felt, who cried *for* me when the pain was too much for me to bear alone."

Killian lifted his chin and stared deeply into her luminous gray eyes. The need to confide, to open his arms and sweep her against him, was painfully real. His whole body was tense with pain. "In my line of work, there aren't many therapists available when things start coming down—or falling apart. There are no safe havens, Susannah. To avoid trouble and ensure safety, I breathe through my nose. It keeps my mouth shut."

He'd said too much already. Killian looked around, wanting to escape, but Susannah stood stubbornly in the doorway, barring any exit. Panic ate at him.

Susannah shook her head. "I felt such sadness around

you," she whispered, opening her hands to him. "You put on such a frightening mask, Sean—"

Angrily he rasped, "Back off."

The words slapped her. His tone had a lethal quality. Swallowing hard, Susannah saw fear, mixed with anguish, mirrored in his narrowed eyes. The words had been spoken in desperation, not anger. "How can I? I feel how uncomfortable you are here with me. I feel as if I've done something to make you feel like that." She raised her eyes to the ceiling. "Sean, I can't live like that with a person. How can you?"

Nostrils flaring, Killian stared at her in disbelief. Her honesty was bone deep—a kind he'd rarely encountered. Killian didn't dare tell her the raw, blatant truth—that he wanted her in every way imaginable. "I guess I've been out in the field too long," he told her in a low, growling tone. "I'm used to harshness, Susannah, not the softness a woman has, not a home. Being around you is...different...and I'm having to adjust." *A lot.*

"And," he added savagely, seeing how flustered she was becoming, "I'm used to bunking with men, not a woman. I get nightmares." When her face fell with compassion for him, he couldn't deal with it—almost hating her for it, for forcing the feelings out of him. "The night is my enemy, Susannah. And it's an enemy for anyone who might be near me when it happens. The past comes back," he warned thickly. Killian wanted to protect Susannah from that dark side of himself. He was afraid he might not be able to control himself, that terrorized portion of him that sometimes trapped him for hours in its brutal grip, ruling him.

Standing there absorbing the emotional pain contained in his admission, Susannah realized for the first time that Killian was terribly human. He wasn't the superman she'd first thought, although Morgan's men had a proud reputation for being exactly that. The discovery was as breathtaking as it was disturbing. She had no experience with a man like Killian—someone who had been grievously wounded by a world whose existence she could hardly fathom. The pleading look Killian gave her, the twist of his lips as he shared the information with her, tore at Susannah's heart. Instinctively she realized that Killian needed to be held, too. If only for a little while. He needed a safe haven from the stormy dangers inherent in his chosen profession. That was something she could give him while he stayed with her.

"I understand," she whispered unsteadily. "And if you have bad dreams, I'll come out and make you a cup of tea. Maybe we can talk about it."

He slowly raised his head, feeling the tension make his joints ache. He held Susannah's guileless eyes, eyes that were filled with hope. "Your naiveté nearly got you killed once," he rasped. "Just stay away from me if you hear me up and moving around at night, Susannah. *Stay away.*"

She gave him a wary look, seeing the anguish in his narrowed eyes even as they burned with desire. Desire for her? Susannah wished that need could be for her alone, but she knew Killian was the kind of man who allowed no grass to grow under his feet. He was a wanderer over the face of the earth, with no interest in settling down. Much as she hated to admit it, she had to be honest with herself.

Killian wasn't going to say anything else, Susannah realized. She stepped back into the hallway, at a loss. Lamely she held his hooded stare.

"It's as if you're saying you're a danger to me."

"I am."

Susannah shook her head. "I wish," she said softly, "I had more experience with the world, with men…"

Killian wanted to move to her and simply enfold Susannah in his arms. She looked confused and bereft. "Stay the way you are," he told her harshly. "You don't want to know what the world can offer."

Susannah wasn't so sure. She felt totally unprepared to deal with a complex man like Sean, yet she was powerfully drawn to him. "Should I follow my normal schedule of doing things around here tomorrow morning?" At least this was a safe topic of conversation.

"Yes."

"I see. Good night, Sean."

"Good night." The words came out in a rasp. Killian tasted his frustration, and felt a heated longing coil through him. Susannah looked crestfallen. Could he blame her? No. Darkness was complete now, and he automatically perused the gloomy area. Perhaps talking a little bit about himself hadn't been so bad after all. At least with her. He knew he couldn't live under the same roof without warning Susannah of his violent night world.

By ten, Killian was in bed, wearing only his pajama bottoms. He stared blankly at the plaster ceiling, which was in dire need of repair. His senses functioned like radar, swinging this way and that, picking up nuances of sound and smell. Nothing seemed out of place, so he relaxed to a degree. And then, against his will, his attention shifted to dwell on Susannah. She had a surprisingly stubborn side to her—and he liked discovering that strength within her. Outwardly she might seem soft and naive, but she had emotional convictions that served as the roots of her strength.

Glancing at the only window in his room, Killian

could see stars dotting the velvet black of the sky. Everything was so peaceful here. Another layer of tension dissolved around him, and he found himself enjoying the old double bed, the texture of the clean cotton sheets that Susannah had made the bed with, and the symphony of the crickets chirping outside the house.

What was it about this place that permeated his constant state of wariness and tension to make him relax to this degree? Killian had no answers, or at least none he was willing to look at closely. Exhausted, he knew he had to try to get some sleep. He moved restlessly on the bed, afraid of what the night might hold. He forced his eyes closed, inhaled deeply and drifted off to sleep. On the nightstand was his pistol, loaded and with the safety off, perpetually at the ready. Killian jerked awake, his hand automatically moving to his pistol. Sunlight streamed through the window and the lacy pale green curtains. Blinking, he slowly sat up and shoved several locks of hair off his brow. The scent of freshly brewed coffee and frying bacon wafted on the air. He inhaled hungrily and threw his legs across the creaky bed. Relief flowed through him as he realized that for once the nightmares hadn't come to haunt him. Puzzled, he moved to the bathroom. Not only had the nightmares stayed at bay, but he'd slept very late. Usually his sleep was punctuated by moments of stark terror throughout the night and he finally fell more heavily asleep near dawn. Still, he never slept past six—ever. But now it was eight o'clock. Stymied about why he'd slept so late, he stepped into a hot shower.

Dressed in a white shirt and jeans, Killian swung out of his room and down the hall, following the enticing smells emanating from the kitchen. Halting in the doorway, he drank in the sight of Susannah working over the old wood stove. Today she wore a sleeveless yellow blouse, well-worn jeans and white tennis shoes. Her hair, thick and abundant, cloaked her shoulders. As if she had sensed his presence, she looked up.

"I thought this might get you out of bed." She grinned. "So much for keeping up with me and my schedule. I was up at five-thirty, and you were still sawing logs."

Rubbing his face, Killian managed a sheepish look as he headed for the counter where the coffeepot sat. "I overslept," he muttered.

Taking the bacon out of the skillet and placing it on a paper towel to soak up the extra grease, Susannah smiled. "Don't worry, your secrets are safe with me."

Killian gave her a long, absorbing look, thinking how pretty she looked this morning. But he noted a slight puffiness beneath Susannah's eyes and wondered if she'd been crying. "I guess I'll have to get used to this," he rasped. The coffee was strong, hot and black—just the way he liked it. Susannah placed a stack of pancakes, the rasher of bacon and a bottle of maple syrup before him and sat down opposite him.

"'This' meaning me?"

Killian dug hungrily into the pancakes. "It's everything."

Susannah sat back and shook her head. "One- or two-word answers, Sean. I swear. What do you mean by 'everything'?"

He gave her a brief look. He was really enjoying the buckwheat pancakes. "It's been a long time since I was in a home, not a house," he told her between bites.

She ate slowly, listening closely not only to what he said, but also to how he said it. "So, home life appeals to you after all?"

He raised his brows.

"I thought," Susannah offered, "that you were a rolling stone that gathered no moss. A man with wanderlust in his soul."

He refused to hold her warm gaze. "Home means everything to me." The pancakes disappeared in a hurry, and the bacon quickly followed. Killian took his steaming cup of coffee and tipped his chair back on two legs. The kitchen fragrances lingered like perfume, and birds sang cheerfully outside the screen door, enhancing his feeling of contentment. Susannah looked incredibly lovely, and Killian thought he was in heaven—or as close as the likes of him was ever going to get to it.

Sipping her coffee, Susannah risked a look at Killian. "To me, a house is built of walls and beams. A home is built with love and dreams. You said you were from Ireland. Were you happy over there?"

Uncomfortable, Killian shrugged. "Northern Ireland isn't exactly a happy place to live." He shot her a hard look. "I learned early on, Susannah, the danger of caring about someone too much, because they'd be ripped away from me."

It felt as if a knife were being thrust down through Susannah. She gripped the delicate cup hard between her hands. "But what—"

With a shrug, Killian tried to cover up his own unraveling emotions. Gruffly he said, "That was the past— there's no need to rehash it. This is the present."

Pain for Killian settled over Susannah. She didn't know what had happened to him as a child, but his words "the danger of caring about someone too much" created a knot in her stomach.

Finishing her coffee, Susannah quietly got up and

gathered the plates and flatware. At the counter, she began washing the dishes in warm, soapy water.

Killian rose and moved to where Susannah stood. He spotted a towel hanging on a nail and began to dry the dishes as she rinsed them.

"You're upset."

"No."

"You don't lie well at all. Your voice is a dead give-away—not to mention those large, beautiful eyes of yours." No one could have been more surprised than Killian at what had just transpired. He hadn't meant to allude to the tragedy. Her empathy was touching, but Killian knew that to feel another person's pain at that depth was dangerous. Why didn't Susannah shield herself more from him?

Avoiding his sharpened gaze, Susannah concentrated on washing the dishes. "It's just that, well, you seem to carry a lot of pain." She inhaled shakily.

"I told you the secrets I carried weren't good ones," he warned her darkly.

"Yes, you did…" she agreed softly.

Disgusted with himself, Killian muttered, "Face it, life isn't very nice."

Susannah's hands stilled in the soothing water. Lifting her chin, she met and held his stormy gaze. "I don't believe that. There's always hope," she challenged.

With a muffled sound, Killian suppressed the curse that rose to his lips. Susannah didn't deserve his harsh side, his survival reflexes. "*Hope* isn't a word I recognize."

"What about dreams?"

His smile was deadly. Cynical. "Dreams? More like nightmares, colleen."

There was no way to parry the grim finality of his view of the world—at least not yet. Susannah softened her voice. "Well, perhaps the time you spend here will change your mind."

"A month or so in Eden before I descend back into hell? Be careful, Susannah. You don't want to invest anything in me. I live in hell. I don't want to pull you into it."

A chill moved through her. His lethal warning sounded as if it came from the very depths of his injured, untended soul. Killian was like a wounded animal—hurting badly, lashing out in pain. Rallying, Susannah determined not to allow Killian to see how much his warning had shaken her.

"Well," she went on with forced lightness, "you'll probably be terribly bored sooner or later. In the end, you'll be more than ready to leave."

Killian scowled as he continued to dry the flatware one piece at a time. "We'll see" was all he'd say. He'd said enough. *Too much.* The crestfallen look in Susannah's eyes made him want to cry. Cry! Struck by his cruelty toward her, Killian would have done anything to take back his words. Susannah had gone through enough hell of her own without him dumping his sordid past on her, too.

"What's on the list this morning?" he demanded abruptly.

Susannah tried to gather her strewn, shocked feelings. "Weeding the garden. I try to do it during the morning hours, while it's still cool. We have to pick the slugs off, weed and check the plants for other insects. That sort of thing." Again, tension vibrated around Killian, and it translated to her. She knew there was a slight wobble in her strained tone. Had Killian picked it up? Susannah didn't have the courage to glance at him as he continued drying dishes.

A huge part of Susannah wanted to help heal his wounds. Her heart told her she had the ability to do just that. Hadn't she helped so many children win freedom from crosses they'd been marked to bear for life? She'd helped guide them out of trapped existences with color, paints and tempera. Each year she saw a new batch of special children, and by June they were smiling far more than when they'd first come to class. No, there was hope for Killian, whether he wanted to admit it or not.

Killian methodically pulled the weeds that poked their heads up between the rows of broccoli, cauliflower and tomatoes. A few rows over, Susannah worked, an old straw hat protecting her from the sun's intensity. He worked bareheaded, absorbing energy from the sunlight. Since their conversation in the kitchen that morning, she'd been suspiciously silent, and it needled Killian enormously.

He had to admit, there was something pleasurable about thrusting his hands into the damp, rich soil. Over near the fence, the baby robin that had previously fallen out of its nest chirped loudly for its parents to bring her more food. Killian wore his shoulder holster, housing the Beretta beneath his left arm. Susannah had given him a disgruntled look when he'd put on the shoulder harness, but had said nothing. Just as well. He didn't want her getting any ideas about saving him and his dark, hopeless soul. Let her realize who and what he was. That way, she'd keep her distance. He wasn't worth saving.

Susannah got off her hands and knees. She took the handful of slugs she'd found and placed them on the other side of the fence, under the fruit tree, below the robin's nest. Not believing in insecticides, she tried to use nature's balance to maintain her gardens. The robins would feed the slugs to their babies, completing the natural cycle.

Usually her work relaxed her, but this morning the silence between her and Killian was terribly strained, and she had no idea how to lessen it. She glanced over at Killian, who worked in a crouch, pulling weeds, his face set. Every once in a while, she could feel him surveying the area, his guarded watchfulness evident.

Susannah took off her hat, wiped her damp brow with the back of her hand and walked toward the house. She wanted to speak to him, but she felt that cold wall around him warning her to leave him alone.

Entering the kitchen, Susannah realized just how lonely was the world Killian lived in. It was sheer agony for him to talk. Each conversation was like pulling teeth—painful and nerve-racking. Tossing her straw hat on the table, Susannah poured two tall, icy glasses of lemonade.

Killian entered silently, catching her off guard. Susannah's heart hammered briefly. His face was glistening with sweat, but his mouth was no longer pursed, she noted, and his eyes looked lighter—almost happy, if she was reading him accurately.

"Come on, sit down. You've earned a rest," she said.

The lemonade disappeared in a hurry as he gulped it down and nodded his thanks.

"More?"

"Please." Killian sat at the table, his hands folded on top of it, watching Susannah move with her incredible natural grace.

With another nod of appreciation, he took the newly filled glass but this time didn't gulp it down. He glanced at his watch. "I hadn't realized two hours had gone by."

Susannah smiled tentatively. Casting about for some safe topic, she waved at the colorful pictures on the kitchen walls. "My most recent class did these. Some of the kids have intellectual disabilities, others have had deformities since birth. They range in intellectual age from about six to twelve. I love drawing them out of their shells." And then, deliberately holding his gaze, she added, "They find happiness by making the most of what they have." Susannah pointed again to the tempera paintings that she'd had framed. "I keep these because they're before-and-after drawings," she confided warmly.

"Oh?"

"The paintings on this wall were done when the children first came to class in September. The paintings on the right were done just before school was out in June. Take a look."

Killian rose and went over to the paintings, his glass of lemonade in hand. One child's first painting was dark and shadowy—the one done nine months later was bright and sunny in comparison. Another painting had a boy in a wheelchair looking glum. In the next, he was smiling and waving to the birds overhead. Killian glanced at Susannah over his shoulder. "Telling, aren't they?"

"Very."

He studied the others in silence. Finally he turned around, came back to the table and sat down. "You must have the patience of Job."

With a little laugh, Susannah shook her head. "For me, it's a wonderful experience watching these kids open up and discover happiness—some of them for the first time in their lives." Her voice took on more feeling. "Just watching them blossom, learn to trust, to explore, means everything to me. It's a real privilege for me."

"I guess some people pursue happiness and others create it. I envy those kids." Killian swallowed convulsively, feeling uncomfortably as if her sparkling eyes were melting his hardened heart—and his hardened view of the world. Her lower lip trembled under the intensity of his stare, and the overwhelming need to reach over, to pull Susannah to his chest and kiss her until she molded to him with desire, nearly unstrung his considerable control. If he stayed at the table, he'd touch her. He'd kiss the hell out of her.

Susannah wanted Sean to get used to the idea that he, too, could have happiness. "You know, what we did out there this morning made you happy. I could see it in your eyes. Your face is relaxed. Isn't that something?"

Leaving her side abruptly, Killian placed his empty glass on the counter, a little more loudly than necessary. "What's next? What do you want me to do?"

Shocked, Susannah watched the hardness come back into Killian's features. She'd pushed him too far. "I... Well, the screen in my bedroom could be fixed..." she said hesitantly.

"Then what?" A kind of desperation ate at Killian. He didn't dare stay in such close proximity to Susannah. The more she revealed of herself, the more she trusted him with her intimate thoughts and feelings, the more she threatened his much-needed defenses. Dammit, she trusted too easily!

"Then lunch. I was going to make us lunch, and then I thought we'd pick the early snow peas and freeze them this afternoon," she said.

"Fine."

Blinking, Susannah watched Killian stalk out of the kitchen. The tension was back in him; he was like a trap that begged to be sprung. Shakily she drew in a breath, all too clearly recognizing that the unbidden hunger in his eyes was aimed directly at her. Suddenly she felt like an animal in a hunter's sights.

Chapter 6

"Look out!" Killian's shriek careened around the darkened bedroom. He jerked himself upright, his hand automatically moving for the pistol. Cool metal met his hot, sweaty fingers. Shadows from the past danced around him. His breathing was ragged and chaotic. The roar of rifles and the blast of mortars flashed in front of his wide, glazed eyes as he sat rigidly in bed. A hoarse cry, almost a sob, tore from his contorted lips.

He made a muffled sound of disgust. With the back of his hand, Killian wiped his eyes clear of tears. Where was he? What room? What country? Peru? Algeria? Laos? *Where?*

His chest rising and falling rapidly, Killian narrowed his eyes as he swung his gaze around the quiet room. It took precious seconds for him to realize that he was here, in Kentucky. Cursing softly, he leaped out of bed, his pajama bottoms damp with sweat and clinging to his taut body. Shaking. He was shaking. It was nothing new. Often he would shake for a good hour after coming awake. More important, the nightmare hadn't insidiously kept control of him after waking. The flashbacks frightened him for Susannah's sake.

Laying the pistol down, Killian rubbed his face savagely, trying to force the remnants of the nightmare away. What he needed to shock him back into the present was a brutally cold shower. That and a fortifying cup of coffee. Forcing himself to move on wobbly legs, he made it to the bathroom. Fumbling for the shower faucet, he found it and turned it on full-force.

Later, he padded down the darkened hall in his damp, bare feet, a white towel draped low around his hips. His watch read 3:00 a.m.—the same time he usually had the nightmares. Shoving damp strands of hair off his brow, he rounded the corner. Shock riveted him to the spot.

"I thought you might like some coffee," Susannah whispered unsteadily. She was standing near the counter in a long white cotton nightgown. Her hands were clasped in front of her. "That and some company?"

Rubbing his mouth with the back of his hand, Killian stood tautly, his heightened senses reeling with impact. Moonlight lovingly caressed Susannah, the luminescence outlining her slender shape through her thin cotton gown. The lace around the gown's boat neck emphasized her collarbones and her slender neck. He gulped and allowed his hand to fall back to his side. Susannah's face looked sleepy, her eyes dreamy with a softness that aroused a longing in him to bury himself in her, hotly, deeply. She remained perfectly still as he devoured her with his starving gaze.

There was fear in her eyes, mixed with desire and longing. Killian not only saw it in the nuances of her fleeting expression, but sensed it, as well. Like a wolf too long without a mate, he ached to claim her as his own. And then, abruptly he laughed at himself. Who was he kidding? She was all the things he was not. She had hope. She believed in a future filled with dreams. Hell, she gave handicapped children back the chance to dream.

"It's not a good time to be around me," he rasped.

Inhaling shakily, Susannah nodded. "It's a chance I'll take." Never had she seen a man of such power, intensity and beauty as Killian. He stood in the kitchen doorway, the towel draped casually across his lean hips, accentuating his near nakedness.

Killian's shoulders were proudly thrown back, and his muscles were cleanly delineated. His chest was covered with hair that headed like an arrow down his long torso and flat belly. The dark line of hair disappeared beneath the stark whiteness of the towel, but still, little was left to the imagination. Susannah gulped convulsively.

Susannah's skin tingled where his hungry gaze had swept across her. Trying to steady her desire for him, she noticed that her hands shook as she turned to put the coffee into the pot.

It had taken everything for Susannah to tear her gaze from his overwhelming masculine image. "I—I heard you scream. At first I thought it was a nightmare I was having, and then I realized it wasn't me screaming. It was you."

Killian remained frozen in the doorway. The husky softness of Susannah's voice began to dissolve some of the terror that seemed to twist within him like a living being.

She shrugged. "I didn't know what to do."

"You did the right thing," he said raggedly. He forced himself to move toward the table. Gripping the chair, he sat down, afraid he might fall down if he didn't. His knees were still weak from the virulent nightmare. He looked up at Susannah. "Didn't I tell you that I wasn't worth the risk? Look at you. You're shaking." And she was. He wanted desperately to reassure her somehow, but he couldn't.

Rubbing her arms, Susannah nodded. "I'll be okay."

Killian felt like hell. He'd scared her, triggered the fear she'd barely survived months ago, and he knew it. "I walk around in a living death every day of my life. You don't deserve to be around it—or me."

The sweat glistening on Killian's taut muscles spoke to her of the hell he was still caught up in. Susannah forced herself to move through her fear and cross to his side. She reached out and gently laid her hands on his shoulders.

Killian groaned. Her touch was so warm, so steadying.

"Just sit there," she whispered in a strained tone. "Let me work the knots out of your shoulders. You're so tense."

He opened his mouth to protest, but the kneading quality of her strong, slender hands as they worked his aching muscles stopped him. Instead of speaking, he closed his eyes and gradually began to relax. With each sliding, coaxing movement of her fingers along his skin, a little more of the fear he carried with him dissolved. Eventually he allowed himself to sag against the chair.

"Lean on me," Susannah coaxed. She pressed her hand to his sweaty brow and guided his head against her.

How easy it was to have his head cushioned against her as her hands moved with confidence on his shoulders and neck. A ragged sigh issued from him, and he closed his eyes, trusting her completely.

"Good," she crooned softly, watching his short, spiky lashes droop closed. Even his mouth, once a harsh line holding back a deluge of emotions, gradually relaxed.

Susannah felt the steel-cable strength of his muscles beneath her hands. He was built like a cougar—lean and lithe. Her feelings were alive, bright and clamoring not only for acknowledgment, but for action. The thrill of touching Killian, of having him trust her this much, was dizzying and inviting. Susannah ached to lean forward and place a soft kiss on his furrowed brow. How much pain did this man carry within him?

As she stood in the moonlit kitchen with him, massaging his terror and tension away, Susannah realized that Killian's life must have been one of unending violence.

"Two years ago," she said unsteadily as she smoothed away the last of the rigidity from his now-supple muscles, "I had a little boy, Stevey, in my class. He had intellectual disabilities and had been taken from his home by Social Services. He was only eight years old, and he was like a frightened little animal. The social worker told me that his father was an alcoholic and his mother was on drugs. They both beat up on him."

Killian's eyes snapped open.

"I'm telling you this for a reason," Susannah whispered, her hands stilling on his shoulders. "At first, Stevey would only crawl into a corner and hide. Gradually I earned his trust, and then I got him to draw. The pictures told me so much about what he'd endured, what he'd suffered through, alone and unprotected. There wasn't a day that went by that I didn't cry for him.

"Stevey taught me more about trust and love than any

other person in my life ever has. Gradually, throughout the year that he was in my class, he came to life. He
truly blossomed, and it was so breathtaking. He learned
to smile, then to laugh. His new foster parents love him
deeply, and that helped bring him out of the terror and
humiliation he'd endured.

"I saw this frightened, beaten child have enough blind
faith in another human being to rally and reach out just
once more. Stevey had a kind of courage that I feel is
the rarest kind in the world, and the hardest to acquire."
Susannah reached out and stroked Killian's damp hair.
"Stevey knew only violence, broken trust and heartache.
But something in him—his spirit, if you will—had the
strength to work through all of that and embrace others
who truly loved him and accepted him for who he was."

Killian released a shaky breath, wildly aware of Susannah's trembling fingers lightly caressing his hair. Did
she realize what she was doing? Did she know that if she
kept it up he'd take her hard and fast, burying himself in
her hot depths? Longing warred with control. He eased
out of her hands and sat up.

"Why don't you get us that coffee?" he said. His voice
was none too steady, and it had a sandpaper rasp. Glancing up as Susannah walked past him, he saw her face.
How could she look so damned angelic when all he felt
was his blood pounding like a dam ready to burst?

Miraculously, the nightmare and its contents had disappeared beneath Susannah's gentle, questing hands.
Killian's eyes slitted as he studied her at the counter,
where she was pouring the coffee. What was it about her?
Grateful that she wasn't looking at him, Killian struggled
to get his raging need back under control. Usually he had

no problem disconnecting himself from his volcanic emotions, but Susannah aroused him to a white heat of desire.

With trembling hands, Susannah set the coffee before Killian, sharply conscious of his perusal of her. His words, his warning, kept thrumming through her. She felt danger and intensity surrounding them. Did she have the courage to stay? To be there for Killian? Forcing herself to look up, she met and held his blue gaze, a gaze that was hooded with some unknown emotion that seemed to melt her inwardly.

Gulping, she sat down at his elbow, determined not to allow him to scare her away. Right now, her heart counseled her, he needed a friend, someone he could talk with.

Killian sat there thunderstruck. Susannah couldn't be this naive—she must realize how he wanted her. Yet she sat down next to him, her face filled with determination as she sipped her steaming coffee. Angry, and feeling at war within himself, he snapped irritably, "Why don't you go back to bed?"

"Because you need me here."

His eyes widened enormously.

Prepared to risk everything, Susannah met and held his incredulous gaze. "You need a friend, Sean."

His fingers gripped his cup, and he stared down at the black contents. "Talking is the last thing I want to do right now."

She tried to absorb his brutal, angry words. "What, then?"

He snapped a look at her. "Get away from me, Susannah, while you can. Stop trying to get close. I'm not Stevey. I'm a grown man, with a grown man's needs. You're in danger. Stay, and I can't answer for what I might do."

There was such anguish in his raspy words, and she

felt his raw need of her. She sat up, her fingers releasing the cup. "No, you aren't like Stevey," Susannah whispered unsteadily. "But you are wounded—and in need of a safe haven."

With a hiss, Killian jerked to his feet, the chair nearly tipping over from the swiftness of his movement. "Wounded animals can bite those who try to help them!" Breathing harshly, he walked to the other end of the kitchen. "Dammit, Susannah, stay away from me. You've already been hurt by a man who nearly killed you." He struck his chest. "I can hurt you in so many different ways. Is that what you want? Do you want me to take you, to bury myself in you, to make night and day merge into one until you don't know anything except me, my arms, my body and—"

With a muffled sound, Killian spun around, jerked open the screen door and disappeared into the night. If he didn't go, he was going to take Susannah right there on the hard wooden floor. The primal blood was racing through him, blotting out reason, disintegrating his control. As he stalked off the porch, he knew she was an innocent in this. She was the kind of woman he'd always dreamed of—but then, dreams never could stand the test of harsh daylight.

Who was he kidding? Killian walked swiftly, his feet and ankles soon soaked from the trail he made through the dewy grass. Moonlight shifted across him in unending patterns as he continued his blind walk through the orchard. He had to protect Susannah from himself—at all costs. She didn't deserve to get tangled up with his kind. It could only end in disaster.

Gradually he slowed his pace as his head began to clear. The night was cool, but not chilly. He realized with disgust that he'd left without his weapon, and that he'd left Susannah wide open to attack if someone was prowling around. As he halted and swiftly shifted his awareness to more external things, he acknowledged that, although unarmed, he was never defenseless. No, he'd been taught to kill a hundred different ways without need of any kind of weapon.

He stood in the middle of the orchard, scowling. Bats dipped here and there, chasing after choice insects that he couldn't see. The old homestead was a quarter of a mile away, looking broken down and in dire need of paint, and also the love and care it would take to put it back in good repair. Killian laughed harshly. Wasn't he just like that old house? The only difference was that the scars he wore were mostly carried on the inside, where no one could see them. No one except Susannah. Why couldn't she be like everyone else and see only the tough exterior he presented to the world?

Killian stood there a long time, mulling over the story she'd told him about the little boy named Stevey. The boy deserved Susannah's loving care. She was the right person to help coax him out of his dark shell of fear. Her words, soft and strained, floated back to him: "You are wounded—and need a safe haven."

How long he stood there thinking about their conversation, he didn't know. When he glanced at his watch, it was 4:00 a.m. Forcing himself, he walked slowly back to the homestead. As he walked, he prayed—something he rarely did—that Susannah had had enough sense to go back to bed. What would he do if she was still up and waiting for him? His mouth was dry, and he wiped at it with the back of his hand. He didn't know.

* * *

Susannah was out in the extensive rose garden, giving the colorful flowers the special food that helped them to bloom. It was nearly noon, and she was hot, even though she wore her straw hat, a sleeveless white blouse and a threadbare pair of jeans. Her mind and heart centered on Killian. She'd gone back to bed around four, and had promptly plummeted into a deep, restful sleep. When she'd gotten up this morning at six, his bedroom door had been shut. Was he in there? Had he gone somewhere else? Susannah didn't know, and she hadn't had the courage to find out.

Taking her one-gallon bucket and the box of rose food, she went back over to the hose to mix the ingredients for the next rosebush. The air was heavy with the wonderful fragrance of the flowering bushes. The rose garden sat on the southern side of the homestead, where there was the most light. There was no fence around it, and the bushes stretched for nearly a quarter of a mile.

Susannah hunched over the bucket and poured the rose food into the pooling water, stirring it with her hand. The water turned a pretty pink color. Pink always reminded her of love, she thought mildly. Then Killian's harsh warning pounded back through her. He *was* dangerous, she thought, feeling the heat of longing flow through her—dangerous to her heart, to her soul. Killian had the ability to touch her very essence. How, she didn't know. She only knew he had that capacity, and no other man she'd ever met had been able to touch her so deeply.

Shutting off the faucet, Susannah set the food aside and hefted the gallon bucket to carry it to the next rosebush, a beautiful lavender one with at least ten blossoms. No longer could she keep from entertaining the idea of loving Killian. Her dreams had turned torrid toward morning, and she vividly recalled images of his hands caressing her body, his mouth ravishing her with wild abandon, meeting her willing, equally hungry lips.

She poured the bucket's contents into the well around the rosebush. What did she want? *Killian.* Why? Because... Susannah straightened and put the bucket aside. She pulled out a pair of scissors and began pruning off old blooms. Was it to help him heal? Yes. To show him that another person could trust him fully, fearlessly, even if he didn't trust himself? Yes. To give him her love in hopes that he might overcome his own fear of loving and losing—and to love her? *Yes.*

Stymied, she stood there, her hands cupped around one of the large lavender roses. She leaned forward, inhaling the delicate fragrance. Life was so beautiful. Why couldn't Killian see that? As she studied the many-petaled bloom, Susannah ached for him. She knew she had the ability to show him the beauty of life. But what then? He would be in her life only long enough to catch the killer who might be stalking her. He'd repeatedly warned her that he wasn't worth loving.

But he was. With a sigh, Susannah pocketed the scissors, picked up the bucket and headed back to the faucet. Her stomach growled, and she realized that it was nearly lunchtime and she was hungry. Placing all the gardening tools near the spigot, Susannah walked back to the homestead. Would Killian be there? And if he was, would he be up yet? Fear mingled with need of him inside her. How would she handle their next confrontation?

Killian's head snapped up at the sound of someone's approach. He was at the kitchen cabinets, searching through them for something to eat. He'd just gotten up and taken a scaldingly hot shower to awaken, then gotten dressed in a dark blue short-sleeved shirt and jeans. He felt like someone had poleaxed him.

Susannah opened the screen door and took off her straw hat. When she saw him, she hesitated.

Killian glared at her.

"Hungry?" she asked, hoping to hide the tension she felt. She continued into the room and placed her hat on the table.

"Like a bear," he muttered, moving away from the counter.

Susannah kept plenty of distance between them. She noticed the stormy quality in his blue eyes, and her nerves grew taut. Scared, but aware that Killian needed courage from her, not cowardice, Susannah said firmly, "Have a seat and I'll fix you what I'm going to have: a tuna sandwich, sweet pickles and pretzels."

Sitting down, Killian tried to soften his growly bad humor. "Okay."

"Coffee or iced tea?"

"I don't care."

Gathering her dissolving courage, Susannah said, "I think you need a strong cup of coffee. Are you always like this when you wake up?" Killian looked fiercely unhappy, his eyes bleak, with dark circles under them. It was obvious he hadn't slept well after their verbal battle last night.

Killian refused to watch her as she moved to the icebox. "I told you I was a bastard."

She forced a laugh and brought bread and a bowl of prepared tuna to the counter. "You really aren't, you know. You're just grouchy because you lost some sleep last night and you haven't had your coffee yet."

"Maybe you're right." Killian watched her hungrily, every movement, every sway of her hips. Susannah had her sable hair swept into a ponytail, as usual, and it shone with each step she took. Her face glowed with the good health of a woman who loved the outdoors. Unhappily Killian folded his hands on the table. Why wouldn't Susannah heed his warning? Why didn't she believe that he was a bastard, someone capable of hurting her badly? He didn't want to hurt her—not her, of all people.

Humming softly, Susannah made coffee, prepared the sandwiches and put together a wholesome lunch. When she turned around, Killian's rugged profile still reflected his unhappiness. He sat tensely, his mouth pursed.

"Here, start on the sandwich. Bears don't do well on empty stomachs."

Grateful for her teasing, he took the sandwich and began eating. But he didn't taste it—all he was aware of was his own intense suffering, and Susannah's sunlit presence. She chased away his gloom, that terrible shadow that always hovered over him like a vulture ready to rip out what little was left of his heart.

Placing the coffee before him, Susannah took her usual seat at his elbow. Her heart was hammering so hard in her chest that she feared Killian might hear it. As she forced herself to eat, the kitchen fell into a stilted silence.

"Earlier, I went down to visit my parents," she offered after a moment, trying to lessen the tension. "They told me my school had called, that the principal wanted me to consider coming back to work sooner." She picked up a pickle and frowned. "I really miss teaching. I have a new class of kids that I've never seen." She watched

Killian raise his head, his blue gaze settling on her. Her pulse raced. Trying to continue to sound nonchalant, she added, "So I called Mr. Gains back—that's the principal—and told him I'd like to return."

"When?" The word came out sharp.

Wiping her hands on a napkin, Susannah said, "Next Monday. I feel well enough now."

Relief shattered through Killian. That, and terrible disappointment. Some stupid part of him actually had held out hope that Susannah would stay, would persevere with him and reach into his heart. Putting down the sandwich, he reached for the coffee. Gulping down a swallow, he burned his mouth.

"Does that mean you're moving back into town? Into your house?"

"I—I don't know." Susannah managed a small shrug. "I really miss my kids, Sean. But I don't know if I'm ready to be alone. Do you know what I mean?"

He nodded and dropped his gaze. "Yeah, I know what you mean."

"I've been doing a lot of thinking this morning, and I guess I'll try to go to work full-time. Mr. Gains said if I have any problems I can split the class and work only half days for a while, until I get back into the swing of things."

"Half a day is enough for now."

She shrugged, not sure.

"Susannah, you're still healing."

And the other half of the day would be spent here, in Killian's intense presence, reminding her constantly of her need of him as a man, a lover. "I don't know," she confided in a low voice.

He set the coffee cup down a little more loudly than he'd intended. Susannah winced. "You aren't ready for all of that yet. You've got to pace yourself. Comas do funny things to people. What if you get flashbacks? Periods of vertigo? Or what if you blank out? All those things could happen under stress. And going back into that classroom *is* stress."

Susannah stared at him, feeling his raw intensity, his care. "Being here with you is stress, too, Sean."

Gripping the cup, he growled, "I suppose it is. I'm not the world's best person to be near. Around you, I shoot off my mouth, and look what it's done."

A soft smile touched her lips, and she leaned over and rested her hand on his arm. "Sean, some kinds of stress aren't bad. I like talking with you, sharing with you. I don't consider it bad or harmful. I feel shutting up and retreating is far more damaging."

"You would," Killian muttered, but he really didn't mean it. Just the cool, steadying touch of her fingers on his arm sent waves of need pulsing through him.

"Everyone needs someone," Susannah whispered. "Your needs are no different than anyone else's."

He cocked his head. "Don't be so sure."

She smiled a little, feeling danger swirling around her. "I'm betting your bark is worse than your bite."

"Oh? Was that the way it was with Stevey?"

Susannah forced herself to release him. "At first, every time I came near him, he lashed out at me."

"And what did you do?"

"I'd lean down, pull him against me and just hold him."

Killian shut his eyes and drew in a deep, shaky breath. "I don't know what to make of you, Susannah. Why would anyone put themselves in the line of fire just to let someone else know that they weren't going to be hurt again?" He opened his eyes, searching her thoughtful gray ones.

"I believe we're all healers, Sean. We not only have the ability to heal ourselves, but to heal others, too. Stevey wanted to be healed. Each time I approached him, he struck out less and less, until finally, one day, he opened his arms to me. It was such a beautiful, poignant moment."

"He trusted you," Killian said flatly.

"Yes, he did."

"You're a catalyst."

"So are you," she said wryly, meeting his wary eyes.

Uncomfortable, Killian wanted to shift the conversation back to her. "So you're going to try class for a full day next Monday?"

"Yes."

"All right, I'll drive you to work and hang around, if you don't mind. I want to get the layout of your school, your classroom. If they've got a contract out on you—and we still don't know if they do or not—I want to have that school, its entrances and exits, in my head in case something comes down."

She sat back, surprised. "Do you really think I'm in danger?"

"Until I can prove otherwise," Killian said roughly, "I'm assuming there's a hit man out there somewhere, just waiting for you. What you can't comprehend is that a contract means anytime, anywhere. A killer doesn't care where the hit takes place. He's been paid to do a job, and he's going to do it. He doesn't care if other lives get in the way."

The brutal harshness of his words sank into Susannah with a frightening chill. "What about my kids? Are they safe?"

Killian shrugged. "I don't know, Susannah. Hit men usually try for a clean one-shot deal. They don't like putting themselves in a messy situation where they could get caught." He saw the color drain from her face. "Look," he added harshly, "let me worry about the possibility of a hit man, okay? I know where to look, I know their usual methods. You'll be safe. And so will your kids," he added, softening his voice for her sake.

Getting up, Susannah moved to the counter. "I—I just didn't realize, Sean…"

"I didn't want you to," he muttered. "It's fairly easy to watch you here, at the farm. But the moment you start driving to work, shopping and doing all the other things normal people do daily, you become more of a target-rich opportunity."

She shivered at the military jargon. *Target-rich opportunity.* Gripping the cool porcelain of the double sink, she hung her head. "I can't—I won't—live my life in fear, Sean."

"Well, then, there's a price to pay for that kind of decision. You deserve to know the chances you're taking. You could stay here, at the farm, and flushing out the hit man would be easier—but it would probably take longer."

Susannah turned around and held his searching gaze. Crossing her arms in front of her, she shook her head. "No. If there really is a contract out on me, let's find out. I'd rather get it over with."

Killian understood only too well. "You're courageous," he said, and he meant it.

"No," Susannah told him, her voice quavering, "I'm scared to death. But I miss the kids. I miss teaching."

Killian slowly rose and pushed back his chair. He brought over his now-empty plate and coffee cup. "Okay, Monday you go to work, but I'll be like a shadow, Susannah. Everywhere you go, I go. I'll explain the situation to your principal. He may decide not to let you come back after he knows the potential danger."

"Then I'll stay away," Susannah whispered. "I don't want to endanger my kids. They're innocent."

He set the dishes in the sink and turned to her. Placing his hands on her slumped shoulders, he rasped, "So are you."

Chapter 7

Uneasy, Killian walked the now-quiet halls of Marshall Elementary School, which was located near the edge of the small town of Glen. All of the children, from grades one through six, were in their classes, the wood-and-glass door to each room closed, and the teachers were busy with their charges. Killian's heart automatically swung back to Susannah, who was happily back at work. The meeting with the principal had gone well. Killian had actually expected him to turn down Susannah's request after hearing about the possibilities.

The principal obviously didn't believe there could be a contract out on Susannah. Nor did she. They didn't want to, Killian thought grimly as he padded quietly down the highly polished floor of an intersecting hall lined with metal lockers.

Dressed in jeans, a tan polo shirt and a light denim

jacket that hid his shoulder holster, Killian had a small blueprint layout of the school and its adjacent buildings. He'd already been in Susannah's room and met her ten handicapped students. The children ranged in age from seven to twelve. He hadn't stayed long—he was more interested in the deadly possibilities of his trade.

At lunch, he planned to meet Susannah and her class in the cafeteria. A story had been devised to explain Killian's presence in Susannah's classroom: He was monitoring the course, a teacher from California who was going to set up a similar program out there. Everyone, including the faculty at the morning meeting, had accepted the explanation without reaction. Killian had discovered that Susannah had, from time to time, had teachers from other states come and watch how she conducted her class, because the children had developed more quickly than usual as a result of her unique teaching methods.

The lunch bell rang as Killian finished circling on the map in red ink those areas where a contract killer might hide. Luckily, there weren't many. He missed Susannah's presence, and he hoped to meet her on the way to the cafeteria with her charges.

Susannah's heart sped up at the sight of Killian moving slowly through the hall, which was filled with hundreds of laughing and talking children. She saw his dark eyes lighten as he met and held her gaze, and she smiled, feeling the warmth of his heated look.

Killian moved to the wall of lockers and waited for her. "Hi," she said breathlessly.

Susannah's eyes shone with a welcome that reached through Killian's heavy armor and touched his heart. An ache began in his chest, an ache that startled Killian. How easily she could touch him with just a look and a soft smile. "How you doing?" Killian fell in step just behind her.

"Fine." Susannah beamed. "It's so good to be back, Sean! I feel like my life's finally coming back together again." Susannah looked tenderly at Freddy, a seven-year-old boy with Down's syndrome who walked at her side, his hand firmly gripping hers. "I really missed my kids," she quavered, looking up at Killian.

Killian had his doubts about Susannah returning to work, about how it might affect her, but he said nothing. Freddy gave her a worshipful look of unqualified love. No wonder Susannah liked working with these special children. They gave fully, in the emotional sense, Killian noted with surprise.

"Are you done with your walk around the school?" Susannah asked as her little flock of children surrounded her. The double doors to the cafeteria were open. She guided her group through them and down the stairs.

"Yeah, I'm done. What can I do to help?"

She smiled and pointed to several long tables with chairs lined up on either side. "See that area?"

"Yes."

"After we get the kids seated, some of the help will bring over their lunches. You go ahead and go through the cafeteria line and meet me over there. I'm going to be pretty busy the next twenty minutes."

Killian sat with his back to the wall. For security reasons, he was glad that the cafeteria was in the basement with no windows. He didn't taste his food—chili, a salad and an apple—or the coffee he'd poured for himself. Instead, he watched Susannah. She wore a bright yellow cotton skirt today, a feminine-looking white short-sleeved blouse, and sandals. Her hair was loose, flowing

over her back. She looked beautiful. And it was clear…
that there wasn't one child who didn't adore her and positively glow when rewarded with her smile, a touch of her
hand, or a brief kiss on the brow.

"Finally!" Susannah sat down with her tray of food.
She tucked several stray strands of hair behind her ear
and smiled across the table at him.

"You've got your hands full," Killian commented.
Lunch was only forty-five minutes long, and Susannah
had been up and helping her kids for close to half an hour.
Now she'd have to gulp her food down.

"I love it! I wouldn't have it any other way."

Killian quietly suffered the din in the cafeteria, his
senses heightened and pummeled at the same time. He
nodded to Susannah, but his concentration was on the
faculty. There was a possibility that the hit man could
pose as a teacher, slip in and try to kill Susannah in the
school. All morning he'd been committing faculty faces
to memory, his gaze roving restlessly across the huge,
noisy cafeteria.

"Well? Did you find what you were looking for?" Susannah asked, eating her chili.

"I located possible sites," Killian said, not wanting to
refer directly to the topic for fear of scaring the attentive,
listening children who surrounded them. "I'll discuss it
with you tonight, when we get home."

With a sigh, Susannah smiled. "Home. It sounds so
nice when you say that."

Avoiding her sparkling gaze, which sent a flush of
heat sheeting through him, Killian nodded and paid attention to the apple he was eating but not tasting. Home
anywhere with Susannah was a dream come true, he decided sourly. Four o'clock couldn't come soon enough

because Killian realized he *wanted* time alone with Susannah. Each moment was a precious drop of a dream that, he knew, must someday come to an end. And, like a man lost in the desert, he thirsted for each drop that she gave him simply by being nearby.

"You're exhausted," Killian told Susannah as they worked in the kitchen preparing their dinner. He'd taken on the salad-making duties, and she was frying some steaks.

"Oh, I'm okay. First days are always that way. I'll adjust."

He glanced at her as he cut a tomato deftly with a knife. Susannah had changed into a pair of jeans and a pink sleeveless blouse. She was barefoot. He frowned as he studied her at the stove.

"Maybe you ought to switch to half days for now."

"No... I'll be okay, Sean. It's just that the first days are overwhelming. The children—" she glanced up and met his serious-looking face "—needed reassuring that I wouldn't abandon them. Handicapped children are so sensitized to possible loss of the people they rely on. They live in a very narrow world, and part of their stability is the fixedness of activity within it. If a teacher or a parent suddenly leaves, it's terribly upsetting to them."

"So you were applying Band-Aids all day?"

She grinned. "You might say that. You look a little tired yourself."

With a shrug, Killian placed the two salad bowls on the table near their plates. "A little," he lied. He'd hardly slept at all last night.

"Is the school a viable target?" she asked as she arranged their steaks on the plates.

Killian heard the quaver in her voice. He sat down and said, "There are pros and cons to it. The only place where you're really a target is the school-bus loading and unloading zone. The gym facility across the street is two stories tall—ideal for a hit man to hide in and draw a bead on you."

Trying to stay calm, Susannah sat down after pouring them each a cup of coffee. Taking a pink paper napkin, she spread it across her lap. "This is so upsetting, Sean."

"I know." The strain on Susannah's face said it all. Killian wished he wasn't always the bearer of such bad tidings.

"It's not your fault." She cut a piece of her steak and gave him a sidelong look. "Do these men hit quickly?"

"What do you mean?"

"Well, if a contract's been put out on me, will he try to get it done quickly, instead of waiting months to do it?"

"They like to get paid. They'll do it as quickly as possible to collect the balance of the money."

Susannah pushed some salad around with her fork. "Have you heard from the police about a possible identification from the sketch I gave you a few days ago?"

"Not yet. I was hoping Morgan or the Lexington police would call me. With any luck," Killian said, eating a bite of the succulent steak, "we'll have more answers by tomorrow at the latest."

"And if you find out who my attacker is, you'll be able to know whether or not he's part of a larger drug ring?"

"Yes."

With a sigh, Susannah forced herself to eat. "I just wish it was over."

"So I'd be out of your life."

She gave him a tender look. "You're something good

that's happened to me, Sean. I don't want you out of my life."

With a disgruntled look, he growled, "If I were you, I would."

As gently as possible, Susannah broached the subject of Meg with him. "Has your sister had any therapy to help her through the trauma she endured?"

Killian looked up. "A little." He frowned. "Not enough, as far as I'm concerned. Ian, her fiancé, wants to come back into her life, but Meg is afraid to let it happen."

Once again Susannah saw the anguish burning in Killian's eyes, anguish and love for his sister. There was no question but that he cared deeply about her. It was sweet to know that he now trusted her enough to reveal a small piece of his real self. Still, she knew she would have to tread lightly if Sean was to remain open and conversant. What had changed in him to make him more accessible? Possibly today at the school, she thought, cutting another piece of meat.

"Ian still loves her?"

Killian's mouth twisted. "He never stopped."

Susannah moved back to the stove. "You sound confused about that. Why?"

"Because Ian is letting his love for her tear him apart years afterward. He won't forget Meg. He refuses to."

"Love isn't something that dries up and goes away just because there's a tragedy," she said gently, passing him the platter of meat.

Killian placed another piece of steak on his plate, then handed the platter back to Susannah. "If you ask me, love is a special kind of torture. Ian twists in the wind waiting for Meg to take him back."

"He loves her enough to wait," Susannah noted. She

saw Killian's eyes harden, the fork suspended halfway to his mouth.

Glancing at her, he snapped, "Love is nothing but pain. I saw it too many times, too many ways, growing up. I've watched Ian suffer. It's not worth it."

"What? Loving someone?" Susannah stopped eating and held his turbulent gaze.

"Yes."

Treading carefully, she asked, "Does Meg allow Ian back into her life in any form?"

"No, only me. She trusts only me."

"Why won't she allow Ian to help her recover?"

Flatly he responded, "Because Meg is disfigured. She's ugly compared to what she used to look like."

Suffering was all too evident on Killian's hard features. Susannah ached for both him and Meg. "She thinks that if Ian sees her he'll leave her anyway?"

"Yes, I guess so. But Ian knows she's no longer beautiful, and he doesn't care. I tried to tell Meg that, but she won't listen."

"Maybe Ian needs to go to Meg directly and confront her about it."

With a snort, Killian shook his head. "Let's put it this way. Our family—what's left of it, Meg and me—are bullheaded."

"She's not being bullheaded," Susannah said softly. "She's sticking her head in the sand and pretending Ian and his feelings don't count."

Killian moved around uncomfortably in his chair. "Sometimes," he muttered defiantly, "running away is the least of all evils."

Susannah met and held his dark blue gaze. "I don't agree. Having the courage to face the other person is always better. You should tell Ian to go to Meg and talk things out."

"If Ian knew where she lived, he'd have done that a long time ago."

She stared at him. "You won't tell him where she lives?"

"How can I? Meg begs me not to. Do you think I'm going to go against her wishes?"

"But," Susannah said lamely, "that would help heal the situation, Sean. Ian wouldn't be left feeling so tortured. Meg wouldn't feel so alone."

Smarting beneath her wisdom, Killian forced his attention back to his plate. He'd lost his appetite. "You're young, Susannah. You're protected. If you'd been kicked around like my family has been, gone through what we've gone through, you wouldn't be so eager for emotional confrontations."

She felt his panic—and his anger. "I know I'm naive," she whispered.

"Life makes you tired," Killian rasped. "Try getting hit broadside again and again and see how willing you are to get up and confront it again. Believe me, you'll think twice about it. If Ian's smart, he'll get on with his life and forget Meg."

The depth of his belief in running and hiding frightened Susannah. How many other women had wanted to love Killian? How many had he left? Upset, she could only say, "If I were Ian, I'd go to Meg. I'd love her enough to find her on my own without your help."

Killian saw the flash of stubbornness in her eyes, and felt it in her voice. He offered her a twisted, one-cornered smile. "Idealism doesn't make it in this world, and nei-

ther does hope. You've got too much of both, Susannah.
All they'll do is hurt you in the end."

Susannah was getting ready to take a bath around ten
that night when the phone rang. Killian was sitting in the
living room, reading the newspaper. His head snapped
up and his eyes narrowed. Forcing herself to answer the
phone, Susannah picked up the receiver.

"Hello?"

"Susannah?"

"Morgan! How are you?"

"I'm fine. Better question is, how are you doing with
Killian there?"

She flushed and avoided Killian's interested gaze.
"Better," she whispered, suddenly emotional. "Much
better."

"Good. Listen, I need to talk to Killian. Can you put
him on?"

"Sure. Give Laura and the kids my love, will you?"

"Of course. Are you doing all right physically?"

Susannah heard the guilt in Morgan's voice and knew
that he blamed himself in some way for her problems.
Her hand tightened on the phone. "I'm improving every
day," she promised.

"The headaches?"

Susannah thought for a moment. "Why," she breathed
as the realization sank in, "I've had fewer since Killian
arrived. Isn't that wonderful?"

"It is."

"I'll put Sean on the phone. Hold on." Susannah held
the phone toward Killian. "It's Morgan. He wants to talk
to you."

Unwinding from his chair, Killian put the newspaper aside.

Just the touch of Killian's fingers on her own as he took the receiver sent an ache throbbing through Susannah. Sensing that he wanted to be alone to talk to Morgan, Susannah left to take her bath.

Holding the receiver, Killian waited until Susannah was gone. "Morgan?"

"Yes. How's it going?"

"All right," Killian said noncommittally, keeping his voice low. He continued to watch the doorway that Susannah had disappeared through. If the conversation was disturbing, he didn't want her to overhear and become upset. "What's going on?"

"That sketch you sent that Susannah drew?"

"Yes?"

"We've got a positive identification from the FBI. His name is Huey Greaves, and he was a middleman stateside for Santiago's ring. So my hunch was correct—unfortunately. Greaves doubles as a hit man for Santiago whenever another cartel tries to encroach on his territory. The man who was killed was there to pick up drugs that were later found in one of the bus terminal luggage bins. He was from another drug ring—one that's been trying to move in on Santiago's territory."

Killian released a ragged breath, cursing softly. Susannah was in serious danger. "You've given this info to the Lexington police?"

"Yes. They've got an APB out on him. They've also alerted the county sheriff who covers Glen and the Anderson farm."

Grimly Killian gazed around the living room, which

was dancing in the shadows created by the two hurricane lamps. "The bastard will hit Susannah."

Morgan sighed. "It's only a matter of time. Santiago—it figures."

"I've got to talk to her about this," Killian rasped. "She's got to know the danger involved. She started teaching today, and under the circumstances I don't think it's a good idea for her to go in tomorrow morning."

"No," Morgan agreed. "We know from experience that Santiago will go to any lengths. His people wouldn't care if there are children involved. Keep her at the farm, Killian. It's safer for everyone that way."

Killian almost laughed at the irony of the situation. No place was safe for Susannah—not even with him. "Yeah, I'll keep her here."

"You know Glen doesn't have much of a police department. The county sheriff is the only one who can help you if you get into trouble. Get the number and keep it handy. With budget cuts, they only have two patrol cars for the entire county, so don't expect too much. A two-hour delay wouldn't be unusual, Killian. I'm afraid you're really on your own on this one. The county sheriff knows who you are and why you're there, and if they see this guy they'll call to let you know—and send a sheriff's cruiser in your direction as soon as humanly possible."

"Good." At least the police and the FBI were working together on this. Still, chances were that when the hit went down it would be Killian against the killer.

"Stay in touch," Morgan said.

"Thanks, Morgan. I will." Killian scowled as he hung up the phone. He wasn't looking forward to telling Susannah the bad news.

* * *

Susannah couldn't sleep. She was restless, tossing and turning on her ancient brass bed. The night air was warm, and she pushed off the sheet. Her watch read 2:00 a.m. It was the phone call from Morgan that had left her sleepless.

With a muffled sound of frustration, Susannah got up. She didn't want to wake Sean. Just the thought of him sent a flurry of need through her as she padded softly down the hall to the kitchen. Perhaps a cup of hot chamomile tea would help settle her screaming nerves so that she could sleep. But, she warned herself, tea wasn't going to stop the simmering desire that had been building in her for days.

Susannah ran a hand through her unbound hair, then opened the cabinet and took out a cup and saucer. Killian had warned her away from him—told her that he was no good for her. Why couldn't she listen to his thinly veiled threat?

"Susannah?"

Gasping, she whirled around, nearly dropping the cup from her hand. Killian stood in the doorway, his drawstring pajamas barely held up by his narrow hips. His eyes were soft with sleep, and his hair was tangled across his brow. Her heart pounding, Susannah released a breath.

"You scared me."

"Sorry," he muttered, any remaining sleepiness torn from him as he studied her in the shadowy moonlight that crossed the kitchen. Her knee-length white gown gave her an angelic look, and the moonlight outlined her body like a lover's caress through the light cotton fabric.

The dark frame of hair emphasized the delicateness of her features, especially her parted lips.

"I—I couldn't sleep." She gestured toward the kettle on the stove. "I thought I'd make some chamomile tea."

"Morgan's call upset you?"

"Yes."

Easing into the room, Killian crossed to the table and sat down. His head was screaming at him to go back to bed, but his heart clamored for her closeness.

"Make me a cup, will you?"

"Sure." Susannah's pulse wouldn't seem to settle down, and she busied herself at the counter, attempting to quell her nervousness. Killian's body was hard and lean. She wondered what it would be like to kiss him, to feel his arms around her.

As Susannah turned, the cups of tea in her hands, the window at the kitchen counter shattered, glass exploding in all directions.

"Get down!" Killian shouted. Launching himself out of his chair, he took Susannah with him as he slammed to the floor. More glass shattered, splintering in rainbow fragments all around them.

Susannah groaned under Killian's weight, her mind spinning with shock. She could hear Killian's harsh breathing, and his cursing, soft and strained. Almost instantly she felt his steely grip on her arms as he dragged her upward and positioned her against the corner cabinets for protection.

Her eyes wide, she took in the harshness in his sweaty features.

"The hit man," he rasped. *Dammit!* He'd left his pistol in the bedroom. He noticed small, bloody cuts on Susannah's right arm.

"But—how?"

Killian shook his head, putting his finger to his lips. Silence was crucial right now. The hit man had to be on the porch. But why the hell hadn't he heard him? Felt him? A hundred questions battered Killian. His senses were now screamingly alert. He had to get to his gun, or they were both dead!

Gripping Susannah's wrist, Killian tugged and motioned for her to follow him. If they couldn't make it to his bedroom, they were finished. The last thing he wanted was Susannah dead. The thought spurred him into action.

Gasping for breath, Susannah scrambled out of the kitchen on her hands and knees. In the darkened hall, Killian jerked her to her feet, shoving her forward and into his room. Instantly he pushed her onto the floor and motioned for her to wriggle beneath the bed and remain there.

Killian's fingers closed over the pistol on the nightstand. The feel of the cool metal was reassuring. Now they had a chance. His eyes narrowed as he studied the window near his bed and the open door to his room.

"Stay down!" he hissed. "Whatever happens, stay here!"

Tears jammed into Susannah's eyes as she looked up into his taut, glistening features. Here was the mercenary. The soldier who could kill. She opened her mouth, then snapped it shut.

"Don't move!" Killian warned. He leaped lightly to his feet, every muscle in his body tense with anticipation. He tugged at the blanket so that it hung off the bed and concealed Susannah's glaringly white nightgown. Swiftly he turned on his heel and moved to the door, his hands wrapped around the pistol that he held high and at the ready.

Killian was angry at himself—angry that he'd dropped his guard because he cared for Susannah. He pressed himself hard against the wall and listened. His nostrils flared to catch any unusual scent. Morgan Trayhern had called him a hound from hell on more than one occasion because of his acutely honed senses. Well, they'd saved his life more than once. Tonight, he had to count on his abilities to save Susannah.

As he ducked out of the entrance and quickly looked up and down the hall, Killian saw no evidence of the hit man. Then a creak of wood made him freeze. There! The kitchen! His heart was a thudding sledgehammer in his chest, his quiet breathing was ragged. The bastard was in the kitchen.

There! Killian heard the crunch of glass. How close to the kitchen doorway was he? He continued down the hall soundlessly, on the balls of his feet. His hands sweaty, beads of perspiration running down his temples, Killian focused like a laser on his quarry. Susannah's killer. Only two more feet and he'd have enough of an angle to peer into the darkened depths of the kitchen. Every muscle in his body stiffened with expectation.

Another crunch of glass. The sound was directional, giving away where the hit man stood. Instantly Killian launched himself forward, flattening himself against the hardwood floor, both hands in front of him, the snout of the Beretta aimed. Seeing the darkened shape of a man move, he squeezed off two shots. The sounds reverberated through the farmhouse. Damn! He'd missed!

The hit man fired back, a silencer on his gun cloaking the sound to light pops. Killian rolled to the left, the

The Rogue

door jamb his shield. Wood cracked and splintered as bullets savagely tore at the barrier. His mind working rapidly, Killian counted off the shots. Six. More than likely the bastard had nine bullets in his clip. Then he'd have to reload.

The scrambling over glass continued. Killian kept low. He realized with terror that the bedroom where Susannah was hiding was directly behind the hit man. If Killian fired, his shots could go through the walls and hit her. Damn!

Breathing hard, his lips pulled away from clenched teeth, Killian grabbed a piece of wood near his bare feet, and threw it into the kitchen.

Two more shots were fired at it in quick succession.

Good! Only one more round before he'd have to take precious seconds to reload. Stinging sweat dripped into his eyes, and he blinked it away.

In those seconds, waiting for the hit man to make his move, Killian realized that he loved Susannah. Where had such a crazy idea come from? Tightening his grip on the Beretta, he rose onto one knee, ready to fire.

An explosion of movement occurred in the kitchen. Before Killian could fire, the table was tipped over, slamming against the doorway and spoiling his shot. The screen door was ripped off its hinges as a dark figure scrambled out. The thudding of running feet filled the air.

Cursing roundly, Killian leaped over the table. The son of a bitch! Sprinting onto the porch, Killian saw the hit man fleeing toward the road, where his car must be hidden. Digging his toes into the soft, wet grass, Killian started after him. The direction the hit man was running was in line with the Andersons' farmhouse, not more than a quarter mile away. Killian couldn't risk a stray bullet hitting the house or its occupants.

Running hard, he cut through the orchard. Ahead, he saw a dark blue car. The hit man jerked the door open, disappeared inside and hit the accelerator.

The nondescript car leaped forward, dirt and clods flying up, leaving a screen of dust in its wake. Killian memorized the license plate number before the car was swallowed up by the darkness. Lowering his pistol, he continued to run toward the Anderson residence. He wanted to report the car's license number to the sheriff and call Morgan. More than likely the vehicle was a rental car, and the hit man had signed for it with an alias at an airport—probably Lexington.

Killian's mind spun with options, with necessary procedures that would have to be instituted quickly.

Reaching the house, he wasn't surprised to find the Andersons still asleep, completely unaware of what had just occurred. Susannah's house was nearly a half mile away with plenty of orchard to absorb the sounds of battle.

Breathing hard, Killian entered the house via the kitchen and found the phone there on the wall. Setting his gun nearby on the counter, he shakily dialed the county sheriff. As he waited for someone to answer, his heart revolved back to Susannah. Was she all right? He recalled the cuts to her right arm, caused by the shattering glass. Anger with himself because he hadn't protected her as well as he should have filled Killian. As soon as he'd reported the incident, he'd get back to the house and care for Susannah.

Lying on her belly, Susannah had no idea how long she remained frozen. Her heart was beating hard, and her fingers were dug into the wooden floor. Sean! Was he all right? What had happened? Did she dare risk coming out from beneath the bed to find out? There had been no sound for about fifteen minutes. Her mind was playing tricks on her. Maybe Sean was bleeding to death on the kitchen floor and she didn't know it. Should she move from her hiding place? Should she stay?

She closed her eyes as tears leaked into them. Sean couldn't be dead! He just couldn't! The attack had ripped away her doubts. She loved Killian. It was that simple— and that complicated. Lying there, shaking badly as the adrenaline began to seep out of her bloodstream, she pressed her brow against her hands. Sean had ordered her not to move—no matter what. But how could she remain here? If he was lying wounded somewhere, how could she not move?

With a little cry, Susannah made her decision.

"Susannah?"

Killian! She gasped as he pulled the blanket away. Her eyes widened enormously as he got down on his hands and knees.

"Sean?"

He smiled grimly and reached for her. "Yeah. I'm all right, colleen. Everything's okay. The hit man got away. Come on, crawl out of there."

Susannah discovered how wobbly she was as she got to her feet. Killian gripped her hands.

"I—I don't think I can stand," she quavered, looking up into his dark, sweaty features.

"I'm not too steady myself," he answered with a rasp. He drew Susannah into his arms and brought her against him. The contact with her was shocking. Melting. Killian groaned as she leaned heavily against him, her arms around him, her head against his shoulder.

"Sweet," he whispered, holding her tightly—holding her so hard he was afraid he was going to crush her. The natural scent of her—a fragrant smell, like lilacs—encircled his nostrils. Killian dragged in that scent, life after the odors of death. He felt Susannah shift and lift her head. Without thinking, he cupped her chin and guided her lips to his mouth.

The meeting was fiery, purging. He felt the softness of her lips, felt them flow open, their heat, their moistness overwhelming his heightened senses. Time ceased to exist. All he was aware of, all he wanted, was her. The warmth of Susannah's breasts pressing softly against his chest, her softness against his hardness, shattered the last of his control.

He groaned, taking her mouth hungrily, sliding against her, absorbing her warmth, her womanliness. His breathing grew chaotic, fevered, as she returned his inflammatory kiss. His fingers sliding into her hair, Killian gripped the silky strands, framing her face, holding her captive as he absorbed her into him like a starving man.

Susannah moaned, but it was a moan of utter surrender mingled with pleasure. She found herself pressed onto the bed, with Killian's tense body against her, driving her into the mattress. The near brush with death—the fear of losing him—overwhelmed her, and she sought blindly to reassure herself that he was alive, that he was safe. There was security in Sean's arms, those powerful bands that trapped her, holding her captive beneath him. With a fierce need, she returned his searching kiss.

"I need you, I need you," Killian rasped against her wet, soft mouth. "Now. I need you now..." He felt her arch beneath him, giving him the answer he sought. He'd nearly lost Susannah to an assailant's bullet. The warmth of her flesh, the eagerness of her beneath him, could have been destroyed in a split second. Sliding his shaky hands beneath her rumpled gown, he sought and found her slender rib cage, then moved upward. The instant his hands curved around her small breasts, he heard her cry out. But it was a cry of utter pleasure, not fear or pain. The husky sound coming from her throat increased the heat in his lower body. Never had he wanted a woman more. Never had he loved a woman as he loved Susannah.

The fierceness of his roiling emotions shattered Killian's ironclad control. He was helpless beneath her hands. They were gliding over his taut back and shoulders as he pulled the gown off her. In moments his pajamas were in a heap on the wooden floor. Her fingers dug convulsively into his bunched shoulders as he leaned down and captured the tight peak of her nipple with his insistent lips. She became wild, untamed, beneath him, moving her head from side to side, begging him to enter her.

The fever in his blood tripled, sang through him as he felt her thighs open to welcome him. He wanted to take it slow, to make it good for Susannah, but the fiery blood beating through him ripped away all but his primal need to plunge deep into her—to bury himself in her life, escaping the death that had stalked them less than an hour earlier.

Framing her face with his hands, Killian looked down into her dazed, lustrous eyes as he moved forward to meet her. He wanted to imprint Susannah's lovely features on his heart and mind forever. The moment he entered her hot, womanly confines, a low, vibrating growl ripped out of him. He couldn't stop his forward plunge—didn't want to. His need for this feverish coupling was like a storm that had waited too long to expend itself.

Killian's fingers tightened against Susannah's face and he stiffened as liquid fire encircled him, captured him, leaving him mindless, aware of nothing but a rainbow of sensations, each more powerful, more overwhelming, than the next. When Susannah moved her hips, drawing him even deeper inside her, he sucked in a ragged breath. Never had he experienced heaven like this. He leaned down, savoring her lips, drowning in the splendor of her sweet, fiery offering.

Then nothing existed but the touching and sliding of their bodies against each other, satin against steel. Susannah was soft, giving, bending to Killian's needs with a sweet suppleness. He was hard, demanding—plunging and taking. Her lilac fragrance surrounded him as he buried his face in the silky folds of her hair. In moments, an explosive feeling enveloped him, freezing him into an immobility of such intense pleasure that he could only gasp in response. As she moved her hips sinuously against him, he could no more control himself than a rain storm could hold back from spending itself on the lush warmth of the earth.

Afterward, moments glided and fused together as Killian lay spent. He raised his head and realized that his fingers were still tightly grasping the thick strands of Susannah's hair, as if he were afraid she'd slip away from him—as if this were one of his fevered dreams, ready to flee when he opened his eyes. Susannah's lashes fluttered upward, and he held his breath, drowning in the glorious gray of her eyes.

The soft, trembling smile that curved her lips sent another sheet of heat through Killian. He felt her hot, wet tightness still around him, holding him, and he groaned.

"I feel like I've gone to heaven," he rasped against her lips. And then he added weakly, "Or as close as I'll ever get to heaven, because I'm bound for hell."

"You *are* heaven," Susannah managed huskily, held captive by him in all ways, luxuriating in his strength and masculinity.

Carefully Killian untangled his hand from her hair and touched her swollen lips. With a grimace, he whispered, "I'm sorry, colleen, I got carried away. I didn't mean to hurt you."

Susannah kissed his scarred fingers. "I'm fine. How could you hurt me?"

He shakily traced her smooth forehead and the arch of her eyebrow. "In a million ways," he assured her.

With a tender smile, Susannah framed his damp features. No longer was the man with the hard face staring down at her. No, this was the very human, vulnerable side of Sean Killian. And she reveled fiercely in his being able to shed his outer shell—to give himself to her in an even more important, wonderful way.

Gently Killian moved aside and brought Susannah into his arms as he lay on the bed. "Come here," he whispered, holding her tight for a long, long time. The moments ran together for him. Susannah's arm flowed across his chest, and one of her long, lovely legs lay across his own. He blinked his eyes several times, trying to think coherently. It was nearly impossible with Susannah in his arms.

"You're all a man could ever dream of having," he told her in a low, unsteady voice as he kissed her cheek, and then her awaiting lips. Lying there with her in his arms, he caressed her cheek.

Susannah melted within his embrace, savoring the feel of his fingers moving lightly across her shoulder, down her arm to her hip. He was stroking her as if she were a purring cat. And wasn't she? "I'll never be sorry this happened," she admitted breathlessly. "Never."

As Killian lay there, his mind finally beginning to take over from the lavalike emotions that had exploded in a volcano lain dormant too long, he tasted bitterness in his mouth. There was Susannah, innocent and trusting in his arms, her eyes shining with such adoration that it made him sick inside. She didn't know his sordid past, didn't know the ghosts that still haunted him.

"I shouldn't have done this to you," he rasped, frowning. Yet he couldn't stop touching her, sliding his hands across her satiny flesh and feeling her effortless response.

"No!" Susannah forced herself up onto one elbow. She reached out, her hand on his chest, where his heart lay. "We both wanted this, Sean. *Both* of us."

He grimaced. "It shouldn't have happened," he said, more harshly.

"Really?" Susannah couldn't keep the sarcasm out of her tone, and she was sorry for it.

Unable to meet her eyes, he shook his head and threw the covers aside. "I was to protect you, Susannah!"

"Loving someone isn't protecting them?"

He glanced at her sharply as he forced himself to get up and leave her side. If he stayed, he'd want to love her all over again, with the fierceness of a breaking thunderstorm.

"I was paid to protect you, dammit!" he flared, moving around the bed and going to the dresser. Jerking open the drawer, he retrieved jeans and a polo shirt.

Sitting up in bed, Susannah suddenly felt bereft. Abandoned. Quiet tension thrummed through the room, and a chill washed over her. Killian put on boxer shorts and the jeans. His face was hard again, his mouth set in a thin line.

"Sean, what's going on? I liked what we shared. I like you. Why are you so angry and upset about it?"

"You'd better get cleaned up, Susannah," he told her tautly, pulling the shirt over his head. "Take a shower and get dressed. The sheriff is sending out a cruiser to check out what happened with the hit man. He'll probably be here in a half hour or so."

Forcing herself to her feet, Susannah moved over to him. His movements were abrupt and tense. She gripped his arm.

"The police can wait," she said hoarsely, searching his dark, unfathomable eyes. "*We* can't."

Her fingers were like small, exquisite brands burning into his flesh. Killian pulled away from Susannah. "There is no 'we'!" he said harshly. It was pure, unadulterated hell looking down at her standing there naked and beautiful before him. "Look at you! Even now you can't protect yourself against the likes of someone like me. It shouldn't have happened, Susannah! It was my fault. I wanted—needed you so damned bad I could taste it." Aggravated, Killian ran his fingers through his mussed hair. "I broke a cardinal rule that I've never broken before—I got involved with the person I was supposed to protect." He gave her a sad look, his voice cracking with emotion. "I'm sorry. I'm sorry it happened. You didn't deserve this on top of everything else, Susannah."

Chapter 8

Susannah had barely stepped out of the shower when the sheriff's cruiser arrived. Going to her bedroom, she dressed in a sensible pair of dark green cotton slacks and a white short-sleeved blouse. Her hair was still damp, and she braided the strands together, fastening the ends with a rubber band. Her hands shook as she put on white socks and a pair of sneakers.

The terror of nearly being killed warred with Sean's reaction to their lovemaking, buffeting her weary senses. Each time she replayed the conversation, it made no sense to her. Why was he sorry he'd loved her? She wasn't. Touching her bangs with trembling fingers, she took one look in the mirror. Her face was pale, and her eyes were dark and huge. And her lips… Susannah groaned softly. Her mouth looked wonderfully ravished, slightly swollen and well kissed.

Entering the kitchen, Susannah saw the damage from the gunfire for the first time. Killian had set the table upright, and he and the two deputies sat at the table, their faces grim. Across the wooden floor, glass lay splintered and glinting in the lamplight.

Killian glanced up. Susannah stood poised just inside the room. He was struck by her beauty, her simple clothing—the luster in her gray eyes that he knew was meant for him alone. Trying to steel himself against his still-turbulent emotions, he got up.

"Come over here and sit down," he invited, his voice rough. "They've caught the guy who tried to kill us."

Gasping in surprise, Susannah came forward. "They did?"

"Yes, ma'am," a large, beefy deputy volunteered. "Thanks to Mr. Killian's quick reporting, we got him just as he was trying to leave the Glen town limits."

Killian pulled the chair out for her so that she could sit down. It hardly seemed possible, but Susannah looked even paler.

"You want some coffee?" he asked. Dammit, why did he have to sound so harsh with her? He was angry with himself, with his lack of control. It was he who had initiated their lovemaking.

"Please." Susannah tried to ignore Killian's overwhelming male presence—to concentrate on the deputy, whose name tag read Birch. But it was impossible. "Deputy Birch, what can you tell us about this hit man?" she managed to say, her voice unsteady.

"Not much. We're putting him through the paces right now back at the station. I do know he'll get put in jail without bail. The judge won't hear his case until nine this morning."

Susannah looked at the wall clock. It was 3:00 a.m., yet she felt screamingly awake. Was this how Sean felt all the time? Did a mercenary ever relax? As Killian moved around the counter, which was strewn with wood and glass debris, Susannah sensed an explosiveness around him.

"How may I help?" Susannah asked the deputies in a low, off-key voice.

"Just give us your statement, Miss Anderson." Birch threw a look at Killian. "I'd say your guardian angel here saved you."

She forced a smile that she didn't feel. "Yes, well, Mr. Killian is protective, if nothing else." Susannah saw him twist a look across his shoulder at her. His eyes were dark and angry. What had she done to deserve his anger? She hoped against hope that, when the deputies left, she and Sean could sit and talk this out.

Killian moved restlessly around the kitchen. It was 4:00 a.m., and the deputies were wrapping up their investigation. Susannah was looking exhausted, her adrenaline high clearly worn off, a bruised-looking darkness beneath her eyes.

"We'll be in touch shortly," Birch promised as the deputies stood up and ended their visit.

"Thank you," Susannah told them wearily, meaning it. She watched as Killian escorted the officers out to the porch, where they talked in low voices she couldn't overhear. Exhausted, she stood up, feeling as if she'd gone days without sleep. As much as she wanted to wait for Sean to return, to discuss whatever problem had sprung up between them, Susannah knew she didn't have the emotional strength for the confrontation. It would have to wait.

In her room, Susannah set the alarm for seven, so that she could call the principal and tell him she wouldn't be able to teach today. She lay down on the bed, not caring that she was still dressed, and fell asleep immediately. In her dreams, Killian loved her with his primal hunger all over again.

Susannah awoke with a start, her heart pounding. Sunlight was pouring in through the curtains at a high angle. What time was it? Groggily she looked at her watch. It was noon! She barely recalled getting up at seven to make the call and going straight back to bed.

Sitting for a moment, she allowed herself time to get reoriented. Had last night been some terrible combination of nightmare and dream? Killian's words about heaven and hell came back to her. That was what last night had been for her: tasting both extremes. It had been heaven loving Sean, feeling the intensity of his need for her. The hell had arrived earlier, in the form of a killer who'd wanted to take her life. Rubbing her brow, Susannah felt the beginnings of a headache. A heartache would be more appropriate. Why was Sean sorry he'd loved her?

When Susannah went to the kitchen, she found it almost as good as new. The only thing missing was the window over the sink. The floor had been swept clean of debris and mopped, the counters cleared of any evidence of the violent episode. She looked around. The splintered wood in the doorway had been removed. Either Killian or her father was busy making repairs.

What couldn't be repaired as quickly were the bullet holes along the kitchen wall. They were an ugly reminder, and Susannah stood there, rubbing her arms absently, feeling very cold.

"It's almost like new."

Gasping, Susannah turned at the sound of Killian's low voice. He stood at the screen door, a piece of wood in his hand. "You scared me to death!" She placed her hand against her pounding heart.

Entering, Killian scowled. Susannah looked sleepy, her eyes puffy, and her mouth—he groaned inwardly. Her mouth looked beautifully pouty, the force of his kisses last night still stamped there. The ache to kiss her all over again, to ease the fear lingering in her eyes by taking her into his arms, flowed through him. Savagely he destroyed the feeling.

"Sorry," he muttered. "I didn't mean to scare you." He stalked across the kitchen and placed the wood against the door jamb. It fit perfectly. Now all he had to do was nail it into place.

"That's okay," she reassured him, a little breathlessly, "I'm just jumpy right now."

"Now you know how a mercenary feels twenty-four hours a day." He gave her a cheerless look. Killian wanted to convey in every way possible the miserable life he led—no place for a decent human being like Susannah. He wished she'd quit looking at him like that, with that innocence that drove him crazy with need.

Forcing herself to move, Susannah poured herself some fresh coffee. "Has the sheriff called yet?"

"Yes. Greaves was the man. The same one that nearly killed you at the bus station. He isn't talking, but I spoke to Morgan earlier, and he's working with the sheriff. The FBI are still in on it, too." Killian placed the board against the wall and went to the icebox. He wasn't hungry, but he knew he had to eat.

Biting down on her lower lip, Susannah glanced over at Killian as he brought out whole wheat bread, lunch meat and mustard. "Is it over, then?"

"I don't know. Morgan is sending a message through a third party to Santiago's cartel in Peru. He's ordering him to lift the contract on you or we'll start extradition procedures against more of the cartel honchos."

"What makes you think they'll lift the contract?" Susannah watched him slap some mustard on the bread and top it with several pieces of lunch meat. His features were unreadable, as usual. What was he feeling? Hadn't their loving meant anything to him? He was acting as if it had never happened!

Killian moved to the table and sat down with his sandwich. "This particular drug family is in plenty of hot water already with the Peruvian government, so they don't need any more attention from the authorities. Besides, Greaves is one of their top men who does dirty work for them in this country. They don't want to risk him spilling the beans to the American authorities on what he knows about the drug shipments to the U.S. He's been in a position to know about a lot of things. No, they'll probably make the deal and take the heat off you."

Turning around so that her back rested against the counter, Susannah crossed her arms. Killian sat, frowning darkly while he munched on the sandwich. "How soon will we know?" she asked softly.

"Morgan says a day or two at the latest. He'll call us."

Her arms tightened against herself. "And if they agree to lift the contract, what will you do?"

Forcing himself to meet her gaze, Killian growled, "I'll leave."

The words plunged into her heart like a dagger. Susannah felt as if someone had just gutted her. Turning away, she realized she was out of sorts, still waking up, in no mental—or emotional—state to discuss last night. Killian was biting into his sandwich as if he were angry with it. His blue eyes were turbulent, and he was markedly restless. Misery avalanched Susannah.

"I'm going into town," Killian said abruptly, rising. He'd choked down the sandwich, not tasting it at all, and now it sat like a huge rock in his stomach. The suffering on Susannah's face was real, and he had no control over his response to it. He'd made her this way with one lousy indiscretion—with his selfish need of her. Killian stalked to the screen door, which he'd recently rehung with new hinges.

"I've got to pick up the new glass for that window. I'll be back later."

Hurt, Susannah nodded. When Killian had left, she remained where she was, her head bowed, her eyes shut. Forcing back tears, she realized that even though he'd made wild, passionate love to her this morning, it had been little more than that. She knew nothing of the mercenary type of man. Was this part of their pattern—loving a woman and then leaving her? Susannah laughed derisively as she opened her eyes. There were a lot of men out there like that, unwilling to commit to a real, ongoing relationship, so they used women, then left them. Was Killian like that?

Her heart cried no, but as Susannah moved around the kitchen, she couldn't come up with a more reasonable answer. Still, Killian just didn't seem the type not to be loyal. Perhaps, when he came back with the window this afternoon, both of them would be more settled after the frightening events of last night, and she could talk to him.

Killian stood back, pleased with the new window gracing the kitchen. He was wildly aware that Susannah was nearby. She'd taken care of the bullet holes, filling them with spackling compound. In a day or two, when they'd dried sufficiently, she would sandpaper them smooth and paint over them. No one would realize the bullet holes were there—no one except them. Some things, he thought with disgust, one never forgot.

As Killian poured himself some coffee and went to sit on the front porch swing, he knew he'd never forget loving Susannah. The swing creaked beneath his weight, the gentle back-and-forth motion taking the edge off his screamingly taut nerves and aching heart. Taking a sip of the hot, black liquid, he narrowed his eyes, seeing nothing in front of him. He loved Susannah. How had it happened? When? He shook his head as a powerful sadness moved through him.

It didn't matter. No woman had ever captured his imagination, his feelings, the closely guarded part of him that still knew how to dream, as she had. More than anything, he wanted to spend the whole day loving her, falling asleep with her supple warmth beside him—waking up to love her all over again. But this time he wanted to move slowly, to savor Susannah, to pleasure her. He doubted she'd gotten much pleasure the first time. He'd stolen from her like a thief, because he'd needed her so badly, he thought sourly.

Reality drenched Killian as he swung slowly back and forth. Susannah could never know how he loved her.

"Sean?"

He snapped his head up. Susannah stood uncertainly at the screen door.

"Yes?" He heard the brittleness in his voice and automatically steeled himself.

"I need to talk with you," Susannah said, and pushed the screen door open. "I was waiting for you to take a break."

His mouth thinning, he picked up his now-empty coffee cup in both hands. If he didn't, he would reach for Susannah, who had come to lean against the porch railing, near the swing.

"The window's in."

Susannah nodded, licking her dry lips. "Yes... It looks good as new." She shrugged. "I wish... I wish we could fix ourselves like that window—be brand-new all over again and not have a memory of what happened last night."

"That's what makes us human, I guess," he answered gruffly. The terrible suffering in Susannah's eyes was beginning to tear him apart.

Susannah nervously clasped her hands in front of her and forced herself to look at Killian. His face was closed and unreadable, his blue eyes narrowed and calculating. "We've got to talk," Susannah began hoarsely. "I can't go on like this."

"Like what?"

Taking in a ragged breath, Susannah whispered, "We loved each other last night, Sean. Doesn't that mean anything to you?"

Wincing inwardly, Killian saw tears forming in her eyes. His mouth going dry, a lump growing in his throat, he rasped, "Dammit, Susannah, it shouldn't have happened!"

"I'm not sorry, Sean, if that's what you're worried about."

He gave her a dark look. "Well, I am. We didn't use protection. For all I know, you could be pregnant."

Startled, Susannah allowed his growling words to sink in. "Is that what's bothering you? That I might be pregnant?"

With a disgusted sound, Killian lunged to his feet, tense. "Doesn't it worry you?" he snapped. Desperate for anything that might force her to understand that there was no possible future for them, he zeroed in on that argument.

Susannah cringed beneath his taunting words. It felt as if Killian could explode at any moment. He stood next to her, tense and demanding. "Well—"

"I didn't think you were looking ahead," he rasped.

"That isn't the issue," Susannah said, forcing herself to hold his angry gaze. "The real issue is whether or not we have something special, something worth pursuing—together."

No one loved her courage more than he did. For the first time, Killian saw the stubborn jut of her jaw and the defiance in her eyes. He told himself he shouldn't be surprised by Susannah's hidden strength.

With a hiss, he turned away. "There is no us!"

"Why? Why can't there be?"

Killian whirled on her, his breathing ragged. "Because there can't be, Susannah!" He glared at her. "There will be no relationship between us." It tormented him to add, "You got that?"

Her lips parting, Susannah took a step away from

Killian. Although his face was implacable, his eyes gave him away. Her womanly intuition told her that at least part of what he was saying was bluff.

"What are you afraid of?" she said, her voice quavering.

Stunned by her insight, Killian backed away. "Nothing!" he lied. His chest heaving with inner pain—and the pain he was causing Susannah—he added savagely, "Stick with your dreams and hopes, Susannah. I don't belong in your idealistic world. I can't fit into it. I never will." His voice deepened with anguish. "I warned you to stay away from me. I warned you that it wouldn't be any good if you got close to me."

Rattled, Susannah whispered, "But I did! And I don't regret it, Sean. Doesn't that make any difference?"

Killian shook his head, his voice cracking. "Listen to me. I told you, I'm out of your life. I'm here for maybe a day or two more at the most. I'm sorry I made love to you. I had no right. It was my fault." He gave a helpless wave of his arm.

Her eyes rounded. How callous, how cold, he sounded. "I don't believe you mean that," she said, her voice beginning to shake with real anger.

He stared at her, openmouthed. "Don't look at me like that, Susannah. I'm no knight on a white horse."

Hurting, fighting not to cry in front of him, Susannah stared up at him. "What man is?" she cried. "We're all human beings, with strengths and weaknesses. You try to keep people at arm's length by making them think you're cold and cruel. I know you're not! You're bluffing, Sean."

Startled, Killian felt panic as never before. But he loved Susannah enough to allow her the freedom she didn't want from him. If only he could explain it to her...

Moving forward, he gripped her arm with just enough force to let her know he meant what he was going to say. "Bluffing? When I leave and you don't hear from me again, that's no bluff, Susannah. I'm sorry I ever met you, because I've hurt you, and I never meant to do that. I swear I didn't." He gave her a little shake. When he spoke again, there was desperation in his voice. "Move on with your life after I leave. Find a good man here— someone who believes in dreams like you do. I've told you before—I'm bound for hell. Well, I got a little taste of heaven with you. It was damned good, Susannah. I'll never forget it, but I'm a realist." He released her and stepped back.

With a little sob, Susannah lifted her hand and pressed it against her mouth. Giving her a hopeless look, Killian spun on his heel and stalked back into the farmhouse.

Swaying, Susannah caught herself and sat down heavily in the swing, afraid her knees would give out entirely. Killian's words pummeled her, cut through her. She felt flayed by his anger. Hell was here, right now. It took a long minute for Susannah to wrestle with her unraveling emotions and force herself not to end up in a weeping heap. Miserably, she wiped the moisture from her eyes. In two days or less, they would know from Morgan whether or not the drug cartel would agree to the deal. If they did, Killian was out of her life in an instant. He wanted to run. He wanted to escape.

Killian slowly finished packing his bag. Morgan had just called to let him know the Peruvian cartel had agreed to lift the contract on Susannah. At least now she would be safe. His hand tightened around the handle of his satchel. The badly beaten leather bag had seen better days—like him, he thought wearily.

Right now, Susannah was out in the garden, barefoot, wearing her old straw hat, doing the weeding. Two of the most miserable days of Killian's life had somehow managed to pass. Never had he suffered so much, known agony as devastating as this. Every fiber of his being wanted to go out and say goodbye to Susannah. He hesitated, torn. If he did, he knew there was a good possibility he couldn't continue his charade. Last night, he'd heard Susannah sobbing softly, as if she were trying to hide her pain by crying into her pillow.

Tears jammed into Killian's eyes. With a disgusted sound, he forced them back. No, he didn't dare say goodbye to Susannah in person.

"Dammit," he rasped, his voice cracking. He scribbled a quick note, then went into the kitchen and left it on the table where Susannah would see it. He took one last look around the old, dilapidated farmhouse. Capturing the memories, he stored and locked them in the vault of his scarred heart.

Taking one last look toward the garden area, Killian saw Susannah down on her hands and knees, still weeding. Dragging in a deep, painful breath, Killian silently whirled around and left. Forever.

Susannah washed most of the dirt from her hands with water from the hose outside the garden fence. It was nearly four, and she knew she had to prepare supper. Where was Sean? She'd hardly seen him in the past two days. And why hadn't Morgan called? It hurt to think. It hurt to feel, Susannah thought as she slipped the straw hat off her head and entered the kitchen.

Almost immediately, she saw the note on the table. Next to it was a glass containing a freshly cut yellow rose. Frowning, her heart doing a funny skipping beat, Susannah went over to the table. Sitting down, she shakily unfolded the note.

Dear Susannah:
Morgan called about an hour ago to tell me that the drug cartel has promised to leave you alone. You're safe, and that's what is important.

By the time you get this note, I'll be gone. I'm sorry I couldn't say goodbye. Being with you was heaven, Susannah. And for a man bound for hell, it was too much to take. Cowardice comes in many forms, and I didn't have the courage to say goodbye to you. You deserve better than me, as I've told you many times before.

You were a rainbow in my life. I never thought someone like me would ever see one, much less meet one in the form of a woman. You deserve only the best, Susannah. I'm not a man who prays much, but I will pray for your happiness. God knows, you deserve it. Killian.

A sob lodged in Susannah's throat. She stared at the paper, the words blurring as tears rose then spilled out of her eyes and down her cheeks. She gripped the letter hard, reading it and rereading it. There were so many mixed messages. It hadn't been the hardened mercenary writing this. No, it had been the very human, hurting man beneath his warrior's facade.

Crying softly, Susannah put the note aside and buried her face in her hands. The school had given her another month's leave to recover from the shooting incident. Lifting her head, she wiped the tears from her eyes. She had a month… Gathering her strewn emotions, Susannah decided to call Morgan and talk to him about Sean. Outwardly, Killian was behaving like a bastard, but a bastard wouldn't have written about her being a rainbow in his life.

Susannah worked to compose herself. She'd gone through so much in such a short amount of time. A huge part of her didn't believe Sean's letter. Never had she felt this way toward a man. She'd been "in love" before, but that relationship hadn't matured. No man had made her feel so vibrant or so alive. Did she even know what real love was? Had Sean touched her heart with genuine love? Susannah didn't know, but one way or another she intended to find out.

She brought the glass containing the yellow rose forward. Touching the delicate petals with her fingers, the fragrance encircling her, Susannah realized that Killian might be tough in many ways, but, like this rose that he'd symbolically left her, he had a vulnerable, fragile underside.

That realization gave Susannah hope as nothing else could have. She'd call Morgan and begin an investigation into Sean and the world he called hell. There was a reason why he'd left her. Something he hadn't told her. Now Sean was going to have to realize that not everything in his life was destined for hell. Nor was every person going to allow him to run away when it suited his purposes—whatever they might be.

Chapter 9

Morgan stood and came around his large walnut desk as Susannah gave him a slight smile of welcome and stepped into his office. When his assistant, Marie, had shut the door, he opened his arms.

"I'm glad you came, Susannah."

Fighting back tears, Susannah moved into Morgan's comforting embrace. She gave him a quick squeeze of welcome and then stepped away from his towering presence.

"Thanks for seeing me, Morgan. I know how busy you are."

He gestured toward the creamy leather sofa in the corner of the spacious room. "You know you aren't getting out of here without staying at least overnight. Laura insists."

Nervously Susannah sat down. "Yes, I told her I'd stay

one night. But she must be terribly busy with this second baby. It's wonderful you have a boy and a girl now."

Morgan nodded, satisfaction in his voice. "A year apart. Katherine Alyssa Trayhern will have a big brother to grow up with. We're very happy about it. She's a real spitfire, too."

Susannah was truly happy for them. Dressed in a navy pin-striped suit, with a paisley silk tie and white shirt, Morgan looked professional, every inch the head of his flourishing company. Susannah and Laura had been close throughout the years, and she knew of Morgan's terrible, torturous past. "Well," she whispered, glancing up at him, "I'm going to need some of that spitfire personality your daughter has."

"I know this involves Killian. How can I help you?" Morgan sat down, alert.

Gripping her leather purse, Susannah held his curious gaze. "I know I was vague on the phone, but I didn't feel this was something I wanted to talk about in detail to anyone except you. And I wanted to do it in person. As I told you on the phone, the school is giving me a month to get my life back in order, and I intend to use it to do just that."

Morgan nodded. "I'm just glad the contract's been lifted. What's this about Killian?"

Susannah's heart contracted in grief. Unable to hold his warm, probing gaze, she felt a lump forming in her throat.

Morgan leaned over and slid his hand across her slumped shoulder. "What's going on, Susannah?"

Fighting to keep herself together, she whispered, "I don't know how it happened or when it happened, but

I've fallen in love with Sean." She gave him a pained look. "It happened so fast…"

Morgan nodded. "I fell in love with Laura the first moment I saw her, although I didn't know it then." He grimaced. "I fought the attraction, the love she brought out in me, for a long time. It was nearly my undoing. Luckily, she hung in there and refused to let me go my own way."

"Mercenaries must all be alike," Susannah muttered unhappily.

"There's probably a grain of truth to that. I met Killian in the Foreign Legion. Did you know that?"

"No, I didn't."

"He was a corporal in the company I helped run." Morgan shrugged. "Many of the men I employ here at Perseus are old contacts out of the Legion. The women who work for me all have a military background of some sort, too."

"What is Sean running from?"

"I don't know. Did he tell you anything about his past? He's always been more tight-lipped about it than most."

"No, it's like pulling teeth to get any kind of information out of him." Susannah sat quietly, staring down at her clasped hands. Softly she said, "Something happened to me when Sean was there protecting me from that hit man. The night we were almost killed, I discovered that I loved him. The fact that we might both lose our lives clarified my feelings for him."

Frowning, Morgan sat up. "I see…"

"Sean ran away from me, Morgan. He left me a note. He couldn't even face me to say goodbye, and that's not fair to me—or to him."

"Men who join the Foreign Legion are always running from something," Morgan said gently.

"I understand that now, but that's not an excuse for his behavior. I need some information," Susannah said firmly. "About Sean. About his past."

Morgan opened his hands. "When men come from the Legion, you don't ask many questions," he said gently. "Each of my employees signs a legal document saying that they aren't wanted criminals in another country before I'll hire them for Perseus. It's their word. I don't make inquiries unless I get a tip-off from Interpol or some other governmental body." He shrugged. "And Killian has been one of the most closemouthed of my men. I know very little of his past."

"Then let me fill you in," Susannah whispered, "because when I'm done with my story I want you to tell me where he lives. He and I have some unfinished business to clear up."

Morgan was scowling heavily by the time Susannah had completed her story. He'd asked Marie to bring in hot tea and cookies, and the tray sat on the glass-topped coffee table in front of the sofa. He'd also had her stop all incoming calls—except for emergencies—and canceled the rest of the day's business.

Susannah couldn't eat, but she did sip some fragrant tea.

"I hate to tell you this," Morgan said, sitting down with her again, "but when Killian came in off your assignment he requested leave."

"Leave?"

"Yes. It's a program I devised when I set up this company. When an operative's out in the field, there are tremendous stresses on him or her. When they come in off a particularly demanding assignment, they can request time off from the company for as long as they need to re-cuperate. Killian came back from Kentucky and wanted leave. I granted it to him, no questions asked."

Susannah's heart beat a little harder. "Where is he, then?"

"Ordinarily, where our people live is top secret. We never give out addresses to anyone, for fear of the infor-mation leaking into enemy hands. But in this case, I'm going to make an exception."

Relief made her shaky. "He won't be expecting me to show up."

Morgan smiled grimly. "There's something about the element of surprise—you might catch him off guard enough to level with you."

"He never has leveled with me, Morgan."

Moving uncomfortably, he said, "Susannah, you're dealing with a lot of unknown factors here."

"He's hurting terribly, Morgan."

Rubbing his jaw, Morgan nodded. "I was hurting a lot when Laura met me," he murmured. "And I can't say I was the world's nicest person around her."

"But you hung in there—together. And look at you now. You're happy, Morgan."

Exhaling, he said, "Susannah, Killian's hurting in a lot of ways neither of us knows. I know you're an idealist, and I know you have a large, forgiving heart. But Killian may not have the capacity to reach out to you, even if he wants to. He may be too afraid, for whatever reason. You have to be prepared to accept that if it happens."

She hung her head and nodded. "I'm not so idealis-tic that I don't know when I'm not wanted, Morgan. But Sean never gave me that chance. He never had the cour-age to sit down and tell me the truth."

"I'm not saying what he did was right," Morgan said, frowning heavily. "We all run in our own way. Luckily, I had Laura's steadfast courage, her belief in me that helped me get a handhold on my own internal problems." Then, with a slight smile filled with sorrow, he added, "I still have problems that overflow into our personal life, our relationship. Mostly because of me, because of my past that still haunts me. It's not as bad now, but believe me, Laura has her hands full some days with me when the past hits me like a sledgehammer." He glanced at the gold watch on his wrist. "Come on, it's time to go home. Laura promised me a special meal because you were coming. Let's not be late."

The loneliness Susannah had felt since Killian's abrupt departure was somewhat ameliorated by Morgan and his happy family. Laura, beautiful as ever with her long blond hair, dancing eyes and ready smile, helped lift Susannah's spirits. Her son, Jason Charles Trayhern, had his father's dark black hair and gray eyes. On the other hand, three-month-old Katherine Alyssa was a duplicate of Laura's ethereal beauty. Just getting to hold her was a treat for Susannah.

After the meal was eaten and the children had been put to bed, Susannah lingered over a cup of coffee with Laura in the living room. Morgan discreetly excused himself and retired to his home office in the basement of their large home.

Laura curled up on the flowery print couch and smoothed her long pink cotton skirt.

"So tell me what's going on, Susannah! You barely ate any of that great supper I fixed!"

"I know, and I'm really sorry, Laura. The roast leg of

lamb was wonderful. It's just that I've got a lot of things on my mind. Well...my heart, to be more honest." She smiled and leaned over, petting Sasha, the family's huge brown-and-white Saint Bernard, who had made herself at home next to Susannah's feet. She'd long since taken off her shoes and gotten comfortable—Laura and Morgan's home invited that kind of response.

"Killian, by any chance?"

"How did you know?"

With a slight smile, Laura said softly, "He's a man who's crying for a woman to help bring him out of his self-imposed exile."

"You've always had such insight into people."

Laura shrugged and smiled. "That's what helped me understand Morgan when I first met him. He was a man trapped in hell, although I didn't understand why for quite some time."

"Well," Susannah muttered. "That's exactly how Sean described himself."

"Chances are," Laura said gently, "he lives in an emotional hell on a daily basis." With a sigh, she sipped the coffee. "Susannah, men who go through a war like Morgan did are scarred for life. It kills a part of them, so they're crippled emotionally, in a sense. But that doesn't mean they can't make the most of what is still intact within them."

"Morgan had you to help him realize all of that."

"We had our love, our belief in each other," Laura agreed quietly. "Sometimes it's still not easy. For Morgan, the war will never really be over. There are days when there's a lot of tension between us." She smiled softly. "Fortunately, we love each other enough to sit down and discuss what's bothering him. Morgan has slowly been opening up more with each year that passes, but it's never easy for us, Susannah."

"You have his trust," Susannah pointed out. "I never had time to get Sean's trust. It all happened so fast, so soon..."

"I understand better than most," Laura whispered. "Men like Killian and Morgan need a woman with strength, with steadiness, because they've lost those things emotionally within themselves. I hope you're prepared for the kind of uphill battles a man like that will put you through."

Susannah glanced at her. "You're not scaring me off, Laura, if that's what you're trying to do."

Reaching over, Laura touched her shoulder. "No one believes in the power of love more than I do. I've seen it work miracles with Morgan—and with me." She lifted her head and looked toward the darkened hall that led to the bedrooms, her eyes misty. "And we have two beautiful babies that reflect that love."

"Ma didn't raise me to think life was easy," Susannah said. "I know the hell I went through with Sean while he was there. He just wouldn't—couldn't—talk."

"And that's going to be the biggest stumbling block when you see him again. Men like that feel as if they're carrying such a horrendous amount of ugliness within them. They're afraid that if they start to talk about it, it will get out of control."

"So they get tight-lipped about it?"

Laura nodded. "Exactly."

With a sigh, Susannah shrugged. "I don't have a choice in this, Laura. I don't want one, anyway. Sean is worth it."

"Well, tomorrow morning, Morgan's driver will take **you to the airport, and you'll fly to Victoria, British Co-**

lumbia, where he lives. It's on a lovely island off the west coast of Canada. There's quite a British flavor to the place. And flowers!" Laura smiled fondly. "The island is a riot of color and fragrance. I've never seen so many roses! You'll love the island."

As she listened, Susannah hoped that her lack of worldliness wouldn't be her undoing. She sat tensely, her hands clasped in her lap. All she had to lead her through this tangled web that Sean lived within was her heart. What would he do when she showed up at his doorstep? As Morgan had said, the element of surprise might work for her—but, she thought, it could also work against her.

Susannah had never needed the kind of strength she knew she would need in order to face Sean Killian bravely. Only Sean could show her if what she felt for him was love. But even if it was, there was no guarantee that he would have the courage to admit it.

Kneeling in the triangular flower bed, Killian stared glumly down at the bright yellow marigold in his hands. The gold, red and yellow flowers assaulted the air with their rather acrid odor. Like the flower in his hand, surrounded by the moist, rich soil, he was alone. Alone and bitter.

Resolutely he dug a small hole with the trowel, and placed the marigold in it. With dirt-stained hands, he pressed the moist earth securely over the roots. Gardening had always helped soothe him. *Until now.*

Looking up from the garden, Killian stared at the calm blue of the ocean, three hundred feet away. His green manicured lawn contrasted beautifully with the glassy water. The pale azure of the sky was dotted with fleecy white clouds. Summer in Victoria was his favorite time.

Luckily, the money he'd earned over the years had gotten him this small English-style cottage when the couple who'd owned it, up in years, could no longer keep up with its landscaping and gardening demands and sold it to him.

Susannah. Her name hung in front of Killian as he caressed the tiny, frilly petals of a pale yellow marigold. The color reminded him of the hope that always burned in her eyes. Hope. He had none. The feeling had been utterly destroyed so long ago. Closing his eyes, he knelt there, surrounded by the lonely cries of the sea gulls that endlessly patrolled the beach and, off in the distance, the hoarse barks of sea lions.

Killian opened his eyes, feeling the terrible loneliness knife through him as never before. Slowly he looked around. He was surrounded by the ephemeral beauty of many carefully constructed flower beds, all geometrically shaped and designed by him, their rainbow colors breathtaking. But Killian could feel none of his usual response to them. Only Susannah could make him feel.

What was wrong? What had happened to him? He opened up his hands and studied them darkly. He'd made love to other women off and on throughout his life, but never had the act—or more truthfully, the feelings—continued to live like a burning-hot light within his body and heart as they did now.

With a shake of his head, Killian muttered under his breath and got to his feet. Brushing off the bits of soil clinging to his jeans, he straightened. The three tiers of flower gardens culminated with at least a hundred roses of various colors. Their fragrance was heavy in the area nearest the rear sliding glass doors to his house.

And it was a house, Killian reminded himself harshly. Susannah's ramshackle, broken-down old place was a *home.* She'd made it feel homey, comfortable and warm with her life and presence. Killian savored the hours spent with her in that antiquated kitchen. Every night when he lay down to try to sleep, those scenes would replay like a haunting movie across his closed eyelids. And when he finally did sleep, torrid, heated dreams of loving Susannah drove him to wakefulness, and a clawing hunger that brought him to the verge of tears. Tears! He never cried!

Stopping at the rose garden, a long, rectangular area bordered with red brick, Killian barely brushed a lavender rose with his fingertips. *Susannah.* No longer did Killian try to escape her memory. The doorbell rang, pulling his attention from his morbid reverie. Who could it be? His housekeeper and regular gardener, Emily Johnston, had left earlier to buy the week's groceries, and she wouldn't be back until tomorrow morning.

Automatically Killian dropped into his natural mode of wariness. Although his address and phone number were known only to Meg and Morgan, he didn't trust his many enemies not to track him down. As careful as Killian was about masking his movements to preserve his sanctuary, he never fooled himself. Someday one of his more patient and vengeful enemies might locate him.

Padding through the fully carpeted house, Killian halted at the front door and peered through the one-way glass. *Susannah!* His heart thumped hard in his chest. What the hell was she doing here? Could he be dreaming? His mind spun with questions. His heart began an uneven pounding. As he closed his hand over the brass doorknob, Killian felt a surge of hope tunnel through him. Just as quickly, he savagely destroyed the burgeoning feeling.

The door swung open. Susannah looked through the

screen at Killian. As usual, his features were set—but his eyes gave away his true feelings. Her palms were sweaty, and her heart was thundering like a runaway freight train. She girded herself for his disapproval.

"What are you doing here?" Killian demanded in a rasp. He glanced around, checking out the surrounding area. Luckily, the street ended in a cul-de-sac, and he knew who his neighbors were and the cars they drove. The white Toyota out front must be a rental car that Susannah had driven.

"We've got some unfinished business," Susannah whispered. It was so hard to gather strength when she felt like caving in and stepping those precious few feet to fall into Killian's arms. The terrible light in his eyes told him he was no less tortured by her unexpected appearance than she was.

"Get in here," he growled, and gripped her by the arm.

Susannah didn't resist. She could tell that Killian was carefully monitoring the amount of strength he applied to her arm. She entered his home. A dusky-rose carpet flowed throughout the living room and hall area, which was decorated with simple, spare, carefully placed furniture. The walls were covered with floor-to-ceiling bookcases. Killian must be a voracious reader.

There were so many impressions she wanted to absorb, to investigate. Each one would give her another clue to Killian. But she didn't have that kind of time. Every word, every gesture, counted. She turned as he closed the door with finality. The grimness in his face made her feel cold. Alone.

"How did you find me?"

"I flew to Washington and talked with Morgan. He

told me where you lived." Susannah saw his eyes flare with disbelief.

Killian took a step back, because if he didn't he was going to sweep Susannah uncompromisingly into his arms. And then he was going to take her to his bedroom and make wild, hungry love with her until they were so exhausted that they couldn't move.

Killian looked down at her vulnerable features. There was real hope in Susannah's eyes, a kind of hope he'd never be able to claim as his own. She was dressed in a summery print blouse—pink peonies against a white background—and white slacks, with sandals outlining her feet. Her lovely sable hair was trapped in a chignon, and Killian had to stop himself from reaching forward to release that captive mass of silk into his hands. His mouth had grown dry, and his heart was beating dangerously hard in his chest.

"All right, what's going on?"

"You and me." Susannah felt her fear almost overwhelming her, but she dared not be weak now. She saw a slight thawing in Killian's narrowed eyes, a slight softening of his thinned mouth. "What made you think," Susannah said in a low, strangled voice, "that you could walk out on me just like that? We made love with each other, Sean. I thought—I thought we meant something to each other." She forced herself to hold his hardening gaze. "You ran without ever giving me the opportunity to sit down and talk to you. I'm here to complete unfinished business." Her voice grew hoarse. "One way or another."

Killian stood stunned. It took him a long time to find his voice. "I told you—I didn't mean to hurt you," he rasped. "I thought leaving the way I did would hurt you less."

Susannah's eyes went round, and anger gave her the backbone she needed. "Hurt me less?" Susannah forced herself to walk into the living room. She dropped her purse and her one piece of luggage on the carpet. Turning, she rounded on Killian. "I don't call running out on me less hurtful!"

Nervously Killian shoved his hands into the pockets of his jeans. "I'm sorry, Susannah. For everything."

"For loving me?"

Killian dropped his gaze and stared at the floor. He heard the ache in her husky tone; her voice was like a lover's caress. He was glad to see her, glad that she was here. "No," he admitted. He raised his chin and forced himself to meet her large, tear-filled eyes. "But I am sorry for the hurt I've caused you."

"You walk around in your silence and don't communicate worth a darn. I'm not a mind reader. Do you know how awful I felt after you left? Do you know that I blamed myself? I asked myself what I did wrong. Was it something I said? Did?" Grimly, her eyes flashing, she said, "I don't have a lot of worldly ways like you. I know I'm a country woman, but I don't question the way of my heart, Sean. You had no right to leave the way you did. It wasn't fair to me, and it wasn't fair to you, either."

Pain knifed through him and he moved into the living room with her. He halted a foot away from her, aching to put his hands on her shoulders, but not daring to. "I was to blame, not you."

To her amazement, Susannah saw Killian thawing. Perhaps Laura was right: He needed a woman to be stronger than him so that he could feel safe enough to open up. Had he never had a woman of strength to lean on? If not, it was no wonder he remained closed, protecting his vulnerability. The discovery was as sweet as it was bold—and frightening. Susannah was just coming out of her own trauma. Did she have enough strength for the both of them? She simply didn't know, but the glimmer in Killian's eyes, the way his mouth unconsciously hinted at the vulnerability he tried so hard to hide and protect, made her decide to try anyway.

"I hope you've got a guest bedroom."

He blinked.

Susannah drilled him with a fiery look. "Sean, I happen to feel that we meant a lot to each other when you were in Kentucky. And after we made love, you ran. I don't know your reasons for running, and that's what I'm here to find out. I intend to stay here, no matter how miserable you make it for me, until we get to the bottom of this—together."

Dread flared through Killian. No woman had ever challenged him like this. "You don't know what you're saying," he warned.

"Like heck I don't! Give me some credit, Sean. I work with special children. I've got to have a lot of insight into them to reach them, to touch them, so that they'll stop retreating."

Killian took another step away, terror warring with his need for Susannah. "You're biting off too much. You don't know what you're getting into," he snapped.

Tilting her chin, Susannah rasped, "Oh, yes I do."

"Now look," he said in a low, gravelly voice, "I don't want to hurt you, Susannah. If you stay here, it'll happen. Don't put yourself on the firing line for me. I'm not worth it."

Tears stung her eyes, but Susannah forced them back. Killian would read her tears as a sign of weakness. "You're wrong. You're a good man, Sean. You've been hurt, and you're hiding. I'm here to show you that you don't need to keep running. You're allowed to laugh, you know. And to cry. How long has it been since you've done either?"

Killian lunged forward blindly and gripped her by the arm. "Dammit," he rasped off-key, "get the hell out of here while you still can, Susannah! I'm a monster! A monster!" He savagely poked a finger at his belly. "It's in here, this thing, this hell that I carry. It comes out and controls me, and it will hurt whoever is around. You've got to understand that!"

She held his blazing gaze, seeing the horror of his past reflected in his eyes, hearing the anguish in his tone. "No," she said. "I'm not afraid of you," she rattled, "or that so-called monster inside of you. For the first time in your life, Sean, you're going to be honest, not only with yourself, but with someone else—me."

Killian took a step back, as if she'd slapped him. He stared down at her as the tension swirled around them like a raging storm. Frightened as never before, he backed away. In place of the panic came anger. He ground out, "If you stay, you stay at your own risk. Do you understand that?"

"I do."

He glared at her. "You're naive and idealistic. I'll hurt you in ways you never thought possible! I won't mean to, but it'll happen, Susannah." He stood there, suddenly feeling very old and broken. His voice grew hoarse. "I don't want to, but I will. God help me, I don't want to hurt you, Susannah."

Swallowing hard, a lump forming in her throat, she nodded. "I know," she replied softly, "I know..."

"This is hopeless," Killian whispered, looking out one of the series of plate-glass windows that faced the flower gardens and the ocean. "I'm hopeless."

Grimly Susannah fought the desire to take Killian into her arms. Intuitively she understood that it would weaken her position with him. He was wary and defensive enough to strike out verbally and hurt her for fear of getting hurt again. As she picked up her luggage, Susannah realized that her love for Sean was the gateway not only to trust, but also to a wealth of yet-untapped affection that lay deep within her.

"You're not hopeless," Susannah told him gently. "Now, if you'll show me where the guest bedroom is, I'll get settled in."

Killian gaped at her. His mouth opened, then closed. "First door on the right down the hall," he muttered, then spun on his heel and left.

Her hands shaking, Susannah put her week's worth of clothes away in the closet and the dresser. Her heart wouldn't steady, but a clean feeling, something akin to a sense of victory, soared within her. She took several deep breaths to calm herself after having established a beachhead in the initial confrontation. Killian's desperation told her, she hoped, how much he was, indeed, still tied to her. Perhaps Morgan and Laura were right, and Killian did love her after all. That was the only thing that could possibly pull them through this storm together. Any less powerful emotion would surely destroy her, and continue to wound Killian.

Straightening up from her task, Susannah took in the simple, spare room. A delicate white Irish lace spread covered the double bed. The carpet was pale lavender, and the walls cream-colored. A vibrant Van Gogh print of sunflowers hung above the bed. The maple dresser was surely an antique, but Susannah didn't know from what era. The window, framed by lavender drapes and ivory sheers, overlooked a breathtaking view of the ocean.

"Well, Susannah, keep going," she warned herself. As much as she wanted to hide in the bedroom, she knew it wasn't the answer. No, she had to establish herself as a force in Killian's isolated world, and make herself part of it—whether he wanted her to or not. And in her heart she sensed that he did want her. The risk to her heart was great. But her love for Killian was strong enough to let her take that risk. He was always risking his life for others; well, it was time someone took a risk for him.

Killian stole a look into the kitchen. Susannah had busied herself all afternoon in his spacious modern kitchen. Although he'd hidden out most of the time in the garage, working on a wood-carving project, the fragrant odors coming from the kitchen couldn't be ignored. As upset as he was, the food she was cooking made him hungry. But it was his other hunger for Susannah that he was trying to quell—and he wasn't succeeding.

"What's for dinner?" he asked with a frown.

Susannah wiped her hands on the dark green apron she had tied around her waist. "Pot roast with sour-cream gravy and biscuits. Southerners love their biscuits and gravy," she said with pride.

"Sounds decent. Dessert?" He glanced at her.

"You really push your luck, don't you?"

He wanted to smile, but couldn't. "Yeah, I guess I do."

"I didn't come here to be a slave who cooks you three meals a day and cleans your house," Susannah pointed out as she gestured for him to sit down at the table. "This food is going to cost you."

"Oh?" Thinking he should leave, Killian sat down. Susannah seemed to belong in the kitchen—her presence was like sunshine. The bleakness of his life seemed to dissolve in her aura.

Susannah served the meat and placed the pitcher of gravy on the table with a basket of homemade biscuits. Sitting down, she held his inquiring gaze. "My folks and I always used to sit and talk after meals. It was one of the most important things I learned from them—talking."

With a grimace, Killian offered her the platter of meat first. "I'm not much of one for talking and you know it."

"So you'll learn to become a better communicator," Susannah said lightly. She felt absolutely tied in knots, and she had to force herself to put food on her plate. Just being this close to Killian, to his powerful physical presence, was making her body betray her head. When his lips curved into that sour smile, Susannah melted inwardly. She remembered how hot, how demanding and sharing, that mouth had been on hers. Never had she wanted to kiss a man so much. But she knew if she bowed to her selfish hunger for him as a man, she'd lose not only the battle, but the war, as well.

"Okay," he said tentatively, "you want me to talk." He spooned several thick portions of the roast onto his plate, added three biscuits and then some gravy. "About what?"

"You," Susannah said pointedly.

"I'm willing to talk about anything else," he warned her heavily.

With a shrug, Susannah said, "Fine. Start anywhere you want."

The food was delectable, and Killian found himself

wolfing down the thick, juicy meat. Still in wonder over this strong, stubborn side of Susannah that he hadn't seen before, he shook his head.

"I didn't realize you were this persistent."

Susannah grinned. "Would it have changed anything?"

The merest shadow of a smile touched Killian's mouth, and the hesitant, pain-filled attempt sent a sheet of heat through Susannah. Taking a deep breath, she said, "I want to know about you, your past, Sean. I don't think that's too much to ask. It will help me understand you—and, maybe, myself, and how I feel toward you."

Again her simple honesty cut through him. He ate slowly, not only hearing, but also feeling her words. He saw Susannah's hands tremble ever so slightly. She was nervous, perhaps even more nervous than he was. Still, his heart filled with such joy that she was here that it took the edge off his terror. "So, if I open up, maybe you'll give me some of that dessert you made?"

Susannah laughed, feeling her first glimmer of hope. She felt Killian testing her, seeing if she was really as strong as he needed her to be. "That coconut chiffon pie is going to go to waste if you don't start talking, Sean Killian."

Her laughter was like sunlight in his dark world. In that moment, her eyes sparkling, her lush mouth curved, Killian ached to love her, ached to feel her take away his darkness. Hope flickered deep within him, and it left him nonplussed. Never had he experienced this feeling before. Not like this. Giving her an annoyed look, he muttered, "I'd rather talk about my flower gardens, and the roses."

"Enough about the roses," Susannah said as she stood up and cleared away the dishes. She saw his eyes darken instantly. Tightening her lips, she went to the refrigerator, pulled out the pie and cut two slices.

"I want you to tell me about your childhood."

Moodily he sat back in the chair, unable to tear his gaze from her. "It's not a very happy story" was all he said.

Susannah gave him a piece of pie and a fork. She sat back down, grimly holding his hooded gaze. "Tell me about it."

With a sigh, Killian shrugged and picked up the fork. "I was the runt. The kid who was too small for his age. I was always scrapping with older boys who thought they could push my younger sister Meg around." He pointed to his crooked nose. "I had this busted on three different occasions in grade school."

"Did you have anyone to hold you?"

Killian flashed her an amused look. "Scrappers didn't fall into their mothers' arms and cry, Susannah."

"Is your mother alive?"

He winced inwardly and scowled, paying a lot of attention to his pie, which he hadn't touched. "Mother died when I was fourteen."

"What did she die of?" Susannah asked softly.

Rearing back in the chair, and wiping his hands absently on his jeans, Killian replied, "A robbery."

She heard the rising pain in Killian's tone, and saw it in the slash of his mouth. "Tell me about it."

"Not much to tell," he muttered. "When I was thirteen, my parents emigrated to America. They set up a grocery store in the Bronx. A year later, a couple of kids came in to rob them. They took the money and killed my parents," he concluded bluntly. Killian bowed his head, feeling the hot rush of tears in his tightly shut eyes. Then he felt Susannah's hand fall gently on his shoulder. Just that simple gesture of solace nearly broke open the wall of grief he'd carried so long over his parents' harsh and unjust deaths.

Fighting to keep her own feelings under control, Susannah tried to understand what that experience would do to a fourteen-year-old boy, an immigrant. "You were suddenly left alone," she said unsteadily. "And Meg was younger?"

"Yes, by a year."

Susannah could feel the anguish radiating from him. "What did you do?"

Killian fought the urge to put his hand over hers where it lay on his shoulder. If he did, he'd want to bury his head blindly against her body and sob. The lump in his throat grew. So many unbidden, unexpected feelings sheared through him. Desperate, not understanding how Susannah could so easily pull these emotions out of him and send them boiling to the surface, Killian choked. With a growl, he lunged away from the table, and his chair fell to the tiled floor.

"You have no right to do this to me. None!" He turned and jerked the chair upright.

Susannah sat very still, working to keep her face neutral. She battled tears, and prayed that Killian couldn't see them in her eyes. His face was pale and tense, and his eyes were haunted.

"If you're smart," he rasped as he headed toward the garden, "you'll leave right now, Susannah."

Stubbornly she shook her head. "I'm staying, Sean."

His fingers gripped the doorknob. "Damn you! Damn you—"

She closed her eyes and took a deep, ragged breath. "You aren't going to scare me off."

"Then you'd better lock the door to your bedroom tonight," he growled. "I want you so damned bad I can taste it. I can taste you." He jabbed his finger warningly at her. "You keep this up, and I don't know what will happen. You're not safe here with me. Don't you understand?"

Susannah turned in her chair. When she spoke, her voice was soft. "You're not even safe with yourself, Sean."

Wincing, he stalked out of the house. Maybe a walk, a long, brutal walk, would cleanse his agitated soul and his bleeding heart. He loved Susannah, yet he feared he'd hurt her. No woman had ever unstrung him as easily and quickly as she did. He strode through the beauty of his flower gardens, unseeing.

Chapter 10

Susannah got ready for bed. She hadn't heard Killian return, and it was nearly eleven. Her nerves were raw, and she was jangled.

Lock the door.

Did she want to? Could she say no if Killian came into her bedroom? Where did running and hiding end? And where did freedom, for both of them, begin? Perhaps it would be born out of the heat of their mutual love... Her hands trembling, Susannah pulled down the bed covers. The room was dark now. Slivers of moonlight pierced the curtains, lending a muted radiance to the room.

Lock the door.

Dressed in a simple knee-length cotton gown, Susannah pulled the brush through her hair. Her own emotions were jumbled and skittish. What if Sean walked through that door? She stared hard at the doorknob. She hadn't locked it—yet. Should she? Was she hesitating for herself or for Sean?

Lock the door.

Trying to recall the nights with Killian at her farmhouse, Susannah realized that she'd been in such turmoil herself that, except for that one night, she had no idea if he generally slept, had terrible nightmares or experienced insomnia. Making a small sound of frustration, she set the tortoiseshell brush on the dresser. No. No, she had to leave the door open. If she locked it, it was a symbol that she really didn't trust him—or herself. Taking a deep, unsteady breath, she slipped between the cool sheets. Getting comfortable, she lay there, her hands behind her head, for a long, long time—waiting. Just waiting.

Lock the door.

Killian moved like a ghost through his own house. All the lights were out, but the moon provided just enough light to see. He was sweaty and tired, having walked miles along the beach in order to purge himself of the awful roiling emotions that were flaying him alive. The forced hike had taken the edge off him, but he hadn't dealt at all with his feelings.

Susannah.

Killian stood frozen in the hallway and finally faced the full realization: He loved her. His hand shook as he touched his forehead. When? Making a sound of disgust, he thought that from the moment he'd seen Susannah his heart had become a traitor to him. Yes, he'd made love to women in his life, but never had he wanted truly to love them. With Susannah, he wanted to give. He wanted to see that velvet languor in her eyes, and the soft curve of her lips as he pleasured her, loved her so thoroughly that they fused into melting oneness.

His nerves raw, more exhausted than he could recall ever having been, Killian forced himself to go to his room for a cold shower. But as he passed Susannah's room, he stopped. His eyes narrowed on the doorknob. Had she done as he ordered and locked her door against him? Sweat stood out on his tense features as his hand slowly moved forward. For an instant, his fingers hovered. A part of him wanted her to have the door locked. He didn't want to hurt her—didn't want to take from her without giving something back. But how could he give, when he didn't even know how to give to himself after all those years?

His mouth tightening, Killian's hand flowed around the doorknob. He twisted it gently. It was unlocked! He stood there, filled with terror and hope, filled with such hunger and longing that he couldn't move. Susannah trusted him. She trusted him to do the right thing for both of them. Just as quietly, he eased the doorknob back to its original position.

Her heart beating wildly, Susannah sensed Killian's presence outside her room. She lay there gripping the sheet, her eyes wide, as she watched the doorknob slowly turn, trying to prepare herself emotionally. If he entered her room, she wasn't sure what she'd do. Her heart whispered to her to love him, to hold him, to allow him to spend himself within her. Loving was healing, and Susannah knew that instinctively. Her head warned her sharply that he'd use her up and eventually destroy her emotionally, just as he'd been destroyed himself over the years.

The seconds ticked by, and Susannah watched the doorknob twist back into place. Killian knew now that she was accessible, that she would be here for him, for whatever he needed from her. The thought was as frightening as it was exhilarating. On one level, Susannah felt as if she were dealing with a wild, unmanageable animal that would just as soon hurt her as stay with her. That was the wounded side of Sean. The other side, the man who possessed such poignant sensitivity and awareness of her as a woman, was very different. Somewhere in the careening thoughts that clashed with her overwrought feelings, Susannah was counting on that other part of Sean to surface. But would it? And in time?

When the door didn't open, she drew in a shaky breath of air and gradually relaxed. At least Killian had come home. She'd worried about where he'd gone, and indeed whether he'd return. Forcing her eyes closed, Susannah felt some of the tension drain from her arms and legs. Sleep. She had to get some sleep. Tomorrow morning would be another uphill battle with Sean. But the night was young, her mind warned her. What were Killian's sleeping habits? Was he like a beast on the prowl, haunted by ghosts of the past, unable to sleep at night? Susannah wished she knew.

Sometime later, her eyelids grew heavy, her heart settled down, and she snuggled into the pillow. Almost immediately, she began to dream of Sean, and their conversation at the table—and the look of pain he carried in his eyes.

Susannah jerked awake. Her lips parting, she twisted her head from one side to the other. Had she been dreaming? Had she heard a scream? Or perhaps more the sound of an animal crying out than a human scream? Fumbling sleepily, she threw off the sheet and the bedspread. Dream or reality? She had to find out. What time was it? Stumbling to her feet, Susannah bumped into the dresser.

"Ouch!" she muttered, wiping the sleep from her eyes. Her hair, in disarray, settled around her face as she glanced at the clock. It was 3:00 a.m. The moonlight had shifted considerably, and the room was darker now than before. Reaching for her robe, Susannah struggled into it.

She stepped out into the hall, but only silence met her sensitive hearing. Killian's room was across the hall. The door was partly open. Her heart starting a slow, hard pounding, Susannah forced herself to move toward it.

Just as she reached it, she heard a muffled crash in another part of the house. Startled, she turned and moved on bare feet down the carpeted hall toward the sound. In the center of the gloom-ridden living room, she halted. Her nerves taut, her breathing suspended, Susannah realized that the sounds were coming from the garage. Killian did woodworking out there. More crashes occurred. Fear snaked through her. She knew he was out there. She had to go to him. She had to confront him. Now Susannah understood what an animal trainer must feel like, facing a wild, untamed animal.

Her mouth dry, her throat constricted and aching, Susannah reached for the doorknob. A flood of light from the garage momentarily blinded her, and she stopped in the doorway, her hand raised to shade her eyes.

Killian whirled around, his breathing raspy and harsh. His eyes narrowed to slits as he picked up the sound of the door leading to the house being opened. He'd prayed that his shrieks wouldn't wake Susannah, but there she stood, looking sleepy yet frightened. Sweat ran down the sides of his face.

"I told you—get the hell out of here!" The words, more plea than threat, tore out of him. "Go! Run!"

Susannah's mouth fell open. Killian's cry careened off the walls of the large woodworking shop. Despite her fear, she noted beautifully carved statues—mostly of children, mothers with children, and flying birds. Some had been knocked off their pedestals and lay strewn across the concrete floor. Were those the crashes she'd heard? Susannah's gaze riveted on Killian. He was naked save for a pair of drawstring pajama bottoms clinging damply to his lower body. His entire torso gleamed in the low light, and his hair was damp and plastered against his skull. More than anything, Susannah saw the malevolent terror in his dark, anguished eyes.

She whispered his name and moved forward.

"No!" Killian pleaded, backing away. "Don't come near me! Damn it, don't!"

Blindly Susannah shook her head, opening her arms to him. "No," she cried softly. "You won't hurt me. You won't…" and she moved with a purpose that gave her strength and kept her fear in check.

Stumbling backward, Killian was trapped by the wood cabinets. There was no place to turn, no place to run. He saw blips of Susannah interspersed among the violent scenes that haunted him continuously. In one, he saw the enemy coming at him, knife upraised. Another flash-back showed his torturer coming forward with a wire to garrote him. He shook his head, a whimper escaping his tightened lips. He was trying desperately to cling to reality, to the fact that Susannah was here with him. He heard her soft, husky voice. He heard the snarl and curse of his enemies as they leaped toward him.

"No!" He threw his hands out in front of him to stop her. Simultaneously the flashback overwhelmed him. His hands were lethal weapons, honed by years of karate training, thickened by calluses, and he moved into position to protect himself. Breathing hard, he waited for his enemy to come at him with the knife as he met and held his dark, angry eyes.

Susannah saw the wildness in Killian's eyes, and she reached out to touch his raised hand. His face was frozen into a mask devoid of emotion; his eyes were fathomless, intent and slitted. Fear rose in her, but she knew she had to confront it, make it her friend and reach Killian, reach inside him.

Just as she grazed his hand, he whimpered. Her eyes widened as she saw him shift.

"Sean, no!" She threw out one hand to try to stop him. "No," she choked out again.

Where was he? He heard Susannah's cry. *Where?* Slowly the flashbacks faded, and Killian realized she was gripping his arm, her eyes wide and brimming with tears.

"No..." he rasped, and quickly jerked away from Susannah's touch. "God... I'm sorry." Bitterness coated his mouth, and he dragged in a ragged breath. "I could have hurt you. My God, I nearly—"

"It's all right. I'm all right, and so are you," Susannah whispered. Dizziness assailed her. She stood very still. When he reached out to touch her, his hand was trembling. The instant Killian's fingers touched her unbound hair, Susannah wanted to cry. There was such anguish in his eyes as he caressed her hair, as if to make sure she wasn't a part of whatever nightmare had held him in its thrall. Gathering what courage she had left, Susannah lifted her hand and caught his. His skin was sweaty, and the thrum of tension was palpable in his grip.

"It was just a nightmare," she quavered, lifting her head and meeting his tortured eyes.

Killian muttered something under his breath. "You shouldn't have stayed," he rasped. "I might have hurt you…" He gently framed her face and looked deeply into her tear-filled eyes. "I'm so afraid, Susannah."

Whispering his name, Susannah slid her arms around him and brought him against her. She heard a harsh sound escape his mouth as he buried his face against her hair, his arms moving like steel bands around her. The air rushed from her lungs, but she relaxed against him, understanding his need to hold and be held.

"I love you," she whispered, sliding her fingers through his short black hair. "I love you…"

Her words, soft and quavering, flowed through Killian. Without thinking, he lifted his head to seek her mouth. Blindly he sought and found her waiting lips. They tasted sweet, soft and giving as he hungrily took her offering. His breathing was chaotic, and so was hers. Drowning in Susannah's mouth and feeling her hands moving reassuringly across his shoulders took away the terror that had inhabited him. Her moan was of pleasure, not pain.

In those stark, naked moments, Killian stopped taking from her and began to give back. Her mouth blossomed beneath his, warm, sweet and hot. How badly he wanted to love her; his body was aching testimony to his need. Tearing his mouth from hers, he held her languorous gray gaze, which now sparkled with joy.

"It's going to be all right," he promised unsteadily. "Everything's going to be all right. Come on…"

Susannah remained beneath his arm, his protection, as he led her through the silent house. In the living room, he guided her to the couch and sat down with her. Their knees touched, and he held both her hands. "You're the last person in the world I'd ever want to hurt," he rasped.

"I know…"

"Dammit, Susannah, why didn't you run? Why didn't you leave me?"

She slowly looked up, meeting and holding his tear-filled eyes. "B-because I love you, Sean. You don't leave someone you love, who's hurting, to suffer the way you were suffering."

Killian closed his eyes and pulled her against him. The moments of silence blended together, and he felt the hotness of tears brim over and begin to course down his cheeks. His hands tightened around her as he gathered her into his arms. Burying his face in her sable hair, he felt a wrenching sob working its way up and out of his gut. The instant her arms went hesitantly around his shoulders, the sob tore from him. His entire body shook in response.

"Go ahead," Susannah whispered, tears in her eyes. "Cry, Sean. Cry for all the awful things you've seen and had to do to survive. Cry. I'll hold you. I'll just hold you…" And she did, with all the womanly strength she possessed.

Time drew to a halt, and all Susannah could feel were the terrible shudders racking Killian's lean body as he clung to her, nearly squeezing the breath from her. He clung as if he feared that to let go would be to be lost forever. Susannah understood that better than most. She tightened her grip around his damp shoulders, whispering words of encouragement, of love, of care, as his sobs grew louder and harsher, wrenching from him.

Susannah was no longer feeling her own pain, she was experiencing his. She held Killian as if she feared that to release him would mean he would break into a million shattered pieces. His fingers dug convulsively into her back as the sobs continued to rip through him. Her gown grew damp, but she didn't care. His ability to trust her, to give himself over to her and release the glut of anguish he'd carried by himself for so long, was exhilarating.

Gradually Killian's sobs lessened, and so did the convulsions that had torn at him in her arms. Gently Susannah stroked his hair, shoulders and back. His spine was strong, and the muscles on either side of it were lean.

"You're going to be fine," Susannah whispered, pressing a kiss against his temple. "Just fine." She sighed, resting her head against his, suddenly exhausted.

Killian flexed his fingers against Susannah's back. Never had he felt more safe—or loved—than now. Just the soft press of her lips against his temple moved him to tears again. He nuzzled deeply into her hair, pressing small kisses against her neck and jaw.

Words wouldn't come. Each stroke of Susannah's hand took a little more of the pain away. The fragrance of her body, the sweetness of it, enveloped him, and he clung to her small, strong form, absorbing the strength she was feeding him through her touch and voice.

Susannah had been hurt by his abruptly leaving her life without an explanation, yet now she was strong, when he had never felt weaker. Her fingers trembled against his hair, and he slowly lifted his head. She gave him a tremulous half smile, her eyes huge with compassion and love for him.

Love. He saw it in every nuance of her expression, in her hand as it came to rest against his jaw. How could she love him? When she reached forward, her fingers taking away the last of the tears from his cheeks, he lowered his lashes, ashamed.

"Tears are wonderful," Susannah whispered, a catch in her voice. "Ma always said they were liquid crystals going back to Mother Earth. I always liked that thought. She said they were the path to the heart, and I know it's true." She smiled gently into Killian's ravaged eyes. "You were brave enough to take the biggest step of all, Sean."

"What do you mean?" he asked, his voice thick, off-key.

"You had the ability to reach out and trust someone with your feelings."

"Crying is a weakness."

"Who taught you that?"

"Father. Men don't cry."

"And they aren't supposed to feel. Oh, Sean—" Susannah stroked his cheek gently. "Men have hearts, too, you know. Hearts that have a right to feel as deeply and widely as any woman's."

He shakily reached over and touched her cheek. "I was afraid that if my nightmares came back and you were around, I'd hurt you." Hanging his head, unable to meet her compassionate gaze, he said, "When I was in the Foreign Legion, I met an Algerian woman, Salima, who loved me. I loved her, too." He shook his head sadly. "I kept having nightmares out of my violent past with the Legion, and it scared her. Finally, I left her for good. I feared that one night I might lash out and strike her." Miserable, Killian held Susannah's gaze. "After that, I swore never to get involved with a woman. I didn't want to put anyone through the hell I put Salima through. I saw what it did to her, and I swore I'd never do it again.

And then you walked into my life. I've never felt such strong emotions for a woman before, Susannah. Those old fears made me leave to protect you from what I might do some night. My God, I couldn't stand it if I hurt you. I nearly did tonight."

She caressed his jaw. "You could have, but you didn't. Some part of you knew it was me, Sean. That's what stopped you, darling."

He lowered his gaze, his voice cracking. "I—I had a nightmare about Peru, about one of our missions. Wolf and I got caught and tortured by a drug lord, and the rest of our team had to go into the estate and bust us out." He squeezed his eyes shut. "That was last year. It's too fresh—that's why I get these nightmares, the flash-backs..."

"And you were having flashbacks after you woke up?" Susannah guessed grimly.

His mouth quirked and he raised his head. "Yes. I was hoping..." He drew in a ragged sigh. "I started screaming in my bedroom, and I got up, hoping I hadn't awakened you. I went out to the garage, where I always go when these things hit. It's safer that way. A lot safer. I'm like a wild animal in a cage," Killian added bitterly, unable to meet her lustrous gaze. His hands tightened around hers.

"A wounded animal, but not a wild one," she whispered achingly as she cupped his cheek. Killian's eyes were bleak; there was such sadness reflected in them, and in the line of his mouth. "Wounds can be bound up to heal, Sean."

He managed a soft snort. "At what cost to the healer?"

Susannah stroked his damp, bristly cheek. The dark growth of beard gave his face a dangerous quality. "As long as you're willing to get help, to make the necessary changes, then I can stay with you, if you want."

He turned to her. "Look at you. Look at the price you've already paid."

Susannah nodded. "It was worth the price, Sean. *You're* worth the effort. Don't you understand that?"

"I don't know what kind of miracle was at work when you reached out for me," he rasped. Killian held up his hands. "I've killed with these, Susannah. And when I mean to defend myself, I do it. The other person doesn't survive."

A chill swept through Susannah as she stared at his lean, callused hands. Swallowing convulsively, she whispered, "Some part of you knew I wasn't your enemy, Sean."

He wanted to say, *I love you, that's why,* but stopped himself. Just looking at her pale, washed-out features told him that he had no right to put Susannah on the firing line. A terrible need to make love with her, to speak of his love for her courage, her strength, sheared through Killian. He gazed down at her innocent, upturned face.

"You're a beautiful idealist," he whispered unsteadily. "Someone I don't deserve, and never will."

"I'll decide those things for myself."

He gave her a strange look, but said nothing. Placing his hand on her shoulder, he rasped, "Let's get you to bed. You need some sleep."

"And you? What about you?"

He shrugged. "I won't sleep."

"You slept like a baby after we made love to each other," Susannah whispered. She reached over and gripped his hand.

"I guess I did."

Susannah held his misery-laden eyes. "Then sleep with me now."

Killian stared at her, the silence lengthening between them. His throat constricted.

"Come," she whispered. "Come sleep at my side."

Chapter 11

A ragged sigh tore from Killian as he felt Susannah's weight settle against him. The darkness in her bedroom was nearly complete. Everything was so natural between them that it hurt. Despite how badly he'd frightened Susannah, she laid her head in the hollow of his shoulder, and her body met and melded against the harder contours of his. Her arm went around his torso, and Killian heard a quivering sigh issue from her lips. To his alarm, after he'd drawn up the sheet and spread, he felt Susannah trembling. It wasn't obvious, but Killian sensed it was adrenaline letdown after the trauma she'd endured.

"This is heaven on earth," he whispered roughly against her hair, tightening his grip around her. Susannah was heaven. A heaven he didn't deserve.

"It is." Susannah sighed and unconsciously moved her hand across his naked chest. The hair there was

soft and silky. His groan reverberated through her like
music. Stretching upward, Susannah placed her lips softly
against the hardened line of his mouth. Instantly Killian
tensed, and his mouth opened and hungrily devoured
hers. She surrendered herself to the elemental fire that
leaped between them wherever their bodies touched.

Sean needed to understand that no matter how bad
the terror that lived within him was, her love—and what
she hoped was his love for her—could meet and dissolve
it. Susannah's fleeting thought was quickly drowned in
the splendor of his mouth as it captured hers with a primal hunger that sent heat twisting and winding through
her. His hands tangled in her thick hair, and he gently
eased her back on the pillow, his blue eyes narrowed
and glittering.

"Love sets you free," she said, and reached up and
drew him down upon her. Just the taut length of his body
covering hers made her heart sing. The gown she wore
was worked up and off her. The white cotton fell into a
heap beside the bed, along with his pajama bottoms. As
Killian settled back against her, he grazed her flushed
cheek.

"You're so brave. So brave…" And she was, in a way
Killian had never seen in a woman before. Knowing gave
him the courage to reach out and love her as he'd tor-
ridly dreamed of doing so many times. As he slid his fingers up across her rib cage to caress her breast, he felt
her tense in anticipation. This time, Susannah deserved
all he could give her. There was no hurry now, no threat
of danger. His mouth pulled into a taut line, somewhere
between a smile of pleasure and a grimace of agony, as
she pressed her hips against him.

The silent language she shared with him brought tears

to his eyes. Susannah wasn't passive. No, she responded, initiated, and matched his hunger for her. When her hands drifted down across his waist and caressed him, he trembled violently. His world, always held in tight control, began to melt as her lips molded against his and her hands ignited him. He surrendered to the strength of this woman who loved him with a blinding fierceness that he was only beginning to understand.

As he slid his hand beneath her hips, Susannah closed her eyes, her fingers resting tensely against his damp, bunched shoulders. Her world was heat, throbbing heat, and filled with such aching longing that she gave a small whimper of pleading when he hesitated fractionally. The ache intensified. Without thinking, guided only by her desire to give and receive, Susannah moved with a primal timelessness that enveloped them. They were like living, breathing embers, smoldering, then blazing to bright, hungry life within each other's arms.

As Killian surged powerfully into her, he gripped her, as if she represented his one tenuous hold on life. In those spinning, molten moments when they gave the gift of themselves to one another, he felt real hope for the first time since he had lost his family. Glorying in his burgeoning love for Susannah, Killian sank against her, breathing raggedly.

Gently he tamed several strands of her sable hair away from her dampened brow. His smile was vulnerable as she opened her eyes and gazed dazedly up into his face. What right did he have to tell Susannah he loved her? Did he dare hope that she could stand the brutal terrors that plagued him night after night? Was he asking too much of her, even though she was willing to try?

Tasting again her wet, full mouth, Killian trembled.

He didn't have those answers—as badly as he wanted them. There was so much to say to Susannah, to share with her. He lost himself in her returning ardor, for now unwilling to look beyond the moment.

With a groan, Killian came to her side and brought her into his arms. "You're sunlight," he rasped, sliding his fingers through her tangled hair. "Hope and sunlight, all woven together like some kind of mystical tapestry."

The words feathered through Susannah. Sean held her so tightly—as if he were afraid that, like the sun, she would disappear, to be replaced by the awful darkness that stalked him. With a trembling smile, she closed her eyes and pressed the length of herself against him. He'd used the word *hope*. That was enough of a step for now, she thought hazily. The word *love* had never crossed his lips. But she had to be patient and wait for Sean to reveal his love for her, if that was what it was after all. Susannah didn't try to fool herself by thinking that, just because they shared the beauty of loving each other physically, it meant that Sean came to her with real love. She would have to wait and hope that he loved her in return. Whispering his name, she said, "I'm so tired…"

"Sleep, colleen. Sleep," he coaxed thickly. As much as he wanted to love her again, to silently show her his love for her, Killian knew sleep was best. He might be a selfish bastard, but he wasn't that selfish. Refusing to take advantage of the situation, he absorbed her wonderful nearness, wanting nothing more out of life than this exquisite moment.

Lying awake for a good hour after Susannah had quickly dropped off to sleep, Killian stared up at the plaster ceiling. How could she have known that he needed this? Needed her in his arms? Her soft, halting words, laced with tears, haunted him. Susannah loved him—without reserve. Didn't she know what she was getting into? He was a hopeless mess of black emotions that ruled his nights and stalked his heels during the day.

His mouth tightening, Killian absently stroked her silky hair, thinking how each strand, by itself, was weak. Yet a thick group of strands was strong. Maybe that was symbolic of Susannah. She was strong right now, while he'd never felt weaker or more out of control.

Sighing, Killian moved his head and pressed a chaste kiss to her fragrant hair. He'd cried tonight, for the first time in his life. Oddly, he felt cleaner, lighter. His stomach still ached from the wrenching sobs that had torn from him, and he absently rubbed his abdomen. The tears had taken the weight of years of grief away from him. And Susannah had paid a price to reach inside him to help him.

Closing his eyes, his arms around Susannah, Killian slid into a dreamless sleep—a sleep that was profoundly deep and healing. His first such sleep since the day he'd become a soldier in the French Foreign Legion.

Killian awoke with a start. *Susannah?* Instantly, he lifted his head and twisted it to the right. She was gone! Sunlight poured in through the ivory sheers—a blinding, joyous radiance flooding the room and making him squint. Quickly he sat up. The clock on the dresser read 11:00. *Impossible!* Killian muttered an exclamation to himself as he threw his legs across the bed and stood up. How could it be this late?

Fear twisted his heart. *Susannah.* Where was she? Had she left him after awaking this morning? Had she realized just how much of a liability he would be in her life? Bitterness coated his mouth as he quickly opened the door and strode across the hall to his bedroom. He wouldn't blame her. What woman in her right mind would stay around someone like him?

Killian hurried through a quick, hot shower and changed into a pair of tan chino slacks and a dark blue polo shirt. He padded quickly down the hall and realized that not only were the heavily draped windows in the living room open, they were raised. A slight breeze, sweet and fragrant, filled the house.

"Susannah?" His voice was off-key. Killian quickly looked around the living room and found it empty. He heard no sound from the kitchen, but hurried there anyway. Each beat of his heart said, *Susannah is gone.* A fist of emotion pushed its way up through his chest, and tears stung his eyes. Tears! Killian didn't care as he bounded into the kitchen.

Everything looked in order. Nothing out of place— and no Susannah. Killian stood there, his hand pressed against his eyes, and gripped the counter for support. She was gone. The shattering discovery overwhelmed him, and all he could do was feel the hot sting of tears entering his closed eyes as he tasted her loss.

The laughter of women vaguely registered on his spinning senses. Killian snapped his head toward the window. Outside, down by the lawn leading to the oceanfront, Susannah stood with his gardener, Mrs. Johnston.

His fingers whitened against the counter, and it took precious seconds for him to find his balance. Susannah hadn't left! She'd stayed! Killian stood rooted to the spot, his eyes narrowing on the two women. Susannah wore a simple white blouse, jeans, and sensible brown shoes. Her glorious hair was plaited into one long braid that hung between her shoulder blades. She stood talking animatedly with the gray-haired older woman.

Relief, sharp and serrating, jagged down through Killian. Susannah was still here. He hung his head, feeling a mass of confused emotions boiling up within him. He loved Susannah. He loved her. As he raised his head, he felt many things becoming clear. Things he had to talk to Susannah about. What would her reaction be? He had to tell her the truth, and she had to listen. What then? Killian wasn't at all sure how Susannah would judge him and his sordid world. What he did know was what he wanted: to wake up with this woman every morning for the rest of his life. But could he ask that of her?

Susannah waved goodbye to Mrs. Johnston as she left. Turning, she went through the front door of the beautifully kept cottage. In the living room she came to a startled halt.

"Sean."

He stood near the couch. The surprise on her features turned to concern. Killian searched her face ruthlessly for any telltale sign that she had changed her mind about him since last night. He opened his hand.

"When I got up, you were gone. I thought you'd left."

Susannah saw the suffering in his dark eyes. "Left?" She moved toward where he stood uncertainly.

"Yeah, forever." Killian grimaced. "Not that I'd blame you if you did."

Susannah smiled softly as she halted in front of him. Killian was stripped of his worldly defenses, standing nakedly vulnerable before her. Sensing his fragile state, she gently reached out and touched his stubbled cheek.

"I'm in for the long haul," she said, holding his haunted gaze. "If you'll let me be, Sean."

A ragged sigh tore from him, and he gripped her hand in his. "Then we need to sit down and do some serious talking, Susannah."

"Okay." She followed him to the couch. When he sat down facing her, she tucked her legs beneath her. Her knees were touching his thigh. His face was ravaged-looking, and his eyes were still puffy from sleep.

"Last night," Killian began thickly, reaching out and grazing her skin, "I could have hurt you." He felt shaky inside, on the verge of crying again as he rested his hand on her shoulder. "After my parents were murdered, Meg and I were given to foster parents to raise. I guess we were lucky, because we had no family left back in Ireland, so Immigration decided to let us stay. Our foster parents were good to us. Meg really blossomed under their love and care."

"And you?"

Sean shrugged. "I was angry and moody most of the time. I wanted to kill the two boys who had murdered our parents. I didn't do well at school. In fact, I skipped it most of the time and got mixed up in gang activities. Meg, on the other hand, was doing very well. She began acting in drama classes at high school, and she was good. Really good."

Susannah saw the pain in Sean's features. No longer did he try to hide behind that implacable, emotionless mask. His eyes were raw with uncertainty and his turbulent emotions. Reaching out, she covered his hand with hers. "How did you get into the Foreign Legion?"

"I joined the French Foreign Legion when I was seventeen, after running away from home. I had a lot of anger, Susannah, and no place to let it go. I was always in fights with other gang members. I saw what I was doing to my foster parents, to Meg, and I decided to get out of their lives.

"The Legion was hard, Susannah. Brutal and hard. It kills men who don't toughen up and walk a straight line of harsh discipline. By the time they found out my real age, I'd been in a year and survived, so they didn't kick me out. Most of my anger had been beaten out of me by that time, or released in the wartime situations we were called in to handle.

"I was only in a year when my company was sent to Africa to quell a disturbance." Killian withdrew his hand and stared down at the couch, the poisonous memories boiling up in him. "I won't tell you the gory details, but it was bloody. Tribesmen were fighting one another, and we had to try and intercede and keep the peace. For three years I was in the middle of a bloodbath that never stopped. I saw such inhumanity. I thought I knew what violence was, because I'd grown up in Northern Ireland, where it's a way of life, but this was a hundred times worse."

"And a hundred times more haunting?"

Her soft voice cut through the terror, through the revulsion that dogged him. When she slid her hand into his, he gripped it hard. "Yeah—the basis for most of my nightmares.

"The Legion has no heart, no feelings, Susannah. No one in the company slept well at night—everyone had nightmares. To combat it, to try to find an escape, I took up karate." He released her and held up his hand, his voice bleak. "All I did was learn how to kill another way. I was a natural, and when my captain realized it, he promoted me and made me an instructor to the legionnaires stationed with me. Just doing the hard physical work took the edge off my time in Africa.

"And then, *Sous-Lieutenant* Morgan Trayhern was transferred into my company as an assistant company commander. He had a lot of problems, too, and we just kind of gravitated toward each other over a period of a year. We both found some solace in each other's friendship. Morgan kept talking about creating a private company of mercenaries like ourselves. He wanted to pursue the idea once his hitch was up with the Legion.

"I liked the idea. I hated the Legion, the harsh discipline. Some of the men needed that kind of brutality, but I didn't. I was getting out after my six-year obligation was up, so I began to plan my life for the future. I told Morgan I'd join his company if he ever wanted to try it." Gently he recaptured Susannah's hand, grateful for her silence. She was absorbing every word he said.

"Then we had trouble in Africa again, and my company parachuted into a hot landing zone. It was the same thing all over again—only the tribes' names had changed. But this time both tribes turned on us and tried to wipe us out."

Susannah gasped, and her fingers closed tightly over Killian's scarred hand.

His mouth twisted. "Morgan was facing a situation similar to the one he had in Vietnam. We lost eighty percent of our company, Susannah. It was a living hell. I thought we were all going to die, but Morgan pulled us out. I saved his life during that time. Finally, at the last moment, he got the air support he'd requested. We were all wounded. It was just a question of how badly. Before both tribes hit us with a final assault, we were lifted out by helicopter." His voice grew bitter. "All the rest, every last valiant man who had died, were left behind."

"How awful…"

Killian sighed raggedly. "Last night I lay awake a long time with you in my arms, reviewing my life." He gently turned her hand over in his, realizing how soft and feminine she was against him. "I was born into violence, colleen. I've done nothing but lead a violent life. Last year, Morgan sent three of us down to work with the Peruvian police to clean up a cocaine connection. Wolf, a member of our team, got captured by the local drug lord. I went in to save him, and I ended up getting captured, too."

Susannah's eyes widened. "What happened?"

"The drug lord was real good at what he did to us," was all he would say. He still wanted to protect Susannah, somehow, from the ugliness of his world. "He had us for a month before Jake, the third member of our team, busted in and brought down the drug lord. Wolf was nearly dead, and I wasn't too far behind him. We got flown stateside by the CIA, and we both recuperated in a naval hospital near the capital. As soon as Wolf regained consciousness, he told Morgan he wanted out, that he couldn't handle being a mercenary any longer."

With a little laugh, Killian said, "At the time, I remember thinking Wolf had lost the edge it takes to stay alive in our business. He's part Indian, so he stayed pretty much to himself. So did I. But I admired his guts when he told Morgan 'no more.' Morgan didn't call him a coward. Instead, he saw to it that Wolf got a job as a forest ranger up in Montana."

With a shake of his head, Killian whispered, "I envied Wolf for having the courage to quit. I wanted to, but I thought everyone would see me as a coward."

Hope leaped into Susannah's eyes, and it was mirrored in her voice. "You want to quit?"

"I can't," Killian said quietly, searching her glowing features, clinging to the hope in her eyes. "Part of my check goes to pay for my sister's massive medical bills. But…"

"What?"

He gripped his hands, thinking how small, yet how strong, she was. "I'm messed up inside, Susannah. Maybe I've done this work too long and don't know any other way." His voice grew thick. "Last night, when I held you, I realized that I needed to get help—professional help—to unravel this nightmare that's eating me alive from the inside out. I swore I'd never put you in that kind of jeopardy again."

With a little cry, Susannah threw her arms around Killian's shoulders. "I love you so much," she whispered, tears squeezing from her eyes. She felt his arms slide around her and bring her tightly against him. Killian buried his face in her hair. "It can be done, Sean. I know it can."

He shook his head, and when he spoke again his voice was muffled. "I don't know that, Susannah."

She eased away just enough to study his suffering features. "I'll be here for you, if you want…"

The words, sweet and filled with hope, fell across his tightly strung nerves. He searched her lustrous eyes. "I don't know…" How badly he wanted to confess his love to her, and yet he couldn't. "Let me feel my way through this."

"Do you want me to leave?" She hated to ask the question. But she did ask it, and then she held her breath.

"I— No, not really." He held her hand tightly within

his. "That's the selfish side of me speaking. The other side, the nightmares… Well, you'd be better off staying at a nearby hotel—just in case."

Susannah had faith that Killian would never harm her, no matter how virulent his nightmares became, but she knew it wasn't her place to make that decision. "I have the next three weeks off, Sean. My principal gave me the time because he felt after all the trauma I'd gone through I needed time to pull myself together again."

Killian's heart thudded, and he lifted his head. "Three weeks?" Three weeks of heaven. There was such love shining in her eyes that he clung to the tenuous shred of hope that had begun burning in his chest when he loved Susannah last night.

"Yes…"

He compressed his lips and studied her long, slender fingers. The nails were cut short because she did so much gardening, Killian realized. Susannah had hands of the earth, hands that were in touch with the primal elements of nature—and her touch brought out so much in him that was good. "I'll take you to a hotel in downtown Victoria," he told her quietly. "I want you to stay these three weeks if you want, Susannah." He lifted his gaze and met hers. "No promises."

She shook her head, her mouth growing dry. "No… no promises. A day at a time, Sean."

Susannah gave him a trembling smile and framed his lean, harsh face between her soft hands. "You slept the whole night last night without those dreams coming back?"

Killian nodded. "It was the first night I've slept that hard. Without waking up." He knew there was awe in his voice at the revelation.

Susannah gave him a tender smile. "Because you trusted yourself on some level. The situation was important enough for you to reach out and try to change it."

There was food for thought in her assessment. A little more of the tension within him dissolved. "I want to live now, in the present," he told her, capturing her hands. "I want to take you sailing this morning, if you'd like." He gestured toward the wooden dock at the edge of the water. "I've got a forty-foot yacht that I've worked on for the past eight years, between assignments. I've always been good with wood, so I began to build the boat as something to do when I got back here."

"Because you couldn't sleep?" Susannah's heart broke for him.

"Partly." He managed to quirk a smile. "Then I put in the rose garden around the house. I find keeping busy keeps me from remembering."

"Then let's go sailing. I've never done it before, but I'm willing to try."

Sunlight glanced off the dark blue of the ocean as the yacht, the *Rainbow,* slipped cleanly through the slight swells of early afternoon. Susannah sat with Killian at the stern of the yacht. He stood proudly at the helm, his focus on the sails as the wind filled them, taking them farther away from the coast of the island. The first time the yacht had heeled over on her side, Susannah had let out a yelp of fear and surprise, thinking the boat would flip over and drown them. But Killian had held her and explained that the yacht would never tip over. Over the past two hours, Susannah had relaxed and enjoyed his company, the brilliant sunlight and the fresh salt breeze that played across the Strait of Juan de Fuca, where they were sailing.

"Here, hold the wheel," he said. Killian saw the surprise in her wide eyes. He smiled and held out his hand. Just being on the water helped to clear his mind and emotions.

"But—"

"I need to change the sails," he explained, reaching down and gripping her fingers. "Don't you want to learn about sailing?" he said teasingly as he drew her to her feet and placed her beside him at the wheel.

"Sure, but—"

Killian stood directly behind her, his body providing support and shelter for her as he placed her hands on the wheel. His mouth near her ear, he said, "I'm going to shift the sails from port to starboard. Be sure and duck when the boom comes across the cockpit. Otherwise, you'll be knocked overboard, and I don't want that to happen."

"Are you sure I can do this?" Susannah was wildly aware of Killian's body molded against hers. The feeling was making her want him all over again. As she twisted a look up at him, she felt her heart expand with a discovery that nearly overwhelmed her. His hair was ruffled by the breeze, and there was real joy in his deep blue eyes. For the first time, she was seeing Sean happy.

"Very sure." He leaned down and pressed his lips to her temple. The strands of her hair were silky beneath his exploration. Susannah invited spontaneity, and Killian reveled in the quick, hot kiss she gave him in answer.

"All right, I'll try," she said, her heart beating hard from his closeness.

"Just remember to duck," he warned, and left her in charge of guiding the yacht.

At two o'clock, they dropped anchor in a small crescent-shaped bay. Thrilled with the way the day was revealing itself, Susannah helped Sean tuck the sails away before the anchor was dropped. He motored the vessel into the dark blue bay, which was surrounded by tall evergreens on three sides. A great blue heron with a seven-foot wing span had been hunting frogs or small fish in the shallows, and it took off just as their anchor splashed into the water.

Susannah watched in awe as the magnificent bird swept by, just above the mast, and headed around the tip of the island. She turned just in time to see that Killian was watching the huge crane, too.

"She was breathtaking," Susannah confided as she moved toward the galley. Killian had promised her lunch, and she was hungry.

Sean nodded. "What I'm looking at is breathtaking," he murmured, and he reached out and captured her. The yacht was very stable at anchor; the surface of the bay smooth and unruffled. Susannah came willingly into his arms, closed her eyes and rested against his tall, lean form. His voice had been low and vibrating, sending a wonderful sheet of longing through her.

Killian absorbed Susannah against him, her natural scent, the fragrance of her shining sable hair, intoxicating him. "I feel like a thief," he murmured near her ear, savoring the feel of her arms tightening around him. "I feel like I'm stealing from you before I get thrown back into the way things were before you stepped into my life."

Gently disengaging from him, just enough that she could meet and hold his gaze, Susannah nodded. Her love for him was so fierce, so steadfast, that she wasn't threatened by his admission. "I remember a number of times in my folks' marriage when they went through stormy times," she confided. "They love each other, Sean, and Ma often told me when I'd grown up and we talked about those stormy periods that love held them together. I like the way Ma sees love, Sean. She calls it a fabric that she and Pa wove together. Some threads were very strong. Others were weak and sometimes frayed or even broke. She saw those weak times as fix-it times. It didn't mean they weren't afraid. But the one thing they clung to throughout those times was the fact that they loved each other."

He rested his jaw against her hair, absorbing her story. "I've never thought of love as a fabric."

"Look at your parents," Susannah said. "Were they happy together?"

He nodded and closed his eyes, savoring her nearness and allowing her husky voice to touch his heart. "Very happy."

"And did they fight from time to time?"

"Often," he chuckled, suddenly recalling those times. "My mother was a red-haired spitfire. My father was dark-haired and closed up tighter than the proverbial drum. When she suggested we emigrate to America, my father balked at the idea. My mother was the explorer, the person who would take risks."

"And your father was content to remain conservative and have the status quo."

Killian nodded and grazed her flushed cheek. Susannah's sparkling gray eyes made him aware of just how much she loved him. "Yes. But in the end, my mother pioneered getting us to America. It took many years to make her dream for all of us come true, but she did it."

Susannah asked soberly, "Do you blame your mother for what happened a year after you emigrated?"

Killian shook his head. "No. I wanted to move as much as she did."

"You're more like your mother?"

"Very much."

"A risk-taker."

"I guess I am."

Susannah held his thoughtful gaze. She could feel Sean thinking, weighing and measuring things they'd spoken about from the past and placing them like a transparency on the present—perhaps on their situation. Did he love her? He'd never said so, but in her heart, she felt he must—or as close as he could come to loving someone in his present state.

"I like," she said softly, "thinking about a relationship in terms of a tapestry. Ma always said she and Pa wove a very colorful one, filled with some tragedy, but many happy moments, too."

Gently Killian moved his hands down her slender arms, and then back up to rest on her shoulders. "A tapestry is a picture, too."

"Yes, it is."

"How do you see the tapestry of your life?" he asked quietly.

She shrugged and gave a slight smile, enjoying his rough, callused hands caressing her. "I see teaching handicapped children as important to my life. I certainly didn't see getting shot and being in a coma or having a contract put out on me, but that's a part of my tapestry now." She frowned. "I guess, having that unexpected experience, I understand how precious life is. Before, Sean, I took life for granted. I saw myself being a teacher, someday meeting a man who would love me, and then marrying. I want children, but not right away. I saw my folks' wisdom in not having children right away. It gave them a chance to solidify and work on their marriage. By the time Denny came along, they were emotionally ready for him. By the time I came along, they were more than ready." She smiled fondly. "I had a very happy childhood compared to most children. But I feel part of it was my parents' being older and more mature, more settled and sure of who they were."

"A tapestry that had the scales of life woven into it," he mused, holding her softened gaze.

"I never thought of it in symbolic terms, but yes, a balancing between doing something I love and having a husband and children when we're both ready for them, for the responsibility of raising them the best we can."

"You've brought balance into my life," Killian admitted, watching her eyes flare, first with surprise, then with joy. "I fought against it."

"Because you were scared."

"I still am," he told her wryly, and eased away.

Susannah followed him into the tight little galley below. There was a small table with a wraparound sofa, and she sat down to watch him fix their lunch at the kitchen area.

"I was scared to come and see you," she admitted.

Twisting a look over his shoulder as he prepared roast beef sandwiches, he said, "I couldn't believe you were standing there, Susannah."

"Your head or your heart?"

Her question was as insightful as she was about him. His mouth curved faintly as he forced himself to finish putting the sandwiches together. Placing the plate of them on the table, he brought over a bag of potato chips. "My head."

Susannah watched as he brought two bottles of mineral water from the small refrigerator built into the teakwood bulkhead. His entire face was relaxed, with none of the tension that was normally there. Even his mouth, usually a hard line holding back some emotional barrage, was softer.

"And your heart?" she asked in a whisper as he sat down next to her.

"My heart," he sighed, "in some way expected to see you." As he passed the sandwich to her, he met and caught her gaze. "I'm finding out that talking about how I feel isn't so bad after all."

With a little laugh, Susannah said, "Silence is the bane of all men. This society has bludgeoned you with the idea that you shouldn't feel, shouldn't cry and shouldn't speak of your emotions. It's a learned thing, Sean, and it's something you can change. That's the good news."

As he bit into his sandwich, Killian felt another cloak of dread dissolve around his shoulders. "You make it easy to talk," he admitted. "It's you. Something about you."

Melting beneath his intense, heated gaze, Susannah forced herself to eat the sandwich she didn't taste. Would Sean make good on his decision to send her away tonight? Or would he have the courage to let her remain? Her heart whispered that if he would allow her to stay with him tonight, his trust in himself and in her was strong enough that he could come to grips with his nightmare-ridden nights very quickly.

Nothing was ever changed in one day, Susannah reminded herself. But life demanded some awfully big steps if one genuinely wanted to heal. If Sean could trust in her love for him, never mind the fact that he might not return her love in the same measure, he could use her support in healing his past.

Only tonight would tell, Susannah ruminated. Being a victim of violence had taught her about the moment, the hour, the day. She would take each moment with Sean as a gift, instead of leaping ahead to wonder what his decision might be.

Just as they entered Sean's home, his phone rang. Susannah saw him frown as he hurried to the wall phone in the kitchen to answer it.

"Hello? Meg?" Killian shot a glance over at Susannah, who stood poised at the entrance to the living room. Surprised that his sister had called, he saw Susannah smile and disappear. She didn't have to leave, but it was too late to call her back. Wrestling with his shock over his sister's call, Killian devoted all his attention to her.

Susannah wisely left the kitchen. Going to her bedroom, she slowly began to pack her one and only bag to leave for the hotel in Victoria. She'd seen shock and puzzlement register on Sean's face over Meg's call. Didn't they talk often? Her heart wasn't in packing her clothes. The bed where they had lain, where they had made love, still contained the tangle of covers. Susannah ached to stay the night, to show Sean that two people could help his problem, not make it worse.

Killian was just coming out of the kitchen after the call when he saw Susannah placing her suitcase by the door. He shoved his hands into his pockets and moved toward her.

Straightening, Susannah felt her heartbeat pick up as Killian approached her. He wore a quizzical expression on his face, and she sensed that something important had occurred. She curbed her questions. Sean had to trust her enough to share, and not make her pull everything out of him.

"The funniest thing just happened," he murmured as he came to a halt in front of her. "Meg just called. I can't believe it." He shook his head.

"Believe what?"

"Meg just told me that she contacted Ian. She's asked him to fly to Ireland to see her." He gave Susannah a long, intense look.

"Wonderful!" Susannah clapped her hands together. "That's wonderful!"

"Yes…it is…"

"What led her to that decision?" she asked breathlessly, seeing the hope burning in Killian's dark eyes.

"She said he'd somehow found out where she was living and sent her a long letter. He talked about his love being strong enough to support both of them through this time in her life. All along, Meg loved Ian, but she was afraid he'd leave her as soon as he saw her disfigurement." Again Killian shook his head. "I'll be damned. The impossible has happened. I'm really glad for her. For Ian. They're both good people, caught in a situation they didn't make for themselves."

Reaching out, Susannah gently touched his arm. "The same could be said of you. Of us, Sean."

He stood very still, hearing the pain, the hope, in Susannah's voice, and seeing it reflected in her eyes.

Risking everything, she whispered, "Sean, you could send me away, just as Meg sent Ian away. Only you would be sending me away just for the night hours that you fear so much. She sent him away for several years, because of her fear that she would be rejected. In a way," she said, in a low, unsteady voice, "you're doing the same thing to me. You're afraid if I stay, you'll hurt me."

Her fingers tightening around his arm, Susannah stepped closer. "I know it isn't true, but you don't. At least not yet. But if you're searching for proof, Sean, look at last night. You didn't have nightmares haunt you after we slept in each other's arms, did you?"

"No… I didn't…" He stood there, assimilating the urgency in her heartfelt words. Realization shattered him in those moments. Meg had finally realized that Ian's love for her was steady—that it wasn't going to be pulled away from her, no matter how bad the situation appeared. He studied Susannah intently. He wasn't really questioning her love for him; he was questioning his ability to love her despite his wounding. Just as Meg had done, in a slightly different way.

Running his fingers through his hair, he muttered, "Stay tonight, Susannah. Please?"

Her heart leaped with joy, but she remained very quiet beneath his inspection. "Yes, I'd like that, darling, more than anything…"

With a groan, Killian swept her into his arms. He buried his face in her hair. "I love you, Susannah. I've loved you from the beginning, and I was too stupid, too scared, to admit it to myself, to you…"

The words, harsh with feeling, flowed across Susannah. Murmuring his name over and over again, she sought and found his mouth. The courage to admit his love for her was, perhaps, the biggest step of all. Drowning in the heated splendor of his mouth, being held so tightly that the breath was squeezed from her, Susannah returned his fire. Tears leaked from beneath her closed eyes, dampening her lashes and then her cheeks.

As Killian eased from her lips, he took his thumbs and removed those tears of happiness. His own eyes were damp, and the relief he felt was sharp and deep. "I want to try," he rasped as he framed her upturned face. "It isn't going to be easy."

"No," she quavered, "it won't be. But our tapestry will be strong, because of our courage to grow—together, darling."

"I'm afraid of tonight, colleen."

"We'll be afraid together. We'll hold each other. We'll talk. We'll do whatever it takes, Sean."

She was right. "One day at a time. One night at a time." Never had Killian wanted anything to work as much as he did this. He'd never admitted loving another woman. He'd been too fearful to do that. Susannah's strength, her undiluted belief in him, was giving him the courage to try.

"There will be good nights and bad ones, I'm sure," Susannah warned. "We can't expect miracles."

He smiled a little. "You're the miracle in my life. I'll do whatever I have to in order to keep you."

His commitment was more than she'd ever dreamed of hearing from him. Somehow Meg's courage to release her past had helped him see his own situation differently. "Just trying is enough," Susannah told him simply. And it was.

Epilogue

Susannah's heart wasn't in her packing. Her three weeks on Vancouver Island had fled by like a blink of the eye. Killian was quieter than usual as he helped her take her clothes out of the closet.

He was thinking about something important, and she could feel it. The days had been wonderful days of discovery, of joy and exploration. The nights had been a roller-coaster ride of good and bad. Together they had managed to confront Killian's nightmare past, and with some success.

More than anything, Killian knew he needed professional help to completely change for good. They'd talked about it and agreed that Susannah couldn't be the linchpin of his healing. He saw her as a loving support, his primary cheerleader. But it wasn't her responsibility to heal him. It was his.

The suitcase was packed, and she snapped it shut. As she turned around, Killian brought her into his arms.

"I've got a few phone calls to make before I take you to the airport."

"Okay." One day at a time, she reminded herself. Sean had not spoken of anything beyond her three weeks at his house. As badly as Susannah wanted to know his future plans and how they included her, she didn't ask.

"I want you to be there when I make the call."

She searched his shadowed face. "Who are you going to talk to?"

"Morgan."

Her heart thudded once. "Morgan?"

"Yes."

"Why?"

Killian cupped her face and looked deep into her wide, loving eyes. "To tell him I'm asking for permanent reassignment to the U.S. only. I'm also telling him I want jobs that don't involve violence. He's got some of those available. Mercenaries are more than just men of war. Sometimes a mercenary is needed just to be eyes and ears. I'm going to tell him I want low-risk short-term assignments." He smiled uncertainly. "That way, I can make my home in Glen, Kentucky, and keep putting my life back together with you."

Tears jammed into her eyes. "Oh, Sean…" She threw her arms around his shoulders.

"It's not going to be easy," he warned her grimly, taking her full weight.

"We'll do it together," Susannah said, her voice muffled against his chest.

Killian knew it could be the worst kind of hell at times,

but Susannah's unwavering support, her love for him, had made the decision easy. He held her tightly. "Together," he rasped thickly. "Forever."

* * * * *

A career Air Force officer, **Merline Lovelace** served at bases all over the world. When she hung up her uniform for the last time, she decided to try her hand at storytelling. Since then, more than twelve million copies of her books have been published in over thirty countries. Check her website at merlinelovelace.com or friend Merline on Facebook for news and information about her latest releases.

Visit the Author Profile page at Harlequin.com for more titles.

A MAN OF HIS WORD

Merline Lovelace

Prologue

Four of the five Henderson brothers stood in a loose semicircle, nursing chilled champagne while they watched their grinning brother waltz his bride of thirty minutes around the dance floor. Tall, tanned, each seasoned as much by his chosen profession as by his youth on the northern Arizona ranch they all still called home, they made a striking collection of broad shoulders, hard muscle and keen blue eyes.

Jake, the oldest of the five and the only other married Henderson male present, shook his head. "Still hard to believe it happened so fast. Of all of you, I expected Sam to hold out the longest. Instead he fell the hardest and the fastest. Molly's gonna lead that boy around more than the dance floor."

Tough, cynical Marsh, the middle brother, grunted in

disgust. "He reminds me of your polled Herefords right now, Jake. Big, moon-faced and completely dehorned."

Even Evan had to agree. Smiling, the attorney tipped his glass in a salute to his newly married sibling. "Sam's got it bad, all right. He told me he would have strangled the bastard who came after Molly with his bare hands if the police hadn't arrived when they did."

Only Reece kept silent. Closest to Sam in both age and temperament, he wavered between a fierce happiness for his younger brother and an equally fierce hope that Sam and Molly could hang on to the love they didn't even try to disguise at this moment.

So few couples did.

Involuntarily his gaze shifted to the vibrant, laughing mother of the groom. Despite her dove-gray hair and the character lines that came with raising five boys and running a twenty-thousand-acre spread in the shadow of the rugged northern Arizona San Francisco Mountains, Jessica Henderson looked almost as young as Jake's wife, Ellen…and so unlike the woman who'd fallen apart one cold, February night that Reece's heart clenched.

None of his brothers knew about that night. About the terror of those dark, desperate hours, when Reece had come home unexpectedly between the engineering jobs that took him all over the world, and found his mother ravaged by loneliness and alcohol and a bitter, corrosive anger. She was almost incoherent when Reece arrived at the Bar-H, but she'd cried and clung to him, begged him not to call a doctor, not to shame her any more than she'd already been shamed.

A grim, shaken Reece had forced gallon after gallon of coffee down her throat. Walked her the length of the ranch house and back a thousand times. Listened to her wrenching sobs and searing anger at the husband she'd buried two years before.

That was when she told him about the letters she'd found hidden in a storage closet…and about the woman his father had carried on an affair with for years. At his mother's fierce insistence, Reece had burned the letters. Many of his illusions about marriage went up in smoke with those blue-edged notes.

Jessica Henderson had bottomed out that night, emptied the well of her self-pity and anger. Soon afterward, she'd turned the ranch over to Jake, who now managed it along with his own spread for the absent Henderson brothers. She'd bought a condo in Sedona and taken up golf, of all things. Now she traveled with her new friends and drove out to the ranch occasionally to visit the old ones. She'd put the terror of that cold, desperate February night behind her…as well as her anger at the husband who'd betrayed her.

Reece was still working on it.

Seeing his mother laughing and his younger brother grinning like a dope at his new bride helped.

What *didn't* help was knowing that Reece had to leave right after the reception to make the long drive back to the sleepy little town of Chalo Canyon in south-central Arizona because of an early-morning meeting with another determined home wrecker.

His champagne goblet hit the bar with a chink of crystal against wood. "I'm claiming a dance with my new sister-in-law," he told his brothers, "then I'm out of here."

Marsh lifted a brow. "You're not going to stay and help us send Sam off on his honeymoon in the hallowed Henderson tradition?"

"Right," Jake drawled, "the 'hallowed' tradition you

clowns started with me. Ellen still shudders when she remembers our wedding night."

"You boys will have to handle this one on your own," Reece said. "I have to be back on-site by dawn tomorrow. I've got a reservoir draining at the rate of eighty cubic feet per second and a dam with some cracks in it waiting for me."

Among other things.

His jaw tightened at the thought of the woman who'd pulled every string in the book to muscle her way into the restricted area behind the dam. She intended to shoot a documentary film of a sunken Anasazi village as it emerged from the waters of the reservoir, or so the letter from the Bureau of Reclamation directing Reece's cooperation had stated.

He knew better. She was returning to Chalo Canyon for one reason and one reason only…to finish what she'd started ten years ago. Everyone in town had told Reece so, including the man she'd begun the affair with.

Well, he didn't have to watch the woman in action. He'd meet with her bright and early tomorrow morning as promised. He'd advise her of his schedule, set some rules of engagement. Then she was on her own. He had more important matters to engage both his time and his attention than Sydney Scott.

Putting the woman firmly from his mind, Reece crossed the floor to claim a dance with his radiant new sister-in-law.

Chapter 1

Arms wrapped around her knees, Sydney sat bathed in warm summer moonlight on one of the limestone out-croppings that rimmed the Chalo River Reservoir. Although she couldn't see the movement, she knew the water level in the vast reservoir was slowly dropping. She'd been gauging its progress for hours now, measuring its descent against the shadowy crevasses on the cliff face opposite.

Another thirty-six hours, she estimated with a shiver of anticipation, forty-eight at most. Then the magical, mystical village she'd first seen as a child would emerge from the dark waters of the reservoir and feel the touch of the sun for the first time in a decade.

Once every ten years, the sluice gates of the dam that harnessed the Chalo River yawned fully open. Once every ten years, the man-made lake behind the dam was drained to allow maintenance and repair to the towering concrete structure. Once every ten years, the waters dropped and the ancient ruins reappeared. This was the year, the month, the week.

Excitement pulsed through Sydney's veins, excitement and a stinging regret that went soul deep.

"Oh, Dad," she murmured softly, "if only you'd had a few more months…"

No! No, she couldn't go down that road. She shook her head, fighting the aching sense of loss that had become so much a part of her she rarely acknowledged it anymore. She couldn't wish another day, another hour of that awful pain on her father. His death had been a release, a relief from the agony that even morphine couldn't dull. She wouldn't grieve for him now. Instead, she would use these quiet, moonlit hours to celebrate the times they'd been together.

With the perfect clarity of a camera lens, Sydney recalled her wide-eyed wonder when her father had first shown her the wet, glistening ruins tucked under a ledge in this small corner of Chalo Canyon. Then, as now, goose bumps had raised on her arms when the wind whispered through the canyon, sounding much like the Weeping Woman of local legend. According to the tale, an ancient Anasazi warrior had stolen a woman from another tribe and confined her in a stone tower in his village. The woman had cried for her lost love, and leaped to her death rather than submit to the man who'd taken her.

A youthful Sydney had heard the legend within days of moving to Chalo Canyon, where her father had taken over as fish and game warden for the state park that rimmed the huge, man-made lake behind the dam. Her dad had pooh-poohed the tale, but it had tugged at his daughter's imagination. So much so that she'd counted the years until she could capture the ruins on film as a special project for her cinematography class.

Sighing, Sydney rested her chin on her knees. How young she'd been then. How incredibly naive. A nineteen-year-old student at Southern Cal, she'd planned the film project all through her sophomore year. Couldn't wait for summer and the scheduled draining of the reservoir. Pop had gone with her that day, too, maneuvering the boat, keeping it steady while she balanced their home camcorder on her shoulder and shot the emerging village from every angle. Sydney had been so elated, so sure this project would be the start of a glorious career in film.

Then she'd tumbled head over heels in love with handsome, charming Jamie Chavez.

Even after all these years, the memory could still make Sydney writhe with embarrassment. Her breathless ardor had by turns amused and delighted the older, more sophisticated Jamie…much to his father's dismay. Sebastian Chavez's plans for his only son didn't include the daughter of the local fish and game warden.

Looking back, Sydney could only shake her head at her incredible stupidity. Jamie was more than willing to amuse himself with her while his fiancée was in Europe. Even now Sydney cringed when she remembered the night Sebastian found her in his son's bed. The scene had *not* been pretty. Even worse, the swing her father took at the powerful landowner the next day had cost him his job. The Scotts had moved away the following week, and neither of them had ever returned to Chalo Canyon.

Until now.

Now Sydney was about to see the ancient ruins for the third time. With a string of critically acclaimed documentaries and an Oscar nomination under her belt, she intended to capture the haunting ruins and the legend she'd first shared with her father so long ago on video- and audiotape. She'd worked for almost a year to script the project and secure funding. The final product would stand in loving tribute to the man who taught her the beauties and mysteries of Chalo Canyon.

Hopefully, she thought with a wry grimace, the docu- mentary would also take her fledgling production com- pany out of the red. Her father's long illness had cut both Sydney's heart and her financial resources to the quick. Even with the big-money financing her recent brush with the Oscars had generated, starting up her own production company had eaten what little was left of her savings. This project would make her or break her.

She brushed at a gnat buzzing her left ear, thinking of all the obstacles she'd overcome to get even this far. The preproduction work had taken almost eight months. She'd started on it just after her dad's leukemia robbed him of his breath and his mobility. She'd shared every step of the process with him during those long, agoniz- ing hours at his bedside. Talked him through the con- cept. Described the treatment she envisioned, worked out an estimated budget. Then she'd hawked the idea to the History Channel, to PBS, to half a dozen indepen- dent producers.

Pop's death had hardened Sydney's resolve into ab- solute determination to see the project through…despite Sebastian Chavez's vehement objections. When Sebas- tian heard of the proposed documentary, he'd used every weapon in his arsenal to kill it. He'd refused all access to the site through his land. He'd flexed his political mus- cle to delay filming permits. He'd even rallied Native

American groups to protest the exploitation of sacred ruins. Evidently the hard feelings generated ten years ago hadn't died.

As a last-ditch attempt to block the project, Chavez had dragged the engineer in charge of the dam repair into the controversy and got him to weigh in against any activity in the restricted area behind the dam.

Sydney had played shamelessly on every connection she had from L.A. to D.C. to overturn Reece Henderson's nonconcurrence. Finally the powerful coalition of PBS, the National Historic Preservation Society, and her wealthy and well-known financial backer, who just happened to have contributed significantly to the president's reelection campaign, had prevailed.

As a condition of the approval, however, Sydney had to coordinate her filming schedule with the chief engineer and shoot around the blasting and repair work at the dam. Henderson's curt faxes in response to her initial queries had set her teeth on edge, but she refused to allow some bullheaded engineer to upset her or her tight schedule. She had only two weeks to capture a legend… and recapture the magic of her youth.

Her chin wobbled on her knees. Weariness tugged at the edges of her simmering anticipation. She should go back to the motel, grab a few hours of sleep before the rest of her crew arrived. She'd learned the hard way that rest and exercise were essential to countering the stress caused by tight schedules, the inevitable snafus, and the sheer physical and mental exhaustion of a shoot. Even more important, she'd need her wits and all her charm in full functioning order when she met with this Henderson guy in the morning.

She'd give herself just a few more moments, she decided. A last stretch of peace before the work began. A quiet time with her father and her dreams.

A rumble of thunder shattered the quiet less than a half hour later. All too soon the moon disappeared behind a pile of dark storm clouds.

Sydney lifted her head, chewing on her lower lip as she eyed the lightning that lit the clouds from the inside out. Damned El Niño. Or maybe it was the depleted ozone layer that was causing the violent, unseasonable storms that had plagued the southwest this summer.

Whatever had spawned them, these storms could wreak havoc with her exterior shots, not to mention her shooting schedule. With luck, this one would break soon, dump its load, and move on so her crew could shoot their preparatory exterior tests tomorrow in bright sunshine. Sydney wanted light. She needed light. Light formed the essence of film and video imagery.

Scowling at another flash of white against the dark sky, she pushed to her feet and headed for her rented Chevy Blazer. She'd taken only a few steps when the wind picked up. The leaves on the cottonwoods lining the canyon rim rustled. The ends of the mink-brown hair tucked haphazardly under her L.A. Rams ball cap flicked against her cheek.

Suddenly, Sydney spun around, heart pounding. There it was! The sigh. The cry. The sob of the wind through the canyon.

Aiiiii. Eee-aiiii.

She stood frozen, letting the sound wrap around and through her. She could almost hear the despair behind the soughing sound, feel the unutterable sadness.

Another gust cut through the canyon, faster, deeper.

The leaves whipped on the cottonwoods. The cry increased in pitch to a wail that lifted the fine hairs on the back of Sydney's neck.

Slowly, so slowly, the wind eased and the eerie lament faded.

"Now that," she muttered, rubbing the goose bumps that prickled every square inch of her bare arms, "was one heck of an audio bite. I wish to heck Albert had caught it."

Her soundman wouldn't arrive from L.A. until tomorrow noon, along with the camera operator and the grip she'd hired for this job. Only Sydney and her assistant, Zack, had come a day early—Sydney to snatch these few hours alone with her memories before the controlled chaos of the shoot began, Zack to finalize the motel and support arrangements he'd made by phone weeks ago.

Sydney could only hope the wind would perform for them again tomorrow afternoon when they shot the exterior setup sequences she'd planned—assuming, of course, this Reece Henderson approved her shooting schedule when she met with him in the morning.

Another frown creased her forehead as she dodged the first fat splats of rain on her way to her rented Blazer. She had enough documentaries under her belt to appreciate the intricacies of negotiating permits and approvals for an on-location shoot, but the requirement to coordinate her shooting schedule galled more than a little. Hopefully, this guy Henderson would prove more cooperative in person than he had by fax.

Sliding inside the Blazer, she shut out the now-pelting rain and groped for the keys in the pockets of the military fatigue pants she bought by the dozen at an Army-Navy surplus store in south L.A. The baggy camouflage pants didn't exactly shout Rodeo Drive chic, but Sydney had found their tough construction and many pockets a godsend on isolated shoots like this one.

One foot on the clutch, the other on the brake, she keyed the ignition and wrapped a hand around the shift knob, wishing fervently she'd thought to specify automatic drive before Zack arranged for rental vehicles. From the way the gears ground when she tried to coax them into first, the Blazer obviously wished so, too.

"Sorry," she muttered, working the clutch and the stick again.

After another protesting *snnnrck,* the gears engaged. With rain pinging steadily against the roof, Sydney eased the Blazer onto the road. She kept her foot light on the accelerator and her eyes on the treacherous curves ahead.

Little more than a dirt track, Canyon Rim Road snaked along the canyon's edge for miles before joining the state road that accessed the dam. The stone outcroppings that edged the road on the left made every turn a real adventure. The sheer drop on the right added to the pucker factor. The deluge that poured out of the black sky didn't exactly help either visibility or navigability. Chewing on her lower lip, Sydney downshifted and took a hairpin turn at a crawl.

A few, tortuous turns later she was forced to admit that it might have made more sense to wait until daylight to drive along the canyon rim. She'd needed this time alone with her memories, though. And there'd been no indication earlier that a storm might—

"What the—!"

She came out of a sharp turn and stomped on the brake. Or what she thought was the brake. Her boot hit the clutch instead, and the Blazer rolled straight at the slab of rock that had tumbled onto the road from the out-cropping beside it.

Choking back an oath, Sydney swung both her foot and the wheel. With the rock wall on the left and the sheer drop-off on the right, there was no room to ma-neuver around the obstacle. The Blazer swung too far out before she jammed on the brake and stopped its roll.

To her horror, she felt the road's narrow shoulder begin to crumble under the Blazer's weight. The vehicle lurched back, dropped at an angle, stalled. Frantic, Syd-ney dragged the stick back to neutral, twisted the key.

"Come on! Come on!"

The engine turned over at the exact moment another piece of the rim gave. The four-wheel tilted at a crazy angle and started to slide backward.

"Oh, God!"

Shouldering open the door, Sydney threw herself out. She hit on one hip and twisted desperately, scrabbling for purchase on the rain-slick earth. Beside her the Blazer gave a fearsome imitation of the *Titanic*. Metal groaned against sandstone. Nose up, headlights stabbing the rain, it slid backward like the great ship slipping into its dark grave, then slowly toppled over the edge.

The echoes of its crashing descent were still ring-ing in Sydney's ears when sandstone and muddy earth crumbled under her frantic fingers and she followed the Blazer over the edge.

Reece Henderson slapped a rolled-up schematic of the Chalo River Dam against his jeans-clad thigh. Jaw tight, he waited while the phone he held to his ear shrilled a half dozen times. He'd started to slam it down when the receiver was fumbled off the hook. Reece took the mumbled sound on the other end for a hello.

"Where is she?"

"Huh?"

"Where's Scott?"

"Whoziz?"

Gripping the receiver in a tight fist, Reece glared at the mirrored calendar on the opposite wall of the office set aside for his use.

"This is Henderson, Reece Henderson. Chief engineer on the Chalo River Dam project. Where's your boss?"

"Dunno." There was a jaw-cracking yawn at the other end of the line. "What time izit?"

"Eight forty-seven," he snapped. "She was supposed to be here at eight."

The irritation that had started simmering at 8:05 was now at full boil. He'd hung around topside waiting for the blasted woman, wasting almost an hour he could have spent down inside the dam with his engineers.

"Did you, like, try her room?" The kid at the other end of the line sounded more alert now, if not more coherent.

"Yes. Twice. There wasn't any answer. The motel operator said you were her assistant and would know where she was."

Actually, Martha Jenkins, who pulled triple duty as owner, operator and day clerk at the Lone Eagle Motel, had provided Reece with more details than he'd either asked for or wanted. Martha hadn't been on duty when Sydney Scott and her gum-popping, green-haired, multiple-body-pierced assistant Zachary Tyree checked in late yesterday afternoon, but things got around fast in a town the size of Chalo Canyon.

"Hang loose."

The phone clattered down. The sound of sheets whooshing aside was followed in quick succession by the snick of a zipper and padding footsteps. Long moments later the phone rattled again.

"She's not in her room."

Reece rolled his eyes. He thought they'd already established that fact.

"Well, if she strolls in anytime soon, tell her I left my brother's wedding early and drove half the night so I would make the meeting she didn't bother to show for. She can call me here at the site. I'll get back to her when and if…"

"You don't understand, dude. She's not here."

Reece felt the last of his patience shredding. "Tell your boss—"

"The blinds in her room were open and I looked in. Her bed hasn't been slept in."

Worry put a crack in the kid's voice. A different sort of emotion put a lock on Reece's jaw.

God! He'd been hearing the rumors and gossip about this Scott woman for weeks. How she'd thrown herself at Jamie Chavez ten years ago. How Jamie's father had all but dragged her out of his son's bed. How *her* father had knocked Chavez, Sr., on his butt the next day. Now she was a big, important Hollywood director, coming back to Chalo River to impress everyone with her success… and to try her luck with Jamie again.

Reece couldn't suppress the disgust that swirled in his gut. The woman had arrived in town only yesterday afternoon and had already spent the night somewhere other than her motel room. Pretty fast work, even for a big, important Hollywood director.

Well, Reece had complied with his boss's direct communiqué. He'd cooperated with the woman, or tried to, damn near busting his butt to get back here in time for their meeting this morning. The ball was in Ms. Sydney Scott's court now, and she could lob it at the net from now until next Christmas for all he cared. He started to hang up when the sharp concern in the kid's voice stilled his hand.

"Syd drove out to the canyon right after we got settled here at the motel yesterday afternoon. She could still be out there."

"What?"

Reece's irritation spiked into anger. He'd made it plain to Ms. Scott in their exchange of faxes that neither she nor any of her crew should go poking around in the restricted area behind the dam until he briefed them on the repair project and the potential hazards during the blasting period.

"Syd said she wanted to check the water level in the reservoir and get her bearings. Told me not to wait up for her. You don't think she, like, got lost or something?"

"I understand Ms. Scott used to live in this area. She should know her way around."

"That was ten years ago, dude."

"The name's Henderson."

"Right, Henderson. Could you, like, drive around and check on her? She sorta gets involved in her projects sometimes and forgets what day it is. I'd go myself, but I don't know the geography, and Syd's got the Blazer, which leaves me, like, without wheels until Tish and the others get here."

Reece wanted very much to tell the kid what he and his boss could, like, do, but he'd assumed responsibility for this project and all the challenges and headaches that went with it. Including, it appeared, Sydney Scott. If she'd entered the restricted area and gotten her vehicle stuck in the mud after that gully-washer last night, she was, unfortunately, his problem.

"All right. I'll drive along the rim and look for her. Take down my mobile phone number. If she walks in, call me."

"Thanks, man!"

After a call down to his second-in-charge to advise him that he'd be on mobile for the next half hour or so, Reece exchanged his hard hat for a battered straw Stetson, legacy of those rare breaks between jobs which he spent at the Bar-H, helping his brother Jake. A moment later, he left the air-conditioned comfort of the office for the blazing heat of a summer Arizona sun bouncing off concrete.

The administration building perched on the east end of the dam, a massive concrete arch that thrust its arms against the steep Chalo Canyon walls. Some 305 feet below, two fully opened spillways poured tons of rushing water into the lower Chalo. Tipping his hat forward to shade his eyes, Reece paused for a moment to assess the reservoir behind the dam. All traces of the thunderstorm that had lashed the area last night had disappeared. Sunlight sparkled on the water's surface, already, he noted with grim satisfaction, sunk well below its usual level.

By tomorrow, he should be able to examine from the outside the cracks that had started stressing the dam from the inside. He'd know then how much work he had ahead of him, and how long this Sydney Scott would have to film her documentary before the reservoir started filling again.

Assuming, of course, that she'd intended to make a

movie at all. Maybe the rumors were true. Maybe this documentary was just a smoke screen, a convenient cover for her personal intentions. Maybe she'd really come back to Chalo River to make nothing but trouble.

If that was the case, she was off to a helluva good start. When and if Reece located Ms. Scott, she might just realize she'd bitten off more trouble than she could chew this time.

He found her twenty minutes later. Or more correctly, he found the spot where the canyon rim had crumbled, taking half the road with it.

Chapter 2

"Hey! You down there! Are you okay?"

The shout jerked Sydney's head back. Never in her life had she heard anything as wonderful as that deep, gruff voice. Keeping a tight grip on the twisted piñon tree that had broken her slide into oblivion seven long hours ago, she shouted to the dark-haired cowboy peering cautiously over the edge of the rim.

"I'm okay. No broken bones that I can tell. Have you got a rope?"

"Yes. I'll be right back. Don't move!"

Don't move. Right. As if she planned on releasing her death grip on the rough-barked trunk or shifting her body so much as a centimeter to either side of the narrow toe-hold she'd found in the canyon wall.

She leaned her forehead against the tree, almost giddy with relief. Then again, this dizzy sensation might have something to do with the fact that she'd just spent seven hours wedged between a tree root and a cliff face hundreds of feet above a narrow river gorge.

She'd been prepared to spend even longer. Sydney hadn't expected Zack to roll out of bed before ten or eleven, much less organize a rescue for his missing boss. Her assistant was worth his 140 pounds in gold once he revved his motor, but getting him going some mornings could take a half-dozen calls that ran the gamut from wheedling to cajoling to outright threats of death and dismemberment. Thank God this was one of his rare self-starting days!

The thump of a rope hitting against the cliff face above her snapped her attention back to the rim. She looked up just in time to take the shower of small stones and dust dislodged by the rope full in her face. Wincing, Sydney spun her head sideways, which caused the tree to shake and its occupant to let out a small, terrified squeak.

"Dammit, don't move!" her rescuer snapped. "I'll work the rope over to you."

Clinging to the tree trunk with both arms, she blew upward in a vain attempt to get the dust and straggling hair out of her eyes. Her Rams ball cap had gone the way of the Blazer during that three-second slide down the cliff face. Sydney only hoped the sacrifice of a hat and a four-wheel-drive vehicle had satisfied the canyon gods.

Her heart in her throat, she watched the thick rope hump and bump its way closer to her precarious perch. Only after it was within reach did she discover that her arms were numb from the shoulders down. She couldn't seem to unlock their tight grip on the trunk.

"Take the rope."

Swiping her tongue along dry lips, she tried again. Her

left arm came unwrapped and dangled like overcooked linguini at her side.

"I need a minute here," she croaked to her rescuer. "I can't seem to feel my arms."

"All right, it's all right." The gruff voice above her gentled. "Don't worry about it."

"Easy for you to say," Sydney muttered to the piñon, her eyes on the rope a tantalizing few inches away. Suddenly it jounced up and out of sight.

"Hey!"

"Hang on, I'm coming down."

He pulled off his hat and looped the rope around his waist. Within moments he was beside her. Black hair ruffled. Blue eyes steady and encouraging in a tanned face. Shoulders roped with reassuringly thick cords of muscle. Altogether he looked big, strong and wonderfully solid.

On second thought, Sydney wasn't so sure big and solid were desirable characteristics in a man whose only connection to terra firma was a length of twisted hemp. Swallowing, she said a silent prayer for the sureness of his lifeline while he propped his boots against the canyon wall. With a cowboy's one-handed ease, he shook out a loop in the length of rope he'd left dangling behind him.

"Bend your head. Let me slip this over you." He spoke slowly, his deep voice calm, confident. "I'm going to lift one of your arms. Got a grip? Okay, now the other. Easy, easy."

The noose tightened around her waist, cutting off most of her breath. The taut, muscled arm the stranger slid around her cut off the rest.

"I've got you. I'm going to swing you in front of me. We'll walk up the cliff face together. Ready?"

Even with the rope and her rescuer's muscled arm

around her, it took a considerable leap of faith to let go of the sturdy little piñon. Swallowing hard, she let him lift her from the tree.

"I've got you. I won't let go."

She managed a shaky laugh. "Promise?"

"I'm a man of my word," he assured her, his breath warm in her ear.

She hoped so. She certainly hoped so.

"Ready?"

She gulped. "Ready."

They crab-walked up the cliff, her bottom nested against his stomach, his arms caging her ribs. Five steps, seven, eight, then a palm on her rear and a heaving shove.

Sydney went over the rim belly down. Panting, she crawled on hands and knees until the ground felt firm enough for her to turn and try to help her rescuer over the edge. Her arms were still so weak she gave up after the first useless tug.

Not that he appeared to need any assistance. With a smooth coordination of brawn and grace, he hauled himself up. Once safely away from the crumbled rim, he untied his lifeline and strode to the Jeep that had anchored it. Sydney gave a little croak of delight when he hunkered down beside her a moment later, a plastic bottle of spring water in his hand. She downed a half dozen greedy gulps before coming up for air. After another swallow or two, her throat had loosened enough to talk without croaking.

"Thanks...for the water and the rescue."

"You're welcome." He picked up his hat and dusted it against his thigh before settling it on his head. "Sure you're not hurt?"

"Just a little weak from hanging on to the tree all night.

I collected a few dents and scrapes on my way down, but nothing that won't heal or cover up."

His blue eyes raked her over from the top of her dusty head to the toes of her dusty boots, performing their own assessment. Evidently he agreed with her diagnosis.

"I saw the wreckage at the bottom of the gorge. What happened?"

"There was a boulder in the road. With the rain, I didn't see it in time and swung too sharply. I got out of the Blazer before it went over, but the rim crumbled beneath me. I thought... I was sure..." She substituted a wobbly smile for the shudder she wanted to let rip. "The piñon broke my fall. How does that poem go, the one about never seeing anything as beautiful as a tree?"

"Beats me." He studied her from under the brim of that beat-up hat, his expression noticeably less comforting and reassuring now that they were back on solid ground. "You're a lucky woman."

She started to point out that not everyone would classify someone who went over a cliff as lucky, but his next comment buried the thought.

"And damned stupid."

"I beg your pardon?"

"Most people would have more sense than to drive along a narrow canyon rim road late at night in the middle of a thunderstorm."

Sydney had come to the same conclusion herself just before she went bungee jumping without a bungee, but she didn't particularly enjoy hearing it from someone else. Still, he'd plucked her out of her eagle's nest. She owed him, big-time.

Ordering her arms and legs to do their thing, she pushed herself to her feet. Her rescuer had to shoot out a hand and catch her before she whumped back down on her rear. Shaking off his hand, she tried to sound grateful.

"Thanks. Again. I'm Sydney Scott, by the way."

"I know who you are."

She flushed at the drawled response, feeling even more stupid than he'd implied earlier. If he was part of a search party, of course he'd know who he'd come looking for.

"And you are?"

"Reece Henderson."

"Oh." The straw Stetson that shaped his head as if made for it had led her to assume he was a local. "You're the dam engineer."

From the way his eyes narrowed, she must have put a little too much emphasis on *dam*. Either that, or their exchange of terse faxes had annoyed him as much as it had her.

"When you didn't show for our meeting this morning," he said curtly, "I called your assistant and woke him up."

So much for the massive search-and-rescue effort Sydney had assumed Zack set in motion!

"The kid told me you'd driven out to the canyon. He seemed to think you might have fallen into an artistic trance and gotten lost."

"I don't fall into artistic trances," she said with another smile, slightly strained but still trying hard for grateful.

One black brow lifted in patent disbelief.

"All right," she admitted grudgingly, "I did leave a pot of red beans and rice on the stove a couple of months ago while I was working a treatment, but the fire didn't do any real damage."

When he only looked at her through those cool blue eyes, Sydney gave Zack a mental kick in the shins. How much had her assistant told this guy, anyway?

"Maybe I did start out for San Diego last week and didn't realize I was going in the wrong direction until I passed Santa Barbara," she said defensively, "but I was outlining a script in my mind and sort of got caught up in it."

With a little snort that sounded suspiciously like disgust, her rescuer strolled back to the Jeep to untie the rope. "Is that what you were doing last night when you drove off a cliff?"

"I was *not* in any kind of a trance last night."

Well, she amended silently, maybe she had let her imagination go for a while, particularly when the wind whistled eerily through the canyon and raised goose bumps all over her body. Henderson didn't need to know that, though.

"As I told you, there was a boulder in the road, a chunk of sandstone. I swerved to avoid it."

"If you say so, lady."

Gratitude was getting harder and harder to hang on to. Sydney folded her arms across her now-scruffy yellow T-shirt.

"I do say so."

He straightened, the rope half-looped in his hand, his eyes as sharp and slicing as lasers. "Then maybe you'll also tell me why you were driving around in a restricted area without a permit? A permit that I had intended to issue at our meeting this morning, by the way."

That "had intended" caught Sydney's attention and shoved everything else out of her mind. The terror of sliding over a cliff, the long, frightening hours alone with only a piñon tree for company, the crab-walk up a sheer rock wall fell away. All that remained was her absolute determination to capture the magic of the ruins on videotape…for her dad, for herself, for the joys and tears they'd shared.

Every inch a professional now, she cut right to the heart of the issue. "I apologize for going around you, Mr. Henderson. I arrived in Chalo Canyon earlier than planned yesterday afternoon. I tried to contact you for permission to drive out to the site, but you were out of town. At a wedding, or so they told me."

"So you drove out, anyway."

"*After* I talked to one of your engineers. He said he thought it would be okay. I believe his name was Patrick Something."

It would be Patrick, Reece thought in disgust. Young, breezy, overconfident of his brand-new civil engineering degree that hadn't yet been tested by thousands of tons of wet concrete and millions of yards of rushing water. Reece finished looping the rope.

"Apology accepted this time, Ms. Scott. Just don't go around me again. I'm chief engineer on this project. The responsibility for the safety of everyone involved, including you and your crew, rests with me."

"It's Sydney," she returned, seething inside at the undeserved lecture, but determined to hammer out a working relationship with this bullheaded engineer.

"Sydney," he acknowledged with a little nod. "Now we'd better get you back to town so you can have those scrapes and dents checked out. In the meantime, I'll get hold of the county sheriff and let him know about the accident."

"I'd prefer to conduct our planned discussion before I hitch a ride into town. If this sunlight holds and the rest of my crew arrives on time, I want to shoot some exterior footage this afternoon."

Reece stared at her across the Jeep's hood. For God's

sake, was she for real? She'd just spent the night perched in a tree. Her baggy fatigue pants and yellow T-shirt looked like they'd been worn by someone on the losing side of the last war. Her tangled, dark brown mane hung in rats' tails on either side of her face…a face, he admitted reluctantly, made remarkable by wide green eyes, high cheekbones and a mouth a man could weave some pretty lurid fantasies around.

Not Reece. Not after all he'd heard about Sydney Scott. He'd make damned sure he didn't weave fantasies of any kind about this particular package of trouble. That tug he felt low in his belly was grudging admiration for her sheer guts, nothing more.

"All right. We'll drive back to the dam and go over schedules." He reached into the Jeep and tossed her the mobile phone. "Here, you'd better call your assistant and let him know you're okay while I block the road."

With the rope looped over one arm, he rooted around in the back of the Jeep for the toolbox he never traveled without. Inside was a thick roll of electrical tape. It wasn't red, but it would have to do as a hazard warning until he could get a crew out here to erect permanent barriers.

"Zack? It's Sydney."

Her voice carried to him at the rear of the Jeep, attractive enough now that most of the croak had disappeared.

"No, I didn't get lost. I, er, drove off a cliff."

She caught Reece's sardonic look and turned her back.

"Yes, I'm fine. Really. Honest. I swear. Just get hold of the insurance company, okay? Make sure our on-location liability coverage extends to rented Blazers that now reside at the bottom of a river gorge. And arrange for another vehicle. I want to do some site shots this afternoon."

Reece turned away, shaking his head. This was one

single-minded female. He'd remember that in future dealings with her.

"It's a long story," she told her assistant, scooping her tangled hair back with one hand. "I'll fill you in on the details later. What have you heard from Tish and the others? Noon? Good! Tell them to be ready to roll as soon as I get back. What time is it now?"

Her little screech of dismay followed Reece to the vertical outcropping a few yards away. Reddish limestone striated with yellow and green pushed upward. Hardened by nature, sculpted by time, it formed a wall of oddly shaped rock. Too often wind and rain toppled smaller segments of these formations and sent them tumbling down, which in turn caused bigger pieces to break off.

Pale gashes showed where the rock had broken loose last night. Reece fingered the marks, frowning, then surveyed what remained of the road at this point. The stone formations butted out, making it almost impossible to see around the curve. A driver couldn't have chosen a worse point to go head-to-head with a fallen rock.

Edging past the narrow neck, he blocked the road off from the other side. He did the same on the Jeep side. His insides still were tight from the narrowness of her escape when he returned.

Sydney buried a sigh at the scowl on her rescuer's face as he strode toward her. She had to work with this guy for the next few weeks. They were not, she decided, going to rank up there among the most enjoyable weeks of her life. With any luck, she and Henderson wouldn't have to see each other again after today.

That hope sustained her during the short, silent ride to the Chalo River Dam. She'd seen the massive structure many times before, of course. During the years her father had served as fish and game warden for the state park that enclosed the reservoir, he'd taken her by boat and by car when he went to check water levels and shoot the breeze with the power plant operators.

And when the reservoir had been emptied ten years ago, leaving the dam naked and glistening in the sun, she'd attempted to capture its utilitarian starkness as well as the Anasazi ruins on film. Of course, she remembered with a wry twist of her lips, that was before her foolish infatuation with Jamie Chavez had blurred both her vision and her purpose.

She didn't have that problem now. Now she saw the curved structure through an artist's eye trained to recognize beauty in its most elemental state. The contrast of whitened concrete against reddish-yellow cliffs made her hands itch for a camera. The symmetry of the arch, with its gated spillways flanking each abutment, pleased her sense of proportion.

The air-conditioned chill of the administration building pleased her even more. Sydney took a moment for her eyes to adjust from dazzling sunlight to dim interior before accepting the mug Reece handed her.

"Thanks."

"You'd better save your thanks until you taste what's in it," he commented dryly. "My guys swear they can use this stuff to patch the dam if we run short of concrete."

The sludgelike coffee carried enough caffeine to make it worth the effort of swallowing.

"Speaking of patching," Sydney hinted broadly, "when do you plan to start?"

He shot her another of those sardonic looks, and gestured to a government-issue metal chair beside an equally nondescript desk. She carried her coffee over with her, careful to keep it away from the charts and clipboards precisely aligned on the desktop.

Tossing his hat aside, Henderson forked his fingers through his pelt of black hair before pulling out one of the clipboards. The tanned skin at the corners of his eyes crinkled with concentration as he skimmed an acetate status sheet filled with grease-pencil markings.

"The water passed the halfway mark just after 6:00 this morning."

Sydney attempted a quick mental calculation. The village nestled in an opening in the cliff face fifty feet or so above the riverbed. If the waters had receded halfway down the cliff face already, they'd reach the ruins when? Eight tomorrow morning? Nine?

Hell! There was a reason she'd routinely cut her science and math classes in college and now carried a really good calculator in her purse at all times. The problem was that at this particular moment both purse and calculator rested amid the wreckage of the Blazer.

"When can I expect to see the ruins?"

"If we don't get any more storms like last night's, the reservoir should empty down to the river level by noon tomorrow. The cave that contains the ruins is some fifty feet above the riverbed. I calculate the village will start to emerge at approximately 9:24."

"Nine twenty-four? Not 9:23, huh? I could probably use that extra minute."

He didn't appear to appreciate her feeble attempt at humor. "I'm an engineer. Precision ranks right up there with timeliness in our book. And safety." He leveled her a sardonic look. "Try not to drive off any more cliffs, Ms. Scott."

"Sydney," she reminded him, shrugging off the sarcasm as her mind whirled. Thinking of the exterior scenes she wanted to shoot this afternoon and the sequencing for tomorrow's all-important emergence, she only half absorbed Reece's deep voice.

"We've detected a stress fracture on the right lower quadrant of the dam's interior. Depending on my exterior damage assessment, we may have to blast some of the old section and pour new concrete. Check in with me each morning before you come out to the site, and I'll let you know the status and whether I want you in the restricted area."

That got her attention.

"Each morning?" she yelped. "What happened to your engineering precision here? I need a little more notice than that to plan my daily takes."

"Call me the night before, then. That's the best I can do until we complete the damage assessment."

"Okay, okay. Give me your number. My little black book with all my contacts is at the bottom of the gorge right now."

Along with all her working files. Thank goodness she always kept complete electronic records of her projects on her laptop, which she'd left back at the motel. She patted her pockets, searching for a pencil before borrowing one from the holder on the desk. Like all the others in the round holder, it was sharpened to a razor tip—another engineering quirk, she guessed.

"You can reach me at the office, on my mobile, or at the Lone Eagle Motel."

Sydney scribbled down the numbers as he reeled them off. "That's where we're staying, too."

"I know."

The dry response brought her head up.

"Chalo Canyon's a small town, Ms. Scott... Sydney. That's the only motel in town."

She was well aware of that fact. She was also aware, as well, of the slight chill in his voice. She had a good idea what had caused it.

"And?" she asked coolly.

His broad shoulders lifted in a shrug. "And people in small towns like to talk, even to strangers. I've been hearing about your return to the Chalo Canyon for several weeks now."

"About my departure from said canyon ten years ago, you mean?"

He leaned back, his long legs sprawled under the desk. The chair squeaked with his weight as he regarded her through eyes framed by ridiculously thick black lashes.

"That, too."

Sydney had come a long way from the hopelessly romantic nineteen-year-old. She wasn't running away this time, from Sebastian or Jamie or herself. Nor, she decided grimly, from this chief engineer.

"Listen, Mr. Henderson..."

"Reece."

"Listen, Reece. What happened ten years ago is, if you'll excuse the lame pun, water over the dam. Something I'd like very much to forget."

"Folks around here seem to want to remember it."

"That's their problem, not mine." She leaned forward, jabbing the air with the pencil to emphasize her point. "And even though it's none of your business, I'll tell you that the only reason I came back to Chalo Canyon is to capture the ruins on videotape. I started the project a decade ago. This time I intend to finish it."

He studied her through hooded eyes. "Why is this particular project so important to you that you'd spend ten years planning it?"

Sydney forced down the lump that tried to climb into her throat. Her father's death was too recent, the scar still too raw, to talk about it with strangers.

"I'm a documentarian," she said with a tight edge to her voice. "Like you, I take great pride in my work. By themselves, the ruins emerging from their long sleep make a good story. Supplemented with historical background material on the Anasazi and the legend of the Weeping Woman of Chalo Canyon, I can craft a good story into a great one."

She pushed to her feet.

"Now if you don't mind, I'd like to hitch a ride back to town. The rest of my crew is supposed to arrive around noon, and I want to be ready to roll as soon as they get here."

It was, Reece decided as he watched her drive off with one of his underlings, an impressive performance.

He might even have believed her if he hadn't been sitting front row, center stage when she made her grand entrance at the Lone Eagle Café some eight hours later.

Chapter 3

Like the clientele it catered to, the Lone Eagle Café made no pretensions to elegance. Most of its business came from locals, the rest from pleasure boaters and fishermen who passed through town on their way to or from excursions on the vast man-made lake behind the dam. Occasionally work crews hunkered in and made the motel and café their headquarters during visits to the hydroelectric plant powered by the Chalo River.

Reece had stayed at the motel during his initial site survey last winter and again during the preplanning phase of the dam's inspection and repair a few months ago. He'd returned three weeks ago to supervise the project itself. By now he pretty well knew the café's menu by heart, and had settled on the rib-eye steak and pinto beans as his standard fare.

The beef came from Sebastian Chavez's spread north

of town, or so he'd been told by the friendly, broad-hipped Lula Jenkins, who, along with her sister, Martha, co-owned and operated the Lone Eagle Motel and Café. The pinto beans, Lula had advised, were grown on a local farm irrigated by water from the Chalo River Reservoir.

"And if you want to keep on shoveling in these beans," she reminded Reece as she plunked his overflowing plate down in front of him, "you'd better see that you get that reservoir filled in time for the fall planting."

"Yes, ma'am."

"Folks hereabouts depend on that water. Depend on the revenues from boaters and fishermen, too."

"I know."

Inviting herself to join him, Lula eased her comfortable bulk into the chair opposite Reece's. Her heavy-lidded brown eyes, evidence of the Native American heritage shared by so many in this region, drilled him from across the green-and-white-checkered plastic tablecloth.

"How long will it take to restock the reservoir with fish after you boys get done messing with the dam?"

Reece's nostrils twitched at the tantalizing aroma rising from his steak. He hadn't eaten since his hurried breakfast of diced-ham-and-egg burritos, wolfed down during the drive out to the dam just after dawn this morning. Despite the rumbling in his stomach, however, he knew his dinner would have to wait a while longer. Lula's question wasn't an idle one. It echoed the worries of a small town that depended on the Chalo River Reservoir for its livelihood.

Reece had prepared detailed environmental- and economic-impact assessments as part of his prep work for the repair project. He'd also conducted a series of meetings with local business and property owners to walk concerned parties through the process, step by step. Slides and briefings didn't carry quite the same impact for the people involved as seeing their water supply disappear before their eyes, though.

As the nation's fifth-largest electric utility and the second-largest wholesale water supplier, the Bureau of Reclamation's network of dams and reservoirs generated more than forty billion kilowatt-hours of electricity and delivered over ten trillion gallons of water each year. One out of five farmers in the western states depended on this water for irrigation to produce their crops. Additionally, hundreds of thousands of sports fishermen and recreationists plied the man-made lakes behind the dams, contributing their share to the economic fabric of communities like Chalo Canyon.

Even more important, the dams harnessed rivers like the Salt and the Gila and the mighty Colorado, controlling the floods and the devastation they'd wrought over the centuries. Born and bred to the West, Reece had grown up with a healthy respect for a river's power. In college he'd double-majored in civil and hydroelectric engineering. After college he'd worked dam projects all over the world. His father's death and the itch to get back to the vast, rugged West where he'd grown to manhood had led to a position with the Bureau of Reclamation's Structural Analysis Group in Denver. The Chalo River inspection and repair project had brought him home to Arizona.

Patiently he addressed Lula's concerns about the project's impact on the serious business of pleasure boating and sports fishing. "My headquarters in Washington began coordinating this project more than a year ago with the U.S. Fish and Wildlife Service and the Arizona Fish and Game Department. The government facility at Willow Bend has doubled its rainbow trout output to resupply the reservoir. The state hatchery will restock channel catfish, black crappie, perch and striped bass. The take won't be as plentiful for a year or more after the lake refills, but it should still provide enough catch to bring in the sport fishermen."

"It better," Lula grumbled. "Things are lookin' pretty thin now, I can tell you. Martha said she doesn't have a single room reserved after your crew and Miss Fancy-Pants Scott's folks leave." The waitress shook her head. "Imagine her driving right off a cliff!"

Reece took a long pull on his beer while Lula rambled on about the accident. Fancy-Pants wasn't exactly how he'd categorize the woman he'd pulled out of a piñon tree this morning. Unless, of course, she wore something decidedly provocative under those baggy U.S. Army rejects.

An image of the leggy, tousle-haired brunette in lacy black bikini briefs flashed into his mind for an instant. Resolutely Reece pushed it out. What she wore or didn't wear under her fatigues was none of his business. His only concern was the safety of her and her crew during their filming around the dam site.

The same couldn't be said for everyone else in town. The imminent arrival of the filmmaker and her crew had dominated the conversation at the café and the town's only bar for weeks. Everyone had an opinion about why she'd come back, and most were only too willing to voice it. Clearly ready for another discourse on the prodigal's return, Lula flapped a hand at Reece.

"Go on, go on, eat that steak while it's still sizzlin'. I'm just keepin' you company while I'm waitin' for them Hollywood people. Did you know that boy with the Scott woman has rings through every part of him that moves, and a few that don't?"

Reece sawed into his steak, not particularly interested in a discussion of Zack Tyree's body parts. It took more than a disinterested grunt, however, to discourage the garrulous Lula.

"Martha says she sneaked a peek at him when she went in to change the bed linens this morning. Couldn't hardly miss him, really. He was prowling around buck naked, wearin' nothing but them rings."

Thankfully, the sound of the door opening sent his hostess swiveling around. A grin beamed across her broad face.

"Hey, Jamie! You're lookin' good, boy, as always."

Tanned, golden-haired Jamie Chavez ushered his wife into the café and guided her across the room to Reece's table.

"Hey, Lula. You're lookin' beautiful, as always." His smile shifted to include her customer. "How's the spill going, Henderson?"

Reece got to his feet, taking the hand Chavez offered in a firm grip.

"It's going," he replied easily. "Another hundred and fifty feet to river level. Nice to see you again, Mrs. Chavez."

The rail-thin redhead at Jamie's side smiled. "Please, call me Arlene. After all the hours you've spent out at the ranch, briefing Jamie and my father-in-law on the dam project, I think we can dispense with formalities."

She was even thinner than Reece remembered from his last visit. Her feathery auburn hair framed sunken cheekbones and hollowed eyes. Skillful makeup softened the stark angles of her face, and her natural elegance drew attention away from her gauntness, but Reece glimpsed the same desperate unhappiness in her shadowed eyes as he'd seen in his mother's not long ago.

Both women had learned to live with the fact that the man they loved had cheated on them. His mother found out about her husband's infidelity after his death. Jamie's transgression occurred during his engagement to Arlene, if the tales of ten years ago held any truth. Now that long-buried embarrassment had come back to haunt her.

Reece had to admit the green-eyed brunette he'd walked up a canyon wall this morning could certainly give this woman something to worry about. Sympathy for the worried wife tugged at him as Lula heaved herself to her feet.

"Did you two come in for dinner? I've got some prime rib-eye in the cooler that was wearin' the Chavez brand not too long ago. I laid in an extra supply for those Hollywood folks, but they said they'd eat light when they got back tonight, whatever 'light' means," she grumbled.

"Probably tofu and soybean salad," Jamie teased.

"Ha!" Lula hitched her apron on her ample hips. "If they're expectin' tofu and such, they're sure as hell not gonna find it at the Lone Eagle Café."

"Where are they?" Jamie asked casually.

Too casually, Reece thought. Arlene evidently thought so, too. She threw her husband a sharp glance.

"Well, they loaded up two vans and took off just after one," Lula told him. "Said they'd be back after the light went, though, so I expect them anytime. If they aren't gonna eat those steaks, I gotta do something with them. What do you say I throw two on the grill for you and the missus?"

Arlene shook her head. "No, thanks. We just stopped by to—"

"Sure," her husband interrupted genially. "Why not? Bring out two more of those beers, too."

"But, Jamie…"

"We don't have to get back to the ranch right away, darling. Mind if we join you, Henderson?"

Reece shrugged. "Of course not. Please, be my guest."

A tight-lipped Arlene slid into the chair he held out for her. She didn't want a steak. That much was obvious. From the nervous glances she darted at the front door every time it opened, it was also obvious she didn't want to be sitting at the Lone Eagle Café when the Hollywood folks, as Lula termed them, returned.

Reece reminded himself that neither Jamie Chavez, his wife, nor the woman who'd almost come between them were any of his business, but that didn't kill the little stab of pity he felt for Arlene when the door swung open twenty minutes later and Sydney trooped in with her crew.

They were certainly a colorful bunch, from the kid with the green hair and the be-ringed nostrils to the statuesque, ebony-skinned six-footer who toted camera bags over each shoulder and sported a turquoise T-shirt with Through a Lens Lightly emblazoned in glittering gold across her magnificent chest. The guy with the earphones draped around his neck like stethoscopes was obviously the soundman. The mousy little female beside him had to be the gofer no crew could operate without, Reece's included.

But it was the writer-director who drew every eye in the café. Reece's included.

She was laughing at something one of her crew had

said. The sound flowed across the room like rich, hot fudge. Her hair looked like chocolate fudge, too, shining and thick and brushed free of the dust and scraggly tangles that had snarled it this morning.

She still wore her boots and baggy fatigue pants. This time, however, she'd paired them with a short-sleeved black top in some clingy material that showed every line and curve of her upper body. The erotic image Reece had conjured up of her earlier popped instantly into his mind. To his disgust, he couldn't quash the startlingly erotic picture as easily as he had before.

He wasn't the only one whose thoughts had focused on Sydney. Arlene Chavez sat with both hands folded into fists in her lap, her lips white at the corners as she took in the director's laughing vitality. Her husband, too, had his eyes locked on the striking brunette.

"Well, well, little Syd's all grown-up."

Jamie's murmur was almost lost in the boisterous group's arrival. Reece caught it, though. So did Arlene. Her gaze wrenched away from the newcomers, and her face filled with such anguish that Reece's heart contracted.

Dammit! Couldn't Chavez see his wife's pain and insecurity?

Evidently not. The man's eyes lit with a gleam that was part predatory and wholly admiring. Tossing his paper napkin onto the table, Jamie rose and strolled forward to intercept the group.

"Sydney?"

"Yes?"

She turned with a look of inquiry that jolted into surprise. Surprise flowed almost instantly into a polite greeting.

"Hello, Jamie."

He took the hand she offered in both of his. "It's been a long time."

"Yes, it has." She freed her hand, eyeing him with the slanting assessment of a person who made her living in the visual arts. "You haven't changed much."

It could have been meant as a compliment or a condemnation. Jamie chose to grin and turn her words back on her.

"You have."

"I'm glad you recognize that fact."

"I heard you almost drove off a cliff last night."

She shook her head, half amused, half exasperated. "Things always did get around fast in this town."

"I'm just glad you weren't hurt." His grin faded. "I also heard your father died. I'm sorry, Syd. He was a good man."

From where Reece sat, it was impossible to miss the change that came over her. She seemed to soften around the edges. Her green eyes grew luminous, her full mouth curved with a genuine warmth.

"Yes, he was."

They shared a small silence, two people bound by the memory of someone they'd both known.

Arlene broke the moment. Rising abruptly with a jerky movement that rattled the glasses and cutlery on the table, she crossed the room to slip her hand into the crook of her husband's arm.

"Is this the famous Sydney Scott I've heard so much about? Why don't you introduce us, darling?"

"This is the one," Jamie replied with unruffled charm. "Arlene, meet Sydney. Syd, this is my wife, Arlene."

Reece wondered how the moviemaker would handle

the awkward situation. So did everyone else in the café. Lula had both elbows on the service window behind the counter, her brown eyes wide. A few of the other local patrons whispered and nudged and nodded in the direction of the threesome. Even the noisy crew Sydney had come in with picked up on the buzz and turned curious eyes on their boss.

To her credit she gave the other woman an easy smile. "I don't know about the famous part, but I am Sydney. It's a pleasure to meet you."

Arlene couldn't let it go there. With her arm still tucked in her husband's, she knifed right to the heart of the matter. "I understand you and my husband were once, shall we say, close friends."

A hush fell over the café. Sydney's ripple of laughter filled the void. "I made a fool of myself over him, you mean. I suppose most girls go through that gawky, hopelessly romantic stage. Thankfully we grow out of it sooner or later."

"Do we?"

"Well, I did, anyway." Her gaze flickered to the fingers Arlene had dug into Jamie's arm. She gentled her voice, as if understanding the woman's need for reassurance. "A long time ago."

Reece stiffened. That was exactly the wrong thing to say around a man like Jamie Chavez. Reece had only met the younger Chavez a few times, but he'd worked with enough men to recognize the type. Handsome, wealthy, restless, chafing a little at having to work with and for his father, despite the fact that he would inherit the vast Chavez ranching and timber empire someday.

That much had been apparent to Reece a few months ago, the night Sebastian Chavez had invited him out to the ranch for drinks and a discussion of the pending dam-repair project. Chavez doted on his only son. He'd displayed a wall of glass cases filled with Jamie's sports trophies and bragged about his keen competitive spirit in both school and business. The bighorn sheep and mountain cat trophies mounted on the den walls, all bagged by Jamie, also indicated someone who loved the thrill of the hunt.

And now a woman who admitted to having made a fool of herself over him laughingly claimed she'd grown out of the infatuation years ago. If Reece had been a betting man, he'd put money on the odds that Jamie would shake loose from his wife's hold…which he did. And that he'd make a move on Sydney…which he now tried to do.

"Not much changes around Chalo Canyon, Syd, even in ten years, but I'd be glad to take you up in my chopper and let you reacquaint yourself with the area. Maybe you can get some shots of the ruins from the air for your documentary."

"I don't think your father would appreciate that, Jamie. He specifically denied me and my crew access to the canyon rim through his land."

Disgusted, Reece lifted his beer. Nothing like telling the man that his daddy was the one calling the shots around here. Didn't she realize that was like waving a red flag in front of a young bull?

His arm froze with the bottle halfway to his mouth. Maybe she did. Maybe she knew exactly what she was doing.

Dammit, he'd wanted to believe her this morning when she'd said she'd come back to Chalo Canyon for one reason only. Now…

"I chopper my own aircraft," Jamie said with a tight smile. "I take up who I want, when I want, where I want."

"Thanks for the offer, but I don't need aerial shots. Or access through Chavez land. I've made other arrangements."

The wrenching heartbreak on Arlene's face as she listened to the byplay between her husband and the moviemaker brought Reece out of his chair. Her expression reminded him so much of his mother's anguish that dark February night. He was still telling himself he was a fool to get involved when he joined the small group.

"Speaking of arrangements, we agreed to get together tonight, remember?"

He kept the words casual, but the lazy glint in his eyes when he looked down at Sydney implied they'd agreed to get together to talk about more than arrangements. To reinforce the impression, Reece aimed a smile her way.

After the first, startled glance, Sydney picked up on his cue. "So we did. Shall we make it your room or mine?" she purred, sliding an arm around his waist.

Whoa! When the woman threw herself into a role, she pulled out all the stops. Reece had to clear his throat before he could push out an answer.

"Mine. I'll clean up while you grab something to eat with your crew."

"I'm not hungry. I just came in with the gang for the company. I'll go with you now. Arlene, maybe we'll get a chance to chat some other time. Jamie…"

Watched avidly by everyone in the café, she searched for a dignified exit line. Once again, Reece stepped into the breech.

"See you around, Chavez."

With a nod to her crew, Sydney preceded Reece out

of the café. Neither one of them spoke as they walked through the heat that was rapidly fading to a sweat-cooling seventy or so degrees as dusk turned the sky purple.

Their footsteps crunched on the gravel walkway. Bugs buzzed the glowing yellow bulbs that hung over the row of motel doors. Sydney halted in front of Number Six. Drawing in a long breath, she turned to face him.

"I don't want to sound ungrateful, but I really didn't need rescuing this time."

"What makes you think I stepped in to rescue you?"

"Then who…? Oh. Arlene?"

"Right. Arlene. She doesn't appear to share your confidence that what happened between you and Jamie is, how did you put it? Water over the dam?"

"I can't help what she believes." She hooked her thumbs in the waistband of her baggy pants, her movements stiff and defensive in the lamplight. "I came here to make a movie, and only to make a movie."

"A lot of people seem to believe otherwise."

"Tough. I can't avoid the past, but I'm certainly not going to let it get in my way."

"The past being Jamie Chavez, or his wife?"

Her chin angled. "Look, this isn't really any of your business. Let's just—"

She broke off, her glance darting past him. Behind him, Reece heard the sound of the café door banging shut.

"Oh, hell!"

It didn't take an Einstein to guess who had just walked out. After a short, pregnant pause, Sydney shot him a challenge.

"Okay, hotshot," she muttered, lifting her arms to lock

them around his neck. "You scripted this scene. We might as well act it out."

Reece would have had to be poured from reinforced concrete not to respond to the body pressed so seductively against his. As slender as Sydney was, she fit him perfectly in every spot that mattered...and at this point that was just about everywhere. Little sparks ignited where their knees brushed, their hips met, their chests touched.

"Let's make it look good," she whispered, rising up on tiptoe to brush her mouth to his.

Reece held out for all of ten seconds before he lost the short, fierce battle he waged with himself. Her mouth was too soft, too seductive, to ignore. Spanning her waist, he slid his hands around to the small of her back.

She curved inward at the pressure, and the sparks sizzling where their bodies touched burst into flames. Reece shifted, widening his stance, bringing her into the notch between his legs.

She drew back, gasping a little at the intimate contact. The glow from the yellow lightbulb illuminated her startled face. The thrill that zinged through Reece at the sight of her parted lips and flushed face annoyed the hell out of him...and sent a rush of heat straight to his gut.

"Are they still there?" he growled softly.

She dragged her gaze from his to peer around his shoulder. "Yes."

"Guess we'd better do a retake."

With a small smile he bent her backward over his arm.

Chapter 4

When Sydney came up for air, her coherent first thought was that Reece Henderson had chosen the wrong profession. If he performed like this on stage or film, he'd walk away with a fistful of Oscars and Emmys.

The second, far-more-disconcerting thought was that she'd forgotten he was acting about halfway through their bone-rattling kiss.

The crunch of car tires on gravel brought her thumping back to earth. She pushed out of Reece's arms, shaken to the toes of her scuffed boots, just in time to see a silver and maroon utility vehicle with the Chavez Ranch logo on the door pull out of the parking lot. Blowing a shaky breath, she turned back to her co-conspirator.

"That was quite a performance, Mr. Henderson. Let's hope it doesn't get back to your wife."

"I'm not married."

"Engaged? Not that I'm really interested, you understand, but I already have something of a reputation in this town. It would be nice to know what I'm adding to it."

He shoved a hand through his closely trimmed black hair. Sydney felt a little dart of wholly feminine satisfaction at the red that singed his cheeks. She wasn't the only one who'd put more than she planned into the kiss…or taken more out of it.

"No fiancée, no significant other, not even a dog," he replied shortly. "My job keeps me on the road too much for anything that requires a commitment."

Was that a warning? Sydney wondered. Well, she didn't need it. She didn't require anything from Reece Henderson except his cooperation for her documentary.

"Well, that's a relief," she replied dryly. "I don't think I've got room on my chest for another scarlet *A*."

His deliberate glance at the portion of her anatomy under discussion had Sydney battling the absurd urge to cross her arms. She never wore a bra…one, because she wasn't well-enough endowed to require support and two, because she didn't like any unnecessary constriction when she was working. Right now, though, she would gladly have traded a little constriction for the shield of a Maidenform. The tingling at the center of her breasts told her she was showing the effects of that stunning kiss. That, and the way Reece's gaze lingered on her chest.

How embarrassing! And ridiculous! She hadn't allowed any man to fluster her like this since—

Since Jamie.

The memory of her idiocy that long-ago summer acted like a bucket of cold water, fizzling out the shivery feeling left by Reece's mouth and hands and appraising glance. She slanted her head, studying his square chin and faintly disapproving eyes.

"When you stepped into the fray tonight and hinted at something more than a casual acquaintance between us, you obviously wanted to send Jamie Chavez a message. Just out of curiosity, why does it matter to you what either he or his wife thinks?"

His jaw squared. "Maybe I don't like to see a wife humiliated by her husband's interest in another woman."

The barb was directed at her as much as at Jamie. Sydney stiffened, but bit back a sharp reply. She refused to defend herself to him...or anyone else...again.

"And maybe it's because I've got a job to do here," he continued. "I made several trips to Chalo Canyon earlier this year to lay the groundwork and gain the cooperation of the locals, including the Chavez family."

"Sebastian Chavez being the most important and influential of those locals?"

"Exactly. Until he learned about your plans to film the ruins, he was willing to work with me to address the worries of the other ranchers and farmers and businessmen. Since then, he's become a major—"

"Pain in the butt?" Sydney supplied with syrupy sweetness.

"A major opponent of any delay."

"Then he doesn't have anything to worry about, does he? I'm as anxious to complete my project as you are yours. Speaking of which, are we still on schedule for 9:24 tomorrow?"

"Nine twenty-three," he corrected with a disconcerting glint in his blue eyes.

Good Lord! Was that a glimmer of amusement? The idea that Reece Henderson could laugh at himself threw

Sydney almost as much as his kiss had. What a contra-
dictory man he was, all disapproving and square-jawed
one moment, almost human and too damned attractive
for her peace of mind the next.

Good thing her work would keep her occupied from
dawn to dusk for the next two weeks. The last thing she
needed at this critical juncture was distraction. This project meant too much to her emotionally and financially to
jeopardize it with even a mild flirtation.

"I want to position my crew on the east rim just after
dawn," she said crisply. "We'll probably shoot most of
the day and into the evening, if the light holds. Any problems with that?"

"No. Just check in with me when you leave the area."

Nodding, she swung around to head back to the café.
She'd better remind Zack to curtail his night-owl TV
watching or it would take a stick of dynamite to roust
him before dawn tomorrow.

"Sydney…"

"Yes?"

He hesitated, then curled that wicked, wonderful
mouth into a real-live smile.

"Steer clear of falling rocks."

"I will."

She'd steer clear of falling rocks and former lovers and
too-handsome engineers. In fact, she swore silently as
she reached for the café's screened door, she'd go out of
her way to avoid any and all possible distractions until
she finished the shoot and shook the dust of Chalo Canyon from her heels forever.

Unfortunately, avoiding distractions and interruptions
was easier planned than done.

* * *

The predawn sky still wore a mantle of darkness sprinkled with stars when Sydney walked out of her room, laden with one of Tish's camera bags and a backpack filled with water bottles. She'd taken only a step toward the parked van when bright headlights stabbed through the quiet of the sleeping town.

Sydney glanced curiously at the vehicle as it pulled into the motel parking lot. She caught a brief glimpse of the silver Diamond-C logo on its side door before the utility vehicle squealed to a stop a few yards away. Her stomach knotted when she saw that the man at the wheel wasn't Jamie Chavez, but his father.

Okay, girl, she told herself bracingly. You knew this confrontation had to come sooner or later.

Yeah, herself answered, but we were hoping for later.

Come on! Get a grip here. You're not the same easy mark you were the last time you faced Sebastian Chavez.

At nineteen, she'd been shamed to her core by Jamie's father. At twenty-nine, Sydney had cradled her own father's hand while he died a slow, agonizing death. The experience put all else in perspective. For that reason she was able to greet Jamie's father with a calm nod.

"Hello, Sebastian."

He slammed the door of the utility, a tall man made aristocratic by fine-boned Hispanic features and rigidly erect carriage. The old man never bent, Jamie had once told Sydney with laughing chagrin. He'd break in two before he yielded so much as an inch of his land or his pride.

Or his son.

Even in the darkness, Sydney could see the disdain in his black eyes. The predawn breeze ruffled his silvery hair as he stared at her coldly.

"You've come back."

Sydney confirmed the obvious with a little nod of her head. "Yes."

"You're not welcome in Chalo Canyon."

"I didn't expect a welcome, Sebastian. Not from you."

Nor had she expected the virulent letters he'd written her financial backers when he learned of her proposed documentary. Chavez had done everything in his power to destroy her credibility, her reputation, and her project. Such hatred…or was it reawakened fear that she would take his son from him? Sydney had no patience with or sympathy for either.

"Did you drive into town this early just to make sure I knew I wasn't welcome?"

His head went back. Regal, scornful, he stared down his nose, taking in her ball cap, her ponytail, the worn navy blue sweatshirt she'd pulled on over her tank top to ward off the early-morning chill.

"I drove into town to tell you to stay away from my son."

Sydney tossed the backpack through the open rear doors of the van. It landed with a clunk beside neatly stowed boxes of equipment. She took considerably more care with Tish's camera bag. Only when it was properly stored and buffered on all sides did she face her old nemesis.

For a moment she toyed with the idea of telling Sebastian that his precious son had killed any feeling she'd had for him when he'd stood back and let his father rip into her that awful, mortifying night. She would cut off her right arm before she'd put herself in such a vulnerable position with Jamie or any other man again, but her pride wouldn't allow her to give Sebastian the satisfaction of knowing he'd gotten to her like that.

"I don't suppose it's occurred to you that both Jamie and I are past the age of allowing you to dictate our behavior?"

His nostrils flared. "You almost sabotaged his marriage to Arlene once. I won't let you do so again."

From what Sydney had seen of Jamie's marriage last night, it was coming apart at the seams without any help from her.

"Fine. You've delivered your warning. Now, if you'll excuse me, I have a crew to round up."

He leaned forward, his lean body quivering. "Don't try to drive through my land to get to the canyon. In case you've forgotten, we shoot trespassers in these parts."

Sydney drew back, shaken and, she was ashamed to admit, just a bit frightened by his intensity. Good God, had her silly infatuation spawned such hatred?

Her prickly pride gave way to a need to make peace. If anything, her father's death had taught her that life was too short, too precious, to squander on unhappiness or despair.

"I didn't come back to make trouble," she said quietly. "Only to make a documentary."

That didn't appear to appease him. Sydney tried again, her voice gentle.

"I won't drive through your lands, Sebastian. It took some doing, but I got permission to access the restricted area behind the dam. I'll shoot the emergence sequence from across the canyon with telephoto lenses."

His mouth twisted. "I know about your permits. I wouldn't…"

The sudden bang of the café's screen door cut off his

bitter words. A still-sleepy Zack joined them, his arms loaded with paper bags.

"Geez, Syd, you won't believe what Lula packed for our lunch. I told her to go light, just sandwiches and stuff, but she must have sliced up a side of beef for these— Oh." He blinked at the figure in the shadows. "Hey, dude, how're ya anyway?"

Sydney bit her lip at the sight of the sloppy, slouchy Zack of the green hair and pierced extremities jumbling brown bags to offer Sebastian a high five. The older man looked the younger up and down, curled his lip, spun on one heel and strode back to his vehicle.

Zack blinked in surprise. "Like, what crawled up his pants?"

"Never mind. Just load the lunches, will you? I'll roust Tish and the others. I want to get moving."

What she wanted was to get her crew in place. To position her cameras and lose herself in the past once again. She ached to feel that secret, soaring thrill as the mystical village slowly emerged from its decade-long sleep. She *needed* to feel it, needed to share the magic with her father a final time. Her heart thumping in anticipation, she strode back to the open doorways of the rooms beside hers.

Statuesque, six-foot Tish strolled out first, her ebony skin a dark shadow in the predawn. Slightly overweight and fastidious to the point of prissiness, Albert followed a moment later.

"Let's get this show on the road!" Sydney urged. "If our senior engineer's calculations are correct, we need to be in place by seven and have the cameras rolling by eight. Tish, are you ready? Albert? Katie?"

It took another ten minutes to locate the infrared lens

Tish had stashed under her bed for safekeeping and five more for Katie and Albert to load the sound console. They wouldn't synthesize sound tracks today, only record them, but Albert preferred to hear the input coming in over the four wireless mikes as he got it, which meant loading up every piece of his equipment every day.

Sydney didn't spare a thought to the physical labor it took to haul the equipment in and out of the motel. With a single camera lens costing upward of five to six thousand dollars, no professional would leave his gear sitting in a van all night, even in a sleepy little town like Chalo Canyon.

Faint streaks of purplish pink hazed the horizon by the time she had both crew and equipment loaded and ready to roll.

"Tish, you ride with me, and we'll talk about settings on the way to the canyon. Zack, you've got the keys to the van?"

"Got 'em." Her assistant ambled to the rented vehicle, his battery-operated Nike shoes flashing. "We'll be right behind you. Just don't drive off any more cliffs, dude-ess."

They made it to the barriers Reece's crew had erected across the canyon rim road just as the eastern sky had begun to glow a reddish gold. In a fever of impatience now, Sydney hustled her crew out of the vehicles and loaded them up for the trek to the vantage point she'd scouted out. As she edged her way around the narrow curve where she'd gone over the cliff, she shot a fond glance toward the piñon where she'd spent the previous night. Once beyond the narrow neck, her boots ate up the dirt track.

Albert was huffing and Zack complaining loudly by the time they reached the point opposite the sunken village. Quiet, mousy Kate went right to work, unpacking sound equipment, spare batteries, videotapes.

Zack flopped down on the ground, arms and legs spread. "Why did I ever throw my lot in with a documentarian?" he grumbled. "I could, like, go to work for Disney and just sit on my butt all day drawing cartoons."

Sydney paid no attention to his grousing. She'd worked with every person on this crew before and knew their strengths and weaknesses. Tish and Albert ranked right up there among the best in the business. Zack… Well, Zack was Zack.

"Okay," she said briskly, "let's go over the shooting script." She knew it almost by heart, but another review wouldn't hurt.

"We'll start with a few wide angles. Tish, as soon as you've got enough light, pan the canyon. I want to convey a sense of its size and scope. I'm also looking for contrasts—dark shadows on red sandstone, the round arch of the cave against the flat cliff face."

"You want contrasts, you'll get contrasts," Tish said confidently, tucking her copy of the shoot script into the pocket of her twill vest. With the loving care of a mother handling a newborn infant, she lifted a long, sausagelike lens out of its case.

"Albert, get me morning sounds. Lots of them. Birds, squirrels, the breeze in the trees. Lazy, sleepy, just coming to life. Let's try for a sense of the world greeting the dawn."

"What you want is your Brigadoon coming awake after its hundred-year sleep."

"Exactly. That's the mood I'm after. A slow awakening. A gentle rebirth. The village slowly emerging from the waters into the sun."

Excitement pulsed along Sydney's nerves, tripping little bursts of energy. This was what she did best. This was what she thrived on. Most people outside the film community thought a documentary simply recorded events as they unfolded. Few realized that a skilled director shaped and shaded the recording to put his or her own artistic interpretation on the footage.

"The next sequence will be the actual emergence. I want a wide-angle shot of the cliff face on camera one, medium close-ups of the village as it clears the water on camera two. As soon as we spot the tower, we'll go maximum zoom. I want to see the stones, the bricks, the empty windows, as they clear the water."

"Got it," Tish said calmly.

"Albert, can you drop one of the mikes to catch some water sounds? Waves lapping against rock, maybe, or a trickle of water running down stone? I know we planned to catch that later, but it would help set the mood…"

The soundman edged to the canyon rim and peered into the dimness below. "How far down is it to the water?"

"More than two hundred feet by now."

"We can try a fishing expedition, but I'm not guaranteeing anything," he said dubiously. "Katie, get that extra roll of cable, will you?"

While her crew set up, Sydney went about her own tasks with a sort of schizophrenic precision. The director in her consulted with Tish on camera placement, studied the light meters that recorded the glow of dawn, listened to the faint whistle of wind magnified through Albert's earphones. All the while her heart pounded and

her anxious eyes watched the water level on the opposite cliff face.

Gnawing on her lower lip, she paced the rim. The
water inched lower and lower. The sky behind her lightened to purple. The sun rose in a majestic golden ball,
painting the cliffs across the shrunken reservoir a rosy
pink. The water shaded to gray, then green.

"I'm panning the canyon now," Tish advised, her hand
sure and steady on the tripod's handle.

Sydney crowded as close to the camera operator as she
could without jostling either her or the equipment. Closing one eye, she followed the camera's tiny video screen
as Tish moved it in a slow sweep.

A lump formed right in the middle of her throat. The
vast panorama of Chalo Canyon waking to the dawn was
magnificent, even framed in a one-inch screen. Light
washed down the sandstone cliffs, painting them a rich
umber. The same morning sunshine outlined the sharp
stone projections and threw the recesses behind them
into even starker shadow. Above the cliffs, the sky blued.
Below, the waters retreated.

The sun rose higher, clearing the mountains behind
them. With agonizing slowness, the shadows on the cliffs
across the canyon separated. Distinct, black streaks appeared on the wall of stone.

"There they are," Tish murmured. "The smoke marks
left by the cook fires."

Sydney eased away from the camera, her heart pounding. Tish knew what to do. They'd talked about it, planned
it. She'd keep one camera trained on those black streaks,
follow them down, wait for the village below to appear.

It was close now, so close.

"I'd better change cassettes," Tish murmured. "I don't

want both cameras to run out at the same time. You'll skin me alive if I miss this."

Swiftly, Tish ejected the thirty-minute Betacam cassette in camera one and substituted a fresh videotape. She could have used a sixty-minute cassette, or even one that ran for two hours. Neither she nor Sydney wanted to exchange quantity for quality, however.

"Better pull out another battery, too," Sydney murmured to Katie.

The grip nodded and rooted in one of the cases for another spare. Then a quiet settled over the crew as they waited for the village to show itself.

Finally it appeared. First, a rounded arch aged by centuries of smoke. Then a shallow depression. The top of a stone tower. A square window in the stone.

"In close," Sydney whispered to Tish. "As close as you can get. Find me a face in that window."

Without taking her eye from the viewfinder, the camera operator smiled. "This *is* only a legend we're documenting, right, Syd?"

"All myths and legends spring from some aspect of real life," she murmured. "They're tied to the cycles of the season, or a woman's passion for her mate, or the birth of a child."

Sydney hugged her arms. This particular legend was tied to more than just the cycles of the season. It was tied to her youth, her coming of age. And to her father. Especially to her father.

Only when a cloud drifted across the sun and momentarily plunged the canyon into darkness again did she remember that the legend of the Weeping Woman of Chalo Canyon also had its roots in death.

Chapter 5

Sydney got in one glorious day and one moonlit night of shooting before a wall of black clouds rolled in. She awoke before dawn on Wednesday morning to the buzz of her travel alarm and the distant rumble of thunder.

Groping for the alarm, she hit the snooze button and buried her face in the pillow. A moment or two later, the significance of the sounds that had awakened her sunk in. She jerked her head up and stared at the curtained window.

"Oh, no!"

Throwing aside the blanket, she wove her way through stacks of equipment she and the crew had brought into the rooms last night for safekeeping. A quick yank untangled her sleepshirt enough to cover her hot-pink bikini panties. Semidecent, she parted the curtains and peeked outside.

Rain sheeted the window, blurring the darkness beyond. Dismayed, Sydney stared at the puddles of light made by the bulbs hanging above the motel doors. Suddenly a streak of lightning zapped out of the sky and lit everything in greenish-white light.

"Yikes!"

She jumped back and yanked the curtains shut in the foolish belief they would keep out the sizzling electricity. She'd seen enough of these high-desert storms in the years she'd lived in Chalo Canyon to have a healthy respect for them.

Scurrying away from the window, she switched on the bedside lamp and dug her schedule out of the canvas briefcase Zack had scrounged as a replacement for the one that now resided at the bottom of the gorge. With legs crossed under her, she studied the schedule.

The crew had arrived on Monday and got in some good footage around the canyon rim. Yesterday, they'd shot the emergence sequence and some good visuals of moonlight playing on the village.

Today, with the reservoir fully emptied, they were scheduled to hike down into the canyon and shoot some close-ins of the ruins. She'd already arranged for a team of locals to haul in the crates containing the ladders and pulleys her crew would need to get themselves and their equipment up to the cave.

Worrying her lower lip with her teeth, Sydney studied her schedule. She'd built in some slippage, but not much. She'd planned on eight good days of shooting. She could live with six. Between trips down to the ruins, she intended to tape interviews with selected local residents to add authenticity and local color to the legend.

And that was the easy part. After the actual shoot would come months of work in her L.A. studio, editing the tapes, synthesizing sound tracks, recording the scripted narrative, adding the titles and graphics that transformed raw footage into a stunning visual statement. If all went as planned, she would finish the first cut by the end of August and the fine cut by mid-September. PBS wanted to view the edited master tape by October fifteenth. Once approved, the documentary would broadcast in the spring, which allowed plenty of time to get it in the running for next year's Oscars.

Another nomination would go a long way toward helping her pay off the loan for her studio. Even more important, completing this project would fulfill her promise to her father. She'd put Chalo Canyon and her past behind her once and for all and get on with her life.

Sighing, Sydney slumped back against the rickety headboard. She missed her dad so much. She wasn't lonely, exactly. Her grief had dulled enough for her to accept his loss, and her various projects kept her too busy to indulge in long periods of introspection or sadness. But at moments like this, with the night still wrapping the world in darkness and rolling thunder threatening her with hours of enforced idleness, she felt the emptiness.

There'd been other men besides her father in her life, of course. But after Jamie Chavez, she'd remained wary. Cautious. In retrospect she probably owed Jamie a real debt of gratitude. He'd taught her a valuable lesson, so much so that she'd kept subsequent relationships light and unentangling. None of the men she'd dated over the years had tempted her into anything more than casual companionship.

Then again, none of them had kissed her the way Reece Henderson had.

The memory of those startling moments outside

her motel room that night slid into Sydney's mind and wouldn't slide out. To her surprise, a tight little flicker of desire ignited low in her belly.

Frowning, she willed it away. *Forget it, girl! He's not your type, not that you have a clue what your type is. Besides, he's convinced you've only come back to Chalo Canyon to wreak havoc among the natives.*

The reminder of the barely disguised disdain she'd glimpsed in Reece's eyes that night irritated her so much that she shot another glance at the clock. Almost six. He should be up by now.

Jamming the receiver to her ear, she punched in the number for Reece's room. The phone shrilled once, twice, three times. She'd just started to disconnect when he picked up.

"Henderson."

Sydney had to admit the man had a voice like cut velvet. Deep. Rich. Sexy smooth, with just enough of a Southwestern accent to hint at cowboys in old Stetsons and tight jeans. Briefly she wondered if he'd ever considered doing voice-overs to supplement his income. Probably not. She had no idea what engineers earned, but from the way his men jumped every time he opened his mouth, he must rank right up there at the top of the pay scale.

"Reece, it's Sydney."

"Yes?"

"It's raining."

There was a moment of dead silence.

"You called me at 5:46 a.m. to apprise me of that?"

Did the man always think so precisely, for heaven's sake?

"Were you asleep?"

"No, I was in the shower. Now, I'm soaking wet, buck

naked, and wondering what the hell you expect me to do about the fact that it's raining."

Sternly, Sydney suppressed a vivid mental image of Reece Henderson soaking wet and buck naked.

"I don't expect you to do anything except give me blanket authority to trek into the canyon when the rain stops."

"Call me when the weather clears. We'll talk about it then."

Her back teeth ground together. "Can't we compromise a little? I've hired a guide and some locals to haul in the ropes and ladders we'll need to get up to the ruins. I hate to waste the whole day if I don't have to. How about at least letting us drive to the access point to wait out the storm?"

"It's not just the rain in this vicinity we have to worry about," he pointed out. "It's been raining north of us, too. I don't want you or your crew caught by a flash flood."

"Neither do I," she assured him earnestly. "One disaster per project is my limit. We'll await your go-ahead before trekking into the canyon."

Another silence followed.

Sydney wasn't above wheedling and cajoling when the occasion demanded. She'd already learned, however, that Reece wasn't particularly wheedlable.

"All right. Call and speak with me personally before you go in."

"Thanks."

She hung up before he could add any further caveats. Dragging up her knees, she looped her arms around them and tried to detail the sights and sounds they would record when they got to the ruins. To her disgust her mind kept zinging back to the vivid and wholly erotic mental image of Reece Henderson's wet buns.

Four rooms away Reece dropped the phone into its cradle and headed back to the shower. He'd been awake for an hour, stretched out in bed, waiting for the lightning to pass before he showered and shaved, thinking about his crew, about the stress fracture, about the exterior-damage assessment he hoped to complete today.

Hell, who was he kidding? He'd spent most of the time trying not to think about Sydney.

He still couldn't quite believe he'd bent her over his arm that night and laid one on her like that. He hadn't experienced such a brainless, idiotic, caveman response to the feel of a woman's body pressed against his since... since...

Since never.

The unpalatable truth stared him in the face, and he didn't much like it. Granted, Sydney Scott could rouse a dead man with those flashing green eyes and supple curves, not to mention the round, neat bottom that had fit so enticingly in Reece's lap, but he'd met his share of enticing women in his time. Once, he'd even thought about marrying one. A brown-eyed Brazilian beauty with a shy smile and a degree in agriculture had kept him in South America long past the time required for the job that had taken him there. She'd shied away from a permanent commitment to a foreigner, however, and Reece had left Brazil with his heart surprisingly undented.

Even then, even with Elena, he'd never felt such a hard, tight slam of lust when he'd taken her in his arms. He'd wanted her, yes, but with a controlled passion, a measured need…totally unlike the urgency that knifed through him when Sydney plastered herself against his chest.

Frowning, Reece turned his face up to the tepid water. Of all the rowdy Henderson brothers, he'd always exercised the most self-discipline in his work, in his finances, in his personal habits. He enjoyed a good fight, sure, and had been known to down his share of brews with his brothers, although the last time any of them had gotten drunk, really, honest-to-goodness, falling down drunk, was just after Jake's high school graduation. All five of them, even eight-year-old Sam, had sneaked off to one of the line shacks with a couple of cases of beer to celebrate Jake's passage into manhood. Their father had found them the next morning and never said a word about their pasty faces and red-veined eyes.

At the thought of his father, Reece stiffened. He still couldn't think of Big John without a tight whip of anger. The fact that the old man had cheated on his wife was bad enough. Leaving those damned letters behind for her to find just when her grief had started to heal made his betrayal even worse.

Reece didn't have any use for a man who would betray his wife. Or for the woman who'd encourage him to do it…which brought his thoughts back full circle to Sydney.

Why had she gone along with Reece's clumsy attempt to save Arlene embarrassment? To discourage Jamie? Or dig the spur in deeper? Make him think he had a rival? Rouse his competitive instincts even more?

Looking back on it, Reece found himself wanting to believe her dry comment that it was all water over the dam. He'd supervised enough men and women over the years to trust his instincts about people, and his instincts were telling him to take Sydney at her word, to accept that she'd returned to Chalo Canyon to make a movie.

Or maybe he just wanted to believe her…because he wanted *her*.

Ducking his head under the pulsing stream, he soaped his scalp. Why didn't he just admit the woman had a mouth made for sin and leave it at that? He didn't have time for any more quixotic gestures or clumsy attempts to salvage anyone's pride, let alone for lusty little interludes with the delectable Ms. Scott.

Comfortable in a blue workshirt, jeans, sturdy boots and his trusty Stetson, he left his room twenty minutes later and joined the men hunched over mugs of coffee and platters of *huevos rancheros* in the restaurant. The accommodating Lula provided the crew with thermoses of steaming coffee to sustain them during the drive to the dam. Headlights on, windshield wipers swiping at the rain, the work vehicles formed a small caravan and headed out.

As they pulled out of the parking lot, the light glowing behind the curtains of Unit Six caught Reece's eye. Resolutely, he put Sydney Scott out of his mind.

The pounding rain had fizzled to foggy mist by the time Sydney and her crew began loading their equipment. They had most of it stowed when the guide she'd hired drove up in a pickup covered with more rust than paint.

A bubble of delight danced through her veins when Henry Three Pines stepped out of the vehicle. She remembered him from the times he and her father worked together—her dad as fish and game warden, Henry as headman of the Hopi clan whose lands bordered the Chalo River Reservoir. Sydney had talked to him again by phone a few months ago. He'd agreed to act as their guide and, she hoped, share some of the lore of the Anasazi who'd inhabited the region.

She had no idea how old he was. He'd seemed as ancient as the earth two decades ago. Now his immense dignity and the sheer visual magic of his weathered face, shadowed by a brown felt hat with rattlesnake skin band, called to the filmmaker in her.

"Henry! It's good to see you again."

"And you, Little Squirrel."

Sydney grinned at the nickname he'd given the pesky, curious, irrepressible nine-year-old who'd dogged his heels her first summer in Chalo Canyon.

His gnarled hands folded over hers. His black eyes spoke to the little knot of pain she carried just under her heart.

"I know you still sorrow for your father, but he lives on in spirit with the kachina."

As an outsider, Sydney made no claim to understanding the complicated and all-pervasive religious structure the Hopi had evolved over the centuries. She knew only that it answered the insecurities of a people living in a harsh environment. She still treasured the hand-carved wooden kachina doll Henry had presented her upon her departure from Chalo Canyon, and took comfort from the understanding in his seamed face.

"He is why you've come back," Henry said softly. "You wish to honor him with this film you make."

"Yes."

"It is good for a daughter to honor her father." His arthritic hands squeezed gently. "It is good for me to help her do so."

"Thank you."

His calm gaze took in the assembled crew. He greeted each of them with grave courtesy, awing even the still-sleepy Zack into a handshake instead of his customary high five.

"Hey, dude, er, Mr. Three Pines, er, sir."

"Call me Henry." He turned back to Sydney, his aged face unflappable. "I am told you hired men to deliver crates to the canyon."

"I did." Frowning, she swiped a look at her watch. "They should have been here by now."

"They do not come."

"What?"

"Sebastian Chavez has told them they must not aid you."

Her jaw sprang shut, effectively stopping a curse.

"If you wish," Henry said calmly, "I'll arrange for my grandsons to carry these crates down into the canyon. They've gone to Phoenix this morning to enroll at the university for the fall semester, but they return later this afternoon."

Swiftly Sydney reordered the shoot schedule. *If* the rain let up, and *if* Reece gave them permission to trek down into the canyon, they could concentrate on more background shots until Henry's grandsons arrived with the heavy equipment. Almost choking with disappointment that she'd have to wait to get into the ruins, she accepted Henry's offer.

With Zack driving the van, Sydney and Henry climbed into the replacement Blazer. This one, thank goodness, came equipped with automatic drive. She didn't even *want* to think about working a clutch on narrow, wet roads.

Denied direct access to the western rim through Sebastian Chavez's property, they had to drive a good twenty miles out of their way. Sydney seethed for a good part of the way over Sebastian's attempts to block her shoot.

Well, no amount of contrariness on his part was going to drive her away. Not this time.

They crossed the river via a bridge south of the dam, then headed north. A few miles later the asphalt road dwindled to an unimproved dirt track. By the time their small caravan reached the narrow path that wound down into the canyon, the rainy mist had begun to dissipate.

Sydney had just picked up her cell phone to check in with Reece when Tish jumped out of the van with an ecstatic shout.

"Omigod, look at that!"

The whole crew froze as the mists parted, revealing a perfect, shimmering rainbow. One end disappeared in the clouds to the east. The other touched down right above the distant cliffs that sheltered the ruins.

Tish dived back into the van, all six feet of her ablaze with excitement. Swooping up one of the video cameras, she darted toward the canyon rim.

With her own swan dive over the cliffs still fresh in her memory, Sydney hotfooted after the camera operator and grabbed the tail of her tan safari shirt. A swift tug yanked her back.

"Not so close to the edge."

The statuesque woman shuffled backward, her eye already glued to the view finder. "Katie! Get the fish-eye lens! No, no, the EF 15! Dammit, where's my tripod?"

"I've got it!" Zack yelled.

Whipping out the telescoping legs, he set the tripod up for her while Katie passed her the wide-angle lens.

Within mere seconds, Tish had the camera stabilized and trained on the shimmering rainbow.

Only then did Sydney notice Henry Three Pines standing apart from all the bustle, his gaze trained on the distant arc of color. A faint memory of ancient lore pinged in Sydney's mind, something about the spirits residing half the year in Hopi villages, then using rainbows as a bridge when they returned to their underground dwelling places for the rest of the year.

"Albert," she murmured. "Give me a hand mike and get ready for a take."

She approached slowly, respectfully. She wouldn't intrude if Henry wanted solitude, nor would she violate his religious beliefs by capturing his image on video. But if he wished to share the legend, she wanted it on tape.

"Will you speak to me of rainbows?" she asked softly.

He smiled, his face folding into a thousand tiny lines. "Yes, Squirrel, I will speak to you of rainbows."

She held her breath, mesmerized by his voice, by his tales of the spirits, of the elemental fusing of earth and sky. Her own spirits soared with the beauty of the moment.

The rainbow dissolved ten minutes later, leaving Sydney filled with the satisfaction of a good take. What started out as a dreary morning had just yielded an unexpected bonus. Now if only Reece Henderson would give them the okay to trek down into the canyon...

He did. Grudgingly. "Just keep the phone with you at all times."

"I will."

"Let me know when you leave the area."

She had to strain to hear him. The signal kept cutting

in and out. She'd better get Zack to dig out the extra battery pack.

"And watch out for snakes."

"Trust me, I'll definitely do that!"

On fire with anticipation, she snapped the cell phone shut, helped her crew load their essential supplies into backpacks and fell in line behind Henry as he picked his way down into the canyon.

The sun came out before they were halfway down. By the time they reached the canyon floor and the banks of the Chalo River, the mists had burned away, and the heat rose in shimmering waves from the limestone.

Throughout the descent, Sydney had the eerie sensation of climbing down to an ocean bottom. Her lively imagination couldn't help likening the experience to what the Israelites must have felt when Moses parted the Red Sea and led them into its cavernous depths.

After ten years underwater, the dark canyon walls gave off a dank smell. Silvery gray lichenlike plant forms made its sandstone slopes treacherous. The cottonwoods that had grown along the riverbank before the dam's construction still remained, their branches stripped of all green.

And it was quiet, unearthly still, without any birds or scurrying desert creatures or even the rustle of wind through the leaves. In fact, there were no leaves or greenery of any kind below the canyon rim. The trees had drowned long ago. Now, their blackened trunks and naked limbs were starkly silhouetted against the sky. The only sound that disturbed the stillness was the river's murmur.

Sweating and red-faced, the crew regrouped at the

riverbank. Tugging off his Australian bush cap, Albert waved it in front of his face to stir some air.

"How far to the cave?" he asked.

"Half a mile as the crow flies. A mile as the river flows."

The portly soundman gulped and beat the air with his hat.

"You okay?" Sydney asked quietly, concerned by the red flush heating his face.

"Yeah. Just a little out of shape."

"We'll rest here for a while."

"No, let's go on."

A professional down to the tips of his designer, ostrich-skin boots, Albert would keel over in a dead faint before he caused a schedule slip. That was one of the reasons Sydney had hired him for this project, and one of the reasons she watched him closely as Henry led them along the riverbed for another mile.

The narrow gorge gradually widened. The river also widened and became more shallow, bordered by a wide ledge of sandstone. Finally the small party stood below the cave that housed the cliff dwellings. Necks craned, they stared up at the wet, glistening ruins. Tish was the first one to break the silence.

"The Anasazi must have been part monkey to climb up and down these cliffs every day."

Sydney had researched the ancient peoples thoroughly as part of her prep work for the shoot. "They used wooden ladders that they could pull up if attacked," she explained. "Or they climbed down from the canyon rim using those hand- and footholds carved into the rock."

Tilting her head back, the camera operator squinted

at the shallow holes carved in the cliff face. A moment later she shook her head.

"You know how much I like working with you, Syd. I didn't object when you decked me out in netting and walked me into that room full of buzzing bees. I didn't like it, but I didn't object. And that time in Peru, when we had to dodge llama doo-doo all during the long climb up to Machu Picchu, did I complain?"

"Yes. Loudly."

"Only when the llama behind me took a nip at my tush," she protested. "But there's no way I'm crawling up that rock wall with all my equipment slung over my back."

"Not to worry," Sydney assured her. "Henry's grandsons will deliver the ropes and pulleys and aluminum ladders we had shipped in later this afternoon. Until they get here, we'll concentrate on exteriors."

She turned a smile at her father's friend.

"And Henry has agreed to tell us of the Ancient Ones who lived here. We'll use his voice for part of the back story narration. So let's get to it, troops. Time and sunlight wait for no man…or woman for that matter."

Within minutes the various members of her crew were hard at it. Sydney, whose background and training had her fingers itching for a camera, forced herself to oversee, to direct, to suggest.

This was the work she loved, and she got into it heart and soul. She thought nothing of squatting in the mud of the riverbank with Tish to study camera angles, climbing halfway up a tree to help Katie hang a mike, or sitting cross-legged beside Henry while an intense, earphoned Albert recorded the old man's tales.

Totally absorbed, Sydney spent the rest of the morning engaged in the craft of weaving dreams into reality. Just past noon the sound of a helicopter shattered the canyon's quiet and brought first Jamie Chavez, then a coldly furious Reece down on her.

Chapter 6

The helo came swooping up the canyon from the south.

Sydney heard it first through earphones. She'd borrowed a set from Albert to listen to the replay of Henry Three Pines's description of the Basket Makers, the earliest of the Ancient Ones to inhabit the canyon. Frowning, she hunched her shoulders and tried to tune out the muffled *whump-whump-whump*.

She couldn't, however, ignore the sudden gust of wind that stirred every piece of paper in the small camp, including her script, the video footage sheets and the loose-leaf pages of notes she'd made of the day's shoot. With a gasp of dismay, she tore off the earphones and lunged for the scattering papers. She managed to catch a handful or two, but the rest swirled and twirled and danced on the now-vicious downdraft. Shouting at Zack and Katie to help, she snatched them out of the air.

Consequently she greeted the pilot who climbed out of the maroon-and-silver helo with something less than civility.

"Thanks a lot! You almost sent my cue sheets and shoot notes flying to the four corners of the canyon."

Jamie blinked, thrown off stride for all of three or four seconds before his charm kicked into gear.

"Sorry 'bout that, Syd."

She planted both hands on her hips, glaring. The roguish grin that had melted her knees ten years ago now had zero effect on her. Less than zero.

"What do you want, Chavez?"

"It's not what *I* want."

His voice dropped, hinted at an intimacy that didn't exist. Never really existed, she knew with the unerring accuracy of twenty-twenty hindsight.

"It's what you want, Syd."

She wasn't in the mood for suggestive innuendoes. "In case I didn't make myself clear last night, I'm not interested in picking up where I left off ten years ago. I came back to Chalo Canyon to make a movie. *Only* to make a movie."

For Pete's sake, how many times did she have to repeat herself? She didn't need this distraction, and she certainly didn't need any more after-hours visits from Sebastian Chavez.

"I'm in the middle of a shoot here, Jamie, which you've just totally disrupted. Why don't you climb back into your little toy and take off?"

"Sure." Unruffled, he torqued his grin up another notch. "Do you want me to leave before or after I unload your crates of equipment?"

Her eyes narrowed. She suspected Sebastian had no

idea Jamie had taken it upon himself to haul in her equipment, and wouldn't like it when he found out about it. Tough! Father and son could work that one out between them. Right now, all she cared about was getting up to the ruins.

"After," she conceded.

"I thought so."

Eager to climb up to the cave, the entire crew pitched in to help Jamie unload two folding aluminum ladders and a large crate containing pulleys and winches. Stripped down to her sleeveless orange tank top and jeans, Sydney helped Zack muscle one ladder into position while Tish and Albert unfolded the other.

They were just about to attack the crates when Reece appeared. He strode along the wide sandstone ledge that formed the river's bank with a sure-footed agility that made a mockery of the far-slower pace Sydney and her crew had managed earlier.

Watching him approach, she felt her heart give a little bump against her ribs. To hell with engineering and building dams. Reece Henderson belonged in Hollywood. That rawhide-smooth voice of his, alone, would earn him a fortune. Paired with his broad shoulders and that lean-hipped, long-legged, outta-my-way stride, he was every woman's fantasy come to life.

Giving in to an impulse that was as natural to her as breathing, Sydney snatched up one of the video cams. She had no idea what she'd do with this footage, but it was too darned good to miss. Framing the man against the red sandstone cliffs, she zoomed in. Only then did she catch the tight-lipped expression on her subject's face.

Oh-oh. Evidently this wasn't a social visit. Sighing, she lowered the camera.

He joined their little group a moment later. The look he zinged from Jamie to her and back again set Sydney's teeth on edge. She would eat dirt before she defended herself against the scorn on Reece's face, or protest yet again that she had no interest in Jamie Chavez.

"I've been trying to reach you for the past hour," he said tightly. "Where the hell's your phone?"

Bristling, Sydney whipped it out of her pants pocket. "Right here."

Too late she remembered the weak battery. She'd gotten so caught up in the trek down the canyon that she'd forgotten to change it. Biting back a groan, she glanced down at the instrument. Sure enough, the liquid crystal display showed a blank face.

"The battery's dead." Feeling like ten kinds of a fool, she handed it to Zack with quiet instructions to dig out the spare battery.

"I'm sorry," she told Reece, bracing herself for the broadside she expected him to deliver. "I'll make sure that doesn't happen again."

"Do that," he snapped.

She ground her teeth, mentally counting to ten. "Why were you trying to contact me?"

"To verify the report I got of a helo touching down close to the ruins." His icy blue eyes sliced to Jamie, then back to Sydney. "I thought I'd made myself clear that all incursions into the restricted area behind the dam had to be coordinated with me."

She wasn't taking the fall for Jamie Chavez. Not this time.

"You did," she replied coolly. "Very clear."

With a careless shrug, Jamie stepped into the breach.

"I thought I'd just help Syd out by delivering her gear. She didn't know I was coming."

"Neither did your father," Reece said shortly.

Jamie stiffened. "You called him?"

"He called me."

From the tight angle to Jamie's jaw, Sydney knew she'd guessed right. Obviously he hadn't told his father about his little excursion to the canyon.

Or his wife, she'd bet.

Her mouth twisted. How in the world had she been so blind ten years ago? How had she let herself fall for a handsome face and a flashing smile, and never spared a thought to the person behind them? She owed Sebastian for opening her eyes. She really did. She'd try to remember that the next time he came down on her with both boots, she thought sardonically.

"Sorry, Henderson," Jamie said with a stiff edge to his voice. "I'm used to doing things my way around here."

"Not this time, Chavez. No more flights into the canyon without my approval."

Jamie's mouth set, and for a moment Sydney wondered if he'd grown enough backbone in the past ten years to challenge the flat order or the man who gave it.

Evidently not. He caved. Ungraciously.

"Yeah, well, I'll give you a call next time I decide to fly in and check on Syd."

"See that you do."

Without her quite knowing how or when it happened, the ground had shifted. The air between the two men took on a charged sensation. Reece made no overt move toward her, as he had at the café the other night, but Jamie seemed to take his challenge personally.

Sydney had the oddest sensation, as if she was an

old soup bone tossed down between two sleek, well-fed hounds. Neither one really wanted her, but neither was about to allow the other too near.

"You boys work this out between you," she said with a snap. "I've got work to do."

Jamie left in a whirl of rotor blades and a flash of sunlight on maroon and silver a few minutes later. If not for the downdraft produced by the helo, Sydney wouldn't have noticed his departure. She was on her knees, helping Zack and the others unpack the crate she'd had shipped in from L.A. Henry Three Pines sat in the shade of the canyon wall, conversing comfortably with Reece and drawing deep, satisfied drags on the cheroot the engineer had produced from his shirt pocket.

Zack had just pried open the lid of the first crate when the flush on Albert's face snagged Sydney's attention. She sat back on her heels, instantly contrite. He wasn't used to this blazing Arizona heat. If she'd been thinking of anything except getting up to the ruins, she would've seen how it affected him.

"Why don't you and Katie pack it in for the day?" she suggested casually. "We've got enough sound takes of the river and the canyon. No sense you two sitting around here just waiting for the wind to pick up. Leave me a recorder and a mike just in case, then take the Blazer back to town."

"Well…" Albert mopped his brow, reluctant but obviously considering the offer.

Sydney threw a look over her shoulder. "Maybe Reece will walk you out of the canyon. He knows the way. Hang loose, I'll ask him."

When she put the question to him, the engineer nodded his assent. "Sure."

He speared a look at the tangle of ropes and blocks in the scattered crates, started to say something, then rolled his shoulders in a quick shrug.

"Tell your man... Al, is it?"

"Albert."

"Tell Albert to gather his gear," he said curtly, still obviously less than pleased with her and her dead battery. "I want to get back to the dam."

"Yes, sir!" She flipped him the Hollywood version of a military salute and marched away with a stiff-kneed goose step.

Reece leaned against the cliff face, trying to hold on to his anger. He *wanted* to hold on to it. He'd been stewing ever since the call from Sebastian, and come to a near boil when he'd spotted Jamie Chavez laying his particular brand of charm on a sweat-streaked, tumble-haired, thoroughly seductive Sydney.

Calling himself a fool for almost believing her when she'd protested that she had no interest in Chavez, Jr., he'd wanted to let rip. Only the rigid self-control his brothers had delighted in putting to the test so many times over the years kept his anger tightly leashed.

He had to admit, though, that Sydney didn't seem particularly concerned whether Chavez stayed or left once he unloaded his cargo. She showed far more interest in the crates than in their deliverer, and didn't appear at all distressed by Reece's dictum barring Chavez from any further unauthorized intrusions into the restricted area behind the dam.

Was that part of her game? Was she still playing hard to get? Or did she really not care about Chavez?

The fact that Reece couldn't make up his mind one way or the other annoyed the hell out of him. He tended to see things in black and white. He admitted it. He preferred to keep business and personal matters neat, well-defined, precisely aligned.

Which was why the engineer in him shuddered as he watched Sydney and the green-haired kid pull a tangle of ropes and pulleys out of the crate and dump them carelessly on the ground.

"Funny," the kid—Zack—commented. "This contraption didn't look, you know, so complicated when the guy in L.A. demonstrated it." Huffing, he lifted a clanking block and pulley. "Or so heavy."

"Does it come with instructions?"

"I dunno."

Sydney bent over, delving into the crate for a set of instructions. In the process, she gave Reece a view of a slender, rounded backside that dried the saliva in his mouth and throat. A moment later she sat back down on her heels, dangling a length of rope in one hand. Frustration pulled her lips into a pout as she eyed the tangle of blocks and pulleys.

"I can take a camera apart and clean it faster than a Marine can field strip his M-16, but this stuff…"

She glanced from the ropes to Reece, calculating, debating. He saw what was coming and steeled himself against the reluctant appeal.

"I don't suppose you'd consider giving us the benefit of your expertise on this thing before you go?"

No. No way. He needed to get back to the dam. The computerized stress simulations should be coming off the Cray supercomputer in D.C. within the next hour. He'd already put a dent in his schedule by driving up here.

Ever after, Reece could never decide whether it was the unsightly tangle of rope in Sydney's hand or the sweat streak between her breasts that changed his mind. Somehow, he couldn't stand the thought of her and her crew wrestling with the heavy blocks in this heat...and making a mess of it. Sighing, he told Albert and the mousy gofer to hang loose for a few minutes, and strolled over to join the small group clustered around the crate.

"This 'thing,' as you call it, is one of the oldest machines invented by man."

Calmly, methodically, Reece helped lay the various pieces of the mechanism in orderly rows on the ground.

"Like the fulcrum and the lever, the pulley trades distance for force or force for distance."

Sydney shot the others a look. "Right. Distance for force."

His professional instincts roused now, Reece tried a more basic, textbook explanation.

"Essentially, all machines are force multipliers. Work equals force multiplied by the distance over which the force acts. Thus, by increasing the distance via a system of block and tackles like this, you increase the mechanical advantage—the ratio of the load-to-overcome versus the effort expended."

Her face arranged in suitably grave lines, Sydney nodded, but Reece couldn't miss the laughter dancing in her green eyes. His stomach muscles did a little force multiplying of their own.

Dammit! How could she tie him up in knots with a single, sparkling glance?

The reminder that she tied Chavez up in exactly the same way did little to loosen the knots. Thumbs hooked in the belt loops of his jeans, Reece scowled at the array of equipment.

"Unless you're planning to lift steel girders to reinforce the walls of some of those ruins, you've got four times what you'll need here. Block and tackles are only necessary for heavy loads."

Sydney and Tish turned accusing eyes on the be-ringed Zack. His skinny shoulders lifted in a defensive shrug.

"Like, I should know that?"

"Well, I guess more is better than not enough," Sydney said, bringing those dazzling green eyes back to Reece again. "If you'll just show us which end of the rope goes where, we'll take it from there."

He winced. Looked at his watch. Struggled valiantly against an overwhelming urge to see the job done right... and lost. With a resigned sigh, he unbuttoned his shirt and pulled it off. Folding it neatly, he laid it on a nearby rock.

"All right. I'll show you which end goes where."

Sydney didn't even notice that her lower jaw had dropped until Tish elbowed her in the ribs. Hard.

"Close your mouth, girl. You're sucking in gnats."

She was sucking in more than gnats. She was sucking in the sight of Reece Henderson's wide shoulders, rippling muscles and intriguingly concave belly with that little twirl of silky black hair just above the navel.

Oh, God! Where was her camera? Why couldn't she ever find extras who looked like this when she needed them? Would he let her capture him stripped to the waist like this on video?

The thought brought reality crashing down.

She hadn't put herself in hock, spent the past eight months lining up funding, and hired an outrageously expensive crew to document Reece Henderson's admittedly spectacular bod. She'd made a promise to her father, and to herself in his memory—a promise she intended to get to work on as soon as Reece finished doing whatever he was doing.

It didn't take him long. Ignoring the heavy wooden blocks, he tied two smaller pulleys to a bundle of hinged wooden struts, then looped a length of rope over his head and shoulders.

"I'll climb up to the ledge and drop a line for the bundle."

"I'll go with you," Sydney said quickly.

She beat him to the aluminum ladder by a second or two. She wasn't about to let anyone set foot in the ruins ahead of her. This was her dream, her and her father's. She'd waited ten years for this moment.

Her heart started pounding the instant she set her foot on the first rung. By the time she swung onto the ledge, it thundered in her ears.

She stood transfixed a few feet from the edge, afraid to move, almost afraid to breathe for fear the ruins would collapse or crumble or otherwise disintegrate before she could explore their secrets. The fear was irrational, she knew. These stone buildings and the people who occupied them had survived hundreds of years under Arizona's blistering sun. After the villagers abandoned their homes and the fields of maize, beans and squash they cultivated on the canyon rim, the deserted village had remained tucked away in this isolated cave for hundreds more. Even decades under water hadn't destroyed them.

Still, Sydney absorbed a sense of ephemeral beauty through every pore of her body. Perhaps the ruins seemed so fragile because they rose from the waters for such a short time, only to sink into oblivion once again when the reservoir filled. Caught up in their spell, she peered through patterns of sunlight on shadow. Above her arched the smoke-blackened roof of the cave. Ahead of her, so close she could touch it, stood a low wall. Hesitantly, tentatively, she reached out. The stone felt cool and dry under her fingertips.

"The cliff dwellers knew what they were doing."

Reece loomed behind her, speaking softly, sounding every bit as awed as Sydney by the ancient ruins.

"They built their homes in cliffs facing east or south to take advantage of solar energy," he murmured. "The morning sun warmed their homes in winter, and the cliffs protected them from the fierce heat of the afternoon sun in summer."

His fingers brushed the same wall Sydney's had.

"Look at this. They chinked the rocks together so tightly the structure held even though the water's eaten away at the mud mixed with straw they used for mortar."

The reverence in his voice brought a smile to her eyes. She didn't know a fulcrum from an inclined plane, but his appreciation for the Ancient Ones' architectural skills she could relate to. Feeling more in harmony with the man than at any other time in their brief acquaintance, she turned to share some of her newly gained knowledge.

The little movement trapped her between the stone wall and Reece's chest. Sydney breathed in his scent, a mixture of hot sun and clean, healthy sweat, and felt her heart do a quick little number against her ribs. If she rose up on tiptoe, if she stretched just a few inches, she could touch her mouth to his.

The idea of drawing him into another of those soul-shattering kisses drove everything, even the ruins, from her mind for a moment or two.

But only a moment or two.

She'd invested too much of herself and her dreams in this project to lose her perspective only seconds after setting foot on the ledge. Recalling herself with a start, she scooted to one side at the precise instant Reece moved the other way, looking every bit as relieved as she at the near miss. With brisk efficiency, he dropped the rope line over the ledge, hauled up the bundle of wooden supports, and set about rigging a simple pulley.

A shout to Tish signaled that the mechanism—correction, the force multiplier—was operational. Following Reece's instructions, the camera operator and Zack attached a case of equipment.

Resolutely Sydney kept her back turned as Reece hauled up the first load. No sense risking another mouth full of gnats by admiring the way the light played over the sweat glistening on his back, or dwelling on the poetry of his lean, muscled torso in motion.

In less than ten minutes, both her reduced crew and their equipment had gained the cave. Eager to get to work, Zack and Tish dug into the packs.

When Reece dusted his hands on his jeans and prepared to leave, common courtesy dictated that Sydney thank him for his efforts. She even offered to buy him dinner later at the Lone Eagle Café in exchange for his help.

"Some other time, maybe." He swung onto the ladder. "If the data I requested comes in this afternoon, I'll be putting in some long, late nights."

"Sure. See you around, then."

As brush-offs went, it was relatively benign. Nothing

like the humiliation Sydney had experienced at Jamie Chavez's hands ten years ago.

Yet for some reason, Reece Henderson's rugged features and casual dismissal of her offer disrupted her thoughts far more than they should have in the hours that followed.

Chapter 7

Sebastian didn't confront his son about his flight into the canyon until the following afternoon. He wanted to remain calm and approach the matter of Sydney Scott rationally, but his distress went too deep…and his fear. Five minutes into the discussion, his cheekbones were singed with red.

"I won't have it!"

He stood ramrod straight, facing his son across the oak trestle table that served as his desk.

"This woman almost destroyed all your plans and dreams ten years ago. You can't allow her to do so again. *I* can't allow it."

"My plans and dreams?" As stiff and unyielding as his father, Jamie gave a huff of derision. "Your plans, you mean. For me. For Arlene. For the convenient joining of your lands with my wife's."

Sebastian reared back, stung. "I wanted only your happiness. That's all I've ever wanted. Since the day your mother…"

His throat worked. Even after all these years, he couldn't speak of his young wife's treachery without tasting bitter gall.

"Since the day your mother went away, I've lived my life for you."

Jamie blew out a long breath. Despite their occasional arguments, neither father nor son ever denied the bond between them. As his belligerence drained, however, guilt took its place. He felt so damned suffocated by his father's all-consuming love, so trapped.

"Yes, I know you have."

Like a hawk, his father moved in to take advantage of his weakening. "Sydney Scott came back to Chalo Canyon to take her revenge on us. You can't trust her."

"No, Dad. *You* can't trust her, any more than you've trusted any woman since Mother walked out on us."

Sebastian gave a hiss of denial, but they both knew it was true. Jamie had heard the story so often, from so many of the ranch hands and residents of Chalo Canyon, that it no longer had the power to sting.

Young, giddy Marianne Chavez had dealt her husband's pride a mortal blow when she'd run off with another man, leaving behind only a few scribbled lines and her five-month-old infant. Since that day, the old man had focused all his devotion, all his ambition, all his burning intensity on his son.

"Whether I trust Sydney or not isn't the only issue at stake here," Sebastian said fiercely. "What if this movie she wants to make garners national attention? She'll focus attention on the ruins. The historical preservationists will get involved. They'll stir up the Hopi, try to save the village, maybe block the refill of the reservoir. Where will that leave us? We use that water for irrigation. The people in town depend on income from pleasure boaters and sportsmen."

"I know, Dad, I know."

"Then why in God's name did you help her by flying her equipment into the canyon yesterday?"

Jamie had his own reasons for choppering into the canyon, but not ones he intended to share with the old man.

"Because your ploy to sabotage her shoot by scaring off the men she'd hired didn't work. I heard that Henry Three Pines intended to press his grandsons into service. I figured the sooner she got her gear and finished her shoot, the sooner she'd leave. That's what you really want, isn't it? For her to leave?"

"I…"

Sebastian hesitated, his black eyes strangely blank for a moment. Only then did Jamie notice the faint blue tinge to his father's lips. His heart jumped. For all their differences, for all he longed to throw off the burden of the old man's constant attention at times, he couldn't imagine a world without his father. Lunging around the edge of the trestle table, he grasped his father's arm.

"Dad? Are you okay?"

Sebastian gave a little shake, as if to throw off his momentary blankness, and lifted a hand to cover Jamie's. The strength of the older man's grip calmed the younger's galloping fears.

"I'm fine. Just worried about the harm this woman can cause you and Arlene. Your wife loves you, Son, with all her heart. That's a gift more precious than gold."

The suffocating feeling returned. Sooner or later, Jamie thought grimly, he was going to drown in all this love.

"I know."

Clawlike, the old man's fingers dug into his. "Promise me you won't go into the canyon again."

Strain put harsh lines in his aristocratic face. Sebastian looked old and tired…and almost frightened.

"I promise," Jamie said quietly.

"Good. Now go find your wife. I'm in the mood for a stiff bourbon and some charming company before dinner."

His heart swelling with pride, Sebastian watched his offspring stride to the door. James Sebastian Chavez was a good man, a son to be proud of. Sebastian had worked diligently over the years to stamp out every trace of his mother. She still surfaced in Jamie's rare flashes of temper or occasional urge to kick over the traces, but not as much of late. The boy had finally started to settle down, taken over more of the ranch and timber-harvesting operations.

Then Sydney Scott had returned to remind Jamie of his youth…and Sebastian of his past.

Gripping the back of his chair, he fought the memories that rose in his mind. Of his laughing young wife. Of his early struggles to provide her the luxuries she craved. Of his joy and her profound disgust when she learned she was pregnant. Of that last ride into Chalo Canyon when she'd been petulant and arguing and Sebastian had been cajoling, begging her as much as his stubborn pride would allow, to reconsider her decision to leave him.

No! He squeezed his eyes shut. He wouldn't remember that time, or the dark, bleak days that followed. She'd given him a son. If nothing else, Marianne had at least given him a son.

In his heart of hearts, Sebastian prayed constantly that Arlene would give Jamie a child. Unlike Marianne, Arlene wanted children. Even more, she wanted to please her husband. She loved him so desperately, starved herself to stay thin, spent exorbitant amounts each time she drove to Scottsdale to shop or have her hair done.

He would talk to Arlene, Sebastian decided. Maybe suggest she see a doctor. It was time, past time, she conceived. The problem, if there was one, had to be on her side, since Sebastian quietly paid a substantial allowance every month to the child Jamie had fathered even before he'd dallied with Sydney Scott.

Damn the woman, he thought again, remembering that near disaster of ten years ago. Damn her for opening the Pandora's box of the past.

Damn the woman!

Arlene dragged a brush through her feathery auburn hair, preparing to join her husband and father-in-law for dinner. With every stroke of the bristles, her thoughts kept returning to Sydney Scott. Damn her for tantalizing Jamie with visions of a world different from Chalo Canyon…and of a woman far different from his wife.

Dropping the brush, she stared into the gilded tri-fold mirror she'd imported from Italy with Sebastian's blessing. Her father-in-law had encouraged her to redecorate, urged her and Jamie to make the addition to the thick-walled adobe ranch house their home.

Now she knew that Jamie considered the luxurious wing a prison.

Her heart aching, Arlene examined her sculpted chin

and pronounced cheekbones from three different angles. She didn't see the hollowed indentations or skin stretched skeletal tight, only the tiny pads in her upper lids. With a trembling finger, she stroked a little fatty fold. Despite her best efforts, it hadn't disappeared with fasting or facial exercise. She'd have to see a plastic surgeon in Phoenix or Scottsdale. She'd call tomorrow and make an appointment for next week. No, she'd wait until Sydney Scott left Chalo Canyon.

Damn the woman!

Ten miles away Reece unknowingly echoed the sentiments of Sebastian and his daughter-in-law. Like a persistent itch that couldn't be reached to scratch, Sydney irritated his thoughts.

Why couldn't he get the woman out of his mind?

He propped a boot on the low parapet that followed the crest of his dam. He'd come up to get some air, take a break before he and his team finished the revised cost estimates he'd promised his boss. Yet his wayward thoughts insisted on drifting to the crew at the ruins. Or more specifically, to the woman who directed them.

He ought to be calculating cubic yards of concrete, additional man-hours, the added economic impact to the surrounding area if the repairs took longer than originally anticipated. He let his gaze roam the now-empty chasm behind the massive concrete dam. At this point Reece couldn't say with any certainty when the reservoir would fill again. After two exhaustive days of e-mails, conference calls and sometimes heated discussions, his boss had decided to crunch the data and construct yet another 3-D finite element model. Since the modified repair program Reece was recommending would run some five million dollars more than originally budgeted for, he could understand Mike's reluctance to rush into it. At this rate, though, the actual repair work would take three years instead of three weeks.

Tomorrow he'd have to meet with a coalition of agricultural, environmental, recreational, Native American and business leaders to explain the added delay before a final decision.

Tonight…

Tonight. He kept wondering how the shoot was going, whether Sydney and her crew had any problems with the pulleys he'd rigged, whether he'd bump into her at the Lone Eagle Café later.

He hadn't seen her since yesterday, had only spoken to her briefly this morning when she'd called for clearance. Yet he couldn't shake the lingering image of her dancing green eyes when he'd tried to explain the rudimentary laws of physics, or his nagging regret that he'd turned down her offer of dinner last night. The more he thought about it, the more regret spiraled into lust. Hard on the heels of that lust came a twist of self-disgust when he remembered his spike of raw jealousy as he'd spotted Jamie Chavez oozing charm all over Sydney yesterday morning.

His boot hit the concrete.

What *was* it with this woman? How had she managed to get under his skin like this, as irritating as a cactus-pear rash and twice as annoying?

With a last glance up canyon, he headed back for the administration building and another bout with Westergaard's added-mass formula for computing incompressible and compressible fluid elements. That, at least, he could comprehend.

* * *

Happily unaware that she was the object of so much intense conjecture and irritation, Sydney loaded her crew and her equipment just as dusk dropped a veil of darkness over the canyon depths.

She hummed contentedly for most of the circuitous drive back to town. They'd had a good day, six full hours of sunlight. Even then, they'd needed artificial lighting for the interior shots. Trailing long, snaking cables, she and Zack and Katie had positioned the lights while a stooped-over Tish clambered through low doorways to pan interiors, even climbing down into a circular stone pit that had once served as a ceremonial kiva. Henry had provided some excellent narration on the secret rites held in the pit, accessible only from a small hole in the roof. She couldn't wait to get back to the motel to review the day's footage and listen to the tapes.

Her only disappointment was that the wind hadn't cooperated. It had gusted for a half hour or so this afternoon, then died without producing the eerie wail she wanted so much to catch on tape. Oh, well, what they had so far with the emergence sequence and the rainbow and today's shoot was good. Darn good!

Once at the motel, Albert pleaded weariness and went back to his room. Zack and Katie disappeared in the Blazer, heading for the nearest McDonald's, thirty-seven miles away.

Sydney and Tish settled in to go over the day's rushes. Changing into comfortable shorts and T-shirts, they left the door propped open to catch the night breeze and sat cross-legged on the floor of Sydney's room. Together they ran through the day's take, playing and replaying the tapes, recording information about the footage, making special note of those frames that caught the best contrast of light and shadow. Sydney would later transfer the information in her log onto her laptop computer. The computerized version made for easy reference when she began editing the raw material into a visual statement.

This was one of the most critical phases of a shoot. Each night she had to step out of her role as concept designer and director and look at what she'd actually shot, as opposed to what she'd intended to shoot. The two were often quite different. If she didn't capture the mood, the feeling she'd been seeking, she'd have to reshoot or alter her approach or perhaps rethink the statement she wanted to make.

"There! Hold it there!" She leaned closer to the video cassette player to copy a stop number. "I want to freeze that shot of the tower and use it as backdrop when we begin the tale of the Weeping Woman."

"Who's doing the narration?" Tish inquired as she jotted the stop number in her own log.

"I've got an actor lined up to read the script when we get back to L.A., but…"

"But what?"

Sydney tapped her pencil against her knee. "But I'm trying to think of a way to talk Reece Henderson into reading the script for me. He's got just the voice I want, all smooth rawhide and rough velvet."

The camera operator snorted. "If I wasn't married to a man who never lets me forget what a good thing I've got, I'd surely to goodness be trying to get Reece Henderson to do more than read to me."

"He's not interested in anything more."

"How do you know?"

"I offered to buy him dinner," Sydney admitted with a wry grin. "He turned me down flat."

"Turned you down? Uh-oh. That means he's either A, engaged…B, married…C, gay…or D, in love with his grandmother."

"According to him, it's not A or B, and from the kiss he laid on me the other night, I'm pretty sure it's not C. I can't speak to D, though."

"For the record," the rawhide and velvet voice drawled from the door, "it's E…none of the above."

Tish's head whipped around. Sydney merely groaned and closed her eyes.

"Tell me it's not him," she begged the other woman.

"Sorry, Syd, no can do." The camera operator's rich contralto vibrated with laughter. "Hello, Reece. Care to come in and join the discussion?"

"Not particularly. I just stopped by to tell your boss that you're clear to shoot tomorrow."

Tish elbowed her in the ribs. "Hear that, Syd?"

"Yes." She unscrewed her eyes enough to shoot her friend a glare before untangling her legs to push up from the green shag carpet.

"And to take her up on her offer," Reece added casually. "If it still stands?"

Sydney almost hit the shag again. Mortified by her clumsiness, she finally managed to get to her feet. The sight of Reece in the doorway, his black hair ruffled by the wind and those blue eyes glinting with amusement didn't exactly help restore her composure.

"Uh, yeah, I guess so."

Oh, that was brilliant! Telling herself to get a grip, she plastered on a wide smile.

"Yes, of course the offer still stands. When did you

want to do it? Have dinner," she added immediately, but not fast enough to head off Tish's snicker.

Those awesome shoulders lifted in a shrug. "Have you already eaten?"

Sydney looked at him blankly. If asked, she could have recited the exact sequence of today's shoot, tossed off the precise amount of video and sound tape recorded to date, and even estimated the cost per minute of what they'd done so far to within a few dollars. But mundane matters like food took a moment to recall.

"No, she hasn't," Tish supplied, unfolding her long legs to rise gracefully to her feet. "She put me to work as soon as we got back to the motel. Now that I think about it, she skipped lunch, too."

"You haven't had dinner yet, either," Sydney pointed out to her too-helpful friend, still thrown off balance by Reece's unexpected appearance but recovering fast. "Why don't we all go?"

"No, thanks. I'm not used to climbing up and down cliffs without llamas nipping at my tush to keep me moving. I'm going to take a long, slow soak, then go over a few more of these reels."

Scooping up three of the minicassettes, she brushed by Reece with a wave of her red-tipped fingernails.

"Llamas?" he inquired.

"It's a long story." Locking her door behind her, Sydney slipped the key into her shorts pocket. "Where would you like to dine, the Lone Eagle Café or the Gas n' Git? Zack tells me the gas station has a tolerable selection of day-old doughnuts and hot dogs smothered in onions and Hormel chili."

"You choose. I'm easy."

Easy wasn't the adjective Sydney would have picked

to describe Reece Henderson. Hard-assed had come to mind after their curt exchange of faxes a few weeks ago. Hard-edged was how she'd thought of him after he'd rescued her from her piñon tree. And yesterday he'd gone all professorial on her when he delivered his little lecture on fulcrums and trading distance for force or whatever.

Then there was that other aspect of his personality, the one that had prompted him to step into an awkward situation a few nights ago to spare Arlene any more embarrassment. And the curious quirk of character that had resulted in a mind-shattering kiss.

Sydney certainly wouldn't mind exploring that particular side of his personality just a bit more. She didn't want to do it at the Lone Eagle Café, though, with Lula Jenkins and the rest of the café's patrons listening to every word. Her disastrous affair with Jamie Chavez had provided the town with enough fodder for gossip to last the previous decade. She didn't want to fuel another ten years' worth.

"Let's hit the Gas n' Git," she suggested, as much to test Reece's resolve as her own. "We'll get our dinner in a bag and have a picnic. I know a great place not too far out of town to watch the stars."

Watching stars wasn't exactly what was on Reece's mind when he turned the Jeep off the road some miles south of town. With the scent of chili and onions teasing his nostrils, he steered the vehicle along a rutted dirt track. Low hanging pines swished their branches against the Jeep's roof.

He still couldn't quite believe he'd given in to the crazy impulse to take her up on her offer of dinner. He wouldn't have even stopped at her room on his way to the café, much less skulked outside her door like a hopeful peeping Tom, if he hadn't heard his name mentioned.

Hell, he wouldn't have stopped even then if he hadn't caught a flash of Sydney's slim, shapely legs stretched out on the pea-green shag carpet…the same bare legs that now tantalized Reece's senses almost as much as the onions and chili.

He'd never considered himself a leg man. He certainly couldn't claim to be a connoisseur like his older brother, Evan. Seeing Sydney in something other than her baggy fatigue pants gave him a new appreciation of Evan's particular fancy, however.

"It's not much farther," she said, breaking into his silent contemplation of her shapely limbs. "Less than a mile. I think."

"You think?"

"It's been a while since I've been out here," she murmured absently. "Ten years, at least."

Which begged the question, Reece thought sardonically, of who she'd watched the stars with the last time. Was she taking him to one of her old trysting places?

The idea that Sydney had driven out to this isolated spot with Jamie Chavez and had ended up rolling around in the back seat shaved the edge right off Reece's concentration. The left front tire dropped into a rut, jouncing him and Sydney and their dinner.

She didn't comment on his driving skills, or lack thereof. With one hand braced against the dash and the other wrapped around the cardboard carryout box containing their dinner, she strained forward. Anticipation shimmered through the body detailed so precisely by that thin T-shirt tucked into thigh-riding shorts.

"Listen! There it is!" She swiveled, her face alive with

eagerness in the scant moonlight filtering through the pines. "Can you hear it?"

Straining, Reece picked up a faint roar. "If you mean the river, I can."

"Not the river. The waterfall."

As soon as the Jeep cleared the trees and rolled to a stop a prudent distance from the river's edge, Sydney sprang out. Leaving Reece and the chili dogs behind, she scrambled up on a flat ledge. Hands shoved in the back pockets of her shorts, she drank in the vista of a tumbling, opalescent waterfall.

The falls weren't the most impressive Reece had ever seen. Having spent most of his adult life on the world's riverways, he'd viewed such spectacular spills as Canada's Churchill Falls and the spot on the border between Argentina and Brazil where the Iguacu River plunged almost three hundred feet over a two-mile-wide escarpment. This narrow fall couldn't be more than a twenty-five or thirty-foot drop, but the utter delight on Sydney's face told him she saw it with the eye of an artist, not a hydrologist.

He joined her on the ledge, almost as unsettled by the way her enchantment affected him as by his irritation of a few moments ago. The thought of her driving out here with Chavez still went down hard.

He might even have simply spent an hour downing cold chili dogs and taken her home if she hadn't turned to him at that moment, her eyes luminous in the moonlight.

"This was one of our special spots," she said softly. "Mine and my father's. Almost as special as the ruins. Since those were underwater most of the time, we'd come here when he wanted to fish or just talk."

"You came here with your dad?"

She nodded. "He was the fish and game warden at the state park while I was growing up. He…"

She swallowed, then tried a smile to hide the other emotions that flickered across her face.

"He died a few months ago."

Reece knew he was in trouble then. Big trouble. He forgot his earlier suspicions. Forgot that he didn't have time for any complications in his life right now. The urge to comfort this woman gripped him and wouldn't let go.

He lifted a hand to stroke her cheek. He kept the touch gentle, soft. "I'm sorry."

Her smile got ragged at the edges. "Me, too. He was a good man. He loved the outdoors, and respected the natural order of things. You…you would have liked him."

As soon as she said it, Sydney knew the reverse was true as well. Her father would have liked Reece, would have admired his chosen profession. He'd often spoken of the utility of dams, of the way they harnessed nature's excesses so that man and river could peacefully coexist without the constant threat of floods or droughts.

But it wasn't the thought of her dad's approval that turned her head and brought her lips against Reece's palm. It was the warmth of his skin, the gentleness of his touch. That and the shivery delight that coursed through her at the contact.

He used his thumb to tip her head back, and the look in his eyes sharpened her delight into a spear of need so strong Sydney shook with it.

A frown feathered his brows. "Cold?"

"No. Yes." Another shiver rippled down her spine. "I don't know."

"The chili dogs might warm you up." His thumb traced her jawline, her lower lip. "Or I could."

"You choose," she whispered, echoing his earlier words to her. "I'm easy."

Chapter 8

As soon as she heard herself, Sydney winced.

Of all the stupid, idiotic, ill-chosen replies! She'd only been playing Reece's words back to him, mimicking his earlier suggestion that she choose their dinner locale, but in this particular situation the attribute "easy" carried a meaning she hadn't intended.

It also conjured up some instant, unpleasant memories. That was only one of the labels Sebastian had hung on her the awful night he'd found her in his son's arms. Chagrined that the memory could still sting, Sydney back-pedaled, hard and fast.

"I know you've been filled in on every detail of my sordid past, but I didn't mean that as an invitation to anything more than a kiss."

"I didn't take it as anything more."

His thumb was at it again, soothing, stroking, distracting. She saw herself reflected in his eyes before they filled with a disturbing gleam.

"Maybe I can change your mind."

"You think?"

"A guy can only try," he murmured.

Sydney stood unmoving under the kiss, determined not to repeat her mistake of ten years ago. She'd tumbled into love…or thought she had…with a charming rogue, and let him distract her the last time she'd tried to film the ruins. She refused to let that happen again.

Maybe she should have thought of that before she'd invited Reece for a moonlit picnic at the falls. And maybe she'd wanted him to kiss her again, his mouth warm and hard on hers, his lips wickedly wonderful. But that insidious want did *not* mean she was going to fall into his bed when they returned to the motel, or invite him into hers.

She knew she had to make that clear when he lifted his head, his eyes at once questioning and rueful at her lack of response.

"I haven't changed my mind," she said quietly.

"Okay." His thumb made one more pass over her bottom lip before he dropped his hand. "Let's eat."

Surprised at his easy capitulation, Sydney watched him make his way back to the Jeep to retrieve their dinner. She hadn't expected him to give in that readily, and couldn't quite suppress an irrational pique that he had.

Telling herself to stop acting like a total jerk, she folded her legs under her, sank down onto the rock shelf and waited for him to join her.

Reece kept his demeanor nonchalant as he returned with the soggy brown bag. Beneath that casual expression, however, frustration ate at him like fire ants at a picnic. It had taken everything he had and then some to walk away from Sydney a few moments ago. His body still ached with wanting her.

She didn't want him, though. She'd made that clear enough. Obviously he'd misread her signals, inferred more from her suggestion to drive out and watch the stars than she'd intended. Even worse, he'd let himself dwell far too much on that kiss the other night. She'd been playing to an audience then, he reminded himself with a twist of his lips. They both had.

Unfortunately, the reminder did nothing to relieve the ache in his lower body. As a result he made no objection when she swiped the last of the chili from a corner of her mouth, tossed her paper napkin and the empty beer cans into the cardboard carrier, and suggested they head back to the motel.

The conversation on the return trip flowed a good deal less freely than it had during the drive out. Reece didn't try to force it. Between the spicy chili and his irritatingly persistent desire for Sydney, both of which seemed to have settled like a lump in his gut, he had plenty to think about. Her annoyed exclamation when they turned into the motel parking lot gave him something altogether different to focus on.

"For Pete's sake!"

Reece slanted her a quick look. "What?"

"One of the crew must have been in my room. They left the door ajar."

Sure enough, a slice of light spilled from Unit Six. Frowning, Reece pulled into the empty space in front of the open door.

"Who on your crew has a key to your room?"

"Everyone. We use it as sort of an on-site studio. We

keep the master logs and the video cassette players in there."

Along with a lot of other expensive equipment, Sydney thought with a slash of worry. Extra strobes. Lenses in fitted cases. Spare batteries and digital sound units. She always upped her theft insurance when she went on-site, but a possible delay in the shooting schedule due to stolen equipment bothered her more than the idea that someone might have broken into her room. She was halfway to the door when Reece caught her arm.

"Stay here," he ordered quietly. "Let me check it out first."

Sydney considered herself a feminist and thoroughly competent in any number of ways, but respected the inarguable differences between the sexes. She had no problem at all with letting a tough, well-muscled male nudge her bedroom door open, flip on the lights and do a quick check before she ventured inside.

"You'd better get in here," he called.

Her heart pounding, she stepped through the door. She barely got a foot over the threshold before she froze. Shock constricted her veins, made each beat of her heart an agony. A low, animal cry rose in her throat.

"No!"

Cassettes littered the bed and the floor. Empty cassettes. Someone had ripped their guts out. Yard after yard of shiny brown tape formed a tangled mound in the middle of the green shag carpet.

Shattered, Sydney dropped down on her knees beside the mound. Her trembling fingers reached out, caught the end of a piece of videotape. It came free of the pile, less than a foot in length. Swallowing, she dug her hand into the tangled mass and grabbed a fistful. Loose ends fluttered like ribbons.

Three days work…destroyed. She'd lost the all important, once-in-a-decade emergence sequence. The rainbow footage. The first view of the glistening ruins. The interiors.

She wanted to cry. She would have…if she hadn't used up a lifetime supply of tears during the months of Pop's illness. Now she could only close her fist over those tattered bits of videotape and squeeze until the knuckles showed white.

"Sydney, I'm sorry."

Reece came down on one knee beside her. Concern darkened his eyes. Anger etched deep grooves on either side of his mouth.

"Did you make any backups?"

It took a moment before she could speak. Her throat worked, forcing out the words.

"Of course. But they're working copies, not good enough to print from."

"I see." He eyed the tangled mess in her hand. "Any chance you can splice it together?"

"The person who did this made sure he didn't leave enough for me to salvage."

"He?"

"Sebastian," she hissed, fury slicing through her dismay.

Wave after wave of hot anger spilled into her. Scalding, raging, a conflagration that consumed her. Her hand shook so badly the ends of the tape danced.

"Sebastian told me I wasn't welcome here, that he wanted me gone, but I never thought he'd stoop to something this…this vicious!"

"We don't know for sure he did it."

"I know," she said savagely.

She looked so wild, so fierce...so damned *hurt*...that the need to comfort her grabbed Reece right by the throat again.

Before he could give in to that need, she surged to her feet. The air around her almost vibrated with the force of her anger.

"I'll check with the others on my crew. Maybe they saw something."

"Good idea," Reece said, reaching for the phone. "While you do that, I'll call the sheriff."

The group that gathered outside Sydney's room over the next half hour included not only her crew and Deputy Sheriff Joe Martinez, but Martha Jenkins, proprietor of the Lone Eagle Motel, her sister, Lula, and several of Reece's engineers and construction workers, drawn by the noise and the flashing strobe lights.

No one, it turned out, had seen or heard anything. But Tish, to her boss's profound relief, reminded Sydney that she'd taken a handful of cassettes to her room. She had the all-important emergence sequence reels and a few of the exterior shots in her possession.

Sydney pounced on them like a hen would a missing chick. "Thank God!"

Clutching the cassettes to her chest, she thought furiously. She could reshoot everything else except the rainbow...*if* Reece gave her unlimited access to the ruins and *if* the rains held off and *if* she worked herself and her crew dawn to dusk for the next six days straight.

She'd have to fly back to Chalo Canyon after the reservoir refilled to shoot the exteriors across the water. If that didn't fit with Tish's schedule, she could shoot that footage herself. That would push her deadline for finishing the first cut up several weeks, and not give her as much time as she'd wanted for the fine cut, but she might still make her October viewing with PBS.

Her eyes narrowed with grim determination. She could do it! She had to do it!

She'd invested all her personal resources, everything she had left after her father's hospital and funeral bills in this project and in her new studio. If pressed, she could give up the studio and try to recoup some of the outlay for all that expensive equipment, but she'd staked more than money on this documentary. She'd made a promise to her father and put her professional reputation on the line with her backers. She wouldn't allow anyone to stop her. Anyone!

She swept the small crowd, saw Reece talking to the deputy sheriff. The same man had taken her statement about the Blazer she'd sent to the bottom of the gorge. His brows had climbed when he'd unfolded his rangy frame from the sheriff's vehicle and seen who waited for him.

Sydney had told him what she could about tonight's incident, but the deputy had aimed more questions at Reece than at her. Probably because Reece had checked the door and windows for signs of forced entry. He was the one who found the jimmied lock on the bathroom window, prevented the others from entering her room and generally kept his cool while Sydney had come so close to losing hers.

Reece had understood her fury, though. Those moments inside the room when they'd knelt knee-to-knee on the floor, she'd heard the sympathy in his voice, seen the outrage on his face. If she was another kind of woman, if this was a different time or place, she could easily have leaned into him, howled out her anger and frustration, drawn from his strength. She'd hidden her feelings for so long, though. Been strong for herself and for her father.

Now…

Now more than ever she had to stick to the decision she'd made back there at the falls. She couldn't let Reece distract her, couldn't give in to this crazy urge to lock the door on the shambles in her room and lose herself and her worries in his arms for a few hours.

"Guess I have all I need here," the deputy said a few moments later, flipping his notebook shut. "I dusted the bathroom window and cassettes for prints. We'll match them against the samples you and your crew gave us, Ms. Scott. In the meantime, you might want to move your things into another room. Martha, you got one available?"

The motel proprietress huffed. "Until that reservoir fills up again, Joe, we've got more empties than I want to think about. I'll go get a key."

"We never had a break-in before," her sister added, her black eyes lively. "You sure do generate your share of excitement round these parts, girl."

The dry observation was accompanied with such a sympathetic hug that the perpetrator of all this excitement could only smile.

"Not by choice, Lula."

She edged past the café owner to speak privately to the deputy. "When do you plan to interview Sebastian Chavez?"

Martinez knuckled his straw sheriff's hat to the back of his head, clearly not looking forward to the prospect of asking the county's most powerful landowner to account for his whereabouts tonight.

"I'll drive out to the Chavez place first thing in the morning."

"Let me know what he has to say."

"Yes, ma'am. In the meantime, I need you to come up with an estimated value of the destroyed property."

Frustration added its bite to Sydney's still-simmering anger. In dollars and cents, the actual value wouldn't run to more than the cost of a dozen replacement cassettes. In lost time and footage, the figure could easily reach five figures.

"I will."

He pulled his hat down onto his forehead, tipped it politely. "Ms. Scott. Reece."

"Get your logs," she told her crew as the squad car pulled out of the parking lot. "We'll do a damage assessment and work out a new shoot schedule as soon as I get the key to another room."

Reece opted to wait beside Sydney until Martha returned.

"You okay?" he asked quietly while the others dispersed.

"Yes." She blew out a breath, still raw, still tense, but no longer shaking with fury. "I'll have to hustle to make up the lost footage."

He got the message. She was going to be busy from here on out. Even more to the point, she wanted unlimited access to the area behind the dam. Unfortunately Reece couldn't grant it.

"I should have a decision on my recommended repairs to the dam by tomorrow," he told her, hoping it was true. "I'll let you know as soon as I can how long you've got to shoot. In the meantime, press ahead."

"Thanks."

Her eyes were solemn, bereft of the dancing light that made them sparkle like sunlight refracted through green quartz. He hated leaving her like this. Hated the idea that someone had gained such easy access to her room. Wondered how the hell her safety had become his personal responsibility since the morning he'd pulled her from that piñon tree.

The memory of her near tragedy curled his hands into fists…and sent a sudden, icy chill into his chest. He went still, thinking back, seeing in his mind once more the hairpin turn, the rain-softened shoulder, the slab of sandstone that had tumbled into the road.

He needed to go back, check that site again before he voiced any suspicions or raised more doubts. In the meantime…

Martha's bustling return broke into his racing thoughts. Reece had time for only a final touch, a brief caution. His hand came up, tucked a wayward strand of mink-colored hair behind her ear. His knuckles brushed her cheek.

"Be careful out there."

"I will."

He waited while the two women inspected Units Twelve and Fourteen.

Sydney opted for Twelve, then bade him good-night. To her continuing consternation, his touch lingered on her skin long after she'd moved her things into her new room.

Dawn hadn't yet broken when Sydney stood at the bathroom sink the next morning, already outfitted in her working uniform of high-topped canvas boots, fatigue pants and a ruby-red stretch top layered with a sweater that would tie loosely around her hips when the sun rose.

She'd drawn her hair back, pulling the tail through the back of her ballcap to keep it out of her face. All she needed was moisturizer to protect her skin and she was ready to start over.

She slathered it on, her busy fingers slowing when they reached the spot on her cheek Reece had touched last night. For a big man, his touch was surprisingly gentle.

Regret flowed, sharp and stinging, before she shrugged it aside. She had work to do!

One by one her crew dragged out of their rooms and began ferrying equipment to the van and the Blazer. They had the vehicles almost loaded when Henry Three Pines drove up in his rusted pickup. Sydney didn't really need the services of a guide any longer. By now, she knew every rock and twist in the path leading into the canyon. When she'd hinted as much to Henry yesterday, however, he merely smiled and said he wished to honor his old friend's memory by aiding his daughter in her quest.

This morning it appeared he wished to do more than honor a memory or merely act as guide. Reaching into the truck, he lifted out a rifle and tucked it in the crook of his arm.

A sleepy-eyed Zack came awake fast, dancing back a step when he spotted the weapon. "Whoa, dude! Is that thing, like, loaded?"

"Why would I carry it if it wasn't?"

"You, er, haven't forgotten how to handle it, have you?"

Henry's seamed face folded into a smile at the folly of youth. "Some things a boy must learn and a man never forgets."

"If you say so," Zack conceded doubtfully, edging around the barrel to dump his load in the van.

Sydney, too, made a cautious circuit of the gleaming gun barrel. She hadn't yet succumbed to the stereotypical L.A. resident's predilection for powerful cars and even more powerful personal handguns.

"What is this?" she asked Henry. "Why are you armed?"

"Reece called me last night and told me what happened. He and I agreed we must remain wary until the one who destroyed your film is caught."

She didn't bother to point out that she was using videotape, not film. Such distinctions meant nothing to people outside the industry.

"Remaining wary is one thing, having you ride shotgun is another. I'm not sure about this, Henry."

"You look to your film," he replied with unruffled calm. "Reece and I will look to you."

Sydney wasn't sure she wanted to be "looked to," even by this longtime friend. The placid expression in Henry's black eyes told her it was a waste of time to argue, however, and time was her most precious commodity right now. The eastern sky already showed the first purple streaks of dawn. She wanted to be in place at the ruins to catch the full sun when it broke over the eastern rim.

She'd talk to Reece later, she decided, make sure he understood that she wanted in on any further decisions regarding her or her crew. Right now, though, she had to get her team ready to roll.

Long fingers of sunlight and shadow slanted across the canyon rim when Reece pulled up at the switchback turn where Sydney's vehicle had parted company with the road. His men had removed the slab of tumbled limestone blocking the road and added a temporary metal guardrail to keep vehicles a safe distance from the shoulder. The road was passable again, but it wasn't the makeshift repairs that interested Reece.

His eyes grim and intent, he climbed the striated cliff that edged the road. It took a few moments to find the scar left when the smaller projection had broken free. As yet unweathered by wind or rain, the slash showed pale white against the salmon color of the cliffs.

Reece fingered the scar, followed it up one side, down the other. He wasn't sure what he was looking for, but he sure as hell knew when he found it.

His jaw tightening, he traced the small gouges. They could have been made by a falling rock hitting against the surface. Or by a chisel or crowbar positioned at precisely the right angle to pry loose a slab of stone and send it tumbling to the road below.

He studied them for long moments before climbing down to the road. Back at the Jeep, he pulled out his cell phone, put in a call to the county offices and settled down to wait for Joe Martinez.

The deputy took almost an hour to arrive at the scene. In the interim, Reece received two calls from his on-site engineer and placed one to his boss. The Bureau of Reclamation's supercomputer had kicked out the latest analysis using the revised data Reece had provided after his visual inspection of the exterior. The powers-that-be didn't feel they warranted a modification to the fix as currently designed and contracted for.

"We've spent most of the night going over the specifications and design," his boss said wearily when Reece got him on the phone. "The specifications that you helped draft, I might point out."

"Those were done using computer-generated models and X-ray scans made by underwater divers. My gut now tells me these stress fractures run deeper than we're seeing."

"The revised data you sent us doesn't support that gut feel. We need to move on this project, Reece. The heavier-than-expected rainfall this summer has elevated water levels all along the Colorado River System. We've got to get this dam up and fully operational again before the next flood season."

"You're not telling me anything I don't know here, Mike."

His long-suffering supervisor vented some of his own frustration. "I'm taking all the flak I can handle on this project, Reece. Every day the dam is out of service is costing the government megabucks in lost power generation and water income. I can't justify additional delays without something more specific than your intestinal rumblings."

It was an old dilemma, one Reece had struggled with since he'd joined the Bureau of Reclamation. Whenever a dam went down, disrupting power and water supply, pressure mounted hourly to get it back in service.

Still, safety was and always had been the first consideration. Reece had worked with Mike long enough to know he'd go toe-to-toe with the Bureau's commissioner, the secretary of the interior, even the president himself if he had the facts and figures to support him.

That Reece hadn't been able to supply those facts or figures churned like acid in his stomach.

"All right," he conceded reluctantly. "I'll notify the contractors to proceed. But I reserve the right to halt work if I find anything at the core that worries me."

"Of course. We want this done, but we want it done right."

Reece flipped the phone shut and tucked it in his shirt pocket. The need to get back to the dam pulled at him. He had to go over the blasting schedule a final time, make sure the subcontractors were ready to roll with the hundreds of cubic yards of cement needed for the repairs, brief the civic leaders in the area…including Sebastian Chavez.

The thought of Chavez kept Reece sitting right where he was. Was the old man behind the destruction of Sydney's videotapes? Had he made those chisel marks in the limestone? *Were* they chisel marks?

Chapter 9

"I don't know," Joe Martinez muttered when he finally arrived at the site of Sydney's near slide into oblivion. Squatting on his heels, he fingered the marks in the limestone. "Could be cuts. Could be gouges made by falling rocks."

"Can you test the surface of the stone for metal traces?"

Martinez pushed his hat forward to scratch the back of his head. "I'll have to check with our crime-scene technical unit, but I doubt they've got that kind of sophisticated equipment. We might be able to send samples to the State Forensics Lab. Depending on their workload, it could take weeks to get an answer."

Reece had expected that answer. "Maybe I can speed things up a little. I worked a mine-flooding problem with a metallurgist on the governor's Science and Advisory

Board a few years ago. She has access to a scanning and transmission electron microscope that would pick up even microstructural traces of metal. Maybe I can talk her into taking a look at this rock."

"Sounds good to me."

"The piece that broke off…or was pried off…is still lying in the middle of the road. If you can get one of your men to haul it down to the Arizona Geological Survey Center in Tucson, I'll call ahead to let Dr. Kingsley know it's on the way."

"Consider it done."

Martinez rose, dusting his hands on his pants. His boots clattered on stone as he inched his way back down to the road. Once on level land, his black eyes rested thoughtfully on Reece.

"Are you thinking the same person who slashed Ms. Scott's tapes last night might have tried to keep her from making them in the first place?"

"The possibility occurred to me. Did you talk to Sebastian Chavez this morning?"

"I talked to both him and his son. Mr. Chavez had dinner at home with his son and daughter-in-law last night, then put in some late hours in his office."

"Anyone see him during those hours?"

"Jamie didn't. He was out in one of the barns with a sick horse most of the night. Mrs. Chavez… Arlene… said she saw the lights on in Sebastian's office when she went up to bed."

"So none of them really has an alibi."

"As yet," Martinez pointed out, "none of them needs one. We matched the prints I lifted from the bathroom window to Martha Jenkins, and those on the videocassettes to Ms. Scott and her camera operator. We have no witnesses and no evidence that one of the Chavez family perpetrated the vandalism."

"Just Sydney's gut feel," Reece muttered, unamused by the irony.

Martinez hitched up his holster and slid into the driver's seat of his dust-streaked vehicle. "I'll see that rock gets to Tucson this afternoon. In the meantime, you might advise Ms. Scott to keep her eyes open."

"I already have."

Reece would do more than just offer advice. Between them, he and Henry Three Pines would do their damnedest to make sure she didn't meet with any more unexpected accidents. He'd talked to the Hopi headman at some length last night, learned more about what happened ten years ago. That debacle had cost Sydney her pride and her father his job. Reece intended to see that it didn't now cost her her life.

His overdeveloped sense of responsibility had kicked in again, big-time. His brothers would have recognized the signs immediately. The slashing frown. The white-knuckled grip on the steering wheel when he climbed into the Jeep. The square angle of his jaw. Only Reece knew that responsibility had gotten all mixed up with something that went deeper than mere attraction, zinged right past lust, and smacked up against want. Or need. Or whatever the hell it was that twisted around inside him whenever he thought about Sydney.

Putting the Jeep into reverse, he made a cautious three-point turn and headed back along the rim road. The deep gorge, empty of the waters that had filled it for the past ten years, stretched for miles on his right. Red cliffs crowded the road on the left. Reece kept a careful eye on the twists and turns, but his mind stayed fixed on Sydney and those gouges in the stone.

He'd talk to her tonight at the motel, he decided. Tell her about the marks, about his talk with Henry and Joe Martinez. His stomach tightened at the thought of the hurt and fear that might come with this latest threat.

As if Reece needed anything else to add to the tension building in him more with each passing hour, storm clouds started piling up just after two that afternoon.

He didn't see them until he walked out of the administration building with the prime contractor, who planned to start blasting tomorrow. The moment they stepped outside, the wind whipped at the rolled schematic in the contractor's hand.

"The front's coming in from the north," he observed, eyeing the bank of black clouds. "Hope it blows through without dumping too much rain in the mountains, or we'll have to work around a gully-washer tomorrow."

"I hope so, too," Reece muttered.

Automatically he leaned over the parapet to check the floodgates. Newer dams were constructed with floating, roller-type caissons that moved up and down to control the water flow. On older structures like this one, the gates were simple up-and-down mechanisms.

They now stood fully open, as they had since the reservoir began draining. Reece's men could drop them quickly if necessary to control flooding, but that would cause a buildup behind the dam and subsequently drown all the equipment the contractor had positioned at the base of the structure in anticipation of beginning repairs.

It could also flood the area behind the dam...up to and including the Anasazi ruins.

Damn!

He considered pulling Sydney and her crew out of the area. He even dug his mobile phone out of his pocket. Only the knowledge of how desperately she needed to remake the destroyed footage kept him from punching in her number.

He would watch the weather reports, he decided grimly. Check the computer every half hour for updates from the various monitoring stations maintained by the Bureau on the water level upriver. That way he could allow Sydney as much time as possible at the ruins. He'd give her a heads-up, though, just in case.

Her voice came over the airwaves, breathless, distracted, impatient. "Rain? What rain? I don't see any clouds."

"They're piling up in the north. Stick your head out of the cave and look."

He heard a thump, the sound of boots on rock, a muffled curse. A moment or two later she came back on, alive with excitement.

"The wind's picked up! Albert's recording just the sounds I want."

"Sydney, the clouds…"

"Listen!"

She must have stuck the phone out the face of the cave. A low whistling moan sounded through the receiver, lifting the hairs on the back of Reece's neck.

"Can you hear the wail?"

"I hear it. Sydney, the clouds."

"Don't worry! I'll watch them. The last time I heard that wail, I took a short slide down a long cliff. I won't let anything distract me so much that I get washed down a river."

"I'll call you when and if I think you should leave."

"Thanks."

"Let me know if you depart the area before that."

"Will do."

She snapped her phone shut, obviously eager to get back to her project. Reece did the same.

To his relief, the rain held off upriver for an hour, then another. By the time he called it a day and sent his crew home just after six, however, the sky to the north had blackened ominously.

He still hadn't heard from Sydney. He didn't doubt she was taking advantage of every hour of light, every shrill whistle of wind. Tossing aside his hard hat, Reece climbed into the Jeep. He could call her, tell her to come in. Or he could make a quick trek down the canyon to check on her progress and suggest she drive back to town with him. That would give him the opportunity to tell her about the marks in the sandstone.

Or so he rationalized as he pulled up beside the Blazer fifteen minutes later. The absence of the van indicated Sydney had sent at least part of her crew back to town. With the black clouds whipping closer by the minute, Reece made his way down the cliffs to the riverbed.

When he reached the film crew's temporary base camp set up below the ruins, Reece discovered that everyone had departed except the earringed, earphoned Zack and Henry Three Pines.

"Is he listening to the wind?" Reece asked, indicating the kid.

Henry's wrinkled face creased even more. "No. I believe he listens to one called Marilyn Manson."

Absorbed in the grunge rocker's lyrics, Zack didn't

hear Reece's approach. He jumped half a foot in the air when tapped on the shoulder. Ripping off the earphones, he spun around.

"Geez, dude, go easy on the heart muscles!"

"Sorry. Where's your boss?"

"Up in the ruins, retrieving the mikes. She sent me down to pack up the rest of the equipment before the rain hits."

"Better get with it."

A pierced eyebrow lifted, but Reece was too used to giving orders and Zack too used to following them to argue.

"I'll have to make two trips," he grumbled. "Albert was feeling punk and left half of his gear for me to haul back to the van."

"Load up what you can carry and head out with Henry. I'll bring the rest and follow with Sydney when she finishes here."

"Thanks, man!"

Sydney still hadn't appeared when Zack and Henry trudged off. Reece waited another fifteen minutes before he lost patience and called out to her. His shout bounced off the cliff wall a couple of times before the now-howling wind caught it and whipped it away.

Muttering, he headed for the aluminum ladder. She was probably lost in her creative visions again, or so determined to capture the wind's wail that she hadn't even noticed how dark the sky had grown.

Reece noticed it, though, *and* the lightning that snaked out of a cloud when he was still a few feet shy of the cave floor. Cursing, he scrambled up the last rungs and threw himself clear of the metal posts a mere second before another flash zigzagged across the sky. Picking himself up, he dusted off and watched as the supercharged ions lit the clouds from the inside out.

Well, hell!

No way either he or Sydney were going back down that ladder until the storm had passed.

Which is exactly what he informed her when she appeared a few seconds later, draped in black wire and assorted mikes.

"You're kidding!"

He shoved a hand through his hair, raking down the wind-whipped spikes. "A lightning bolt peaks at about twenty thousand amps. That's not something I'd kid about."

"Twenty thousand?" She threw the darkened sky a wary, respectful look. "Guess we'll have to make ourselves comfortable and wait this one out."

Lifting the wires from around her neck, she started to settle in the shelter of a half-standing stone wall. Reece caught her elbow.

"We'd better go farther back into the ruins, away from the ladder."

More than happy to put as much stone as possible between her and the potential to end up as stir-fry, Sydney wove past crumbled wall and ducked under a low lintel, plunging instantly into inky blackness.

Reece followed more slowly, letting his eyes adjust to the gloomy interior as he picked his way over fallen chunks of shale.

"Back here!"

Her voice echoed through the ruins, luring him on. After the first few paces, the walls closed in. Ceilings dropped, crowding so low he whacked his head against lintels twice. The only light came from the occasional brilliant flashes that lit the narrow window slits. Even after three days in the sun, the village smelled dank from its long, underwater sleep.

"This room's relatively intact," Sydney announced when he bent almost double to enter a small chamber.

It was tucked away under the lowest portion of the overhang. A single narrow window looked out over the canyon. Reece stumbled and almost tripped in a smooth, oblong depression in the stone floor. The trough gave him a clue to the room's use. It was probably a kitchen or a storeroom, he guessed. A place where the Anasazi ground and stored their maize.

Wary of the low ceilings, he felt his way along the wall until he spotted the pale blur of Sydney's face.

"Didn't you bring a flashlight up here with you?" he asked.

"Several, but they're in my backpack, which at this moment is sitting a few feet from the ladder." She looked up at him hopefully. "I don't suppose you have anything to munch on with you?"

"Sorry." He dropped down beside her, his back to the wall. "Don't you ever eat regular meals?"

"I don't have time for them when I'm on location." She thought about that for a moment. "Or when I'm at home. Food isn't real high on my list of priorities."

"Except at moments like this, when you can't work," he guessed.

Her teeth gleamed white in the murky gloom. "Especially at moments like this. That's why I keep Zack on the payroll. He generally remembers to order in a pizza or go pick up Chinese."

"Just out of curiosity, what currency do you pay him in? Silver nose rings?"

"That, and one-on-one instruction in the art of documentary filmmaking. Don't let his appearance fool you. He's an honors grad of UCLA's cinematography school."

"He could use some work on his professional image," Reece returned, stretching out his legs.

"Couldn't we all? Take you, for instance. When I first saw you in your jeans and straw cowboy hat, I didn't connect you with an engineer."

"You mean the day you drove off the cliff? Your appearance was a little misleading, too. Anyone seeing you then might have mistaken you for a ditzy, artistic type."

"I did *not* drive off that cliff. And as I recall, that's exactly how you thought of me."

It was the perfect lead-in to tell her that her accident might have been staged. Reece had set up the intro with deliberate casualness. He hated to frighten her or put that fierce, hurt look in her eyes again. Not that he could see her eyes at this moment, but he hadn't forgotten the anguish in her face last night.

He'd just opened his mouth to tell her about the gouges in the stone when nature accomplished exactly what he was trying to avoid. In one thunderous boom, it scared the bejebers out of the woman next to him.

The sky split. Lightning cracked seemingly right outside the window. The tiny chamber lit with brilliant white light, causing Sydney to scream like a banshee and give a credible imitation of a badger trying to burrow inside Reece's shirt.

He wrapped his arms around her, soothing, stroking, wincing when her elbow augered into his hipbone. After a long, booming roll of thunder, he gave her the all clear.

"It's okay. Sydney, it's okay."

"That's what you say now!" she muttered into his shirt

pocket. "A moment ago you were talking twenty million amps!"

"Twenty thousand."

"Whatever."

He might have convinced her to dig herself out of his shirt if the rain he'd anticipated all afternoon hadn't broken loose at that moment. It came down in sheets, driven by the howling wind, and blew sideways through the slitted window.

With the tested reflexes of a man who'd grown up with four rough and ready brothers, Reece rolled away from the drenching spray, taking Sydney with him.

She ended up in his lap. For the life of him, Reece couldn't say whether that was intentional or not on his part. However she got there, she stayed right where she was, her shoulder pressed his chest, her hair damp and silky under his nose.

He'd tell her about the gouge marks on the stone later, he decided. Right now he'd simply share his warmth and hold her until she lost the shivers generated by fright or by the chill brought in by the rain and the darkness.

His good intentions lasted exactly as long as it took for Sydney to shift to a more comfortable position in his lap. Her body contacted his everywhere it shouldn't. Reece went from loose and relaxed to hard and tight in two and a half seconds flat.

She couldn't miss his sudden stiffening. She shifted again and caused a sort of chain reaction. Her head came up, cracking Reece on the underside of his chin. Her elbow did its thing on his hip again. Her breast pushed into his chest, and he got even harder.

Flattening her palms on his chest, she pushed upright. He couldn't see her expression clearly in the darkness, only hear her quick, uneven breath. He was trying to think of some way to pass off the awkward moment when her voice came to him, soft and edgy and just a little breathless.

"Reece?"

"Yes?"

"Last night, at the waterfall?"

A charged silence filled the chamber. Reece had to speak carefully around the jagged shards of heat slicing into his throat.

"What about last night at the waterfall?"

"I wanted you to kiss me. Almost as much as I want you to kiss me now."

He resisted the driving urge to do just that. "I hear a 'but' in there."

She took his face in her palms, her own a pale blur in the darkness. "But I want to be honest with you. Trust me when I tell you that you don't have to worry that I'll repeat my mistake of ten years ago. I won't tumble into love with you just because I...because we..." Her breath left on a long, determined sigh. "Because of this."

For reasons totally beyond Reece's comprehension, Sydney's earnest assurance that she wouldn't fall in love with him scratched his pride. He didn't *want* her to fall for him, for Pete's sake! Until this moment his only thought was to lock her body to his, to slide her under him and hear her gasp and pant and cry out in a fever of delight.

Now he wanted more, but with Sydney's soft, moist lips and eager hands destroying his concentration, not to mention his control, he was damned if he could decide what.

Later, he decided. He'd deal with this irrational response to her declaration later. Right now, the woman leaning into him, her mouth hungry on his, was all he could handle.

He tumbled back, taking care that she landed atop him, cushioning her from the hard rock. Tongues met. Knees tangled. Hands slid, shaped, cupped. The cave's darkness, split at intermittent moments by flashes of light, wrapped around them. Rain shot through the narrow window and sizzled on stone. Reece didn't notice the damp, didn't worry about the rain. Sydney filled his senses. Like a wild, powerful river rushing through giant turbines, she roared in his ears, churned his blood, set him on fire at every pulse point in his body.

She was all long legs and soft breasts, hungry mouth and sweet, tart tongue. Reece stroked and nipped and sucked the skin of her jaw, her throat, the curve of her neck. Each taste increased his hunger, each glide of his fingers on her hips and waist sparked small fires. He rolled her a little to one side, found the soft mound of breast flattened against his chest.

Stretched atop Reece, her legs tangled with his and her body fitted to his, Sydney marveled at the magic he created with every touch, every scrape of his teeth and tongue. She'd never burned like this. Never wanted so badly. The realization worried her enough to pull back for a moment, her breath almost as loud and harsh as the rain gusting through the window.

"Reece…"

"I know," he growled. "You don't want to repeat your mistake of ten years ago."

His hands tangled in her hair, holding her head still. Even in the dim light, Sydney saw the blue fire in the eyes that blazed up at her.

"Just for the record, though, I'm not Jamie Chavez."

She sucked in a shocked breath. "I know that. I never thought… I didn't mean to imply—"

"And this isn't ten years ago."

He dragged her head down and kissed her with stunning intensity. His mouth ravaged hers as if to prove his point that he was nothing like her charming, feckless first love. She felt swamped, consumed, almost savaged, and something primitive in her stirred. In this cave, in this darkness, with lightning crashing outside and hard stone beneath, she had a fleeting sense of what the Anasazi women must have felt centuries ago when their men came back from the hunt to claim them.

For a moment the line between reality and fantasy blurred. The present merged into the past. A feeling of powerlessness invaded Sydney. Almost panic. Like the Weeping Woman of Chalo Canyon, she felt trapped, bound to this hard, muscular man with something stronger than rope, more binding than chains.

She could stop what was happening with a word, a single push on his shoulder. She knew that. Reece wouldn't follow this savage kiss with an equally savage possession if she dragged her head up and gasped out a protest.

She tried to do it. Even managed to lift her head an inch or two before the primal need stirring in her belly smothered the protest. Instincts deeper than thought, older than time, drove her. She wanted to feel him, run her hands over his arms and back and shoulders, taste his salty skin. Surrendering to that dark, primal need, she tugged at his shirt, dragging the tail free of his jeans so she could slide her hands under it. He made a sound that could have been hunger, could have been triumph. Before she could decide which, he'd stripped off her tank top.

The stretchy top ended up under her, wadded into a ball, cushioning her shoulders from the hard stone. His shirt followed a moment later, providing a pad for her hips. She'd barely registered the cool, damp air on her skin when Reece dipped his head for a hot, greedy exploration of her breasts. He took the peaks between his teeth, teasing, worrying, raising stinging needles that arched her back and had her panting.

She was slick with sweat and wet with need when his hand went to the zipper on her shorts. The brush of his knuckles on her belly hollowed her stomach. She wanted to mate with this man. Wanted to take him into her, feel him inside her, test her will and her femininity against his awesome strength. Yet even the primal instinct that drove her couldn't completely subdue her twentieth-century common sense.

"We can't," she panted, her voice raw with regret. "I want to. Believe me, I want to! But I'm not—I haven't—I don't have any protection," she ended on a wail.

Above her, his mouth curved in a slow, wicked grin. "Didn't I tell you about my brothers? I have four of them, one younger, three older."

This wasn't exactly the moment Sydney would have chosen to exchange family histories. She could barely breathe, much less pretend an interest in anything other than the fingers making small circles just above her bellybutton.

"From the time I was twelve," he murmured, watching the rapid rise and fall of her stomach with great interest, "Jake and Evan and Marsh made sure I left the house prepared for any eventuality."

She managed a shaky laugh. "Twelve, huh?"

"We Hendersons matured early," Reece explained, his

grin deepening to a slash of white teeth and unabashed masculinity.

Early or late, they'd certainly matured. This one had, anyway. Sydney couldn't help noticing how much when he shed his jeans. He was, to put it simply, magnificent. Rippling skin stretched tightly over corded muscles and lean hips. A dusting of black hair created shadows on his chest and lower belly.

When he stretched out beside her, the instincts Sydney had fought to subdue just a moment before went out of control. She lifted her hips so he could slide off her shorts, taking her panties with them, and welcomed him eagerly when he covered her. His knees nudged hers apart, his mouth descended once more, hard, demanding.

When his hand slipped between her legs, desire burst into a blinding, white-hot flame. Within seconds the flame became a raging inferno. To Sydney's astonishment and complete mortification, she felt herself climaxing. She stiffened her legs. Tried to fight it. Couldn't stop the spiraling sensations.

"Reece!"

"It's all right." His mouth was hot on hers, his hand so skilled that a groan ripped from the back of her throat. "Let it go."

"As…if…I…have…any—" Her head went back. Her body arched. "Oh! Ooooh!"

Her last coherent thought was that Reece had chosen the right profession after all. He certainly knew his way around dams. With one wicked twist of his fingers, he opened all the floodgates. Pleasure roared through and over and around Sydney, until she was sure she'd drown in it.

She was still gasping for air when he thrust into her.

Skillfully, sinfully, he filled the reservoir once more, bringing her to another shattering release before following her over the crest.

Chapter 10

Sydney didn't notice that the storm had passed until she stretched, replete and catlike in her languorous contentment. The lazy twist brought her head around and the window into view. She stared at the narrow slit for long moments before recognizing the whitish glow outside as moonlight.

The pale wash of gold stirred her. She'd love to capture the ruins in this light. Reece had told her that he'd sent Zack and Henry back to town with most of the equipment. Maybe they'd left a minicam behind. Not one of Tish's expensive Cannons. She'd have taken those with her. But Sydney's personal camera, snug and safe in its waterproof case, might still be there.

Yet, as much as the moonlight tugged at her, she couldn't bring herself to move. She didn't want to untangle her arms and legs, or relinquish the damp heat of Reece's powerful body pressed so intimately on hers.

Even more to the point, she wasn't ready to examine the nagging little worry that crept into her head. Maybe, just maybe she hadn't learned her lesson of ten years ago as thoroughly as she thought she had.

She could love this man, she thought with a catch in her throat. Easily. After their explosive joining, Sydney knew instinctively that she could make love with Reece Henderson again and again and never lose the wonder of it, the sheer, carnal delight.

The thought scared the heck out of her and made her writhe inside when she remembered how she'd promised Reece she wouldn't go all gooey-eyed on him. Swallowing a groan, she eased out from under the heavy leg thrown across both of hers and groped for her panties.

What *was* it about Chalo Canyon that clouded her thinking, made her so damned vulnerable to a handsome face?

No, not just a handsome face. As Reece had so forcefully reminded her, he wasn't Jamie Chavez. Like she needed a reminder! Reece Henderson didn't operate on the same plane, or even in the same sphere as the careless, casual Jamie.

Resolutely she pulled on her wrinkled top. When her head pushed through the neck opening, she found Reece with his hands hooked comfortably under his neck, his eyes on her breasts, and a sexy smile on his lips. As if remembering the pleasure they'd experienced at the touch of those lips, her nipples peaked.

For heaven's sake! One look from the man and she was ready to throw herself on top of him again and devour him whole. So much for her promise not to make a fool of herself!

"The storm's passed," she muttered, embarrassed by her body's involuntary reaction.

"I see."

Yanking down the hem of her tank top, she pointed out more of the obvious. "It's late. The moon's up."

He nodded solemnly.

A little desperate, she tugged her shorts from under his hip. "At least we'll have some light for the trek out of the canyon."

"You don't have to worry, Sydney. I'll get you home safely...if and when you're ready to leave."

She bit down on her lower lip, both seduced and appalled at the invitation in his tanned-leather voice. She couldn't blame him for wanting seconds. She wanted them, too. So badly her stomach curled in on itself. And she couldn't blame anyone but herself for that lazy, predatory gleam in his eyes. She'd set this whole situation up, promised him a roll in the hay—or in this case, a roll on the rocks—with no strings attached.

"I'm not worried," she assured him. "I just want to take advantage of this glorious moonlight to shoot a few exterior angles."

His sexy little smile faded at her swift transition from passionate lover to equally passionate moviemaker.

"I just hope Zack left some of the high-speed film," she added under her breath, scrambling into her shorts with more haste than dignity.

"Wait a minute. We have to talk."

"No, we don't." She summoned what was probably the world's most insipid smile. "We talked before I jumped your bones, remember? I promised you I wouldn't make the same mistake I made ten years ago, and I won't."

He dragged on his jeans. "Dammit, Sydney…"

"It's okay." She backed away, groping behind her for the opening in the stone that formed the door. "I'm not expecting any declarations of undying love, and I certainly won't lay any on you."

On that firm note, she ducked under the stone lintel and disappeared through the doorway, leaving Reece to glower at the dark rectangle. Five minutes ago he'd roused from a lazy state of satisfaction to the glorious sight of Sydney nearly naked, her mouth still swollen from his kiss and her eyes filled with confusion as she tried to sort out the ramifications of what they'd just shared.

Reece could appreciate her confusion. He was tasting its sharp tang himself. He'd pulled Sydney into his arms with only a vague, hazy worry about where they'd go from here, but now…

Now, what?

Now he wanted her even more fiercely than he had an hour ago. He'd just admitted it to himself when she'd brushed him off with that casual assurance that she wouldn't fall in love with him. Somehow, that wasn't what he wanted to hear right now. Casual didn't come close to describing his feelings for Sydney Scott at this moment.

He yanked on his clothes, trying to catalogue and arrange the sensations she evoked in him in ascending order of importance.

Irritation. Lust. Admiration. Worry.

Especially worry.

His face grim, he yanked on his shirt and ducked through the low door to retrace his steps through the dark, winding ruins. Pushing upright outside the last building, he scanned the cave's mouth.

Silhouetted against a midnight-blue sky studded with thousands of stars, Sydney picked her way through the ruins toward the ladder. Reece reached her just in time to bar her descent.

"We need to talk. *Not* about what just happened between us," he added quickly when she opened her mouth to give him what he guessed would be another of her thanks-it-was-fun-and-I'll-call-you-sometime speeches. "We'll discuss that later. Before we do, I need to tell you what brought me into the canyon tonight."

So much for her fatal attraction, Sydney thought wryly. She'd gotten so caught up in the moment…and in his arms…that she hadn't even questioned Reece's unexpected appearance at the ruins.

"Did you get the results back on your computer simulations?" she asked, cutting to what she assumed was the key issue.

His mouth settled into a tight line. "Yes, I did."

"Not good?"

"Let's just say they weren't what I expected. We start blasting tomorrow. You won't be able to access this part of the canyon for the next couple of days."

She bit back her instinctive protest. She'd agreed to work around his schedule. But two days! Two precious days in which she'd planned to retake the footage lost to the slasher.

Her mind raced. She could still make her deadline. She'd do the interviews in town, rerecord Henry's stories. Maybe go over the stock tapes on the Anasazis she'd purchased from the State Historical Archives to see how and where she could flesh out her own footage. Absorbed in her mental calculations, she almost missed Reece's next comment.

"I talked to Martinez this afternoon. Out on Canyon Rim Road, at the spot where you drove over the cliff."

No one seemed to make the fine distinctions she did about that particular incident. She folded her arms, determined to set the record straight once and for all.

"Swerving to avoid a rock in the road and having the road crumble beneath you is *not* the same as driving over a cliff."

"That's true," Reece admitted.

She barely had time to savor her little victory in the war of words before the ground started to crumble beneath her feet again.

"Some people are questioning how that rock got into the road," he said slowly.

Her arms dropped. "Like who, for instance?"

"Like me."

"I thought…" Reeling, Sydney struggled to grasp the implications of that terse reply. "I assumed—"

Oh, God! She'd assumed that slab of limestone had simply fallen from the cliff beside the road, an accidental product of rain and the eroding wind that whistled through the canyon.

"Are you saying someone pushed that rock into the road deliberately? Someone who knew I'd be driving along that stretch of the canyon after dark?"

"I'm saying it's possible." He kept his eyes on hers, as if to gauge her reaction. "I found some marks on the stone that could have been made by a chisel."

"A chisel," Sydney echoed, feeling sick.

"Or by another falling rock," he added sharply. "Martinez shipped a piece of it to a metallurgy lab in Tucson. We should hear from them within a day or two."

Wrapping her arms around her waist, she fought the sudden chills that started at her fingertips and worked their way inward toward her heart.

"Sebastian."

A shiver danced like a nervous spider down her back.

Seeing the shudder, Reece felt his jaw tighten in its socket. He hated scaring her like this, hated seeing that grim, determined look in her eyes.

Restraining the urge to fold her into his arms, he was obligated to repeat the deputy's caution. "As of this point, there's no proof that any of the Chavez family was involved in either your accident or the malicious destruction of your cassettes."

"It was Sebastian."

Silently Reece could only agree with her low, reverberating assertion. Arlene might have slashed her perceived rival's tapes out of desperation, but only Sebastian possessed the strength or the ruthlessness to arrange such a clever and convenient obstacle on Canyon Rim Road.

If it was arranged.

They wouldn't know for a few days, Reece reminded himself. In the meantime he and Henry would keep Sydney and her crew under close surveillance. Very close surveillance.

And Reece would take the night shift.

The quiet that stretched between him and Sydney during the drive back to town told Reece that he'd be keeping watch over her tonight from a distance. The mind-shattering intimacy they'd shared during that hour in the cave dissipated a little more with every mile. By the time he pulled into the Lone Eagle Motel's gravel parking lot, a quiet, withdrawn woman had completely effaced the one who'd shattered into a million pieces in his arms.

Reece missed her…more than he was ready to admit.

They had just climbed out of the Jeep when a door banged open and Zack sauntered out.

"Where you been, boss? I was, like, getting worried."

"We got caught by the storm."

The kid's gaze drifted from Sydney's tangled hair to Reece's half-buttoned shirt. A smirk tilted down the corners of his mouth.

"Musta been some storm."

"It was."

She shoved her key in the lock and pushed open the door of her room. Reece brushed past her. A quick search of the bedroom and the bathroom beyond revealed no destruction or uninvited guests. Satisfied, he went back outside to unload the Jeep.

"Here, I'll take those," she said.

Lifting the cases from his hands, she muttered a stiff good-night. A moment later the door banged in his face.

Reece stood on the stoop, debating whether he should pound on the door and inform Ms. Scott that they still had unfinished business to discuss or just open the blasted thing and walk in. He didn't want to leave her alone and shaken like this. Hell, he might as well admit it. He didn't want to leave her at all.

What he wanted was Sydney. Any way he could have her. The truth hit him right between the eyes just seconds before Zack hit him right between the shoulder blades. The friendly thump carried more force than the kid's thin frame and lank manner would suggest he possessed.

"You look like you could use a beer. I know I could. I'll keep you company if you'll buy."

Reece slanted him an assessing look. "Are you old enough to drink? Legally?"

"I'm old enough to do anything legally. It's the illegal stuff that gets me in trouble. Hey, man," he added when his prospective drinking companion didn't jump at the offer, "I'm twenty-five and then some. Ask Lula if you don't believe me. She's already carded me twice."

"Once wasn't enough?"

"She had a few doubts about my driver's license the first time I showed it to her," he admitted. "On closer examination, she finally decided that geek with the glasses and the greased-down hair was really me." He palmed his green-tinted spikes. "Took me a while to convince her that people do change over the years."

Years, hell. Reece had changed profoundly in the past few hours. He just wasn't sure how, yet.

He fell in beside the kid, too edgy and wired to hit the sack. He could see the entire motel courtyard from the café. He'd have a beer, draw the kid out, maybe learn a little about the prickly woman who'd just slammed the door in his face.

What he learned about Sydney went down as easily as the beers…at first.

"She's one of the best," Zack said sometime later, his slang giving way to a quiet intensity. "We studied her *Buccaneers* at UCLA. That was one of her first projects for The History Channel. It's a classic, a superb blending of historical fact and popular lore about the pirates who pillaged the seas. She completely debunked those scumbags' romantic image without destroying the myths that surround them. The way she fed those black-and-white stills into her color footage…" He shook his head, his face a study in awe and envy. "You ought to see it."

"I have. I just didn't know it was hers."

"She did that one on her own, with only a minicam and rented stills."

"Sounds like she's come a long way." Reece swirled his beer, thinking of the woman who'd left Chalo Canyon in disgrace and come back an accomplished, accredited filmmaker. "Now she owns her own studio."

"Almost owns her own studio," Zack corrected with a shrug. "She's put everything she has into it. Everything she had left after her dad's hospital bills, anyway. She's got to wrap this project and produce *The Weeping Woman of Chalo Canyon* as promised or she'll lose the projected broadcast date, not to mention a chance at another Oscar nomination this cycle. Even worse," he said morosely, staring down at the amber dregs in his glass, "she'll sacrifice her dream."

"What dream?"

The kid tipped him a curious glance. "She didn't tell you? I'm not surprised. Sydney's still tight about her father and what this project meant to him. To them both. She'll do anything to wrap it. Anything."

The look in the kid's eyes went from curious to speculative and stayed that way just long enough to plant an ugly little doubt in Reece's mind. He shoved it out immediately. "Anything" did *not* include flashing ten-megawatt smiles at the chief engineer to assure access to the dam site…much less seducing him. His insides were still tight with the memory of those hours in the cave, when Zack pushed his chair away from the table.

"I'd better zone out. No doubt Syd will want us all up and on our way to the canyon by dawn."

Reece didn't say anything. It wasn't his place to inform Sydney's crew that they wouldn't be shooting onsite tomorrow. She'd advise them of the change in locale in her own time, her own way.

With a nod to Lula, Zack sauntered out. A few moments later, the generous-hipped waitress plopped down in the vacated chair. A frown creased her broad face.

"What's this I hear 'bout Sydney's accident bein' no accident?"

Beer sloshed over the rim of the glass as Reece shot upright. "How did you hear about that?"

The café's proprietress waved a plump hand, as if the mechanics of her widespread communications network weren't important, only its accuracy. "Arlene came into town this morning, looking as shook up as I've ever seen her. I made her guzzle some coffee and a piece of pie." Lula's head wagged. "That woman's gonna dry up and blow away if she doesn't watch herself. I've tried to tell her staying skinny as a bag of bones won't keep Jamie if he's a mind to stray, but…well…"

With a shrug of her rounded shoulders, she got back to the real meat of the matter. "While Arlene was here, she let drop 'bout Joe Martinez coming out to the ranch and askin' for alibis."

Let drop, his left foot! Reece suspected Lula pried the information out of Arlene with the same ruthlessness Torquemada extracted confessions from the victims of the Spanish Inquisition.

The café operator's brown eyes fixed on Reece. "I've known Sebastian Chavez a long time. Both Martha and I had our eye on him before he married that silly piece of fluff who ran off and left him with a baby to raise. He's hard and he's proud and he dotes on that boy."

Reece didn't mention the fact that the "boy" was now a man, full grown and more than capable of making his own decisions.

"Hard and proud enough to shame the nineteen-year-old girl he didn't think was good enough for his son into leaving town?" he asked.

"And then some."

"Hard enough to arrange her death when she came back ten years later and threatened to destroy his family?"

Lula scratched the plastic tablecloth with a short, stubby finger. Her brown eyes were grave when she met Reece's gaze.

"There's some 'round here that might think so."

He leaned forward, his beer glass forgotten. "What about you? What do you think?"

"I think I'll sleep better now that I've had new dead bolts put on the door to Sydney's unit." The seriousness in her face eased into a knowing smirk. "Thought you might want to know that, since you seem to have taken such a shine to that woman. What were you two doin' out at the ruins so long, anyway?"

Sydney had already provided the residents of Chalo Canyon with enough gossip to last a lifetime. Reece wasn't about to give them more.

"Waiting out the storm."

Lula's keen brown eyes roamed his face and the hair Reece hadn't taken the time to comb.

"If you say so."

Lifting her bulk from the chair, she dug into her pocket. A room key landed on the table with a little jangle of metal on plastic.

"Henry Three Pines stopped by earlier and asked Martha to move you into Unit Eleven. He seems to think you wanted to stay close to Sydney. Real close. We've already moved your gear."

Reece closed his fist over the key. "Thanks."

"It connects to Unit Twelve." Her face deliberately bland, Lula started back to the kitchen. "The door locks on both sides."

Chapter 11

Squeaky clean and feeling almost human after a long, stinging shower, Sydney wrapped herself in one of the Lone Eagle Motel's skimpy bath towels and tucked the edges tightly around her breasts. Steam filled the tiny bathroom, fogging the glass surfaces. Slowly, her mind drifting, she rubbed a clear space on the mirror, turned on the taps and picked up her toothbrush.

Here, alone in her rented room, with only the quiet of the night outside and the rush of water through the faucets to disturb the silence, the doubts she'd held at bay during the ride into town rose up to haunt her. Maybe she should call it quits. Pack up her crew and her dreams and head back to L.A. while she still could. If Reece's suspicions proved true, and someone had really engineered that accident on Canyon Rim Road...

A shudder shook her. For a moment her hand trembled

so badly Sydney couldn't trust herself to squirt the toothpaste onto the brush. Her face looked distorted, frightened, in the dew-streaked mirror.

The image disgusted Sydney.

"You tucked your tail between your legs and scuttled away from Chalo Canyon once, girl. You're not running again." Her chin came up. "Sebastian Chavez is a tough old buzzard, but you're tougher."

A lot tougher. After watching her father die by painful degrees, she could handle anything that either of the Chavez men threw at her.

That fierce advice to herself was still ringing in her ears when she walked into the bedroom a few moments later, wrapped in her towel. Without that infusion of spunk and determination, the faint, almost inaudible snick of the lock on the connecting doors might have sent her terrified into the night. Instead, the tiny sound and an accompanying surreptitious twist of the round door knob fired a surge of fury.

"Bastard," she hissed, her heart jackhammering under the thin shield of cotton. "You're not getting in…or out… without a few lumps this time."

Her bare feet flying over the pea-green shag, Sydney rushed across the room to dig through the equipment piled beside the front door. Battle fever pulsed through her blood as her fist closed around a telescoped tripod.

She swished the heavy stand through the air twice, testing its weight and balance, and was back at the door within seconds. Attack, Sydney remembered from the innumerable John Wayne war movies she'd watched with her father, was always the best defense.

Positioning herself so the door would screen her when it opened, she hefted the tripod in one hand and reached

out with another. With a quick twist of the dead bolt, a
hard yank on the doorknob, and a vicious swing, Sydney let fly.

"What the...?"

The would-be intruder ducked just in time. The tripod missed his head by inches and crashed into the door
frame, gouging out great chunks of the wood. At the
impact, shock waves eddied up Sydney's arm. She had
already pulled back for another swing before she recognized the astonished man who shot up a hand and
grabbed her weapon.

"Reece!" Outraged and relieved, she screeched at him.
"You scared the hell out of me!"

"Yeah, well, you've just taken a year off my life span."
His narrowed gaze swept her bare flesh. "Maybe two."

Releasing her grip on the tripod, she snatched at the
towel that had worked loose in the near melee.

"What are you doing?" she demanded, quivering with
indignation.

"I was testing the locks between our rooms." He hefted
the tripod, eyeing it with a scowl. "Care to tell me what
in blue blazes you intended to accomplish with this?"

"I *intended* to bash your head in. I'll do it, too, if you
ever scare me like that again."

"I thought you were in the bathroom," he said shortly,
obviously as pumped by the near miss as she was.

"I was." Frowning, she caught a glimpse of the clothing hung neatly in the room's small closet. "I thought
this unit was empty."

"I just moved in."

Sydney's gaze whipped back to his. He'd moved in
next to her? Only a connecting door away? The implications sent a wave of heat through her body. Did he think

that she wanted to pick up where they'd left off this afternoon? More to the point, did she?

"I'm a light sleeper," he said, cutting into her chaotic thoughts. "I thought you might want someone close at hand in case you get any more unwanted visitors."

"Oh."

The idea of Reece bedding down right next door, only a few feet away, rattled her all the way down to her toes. Almost as much as the idea that he'd switched rooms to keep watch over her.

She'd been on her own for so long, been strong for herself and her father for so long, that Sydney couldn't decide how to respond to Reece's unexpected protective streak. Not that she trusted herself to say anything coherent at this moment.

It had just sunk in that he wasn't wearing much more than she was.

Bare-chested, barefoot, his jeans slung low on his hips, he radiated even more of the potent masculinity that had melted her bones in the cave. Remembering the way she'd fallen all over him only a few hours ago, Sydney flushed.

"Reece, about what happened at the ruins…"

"When you came apart in my arms, you mean?"

Her flush deepened. "As I recall, we both did a little coming apart."

"So we did."

"But I don't… You don't…"

He let her stumble for a moment or two before he asked with a curious bite to his voice, "Is this another one of your attempts to reassure me that you have no intention of falling for me?"

"Something like that."

"Save the speech, Sydney." He stepped through the

opened doorway, his eyes dark behind his black lashes. "What happened this afternoon confused the heck out of me, too, but I'm not making any promises."

Under the thin cotton towel, her heart did a number on her ribs. She held her breath as he lifted a hand to tip her face to his.

"I don't know where we go from here," he said gruffly, "but I'm willing to explore the possibilities."

"You understand the risk? The last time I got involved with a man in Chalo Canyon, the whole town got involved with me."

Her attempt at humor went wide of the mark. Reece didn't crack a smile.

"I told you, I'm not Jamie Chavez."

"I do believe you mentioned that already."

"I want to make sure we're clear on that point."

"We are," she breathed. "Very clear."

Bound and blindfolded, Sydney couldn't confuse this man with Jamie or anyone else. His scent, his touch, the unconscious air of authority he carried like a second shadow set him apart.

"And this isn't ten years ago," he told her fiercely. "You're not alone in this."

"In what, Reece?"

He stared down at her, his rugged features set. "Damned if I know."

The muttered reply formed a tight band around Sydney's chest. To tell the truth, she had no idea where the sparks that sizzled under her skin every time he touched her would lead them, either. Feeling slightly overwhelmed by all that had happened between them in such a short time, she tried for a smile.

"Let's just take it a day at a time."

Reece didn't answer for a moment. He couldn't. His entire body had gone hard at the thought of tumbling her back on the chenille spread, kissing that full mouth and taut body until they both shot to the stars again.

The purple shadows under her eyes put the brakes on his rampaging need. She'd gotten up before dawn, he remembered. He remembered, too, how she'd fallen asleep in his arms during the storm.

"One day at a time," he echoed slowly. "Starting tomorrow."

"Starting tomorrow," she agreed, coming up on tiptoe to seal the bargain with a brush of her lips against his. He shuddered at the featherlight touch.

"Reece…?"

"Don't worry," he half groaned, then managed a grin. "I'm a man of my word. We'll take this slow."

Even if it killed him.

He shut the door between their rooms a moment later, wondering just what in God's name they were starting… and how they'd finish.

Reece woke well before dawn, driven by the realization that this day would see the start of more than a hazy, yet-to-be-defined relationship with Sydney Scott.

The repair project he'd sweated over for more than ten months was about to enter its most critical phase. The contractor and his crew would begin placing the small, densely packed charges this morning. If all went as planned, the weakened quadrant of the inner wall would be exposed by afternoon. For the first time, Reece would see the stress fractures with his own eyes.

He showered and slathered on shaving cream, listening for sounds that would indicate Sydney was awake.

Briefly he toyed with the idea of going down to the café for coffee. He could bring some back for her. Serve it to her in bed. Join her under the covers for a few minutes.

Yeah, right. As if he could climb in and out of bed with her in less than an hour or two. Or three.

Or ever.

The razor slipped down his chin, taking a patch of skin with it.

"Ouch!"

Grabbing a wad of toilet tissue, Reece dabbed at the cut. The thing wouldn't stop bleeding. He walked out into the sharp, predawn chill sometime later sporting a crusted bit of toilet paper on his chin.

Henry Three Pines drove up in his rickety pickup while the dam crew was still assembling. His eyes were almost lost under wrinkled folds of lid, but Reece trusted the man's eyesight and instinct.

"You'll stay with her?"

"She is my friend and the daughter of my friend. I will stay with her."

Reece threw a quick glance at the door to Unit Twelve. "I'll get back as soon as I can tonight. We'll be blasting today, so it may be late," he warned.

"I will stay with her."

The Hopi headman was in the café when Sydney strolled out of her room an hour later, her arms filled with a load of equipment. She spotted him through the brightly lit glass, dumped her load in the van and joined him for a quick cup of coffee.

"What do we shoot today?" he asked when she'd settled beside him with a steaming mug.

"Local interviews. I want to get a feel for the people

who now inhabit the land of the Ancient Ones. Hopefully I'll also get them talking about the Weeping Woman." She aimed a smile at the woman busy wiping down the counter. "I'll tape Lula and Martha when we get back this evening, after the supper rush."

Henry's wrinkled face folded into a smile. "They would never forgive you if you did not include them in this film you make."

"I know."

Sighing, Sydney sipped her coffee. She'd conducted hundreds of interviews over the years. The hardest ones were with friends and acquaintances.

Good documentarians constructed an invisible wall between their crews and the subjects. The *really* good ones maintained that wall throughout the entire interview process. The object was to avoid influencing the subjects' behavior or nudging them too hard down the paths you hoped they would go.

That could get a little difficult when said subjects had known you all your life.

"I also want to interview Mrs. Brent. Does she still have her 'visions'?"

"Whenever the moon is full."

Henry's own culture was too steeped in spiritualism and kachinas to ridicule the woman half the town referred to as Crazy Lady Brent. The eccentric recluse had terrified and totally intrigued the wide-eyed, nine-year-old Sydney the first time they'd come face-to-face during one of Mrs. Brent's lonely walks across the mesa. If anyone could produce the eerie feel Sydney wanted for her film, the gray-haired widow could. The trick would be to get her to recount some of the tales about the Weeping Woman of Chalo Canyon in front of a camera.

"I've got Buck Sanders and Joe Smallwood lined up this morning," she told Henry, referring to two local ranchers. "Mrs. Brent said we could come out to her place after lunch. I'll shoot the supper crowd at the café before we set up for Lula and Martha."

"We'll be busy," Henry commented with a smile.

"We will."

Impatient now to get to work, Sydney roused her crew. She used the drive out to Buck Sanders's isolated ranchero to review her notes for the interview. Like Henry, Buck was a member of the Hopi tribe and could speak authoritatively on the farming and irrigation techniques their people had learned or stolen from the ancient Anasazi. That would fit right in with a central theme of Sydney's documentary, which was to show the blending of ancient ways into modern culture as well as the mix of reality into myth.

Under other circumstances, she would have begged an interview with Sebastian Chavez. His family had lived in the Chalo Canyon area for as long as anyone could remember. The proud blood of the Spanish and equally proud blood of the Hopi mingled in his veins. With his white hair, hawk's beak of a nose and haughty bearing, he made the kind of visual impact that ordinarily made Sydney's fingers itch for a camera.

Now, just the thought of capturing him on videotape raised goose bumps.

Could he hate her so much? Fear her so much? Had he tumbled that slab of rock into Canyon Rim Road in a deliberate attempt to harm her?

The questions haunted Sydney as Henry guided her and her crew over narrow, dusty back roads. Finally Buck Sanders's place came into view. Tucked under an overhang of granite, the adobe ranch house looked exactly like what it was—a small, working homestead. They'd shoot outside, Sydney decided. Take advantage of the natural light and great visuals.

She made it a point to conduct interviews on the subject's home ground whenever possible. She wanted them to feel comfortable, without the constraints that too often inhibited them in a studio or an artificial set. That meant lugging extra lighting from location to location, of course, but the results generally justified the extra effort.

Generally.

Today might prove the exception. Despite Sydney's best efforts to put the taciturn Buck Sanders at ease, he couldn't relax. He kept a death grip on his coffee cup, looked straight at Sydney instead of the camera, and waited for her questions, which he answered with as few words as possible. The result was a stiff, stilted interview and several hundred wasted feet of videotape.

She had better luck with Joe Smallwood. Bright-eyed and leathery from his years under the Arizona sun, he spat out a chaw and waxed eloquent about the irrigation ditches that had delivered precious water from upriver to the mesa above the ruins more than a thousand years ago.

"Those ditches run some twenty, thirty miles," he ruminated in his tobacco-roughened caw. "Folks 'round here were still using stretches of 'em before the Chalo River dam went in."

She'd have to get some footage of the dam, Sydney thought as she and her crew drove to the next location. Maybe she'd tie the massive structure to both the drowning of the Anasazi village and the salvation of the farmers who came after them. The Bureau of Reclamation could probably dig some stock footage of the dam's construction out of its archives for her.

Or…

She could ask Reece for a private tour of the structure. That would give her the opportunity to observe him in action, maybe help her understand this project that consumed him almost as fiercely as Sydney's did her. She would talk to him tonight, she thought with a shiver of anticipation, about shooting some footage at the dam.

Among other things.

It took a surprising effort of will to blank those other things out of her mind and prepare for the afternoon's interview. Luckily the hollow-cheeked retired schoolteacher-turned-eccentric needed little prompting to talk about the Weeping Woman. Laura Brent closed her eyes, transporting herself from a living room crowded with knickknacks and photographs, not to mention floodlights, cameras and sound equipment, to a place inhabited only by her imagination.

"I hear her often," she murmured. "Whenever the wind blows from the north and she cries for her lost love. Some say she was Zuni, stolen away from her home to the north. Yet the words, the lament, are Hopi."

Her voice rose, thinned.

"Aiiiiii. Eee-aiiiii."

It was the cry of the wind, the wail of a desperate woman. With all her heart, Sydney prayed Albert was getting this.

"I heard her the week after I lost my husband to a perforated ulcer," Laura said sadly, as if the long-ago event had happened just yesterday. "She cried for me."

"This is good," Albert muttered as he played with the levers and dials on his unit. "This is good."

Better than good, Sydney thought exultantly. It was great. The sound take echoed the one they'd recorded in the canyon the other night with uncanny precision. During the postproduction editing process, Sydney would cut from Brent's bright living room to the dark cave. Juxtapose the modern woman with the ancient one. Synthesize recent grief with ancient heartbreak.

She was still on a high from the great visuals and audio when the crew set up in the motel's lobby for the interview with the Jenkins sisters later that evening. The two women turned out for the shoot in their Sunday best. Adorned in squash-blossom necklaces and elaborate earrings, they made a study in contrasts. Through the camera lens, Lula came across as plump, dark-eyed and ready to dish out a healthy dose of laughter. Martha appeared thin, nervous and twittery.

While Albert ran sound checks and Tish adjusted the lighting, Sydney chatted with the two subjects. They talked about the weather and the unseasonable rain, about business at the motel, about the ingredients in Lula's own brand of steak marinade. Sydney didn't hesitate to use audiotape lavishly in these preinterview sessions. Often she got plenty of good sound to use as off-camera fill if the on-camera interview went badly.

When she sensed the sisters were comfortable, she surreptitiously signaled Tish to start shooting. Caught up in their dialogue, Lula and Martha didn't realize they were being recorded on videotape. Slowly, imperceptibly, Sydney withdrew behind the glass shield that separated her from her subjects. Sitting off to one side, content behind her invisible wall, she listened while they poured out tales composed of equal parts gossip, personal accounts and dubious historical fact. Hands moving, heads nodding, they spoke of their ancestors. Of the town of Chalo Canyon. Of the Weeping Woman.

Following their cue, Sydney eased into her role as interviewer for a moment. "Do you remember when you first heard about the legend?"

Martha cocked her head. "Seems like I've heard about the Weeping Woman all my life."

"All your life? From the time you were a small child?"

"Well, I'll have to think about that..."

Lula jumped in at this point. "I don't! I know the very day I first heard about the Weeping Woman. It was thirty-six years ago."

"How the heck can you remember that?" her sister demanded. "You can't even remember to let the dog out in the morning."

"That's now. This was then."

With that somewhat confusing but firm declaration, the younger Jenkins sister launched into her tale.

"Sebastian told me the story one night when he stopped in for a beer, 'bout six months after his wife ran off. He was red-eyed with fatigue and with carin' for his ranch and the boy. We talked about cattle prices and the hay crop and the fierce wind that whistled through the canyon. He went all bitter and hard when I said it sounded like a woman wailing, but before he left the café he unbent enough to pass on the story of the Anasazi woman that his grandfather had told him."

Sydney leaned forward, her heart pounding. Sebastian was the original source of the legend? Damn, she wished she could interview him.

"I sure never wanted to trek down to the ruins again after he told me how that poor woman jumped out of the stone tower," Lula added, grimacing. "Then the dam went in, the canyon flooded, and the Weeping Woman became part of local lore."

Martha appeared struck by her sister's account. "You know, I believe you're right."

"I know I'm right. I always am."

"Ha!" The elder Miss Jenkins shattered the glass wall by appealing directly to Sydney. "Ask her who was right about that Buick she insisted we buy? The thing ended up in the junkyard less than a year after we drove it off the lot down in Phoenix."

"If you'd ever learned how to drive," her loving sister retorted, "it would have lasted a sight longer."

Wisely, Sydney stayed out of the heated debate that followed. She terminated the interview some moments later, not that either sister noticed. The Jenkinses were still arguing over who ran the Buick into the ground when the crew packed up their equipment and left.

Agreeably tired from the long day, Sydney trailed out of the lobby a moment later. She found Henry outside under the café's awning, with his chair tipped against the motel wall and his face turned up to the darkening sky.

"Thanks for coming with us today," she told him with a grateful smile. "I doubt if I could have found Buck's ranch on my own."

"You would've found it, Little Squirrel." He pushed to his feet. "You have the heart to always find your way. So," he added, glancing over her shoulder, "does he."

Sydney spun around. When she spotted Reece climbing out of his Jeep, his hair and eyebrows coated with a whitish dust, the heart Henry had just referred to started knocking against her ribs.

Reece didn't notice her and Henry under the awning. His stride long and swift, he headed toward his room.

After a quick goodbye to Henry, Sydney did the same.

Chapter 12

Reece closed his room door behind him, fully intending to honor his promise to Sydney to take things slow.

He'd spent the past fifteen hours struggling to douse the simmering heat that rose under his skin whenever she slipped into his thoughts. With the noise and distraction that came with blasting away three thousand cubic yards of concrete, he'd pretty much managed to keep her firmly at the back of his mind.

Gritty and bone-weary after all those hours in the heat and the sun, he'd climbed into his Jeep for the long drive back to town. Only minutes after the majestic curve of the dam disappeared from the rearview mirror, Sydney had pushed right to the forefront of Reece's worries.

Deputy Sheriff Martinez had called earlier to confirm that his people had delivered the sample slab of sandstone to the Department of Mine Engineering's metallurgy lab in Tucson. Reece himself had contacted Jan Kingsley, who promised to get the sample under the electron microscope within the next twenty-four hours.

In the meantime…

Reece smiled grimly, crinkling the grit at the corners of his eyes. In the meantime, he and Sydney would slow down, temper the heat that sizzled between them, find the balance between her schedule demands and his. Learn more about each other. He'd take time to understand the artistic vision that took her down into a canyon with thirty pounds of equipment on her back, maybe even share a few more laws of physics with her.

Like the inclined plane.

And the simple lever.

Groaning, Reece banished the instant, erotic image of her inclined and him levering. How in blazes he was going to manage slow escaped him at this moment, when all he could think about was a hot shower, a cold drink, and Sydney in his arms.

That question came to the fore when she pounded on the connecting door between their rooms just moments later. She smiled up at him, her face almost as dusty as his, her hair a wind-tossed mass of mink under a red L.A. Dodgers ball cap.

Instantly, his priorities rearranged themselves. To hell with the cold beer, he decided on a surge of need. It would probably just mix with all the dust he'd swallowed today and harden into concrete in his stomach. And the hot shower could wait. The feel of this woman in his arms couldn't. Not for long, anyway. Particularly when her smile delivered the same wallop as the roughhouse punches he and his brothers used to lay on each other.

"Hi."

The simple greeting contracted Reece's stomach. "Hi."

"How did it go today?"

"We hit the inner core in the lower-right quadrant."

"Is that good?"

He grinned. "Very good. We expected that it would take at least two days to expose the core, but the contractor had a real pro setting the charges."

"So they're done blasting?"

"Looks like it."

He knew what was coming before she slanted him a quick, speculative look.

"Does that mean I can take my crew back down to the ruins tomorrow?"

Reece hesitated, reluctant to break the unwelcome news that more violent thunderstorms were headed their way. The Upper Colorado region had already received record rainfalls for the year. From all indications, the Lower Colorado basin would soon do the same.

Spurred by the latest forecasts, the subcontractor had performed the near impossible and finished the blasting in a single day. Now all Reece had to worry about was the possibility of flash floods raging through the canyon and taking out his crippled dam, not to mention Sydney and her crew.

"Why don't we talk about schedules after I clean up?" he suggested.

She eyed him suspiciously, probably guessing that he was the bearer of bad news, but didn't push it. "Okay by me. I'll get a couple of beers from the café. You look like you could use something cold and wet."

Just in time, Reece bit back the observation that he was far more interested in something warm and wet. Like her lips. Or the curve of her neck. Or any part of her she wanted to make available.

"You," he announced instead, sliding a palm around her nape, "are a woman of remarkable intelligence and perception."

"You've noticed that, have you?"

Her smug little smile almost destroyed what was left of his control. It took a severe effort of will to keep the pacing deliberate, the touch light.

Just one taste, he told himself as he lowered his head. A small sampling.

The moment his lips covered hers, Reece knew one sampling wouldn't be enough. She smelled of wind and woman, of sunshine and Lula's special brew of super-charged coffee. Her mouth shaped instantly to his, as though she'd learned the angle of his jaw, the contours of his face.

Despite his clamoring body's protest, Reece managed to keep to just the one kiss. When he pulled back, she gave a shaky little laugh.

"You taste like cement."

He cocked a brow. "Have you ever tasted cement before?"

"No, but there's a first time for everything."

"So they say."

The small blue vein in her throat drew both his gaze and his touch. He edged his thumb down the faint line, felt her pulse fluttering under his thumb pad.

"Maybe they're right," he murmured.

This tight, driving need was definitely a first for Reece. Lying awake, listening to the whistle of the wind last night, he'd gone over every minute of those hours in the ruins. By the time he'd dragged himself out of bed, he'd almost been convinced that he'd imagined his grinding need. That Sydney hadn't arched under him and exploded in that shattering release.

Now he knew he hadn't imagined anything. Her blood pulsed under his thumb. Her skin felt like satin under his touch. God, he wanted her. Needed her the way a chocaholic needed his sweet, dark fix. The hours he'd spent with her had drowned his doubts, his half-formed, almost subconscious disdain for the woman everyone in Chalo Canyon had painted as a homewrecker.

An engineer down to his steel-toed boots, he was still trying to measure her impact on his internal Richter scale when she backed away. To Reece's immense satisfaction, her breath came as hard and fast as his.

"I'll… I'll get the drinks," she gasped. "Pound on the door when you're ready."

He was ready, more than ready, even before he stepped into a cool, stinging shower. *Slow,* he reiterated through gritted teeth. They were going to go slow. Even if it crippled him, which seemed a definite possibility at this point.

He soon discovered that Sydney's definition of *slow* differed considerably from his. She answered his knock fifteen minutes later with a dew-streaked bottle and a kiss that completely destroyed the effect of his cold shower.

Twenty minutes later they tumbled onto her bed, naked and panting.

"I thought about you all day," she admitted between hard, hungry kisses. "You got in the way of my shoot."

Since her tongue was busy exploring his ear at that point, Reece ignored the faint but unmistakable accusation.

"I thought about you, too, between detonations."

"You did, huh?" Her breath fanned his ear, hot, damp, incredibly arousing. "Why don't we see what we can do to set off a few more explosive charges?"

Her tongue got busier. Instantly Reece got harder. Groaning, he hunched a shoulder. Wrapping both hands around her waist, he slid her down a few inches. The friction of her breasts on his chest, her hips on his pelvis, set off more than just a *few* explosions. The ache that had started low in Reece's belly grew hotter, tighter, wilder with each taste, each teasing, wondering touch.

In the dimness of the ruins yesterday, she'd set him on fire. In the puddle of light thrown by the lamp beside the bed, she was gloriously greedy in her want, spectacularly generous in her giving. He dug his hands in the dark hair that spilled over her shoulders, lost himself in the damp, smooth heat of her mouth.

They were both slick with sweat when Sydney slid a leg over his and rose up on her knees. Yesterday he'd pleasured her so thoroughly, so skillfully. Today, the urge to do the same brought her upright, her hands on her thighs, her hips straddling his.

Her throat closed with the sight of him stretched out beneath her, his muscled shoulders bunched and tight, his chest matted with sworls of black hair. Those lean hollows and flat planes could only come from hard labor and rigid discipline. This was no weekend jogger, no desk man with privileges at an exclusive spa. He lived as he worked, she suspected. Rigorously. Strenuously.

But it was his eyes that transfixed her. Blue, fierce with hunger, dark with anticipation as she eased onto his rigid shaft.

When they joined, he sucked in a sharp breath, holding himself still while she slid down his length. Slowly, so slowly, she lifted. Came down. Rose again.

Eyes narrowed to glittering slits, he dug his fingers into the soft flesh of her hips to guide her. His breathing grew harsh, ragged, picked up the same fast tempo as Sydney's. His hips came up to meet hers, his thighs twisted like steel under hers. She felt each slide, each thrust, each clench of her muscles and his.

"Did I say…you were a woman…of remarkable intelligence?" he rasped.

"I believe you mentioned it, yes."

"Make that…just plain…remarkable."

At the ragged edge to his voice, a thrill of feminine satisfaction pierced the silky curtain of pleasure wrapping itself around Sydney. The wanton, wicked urge to shatter Reece's control into a million tiny pieces spurred her. He looked so determined to hold back, so unused to relinquishing command of any situation.

She leaned forward, planting her hands on his shoulders to give her additional leverage. He didn't hesitate. With swift, unerring skill, he took the tantalizing target she offered. When his mouth fastened on her breast, needles of pure sensation shot from her nipple to her chest to every part of her body. Gasping, writhing where their bodies locked, Sydney rode him.

He climaxed first, shooting up under her, wrapping an arm around her waist to thrust her down, down, until she felt herself splintering.

Reece possessed, Sydney mused lazily some time later, a scent all his own—one she suspected she'd never forget.

She lay sprawled beside him, her cheek on his ribs,

her nose tickled by the curly hair on his chest. With each breath, she drew in the tang of soap mixed with sweat, of healthy male. A smile tugged at her when she spotted the thin film of gray dust rimming his belly button. Evidently he'd missed that vital spot in his hurried shower.

Sydney felt the craziest urge to slide down and swipe it clean for him. Funny how she'd developed a taste for cement all of a sudden. She was contemplating what else she'd developed a taste for when a long, low growl rumbled just under her ear. She lifted her head to find Reece grinning sheepishly.

"Was that you or me?" he asked.

"You."

"Are you as hungry as I am?"

"Hungrier," she replied, matching his grin with one of her own. "I did all the work."

"Is that right?" Giving her hair a playful tug, he eased her onto her back. "Then I guess it's only fair for me to do the catering. Stay right where you are"

As if she could move! Sydney couldn't remember the last time she'd felt so totally boneless. In fact...

She couldn't remember ever feeling like this. She owed this silly, satisfied sensation in part to the burst of splendor she'd just experienced, and even more to the man now zipping up his jeans.

He dropped a kiss on her nose. "I'll be right back."

He disappeared through the connecting door. A moment later Sydney heard the door to his room slam shut. Sighing, she dragged up the spread and tucked it under her arms. Reece's scent came with the well-washed chenille, as masculine and vital as the man himself.

Okay. All right. She might as well admit it. Despite her earnest promises to the contrary, despite her determination not to make a fool of herself by tumbling head over heels in love with a man she'd met little more than a week ago, she was teetering on the edge and about to go right over.

But this time was different, her heart whispered. As Reece had pointed out so fiercely, he wasn't Jamie. He wouldn't play with her, tease her into loving him, then walk away and leave her burning with humiliation. He was like the dam he worked on. Strong. Solid. Built on a foundation of solid bedrock.

More than ever she wanted to see him in action, understand the project that took him out before dawn and brought him back late at night. They were so alike in their drive to succeed, each in their differing fields and disciplines. Eager to learn more about him and his milieu, Sydney made a mental note to ask him when he could take her down into the Chalo River Dam.

The opportunity came sooner than she expected. Cross-legged on the bed, she felt her own stomach rumbling as Reece handed her a plastic bowl brimming with pinto beans. Sopped up with huge chunks of Lula's crusty corn bread and washed down with beer, the beans made for a succulent feast. She'd gobbled down a good portion of her share when Reece brought up the forecast for tomorrow.

"There's another front moving in," he said between bites. "A big one. They're predicting severe thunderstorms for the next several days."

A big chunk of sopping corn bread froze halfway to her mouth. "Oh, no!"

"They've had some flash flooding north of here. We're watching the river levels closely." His eyes grave, he delivered the blow she'd been expecting. "It doesn't look like you should go down into the canyon for another two, possibly three days."

Sydney took a quick gulp of her beer to hide her dismay. She'd shot most of the interviews she wanted, and racked up enough exterior footage to recover from the damage done by the slasher. What she needed now were the interior shots of the ruins, particularly interiors of the stone tower the Weeping Woman of legend threw herself from.

But she couldn't afford to keep her crew twiddling their thumbs for two or three days, not at union scale. Given the prospect of additional delays, her most sensible option was to terminate the on-site shoot. She could shoot the rest of the interiors herself, as well as the final sequence when the reservoir filled and the ruins slowly disappeared beneath the water once more.

Surprisingly, the idea of finishing the takes herself didn't disturb her as much as it might have. When she'd first started out in the business, she'd shot all her own footage. She knew how to handle a minicam.

Added to that was the fact that she'd have time on her hands to explore Reece's world. Besides getting to know him better, she might come up with a different angle on her story, or germinate ideas for a whole new documentary.

With that thought in mind, she was able to swallow her disappointment with her beer and shift the conversation from her project to his.

"What will the rain delays do to your repairs?"

"We'll still pour. We have to. Like you, we only have a designated window of opportunity to complete this project."

"How will you keep the wet concrete from getting, er, wet?"

She braced herself for another physics lesson. Instead, she got a quick grin and a simple layman's explanation.

"We'll erect more scaffolding and use plastic sheeting to shield the fresh-poured concrete."

"When does this production begin?"

"The contractor will have a good-size fleet of cement trucks rolling in here from Phoenix in the morning."

Her ear attuned now to the voice she still wanted to capture on audiotape, Sydney detected a small sting in his reply.

"Are you being pushed?" she asked curiously.

"You might say that."

"Who by?"

He hooked a brow. "You want the whole list or the abbreviated version?"

"Start at the top and work your way down."

"At the top is the secretary of the interior, who's determined to keep his department in line with the budget cuts announced by his close buddy and golfing partner, the president."

"Of the United States?"

"Of the United States. Then there's the commissioner of the Bureau of Reclamation, who's promised his counterpart in the U.S. Fish and Wildlife Service that we'll get the reservoir refilled and restocked as soon as possible."

He stretched out on the bed, the bowl of beans balanced on his stomach. Sydney found her concentration wavering between that lean, flat plane and the list of officials watching over Reece's progress on the repairs to the Chalo River Dam.

"Let's not forget the head of the Arizona Electrical Co-

Op, which purchases about half of the electricity the dam generates," he said with a grimace. "Or the presidents of the Arizona orange and pecan growers associations, who are worried about irrigation for their commercial farms in the area. Then there's Western Region EPA office. They're monitoring the impact on the riverine environment every day we keep the dam down."

Sydney gave a long, slow whistle. "And I thought I was under pressure."

"I won't go into lurid detail about the letters we got from the Bass Anglers Sportsmen's Society, Trout Unlimited, and Outdoor America," he said dryly. "They had to cancel annual sporting events in the area. Or about my meetings with the local ranchers and farmers. Or the lectures I get every day from Lula, who reminds me every day about the business she and Martha are losing each hour the dam is down."

"Good grief! How do you sleep at night?"

"I manage." He stretched out a hand, brushed a knuckle down her cheek. "Something tells me I'll manage even better tonight."

The look in his eyes curled Sydney's toes. The corn bread fell apart in her hands, the crumbs falling unheeded to the spread.

Uh-oh! She was in trouble here. Serious trouble.

She didn't realize how much, however, until Reece took her into his arms once more. And down into his dam the next afternoon.

Chapter 13

Sydney woke the first time when Reece brushed a kiss on her cheek and told her to call him later at the dam. Prying one eye open, she peered at the clock beside the bed, saw that it was 4:20, mumbled a response, and burrowed into the covers.

She woke the second time to a distant growl of thunder. Grimacing, she lay amid the tangled sheets, listening to the rumble. Why the heck did the forecasters have to be so darned accurate in recent days, when they missed so many other predictions? Could she take another extended on-site delay?

Wide awake now, she debated once again the pros and cons of shutting down the shoot and sending the crew home early. She'd pay Albert and Tish and Katie for the sound and videotape they'd shot, as well as the standard early-wrap-up bonus. Albert had another job waiting for him, she knew, and Tish's husband would no doubt be happy to see her come striding in the door with that long-legged gait of hers. Zack... Zack, she'd start on the postproduction work. Torn, she finally admitted she had no choice. She couldn't afford to keep the crew idle.

The rain started just before nine, confirming her decision to shut down operations. Sydney spent the rest of the morning going over the postproduction schedule with Zack while Albert and Tish loaded their equipment into the van. By noon they were packed up for the hour-long drive to Phoenix, where they'd catch a flight to L.A. Several wrapped and sealed cases of videotapes would go with them. With rain splatting down on the oversize red-and-green golf umbrella Zack insisted on leaving with her, she saw the crew to the van.

"Guard those originals with your life," she warned her assistant.

"I will, I will."

"Make two copies of the window-print."

"Got it covered, Syd."

She knew he did. She'd trained him herself. Still, she preferred to personally oversee even this grunt-work part of the process. According to her best estimates, it would take Zack a day at least to make the window-print dubs... copies of the picture and sound from the original videotape with an electronic window inserted that displayed the running time in hours, minutes, seconds, and frames. Another couple of days, she knew from long experience, to label all the originals and dubs, sort through the background information they'd collected, and file and label that as well.

When those tasks were completed, Sydney could begin the arduous task of logging all the footage with the time code of each shot, scene numbers, a brief description of what happened in that scene, and notes about how the shot could be used in the final mix. Only after all that material had been entered into the computer could she use the data to begin the editing process that translated raw footage into a visual statement.

"I'll go over the dub log with you as soon as I get back," she told Zack.

"Which will be, like, when?"

"I don't know. Three days, maybe four. Everything depends on the weather."

"Su-u-u-re it does," Tish put in with a grin as she gave Sydney a quick hug and climbed into the van. "I'm leaving you the Canon two-twelve. Be sure to get some good shots of the dam, girl."

"I intend to."

"Call me if you decide to shoot that documentary on the harnessing of America's rivers."

"I will."

"And don't go, like, driving over any cliffs," Zack begged, only half in jest. "See you, Henry."

Sydney spun around, unaware that her father's old friend had lingered at the café. She'd informed him earlier that she was sending the crew back to L.A., and promised she'd call him when Reece gave her the all-clear to go down into the canyon again. Henry had simply nodded and told her he would wait for her call. She hadn't realized that he intended to do his waiting at the café.

"I have business that keeps me in town," he said simply when she asked him about it.

She was too polite to inquire into his business, but she had a good idea that it concerned her. Henry confirmed her suspicion in the next breath.

"While I'm here, I'll watch over you."

He delivered that pronouncement so calmly, so generously, that Sydney swallowed her instinctive protest.

"Thank you."

Rain dripped from the brim of Henry's felt hat onto his face. "What will you do now?"

"Now, I'm going to call Reece. He offered to take me down into the dam. If he's not up to his ears in wet cement, maybe he could give me a quick tour."

He could, he informed Sydney when she reached him a little while later. As long as she got out there within the next hour.

With Henry dozing in the Blazer's passenger seat, Sydney made tracks out to the dam. En route, she passed a convoy of dump trucks loaded with rubble heading in the opposite direction. They weren't wasting any time clearing out the debris from yesterday's blasting.

The sun poked out between patches of dark clouds just as she made the final, twisting turn down to the dam, giving her a bird's-eye view of the site. Scaffolding draped with great sheets of orange plastic covered the western quadrant, from the crest all the way down to the base. She caught only a glimpse of the gaping wound near the bottom.

Henry opted to doze in the Blazer while one of Reece's men handed Sydney a hard hat and high rubber boots, then escorted her to the elevator that went down inside the dam to the power plant. En route, her natural curiosity prompted her to ask him about the massive crane in operation at the base of the dam.

"How did you get that monster down into the narrow gorge?"

"It was shipped here in sections and lowered piece by piece to the riverbed," her guide explained. "We're using it to clear the debris from the blasting so it doesn't block the inlet channels."

Sydney could only marvel at the detailed planning that had gone into this repair project. No wonder Reece got up before dawn and worked late at night to execute the plan, she thought as she stepped into the tiny elevator cage.

Only eight feet wide at its crest, the dam measured more than fifty-seven feet thick at its base. The deeper Sydney went into its depths, she could feel those fifty-seven feet pressing in on her.

They stepped out of the elevator in the power plant, a long, low building that housed four massive turbines. Flooded with fluorescent lighting and spotlessly clean, the cavernous chamber echoed hollowly as Sydney and her escort crossed it to join the men at the far side.

Even if she hadn't imprinted Reece's face and form on every cell in her body, she could have picked him out instantly as the person in charge. Tall, commanding, sexy as hell in his hard hat and blue workshirt with rolled-up sleeves, he listened intently to the various players before issuing a series of crisp orders.

Sydney waited quietly with her guide until he finished. Welcoming her with a smile, he introduced her to those of his crew she hadn't met, as well as to the contractor and a few of his subs.

"Hey, we've heard about you," one of the subs said. "Are you going to put us in one of your movies?"

"As a matter of fact…" Pulling the hand-held mini-cam out of the canvas bag slung over one shoulder, she asked Reece, "Do you mind if I shoot some footage?"

"Fine by me. If you decide to do anything with the

footage, though, we'll have to run it by the Bureau's public affairs officer."

"Of course."

While the others dispersed, Sydney started having second thoughts about her request for a tour. "Are you sure you have time to show me around right now?"

"This is probably the only time I'll have for the next few days," he replied, scraping a hand across a chin that had already sprouted dark bristles. "What do you want to see first?"

"Whatever you want to show me."

"Why don't we start with the power plant, since we're right here?"

With a hand on her elbow, he guided her to the turbines. Round, green and more than two stories high, they looked like giant mandarin hats with little red buttons on top.

"When these babies are running, you can't hear yourself think," he explained. "Combined, they generate a little over 250,000 kilowatt-hours."

Sydney looked suitably impressed.

Grinning, he put the number into perspective for her. "That's about five percent of all the power generated in the seventeen western states."

"Five percent. Got it. How do these suckers work?"

"They use the simple laws of physics."

She groaned. "Now why doesn't that surprise me?"

"They're nothing more than sophisticated water wheels," he explained, his grin widening. "Water from the reservoir flows through large tubes called penstocks under great pressure and spins the turbines. They, in turn, drive the generators which produce electricity."

Walking her past the towering turbines, he showed her

where the water flowing through them would normally empty into the river below the dam. With the reservoir drained and the spillgates fully opened, the Chalo flowed through in a lazy trickle.

"Providing power was really a secondary motivation in constructing this and the other dams in the Colorado River System," Reece continued as he steered her toward a map mounted on the wall. "The primary concern was and is still flood control."

Propping a boot on a handy storage box, he swept a hand over an area encompassing the states of Colorado, Arizona and Nevada. Unobtrusively Sydney stepped back and lifted the minicam. Thank goodness for the bright lighting. With her high-speed film, she should get a usable image.

"For the millions of years the Colorado has wound its way from the Rocky Mountains to the Gulf, whole cultures have depended on it for life."

God, he looked great through the viewfinder! Tough, rugged, a man who obviously loved his work. She only hoped the echoes in this cavernous chamber didn't distort his deep, drawling narrative.

"Swollen by melting snows, the Colorado and its tributaries had a history of flooding their banks in spring and early summer. In other years, when the snow fell lighter in the northern reaches, the rivers would run dry and great droughts would occur.

"The Indians understood the annual cycles. They retreated before the floods, and when the waters subsided, they planted crops in the rich silt deposits. There wasn't much they could do to compensate for a drought, though. If it lasted too long, they moved on. Some scholars think that's what drove Anasazi out of this area."

This was good! Sydney thought excitedly. Better than good! She'd use Reece's narration as one explanation of why the Ancient Ones abandoned their homes in Chalo Canyon.

"The farmers who followed them seriously underestimated the Colorado's force. In 1905, it flooded for hundreds of miles and rampaged for nearly two years, destroying homes, livestock, whole communities. That disaster led to the establishment of the Bureau of Reclamation and the eventual network of dams that tamed the mighty Colorado."

He dropped his foot and continued the tour, guiding Sydney toward a narrow tunnel.

"This is pretty low in spots. Watch your head."

Thankful for her borrowed hard hat, Sydney followed him into a dimly lit passageway. As the glow from the powerplant faded behind them, she entered a dark, subterranean world. The floor rose in uneven patches where concrete swirled around limestone. Water dripped from the roof of the tunnel. If she hadn't known that the reservoir was drained and not pushing millions of gallons against the tunnel, those shimmering drops would have made her distinctly nervous.

They followed the curve of the base to the canyon wall. Two spotlights were trained on the spot where concrete met sheer rock.

"See those?" Reece pointed to faint striations in the cement some feet above their heads. "Those are the stress fractures I told you about. A minor earthquake hit the area several years ago and pushed the canyon wall into the concrete. You can see the cracks more clearly from the outside now that we've blasted through the exterior wall."

Sydney eyed the hairline fractures with distinct unease. "They're not going to, uh, crack any further in the immediate future, are they?"

"The computers say no."

"What do you say, Reece?"

He hesitated, and her vivid imagination took off. She could almost feel the floor beneath her feet tremble, hear the canyon wall shriek and groan as it rubbed against concrete. Another minute and she'd be feeling millions of tons of cement tumble down on top of her.

As if sensing her growing discomfort, he took her elbow and steered her back the way they'd come. "I say we'd better go topside. You look a little green around the gills."

Sydney had to admit the fresh air and wind whipping down the canyon soothed her jangled nerves. The sky had started spitting again, but not so hard and fast that they couldn't pause for a few moments on the walkway that led along the crest. Hard hat tipped back to catch the breeze, Reece leaned his palms on the parapet and gazed at the scurry of activity below. Sydney was content to simply hitch a hip on the wall and gaze at his profile.

It was strong and clean and almost as stubborn as the forces of nature he worked to harness. Small white squint lines showed in the tanned skin at the corners of his eyes. A faint stubble shadowed his cheeks and chin.

The artist in Sydney wanted to capture the rugged male in his natural element, silhouetted against the pewter sky and the gray sweep of his massive dam. The professional in her admired his awesome intelligence and the dedication that got him up and out to his work at 4:00 a.m. The woman in her just wanted to reach out and stroke that bristly cheek.

"What's next for you after you finish this project?" she asked curiously.

He turned then, his blue eyes lazy on her face. "I'll spend the next couple of months at our Technical Support Center in Denver, working the structural analysis on another critical repair project. My deputy will go into the field on that one, though. I haven't taken any time off in months, and I promised my brother Jake that I'd come home to help bring the cattle down from the north pastures before the snows hit."

"Where's home?"

"A cattle ranch tucked in the foothills of the San Francisco Mountains, just north of Flagstaff. Our folks owned a spread there while I was growing up. Jake manages it now."

"They *owned* it? Did you lose your parents, too?"

"My father died a few years ago. My mother moved off the Bar-H shortly after that."

Keenly sensitive now to this man, Sydney wondered about the edge that had slipped into his voice. Did he still hurt with the loss of his father, as she did? Before she could probe further, he continued.

"Jake manages the spread now, along with his own place. My brothers and I try to make it home for either the spring calving or the fall roundup." He pushed upright, his eyes intent now as he stared down at her. "What about you? What's next?"

"I'm looking at four to five weeks of postproduction work in my studio in L.A. Then…"

She lifted her shoulders. She had several projects in various stages of planning and development. None of them consumed her like the Weeping Woman of Chalo Canyon. And none, she realized, pulled at her as much as the need to take the next step along this magical, sensual journey of discovery with Reece.

"Maybe you could come up to the ranch," he suggested slowly.

Her heart thumped. "Maybe I could."

He moved toward her then, only a step, but Sydney's pulse skittered and spun like a videotape on Rewind. To her intense frustration, one of his men chose that moment to step out of the administration building.

"Hey, Reece! I've got the results of the flownet pressure analysis you requested of the exposed core. You wanted to go over it before we give the contractor the green light to start pouring."

"I'll be right there." The light in his eyes went from dark and intriguing to rueful. "I'm sorry."

"Don't be. I understand pressures and deadlines."

"So you do."

He swept the parking lot beside the building for Sydney's Blazer, noting Henry still ensconced in the front seat, before turning back to her.

"We'll continue this later."

She couldn't act coy if she tried. Making no effort to disguise the hunger that leaped into her veins, she rose up on tiptoe to brush a kiss across his mouth.

"Later it is."

"It'll probably be around eight-thirty," he warned. "We're going to keep going until darkness shuts us down."

"I'll be waiting."

This time, Sydney decided as she stepped into the shower just after eight that night, she intended to pull out all the stops. Reece had seen her in her boots and fatigue pants, in a towel and in nothing at all. Tonight, he was going to see a different woman, one who'd learned the art of skillful, understated makeup from one of Hollywood's masters.

Unfortunately, she hadn't brought anything elegant to wear. Something shiny and slinky and red, like the gown she'd splurged on for the Oscars. The best she could come up with after digging through all her available options were a pair of thigh-skimming flared shorts and a bright red T-shirt cut off just below her breasts, both souvenirs of a weekend at Santa Monica Beach. The shorts she'd purchased before she realized she couldn't bend over in public while wearing them. The short, midriff-baring shirt was more cool and comfortable than sexy. Taken together, however, they made a potent combination.

Humming in anticipation, she dumped the meager supply of makeup she'd brought with her into the sink and went to work. A stubby eye-liner pencil added length and depth to her eyes, careful shadows and a few, feathery strokes to the line of her brows. Lipstick, daubed lightly on her cheeks and rubbed in, doubled as blusher. Her trusty lip balm added a layer of shimmering gloss over the red she swiped on her lips.

That done, she attacked her hair with the hair dryer and boar's bristle hairbrush she never traveled without. The heavy, shoulder-length mass took forever to dry, but each stroke of the brush added to its crackly shine. When it felt like raw silk in her hands, Sydney twisted it up and clamped it on top of her head with a plastic clip. Carefully she teased loose a few strands to frame her face.

Hands on hips, she surveyed the results. The overall picture didn't compare to one she'd made after four hours at one of Beverly Hills' most exclusive salons the day of the Oscars, but it would do. It would definitely do.

Humming, she padded into the bedroom. The bottle of wine she'd picked up at the Gas n' Git on the way back from the dam sat in a gray plastic bucket of ice. The man-size subs heaped with cheese and cold cuts Lula had prepared waited beside the wine.

Deciding to get a little head start, Sydney unscrewed the cap on the wine and poured a half glass. Not bad, she mused after the first sip, considering it had cost all of three ninety-nine. Wineglass in hand, she slipped the cassette from the mini-cam and slid it into the VCR that went everywhere with her.

After a long leader, Reece's face jumped out of the screen. The high-speed tape made for a slightly less vivid image than she liked, but even that small distraction didn't diminish his magnetism. Sighing with satisfaction, Sydney sank onto the bed, plumped the pillows behind her and gave herself over to the unabashed pleasure of listening to Reece explain the simple laws of physics as demonstrated by the turbines.

She had just rewound the tape and started it again when she heard a car door slam right outside. Her eyes flew to the digital clock on the nightstand. Eight twenty-seven. How like Reece to hit it almost exactly on target!

Her stomach clenching with anticipation, Sydney jumped off the bed. The soft rap of knuckles on wood had her reaching for the dead bolt and chain.

"I've got wine chilled and—"

She stopped, her throat closing in shock and dismay. Too late she realized she'd opened her door to the wrong man.

Chapter 14

"Hello, Syd."

Keeping a tight grip on the doorjamb, Sydney eyed Jamie warily. "What do you want?"

The naked bulb over the door cast her visitor's face in stark lines. Rain glinted on his hair, burnishing it to deep gold.

"I need to talk to you. Can I come in?"

"I don't think that's a good idea."

Hitching his shoulders, he shoved his hands in his pockets. A fine edge of desperation seemed to sharpen his features.

"It's important, Syd."

Her instincts shouted at her to slam the door in his face. Jamie Chavez meant nothing but trouble for her.

"Just for a moment. Please." His jaw went tight. "It's

about Arlene. I just found out that she's the one who destroyed your film."

Sydney sucked in a sharp breath and stepped aside. Jamie brushed past her, looking older and more careworn than she'd ever seen him. Just to be safe she left the door open an inch or two. A single piercing scream would bring half the occupants of the motel running, not to mention Lula and Martha.

She turned to find Jamie standing in the middle of the room, his gaze snagged on the video she'd left running on the TV screen. His eyes held a cynical, knowing look when he turned them from Reece to Sydney.

"I thought you came here to document the legend of the Weeping Woman. Looks like you've found another subject that interests you."

She ignored his barbed comment. She wasn't about to discuss what was between her and Reece with this man. A quick flick of the remote killed the video playback. Tossing down the remote, she folded her arms.

"I thought *you* came here to talk about Arlene."

"I did."

"So talk."

He couldn't seem to figure out how to start. "This is hard for me. I didn't think… I didn't know…"

"How much you've hurt your wife over the years?" Sydney supplied with a lift of one brow.

"I didn't know how much she loved me," he said finally. "Or how desperate she's become."

He reached down and helped himself to a glass of wine. Sydney's lips tightened, but she bit back her automatic protest. The sooner he finished, the sooner she'd get him out of here. She had no desire to prolong his visit by indulging in petty arguments or recriminations.

Throwing back his head, Jamie tossed down the white zinfandel like it was water. He stared at the empty glass for a moment before continuing.

"Arlene broke down tonight. The combination of two martinis and those damned diet pills she gobbles like candy got to her, I guess." He shuddered. "It wasn't a pleasant scene."

Poor baby, Sydney thought cynically. He was finally having to face up to reality.

"She poured out doubts and insecurities I didn't even know she had." Obviously shaken, he paced the small space between the bed and the door. "She even told me that she's been seeing a shrink in Phoenix. All this time I thought she was going to have her hair and nails done. She's been in therapy and never told me."

He looked across the room, his eyes beseeching. "I didn't know I'd done that to her, Syd. I never realized she was so fragile."

Sydney bit back the retort that he only had to look at his wife, really look at her, and he would have seen how fragile she was. Reece had seen it, had even pretended a relationship with a near stranger to save Arlene the embarrassment of watching her husband put the make on another woman. But then, Reece wasn't Jamie.

Thank God!

Her visitor seemed lost in contemplation of his empty glass.

"Arlene admitted that she destroyed my film?" Sydney prompted when it seemed as though the silence would stretch indefinitely.

He nodded, lifting his head. "She's jealous of you. Of your success and your looks. She can't forget what happened between us ten years ago."

"Well, I have. And I hope to heck you told her that you have, too."

"I tried." He blew out a long breath. "She's sorry about the videotapes, Syd. Really sorry. We want to cover any extra expenses you might have incurred as a result."

Relenting, Sydney sighed. "I don't care so much about the cost as the lost footage."

He fidgeted with his glass, then poured himself another helping. "Look, I'd appreciate it if you'd call the sheriff's office and tell them you don't want to press charges."

"Ah, now the real reason for your visit comes out." A hint of anger crept into her voice. "The proud Chavez family don't want to see one of their own charged with malicious destruction of property."

"*I* don't want to see my wife charged."

"And your father doesn't play in this, I suppose?"

"He doesn't know anything about it, or that I was coming to see you. I didn't even tell Arlene."

Suddenly she was tired of the whole mess. She couldn't believe she'd ever thought herself in love with this man. Even more to the point, she'd discovered that what she'd felt all those years ago hadn't even come close to love.

She had a pretty good idea now of what comprised that all-consuming emotion. The basic ingredients included listening to a man talk about his work in the claustrophobic confines of a narrow tunnel and thrilling to his passion for what he did. Wanting desperately to hear his low growl of laughter, to feel his hands on her body. Tingling with excitement at the thought of going home with him to a ranch tucked in the foothills of the San Francisco Mountains.

Impatient now to be rid of Jamie, she plucked the glass out of his hand and escorted him to the door.

"I'll call Martinez tomorrow and tell him I won't press charges in the matter of the destruction of the tapes. I can't say I'll feel as forgiving if it turns out Arlene engineered my accident on Canyon Rim Road."

Jamie stopped dead in his tracks. "What are you talking about?"

"Reece thinks someone may have helped that slab of limestone fall, right where the road hairpins around a curve."

"The hell he does!"

"In light of what you've told me tonight, Martinez will want to talk to Arlene about where she was the day of the accident."

High spots of color flagged Jamie's cheeks. Before Sydney could evade them, his hands whipped out and wrapped around her forearms.

"Are you saying you think my wife tried to kill you?"

"Your wife...or your father," Sydney shot back, twisting in his grip.

"You're crazy!"

"And you're starting to annoy me. Big-time. Let me go."

Instead his fingers dug deeper into her arms. His voice rose to a furious shout. "My wife wouldn't hurt a flea!"

"She did a heck of a number on my tapes!"

Incensed at the manhandling, Sydney tried to jerk free. When that didn't work, she aimed a kick at his shins. In self-defense, he hauled her up against his chest.

"Dammit, Sydney, calm down!"

"Go to hell, Chavez!"

She managed to get an arm free and aimed an awkward swing at his chin. He caught her fist just before it connected, and twisted her arm behind her back.

"For God's sake, you always were a hothead! You and your father. He had no business taking a swing at my father the way he did."

"Is that right?"

Her arm pinned against her back, her hair tumbling from its clip, Sydney could barely speak over her fury. Jamie could badmouth her all he wanted, but no one, *no one* put down her father and lived to tell about it.

"I have a lot more respect for a man who would defend his daughter than one who'd tuck his tail between his legs and scurry away at *his* father's command."

Scorn dripped from every word. The flush staining Jamie's cheeks grew brick-red. Before he could get out the hot retort that bared his teeth, however, a heartbroken cry spun his head around.

"Jamie! Oh, God, Jamie!"

He froze. His expression would have been comical in its dismay if anyone was in the mood to laugh.

"Arlene!" A hoarse denial ripped from his throat. "This isn't what it looks like."

Sebastian's outraged voice rose above the anguish coming in little, choking cries from Arlene.

"I knew it! I knew that woman would try to get her claws in you!"

The woman in question fought a groan. She couldn't believe it! Talk about déjà vu! It was ten years ago all over again.

"You ass," she hissed at Jamie. "Let me go."

"What?"

Stunned by the turn of events, he stared down at her

blankly. She opened her mouth to repeat the furious order, but it got lost in a new commotion outside.

Doors slammed. Footsteps pounded. Lula's voice came screeching through the air. "We heard the shoutin'! What's going on?"

Martha added her squeaky demand to her sister's. "What are you doing in Sydney's room, Sebastian?" The footsteps skidded to a halt. "Arlene! You're here, too? And Jamie? Oh, my! Oh, my goodness!"

Enough was enough. Her face flaming, Sydney yanked free of Jamie's hold. She was damned if she was going to explain or apologize or burn with humiliation. Not again. Never again.

"You said you didn't love her!" Arlene cried. She clung to Sebastian's arm as if she couldn't support herself. "Just tonight, just an hour ago, you told me that you'd never loved her."

"I didn't." Jamie swallowed painfully, his face now as pale as it had been red a few moments ago. "It was just a summer fling."

Sydney had found that out the hard way ten years ago. She didn't particularly enjoy having it rebroadcast for public consumption, however.

"Then what are you doing here?" Arlene sobbed. "Why are you in her room?"

Ha! That put him on the spot. Folding her arms, Sydney let Jamie find his own way out of that one.

"I came to talk to her about the videotapes."

Sebastian's aristocratic face sharpened. Shaking free of his daughter-in-law's hold, he strode into the room to stand between Sydney and his son.

"What about the tapes?"

The younger Chavez squared his chin. "I destroyed them and I—"

"You!" Sebastian's head reared back.

Arlene's sobs caught in her throat. She gaped at her husband, her eyes wide and confused. "Jamie…"

He cut her off sharply. "It was a stupid thing to do. I have no rationale, no reason."

Except the desire to protect his wife, Sydney thought. Grudgingly she recognized what Jamie himself didn't seem to. He cared enough for Arlene to want to spare her public humiliation. He certainly hadn't cared that much for Sydney ten years ago.

"I came here tonight to ask her not to press charges," he finished stiffly, his eyes cutting to Sydney as if daring her to contradict him…or bring up the business of the accident on Canyon Rim Road.

She did neither. She was heartily sick of the whole Chavez clan. She would let Deputy Martinez sort out their assorted stories. That was his job. She had just started to tell them so when the sound of brakes screeching brought all heads around.

Reece!

Sydney's heart jumped with relief, with dismay, with the almost farcical irony of the situation. Reece had heard all the stories about her scandalous past. His blue eyes tinged with disgust, he'd stepped in personally to divert Jamie's attention that first night at the café. Would he believe Chavez had come to her room tonight just to talk, or automatically assume the worst, as everyone else had?

Would he walk away from her, as Jamie had once done?

No, he wouldn't walk away. Not Reece. Still, Sydney's chin tipped in anticipation of the explanations she knew he'd demand.

Reece had spotted the crowd milling around the door to Unit Twelve the moment he turned into the parking lot. He was out of the Jeep and running before it had rolled to a full stop. His heart hammering, he shouldered his way through the crowd at the door. He didn't pull in a whole breath until he spotted Sydney, her hair tumbling down and her eyes fierce.

She looked like a mountain cat cornered by a pack of hungry wolves. Her eyes spit green fire. Her claws were unsheathed. She wasn't going down without a fight.

His only thought as he walked into the room was to get his woman away from the voracious pack. He took in the two wineglasses, the rumpled bed, the tears streaking Arlene's face in a single, sweeping glance.

"Are you okay?" he asked Sydney quietly.

"Yes."

The stiff little response spoke volumes. She was writhing inside, but too damned proud to show it. Now that he knew she was safe, Reece decided the first order of business was to clear the room and give her some breathing space.

"Okay, folks. The show's over. Why don't we all call it a night."

The casual order carried an underlying note of steel. Those outside the door drifted away, murmuring. His expression almost as fierce as Sydney's, Jamie Chavez gave Reece a hard look, then walked across the room to slide an arm around his wife's waist. She collapsed against him, crying into his shoulder as he led her away.

Only Sebastian Chavez remained. Rigid. Unyielding. His black eyes cold and scornful in his proud face.

"She's a slut, Henderson. She seduced my son ten years ago and came back to Chalo Canyon to finish what she started then."

Reece rocked on the balls of his feet, his hands curling into fists. "The only reason I don't flatten you right here, right now, Chavez, is the fact that I carry forty pounds more in weight than you and thirty fewer years. I might forget those fine distinctions, however, if you don't get the hell out of here."

"She'll destroy you, too, if you let her."

Reece took a step forward. "Now, Chavez!"

Sebastian's nostrils flared. He glared at Reece for another few seconds, shot Sydney a venomous look, then spun on his heel and stalked out. Reece shut the door behind him, noting that the locks showed no signs of forced entry. Evidently Sydney had let that parade from her past into her room.

He would talk to her later about that bit of foolishness, he decided. Right now he figured she needed one thing, and one thing only. The same thing he did.

He strode back to her, dipped, and swept her up in his arms. The single chair in the room looked too rickety to hold them both, but Reece decided to chance it.

Sydney lay stiff against his chest for several long moments. He could feel her trembling. Subduing his seething fury at the Chavezes for subjecting her to this public debacle, he held her loose against his chest.

Finally she twisted upright in his lap. "Don't you want to know what happened?"

"I can pretty well figure it out."

Her chin came up. A militant sparkle lit her eyes. She was still feeling the sting of Sebastian's parting shot, Reece guessed.

"Just what have you figured out?"

"Jamie came knocking on your door and talked his way inside."

"And?"

The belligerence in her tone tugged at Reece's heart. She'd gone down this road once before.

"And," he said calmly, "Chavez Jr. proceeded to make a total ass of himself. You were in the process of showing him out when his wife and father and everyone else in town arrived on the scene."

She stared at him, waiting for him to continue. When he didn't, her brows snapped together.

"That's it? That's what you think happened?"

"I don't think, Sydney. I know."

"How?"

He smiled at the blunt demand. A week ago, even a few days ago, he might have asked himself the same question. He'd heard all the stories about her. Had formed a less-than-flattering picture of her in his mind before he'd even met her. Since then he'd gained a deeper insight into this vital, vibrant woman. He'd seen her single-minded dedication to her work, her lively curiosity about anything and everything, even his dam. He'd laughed with her, loved with her. He couldn't imagine how he'd believed, even for a moment, the stories that painted her as the cold-hearted other woman.

Sliding fingers into her tumbled hair, he cradled her face in his palms. "I know that's what happened, because I know you."

Sydney went into the kiss stunned by his simple declaration. She came out of it aching with a love that started deep in her chest and spread at warp speed to every finger, every toe.

It was several breathless moments before she remembered Jamie's reason for knocking on her door. She struggled upright in Reece's lap once more.

"Jamie came to town tonight to tell me that Arlene slashed my videotapes."

"He ratted on his wife?" Reece's lip curled. "Nice guy."

Much as it went against the grain to defend the man, Sydney had to admit the truth. "No, he didn't come to rat on her, only to ask me to drop the charges."

The last of her old resentments slipped away as she related how Jamie had leaped to Arlene's defense. He loved her, even if he didn't know the extent of that love. He'd always loved her. Sydney could only blame her own foolish infatuation on the fact that she hadn't recognized that fact any more than Jamie had.

"So are you?" Reece asked. "Going to drop the charges?" he added when she looked at him blankly.

Smiling, she shook off the past forever. "Of course. I don't want to hurt Arlene. I never did."

Looping her arms around his neck, she brushed his mouth with hers. With the touch came a gradual awareness. She *didn't* want to hurt Arlene. She didn't want to hurt anyone. She drew back, her eyes filling with regret.

"Maybe Sebastian was right."

Reece's palm slid around her nape. His thumb tipped her chin. "Not hardly."

The snarl warmed Sydney's heart.

"I didn't come back here for revenge or intending to destroy Jamie's marriage, but I've certainly added to the stresses. If my presence pushed Arlene to such destructive, vengeful acts, I think—No, I know. I need to go back to L.A. and leave them in peace."

He didn't say anything.

"I'll pack up tomorrow, Reece."

"What about your documentary?"

She let out a long gust of breath. "I'll use what footage I have and exercise my creativity to fill in where I have to."

Reece didn't even try to dissuade her. After seeing the look in Sebastian's eyes, his gut told him that the old man's hatred went far deeper than Arlene's. Or maybe it was fear. Whatever drove him, Reece wanted Sydney out of the line of fire.

He knew what leaving would cost her, however, and how much this documentary meant to her. The fact that she'd pack up before she completed her shoot opened a crack in his heart.

"I'll come get you in L.A.," he said with a smile that promised everything he didn't have the words to express, "and take you home to meet my brothers."

"Are they as tough as you?"

"Tougher."

"As big?"

"Bigger."

She traced a fingertip along his jaw. "As handsome?"

"No, ma'am," he said without a blink. "They're ugly as sin and twice as mean. I'm the best of the lot."

Laughing, she dropped a kiss on his mouth.

"I'll remember that."

Chapter 15

Sydney said goodbye to Reece in the predawn darkness. The farewells took longer than either of them anticipated, particularly since they involved an unexpected detour back to bed.

Finally Reece groaned and pulled himself out of her arms. "I'll see you in L.A. within a week. Two, at most. If the repair work takes longer than anticipated, I'll fly in for a night at least."

"Is that a promise?"

"That, sweetheart, is a promise."

Every nerve in Sydney's body hummed with pleasure at the look in his eyes. He was, she now knew, a man of his word. This time she wasn't leaving an aching heart behind when she left Chalo Canyon.

She was still languid with pleasure when she rolled out of bed a few hours later, showered and began to pack her things. She stepped outside to a spitting rain and went down to the café for coffee and a quick breakfast.

Henry Three Pines was waiting for her, his gnarled hands folded around a mug of Lula's dark, steaming brew.

"We will not need the snakes to ask the kachinas for much rain this year," he observed when she joined him.

"Not this year," she agreed.

Someday, Sydney thought, she should document the famous Hopi snake dance that took place each summer after eight days of secret rituals. But she'd only shoot from a distance. She had no desire to get in close to the dancers who snatched up live rattlesnakes and carried them around in their mouths before releasing them to carry the tribe's pleas for rain to the gods.

She and Henry sat in companionable silence for a few moments, each contemplating the rain outside, before Sydney sighed.

"I'm going home today."

"So I have heard. I will send my grandsons down into the canyon this morning to remove the ladders and equipment you rented."

"Thank you."

His calm gaze settled on her face. "It's a wise decision, Little Squirrel. You have found what you sought when you came back here."

A blush started at her neck and worked its way to her cheeks. Under the brim of his brown felt hat, Henry's weathered face folded into a million wrinkles.

"I meant the peace your spirit needed," he said with a grin. "But it is good that you found Reece, also." His hand closed over hers. "Your father would be happy for you."

"I think so, too."

* * *

Sydney thought about Henry's words as she settled her bill and made her farewells to Lula and Martha. Despite the fact that she had gaping holes in her documentary and would have to scramble to fill them with stock footage, she was leaving Chalo Canyon feeling far more serenity than when she'd arrived.

Serenity…and a simmering, sizzling joy.

As if to echo her mood, the sun broke through the clouds unexpectedly just as she hit the two-lane road that led out of town. The Blazer hummed along for another few miles, soaking up the hazy sunshine. As it approached a Y in the road, Sydney eased up on the accelerator.

She could cut right and take the private road through Sebastian's land to save herself twenty miles, or detour around his property as she'd done for the past ten days. The temptation to thumb her nose at him and drive across his land tugged at her, but she swung left and took the longer route. The last thing she wanted was another encounter with any of the Chavez clan.

A few miles down the road, she approached the State Road that ran north and south. South would take her to Phoenix and the airport. North…north would take her to the canyon rim and the pull-off where she and her crew had parked their vehicles before trekking down into the canyon.

The Blazer slowed to a stop. Crossing her hands over the wheel, Sydney contemplated the black-topped road. The sun still shone through the gray clouds, but the light was getting weaker by the moment. She chewed on her lower lip, aching for one last shot at the ruins. She had time. Her flight to L.A. didn't take off for another four hours.

Digging in her purse, she pulled out her cell phone and punched in the number for Reece's. She'd just about given up hope that he'd answer when his voice snapped.

"Henderson."

She could barely hear him over the roar of machinery in the background. He must be down at the base of the dam, near that monster crane.

"Reece, it's Sydney. I'm on my way to the airport."

"Drive safe. Let me know when you get there."

"I will. Listen, I'm only a few miles from the path that leads into the canyon. I'm going down for one more shot while this light holds."

"What?" He had to yell over the ear-splitting noise in the background.

"I'm going to make a brief stop at the ruins."

"That's not a good idea!"

"Everyone thinks I've left town. It's safe."

"No, it's not. Those clouds…" He broke off, cursing as gears shrieked like the demons of hell. "Those clouds to the north have dumped a lot of rain on the mesas. Our recorders haven't registered any measurable threat of flooding yet, but—What? Okay, okay," he shouted in an aside. "I'll be right there."

"I'll only stay a few minutes," she assured him when she had his attention again. "Just enough for some shots of the tower where the Weeping Woman was imprisoned. I won't get the interiors I need, but at least I'll have a few exteriors focused exclusively on the tower and the window she supposedly jumped from. I'll be in and out of the canyon in an hour and a half."

"All right," he conceded with heavy reluctance. "Just

keep your phone handy and hotfoot it out of there immediately if I call and tell you to."

"I will."

Eager for a chance to showcase the tower in a last, dramatic sequence, Sydney grabbed the hard-sided case that held the minicam and its assorted lenses, locked the car and stuffed the keys in one of her many pockets. The cell phone went in another. Thank goodness she'd opted for the comfort of her baggy pants and sneakers for the return trip to L.A.! Slinging the strap of the camera case over her shoulder, she hurried down the path. She'd made the trek in and out of the canyon often enough by now to know every bump and turn and slide of rocks by heart.

Hurrying, she reached river level within ten minutes, the ruins in another fifteen. Sweaty from exertion and the muggy dampness of the impending rain, she gave a silent prayer of thanks when the wind started to pick up. The frisky breeze lifted the damp hair off her neck and tossed stray tendrils at will. Within moments, she had the viewfinder to her eye and was trying to find just the right angles.

Intent on her task, Sydney moved sideways along the river bank, shooting a series of shorts, longs and wide angles that focused on the shadowy window at the top of the square tower. She wished to heck she could climb up to the cave and get inside the Weeping Woman's supposed prison, but Henry's grandsons had already picked up the ladders, and there was no way Sydney was going to attempt those shallow handholds dug into the cliff face.

She finished one thirty-minute Betacam tape, dropped it in her pocket and was just getting ready to insert another when the wind began to whistle down the canyon in earnest. Rising. Falling. A soughing cry.

Aiiiii. Eee-aiiiii.

One by one, the hair on the back of Sydney's neck lifted. It sounded just like the tiny, hollow-cheeked retired schoolteacher turned eccentric, Laura Brent, calling to her. Sydney had already decided to pack it in when the rumble of thunder brought her head up with a jerk. Even as she watched, billowing clouds rolled across the sun. The sky darkened instantly to an angry gray.

"Whoa! Time to make tracks, girl!"

Where there was thunder, lightning was sure to follow. Or was it the other way around? In either case, she had no desire to get zapped by those two zillion amps Reece had talked about.

He confirmed her decision when he called a moment later.

"Get out of there!" he barked. "Now! The rain's coming down in sheets north of here."

"I'm on my way."

"Call me as soon as you're on the path up to the rim."

"I will."

She was fitting the minicam into its case when another sound carried over the eerie cry of the wind. A faint slide of rock on rock. A heavy tread. She spun around and went rigid with shock.

Sebastian moved toward her. Slowly. Steadily. His silver hair whipped in the wind, but the evil-looking automatic pistol in his hand didn't waver. The hatred in his black eyes caught Sydney by the throat.

"I knew you were lying about leaving Chalo Canyon."

She didn't bother to ask how he knew about her abrupt departure. Gossip traveled at the speed of light in a small town. Besides, she wasn't sure she could speak around the baseball-size lump in her throat.

"Your kind always lies."

"No, it's true. I'm leaving. Today. Right now, if you'll just…"

She swallowed her disjointed words and stumbled back a pace as he came nearer. Her fingers gripped the strap of the camera case as if it were a lifeline to reality, sanity. Safety.

"Didn't you see my car? The Blazer?" she asked desperately. "It's all packed."

"I saw it. That's how I knew you had come down into the canyon."

"How could you miss the suitcases and the equipment in the back? I'm leaving Chalo Canyon, Sebastian. I swear, I'm leaving."

He smiled then, a slight rearrangement of his facial muscles that churned Sydney's mounting terror into bile.

"That's what Marianne said."

"Who?"

"My wife. She was a slut, like you. The only thing she did right in our short marriage was give birth to Jamie." His smile slipped into a fury that was all the more frightening for being so cold, so implacable. "Even then, she taunted me, tried to tell me he wasn't my son."

With a calm detachment that horrified Sydney, he pulled back the automatic's slide and cocked it. Hands out, camera case dangling from one wrist, she made a desperate attempt to reason with the man.

"Sebastian! Wait! I didn't come back to Chalo Canyon to hurt you or your son, only to make a documentary. You have to believe me!"

"I believe you," he said grimly. "I've believed you all along."

"Then what…why…?"

"Why do I have to kill you? Because I don't want that film made."

Sydney's hair whipped in her face, stinging her cheeks. She didn't dare reach up to clear it for fear the movement would trigger a reaction from the man only a few yards from her.

"My documentary won't dishonor the Anasazi! If anything, it might stir interest in the Ancient Ones."

"You fool! Haven't you realized that's exactly what I fear? Your cursed movie will bring a horde of archeologists and anthropologists down on the ruins every time the reservoir drains. Maybe even scuba divers during the years the village is underwater, poking around in the ruins, trying to find artifacts."

"But…"

Suddenly his eyes blazed. "Don't you understand? I don't want them up there! I didn't want you up there, disturbing old ghosts!"

"You mean the Weeping Woman? But that's just a legend."

The smile came back, so cold, so terrifying, that Sydney's heart froze.

"Is it?"

Her mind went blank for several seconds. Absolutely, totally, completely blank. Then the bits of gossip mixed with local lore she'd picked up exploded into her thoughts, ripping through her imagination like shrapnel.

"Oh, my God! She's up there, isn't she? Your wife? Lula said…" Frantic, Sydney tried to recall the on-camera interview with the Jenkins sisters. "She said she first heard the legend of the Weeping Woman about thirty years ago. From you…not long after your wife disappeared."

She wet her lips, her horror mounting as she fit the pieces of the puzzle together. "The story shook Lula so much she never trekked down into the canyon again. That's what you intended, isn't it? That's why you made up the tale about the Weeping Woman? To scare people away from the ruins."

"I didn't make it all up. I'd heard a similar tale as a child and simply embellished it."

His lip curled. The face Sydney had always thought of as aristocratic became a twisted mask.

"Appropriate, don't you think? Marianne planned to leave me for someone else. I never learned who. When she threatened to take Jamie away with her, I knew I could never let her leave Chalo Canyon alive. She became the Weeping Woman, crying for her lost love."

"Sebastian…"

"She's been buried under the rubble in that tower for more than thirty years. She would have slept for eternity if you hadn't decided to poke around in the ruins and make your damned—"

Without warning, the skies split. Lightning cracked. Instinctively Sebastian hunched his shoulders and whipped his head around for a second to see where it hit. Only for a second.

Sydney knew that second was all she'd get. In an explosive burst of fear and adrenaline, she fisted her hand around the camera case strap and swung with every ounce of strength she possessed.

The hard-sided case hit Sebastian's arm with a glancing blow, knocking it in a wild arc. The automatic flew out of his hand and clattered against stone. Before he could recover his balance, she followed up with another, even more vicious swing. This one slammed into his right temple. He grunted, then crumpled to the earth.

Her blood roaring in her ears, Sydney stood over him. Panting, gasping, swimming in adrenaline, she hefted the case again, held it high above her head, her arms shaking with the strain, until she felt sure he wasn't feigning.

He was out cold.

For how long, she couldn't guess. And she sure didn't intend to stick around to find out. Scrambling in the direction the gun had flown, she searched desperately for a sight of its gleaming blue steel. She didn't want to leave it behind for him to find if and when he came to and started after her. She'd taken only a single step when her cell phone shrilled, almost stopping her heart.

Sucking in air, she kept a wary eye on Sebastian, dug in her pockets for the phone and tried to find the damned automatic, all at the same time. Finally she fumbled the phone free and flipped it up.

"Sydney!" Reece roared. "Where are you?"

"At the ruins. Sebas—"

"I told you to get out of there!"

"I was on my way, but—"

"You don't have time to make it to the path. You'll have to go up the cliff face! Now!"

She shot an incredulous look at the handholds carved into the rock. "Are you crazy?"

"Listen to me. I just got a call from the water-monitoring station twenty miles north of here. An arroyo that used to drain into the west mesa crumbled and changed course. Its spill is now pouring into the Chalo. There's a wall of water and mud eight feet high roaring down the canyon. I've called in a chopper for you, but—"

She didn't like the sound of that "but." She didn't like the sound of any of this!

"I'll take the Jeep and get to you as fast as I can. Just get up that cliff face!"

"Reece, Sebastian's here." She wrapped both hands around the phone, her hair whipping wildly. "He tried to shoot me. I knocked him out."

"Oh, God!" His breath exploded in her ear. "I've got a rope in the Jeep. I'll come down for Sebastian when I get there. Start climbing, Sydney. Now!"

Abandoning all thoughts of the gun, she ran for the cliff. Halfway there, she stumbled to a halt. She swung around, panting, to stare at Sebastian's unmoving form. She couldn't just leave the bastard there to drown. Could she?

Cursing a blue streak at her own idiocy, Sydney raced back to the comatose man and grabbed his arm. Grunting, panting, she dragged him toward the cliff. She didn't have the faintest idea how she'd get him up the sheer rock face.

She'd figure that out when she got there.

Down canyon, Reece slammed the phone shut and raced along the dam's thick, curving base. He'd already activated the emergency flood-warning-alert system, but the responsibility for the safety of the men working on-site as well as the residents of the towns downriver sat on his shoulders like a ton of concrete. He had only seconds to think, to analyze the situation, only moments to decide what to do.

In a flash flood situation like this, the correct procedure was to close the spillgates and trap the rushing water behind the dam. The massive structure would contain it, keep it from rushing on and ravaging the towns down-river. The dam had been constructed all those years ago for just that purpose.

In this case, however, the rampaging floodwater would hit an exposed core, one already weakened by stress fractures. The whole dam could give under the sudden, added force.

And it would! Reece knew it with everything in him. Despite the computer analyses, despite X-rays and geophysical in-situ testing, Reece knew the base wouldn't hold without some kind of reinforcement. Worry and fear for Sydney gnawing at his gut, he raced for the two men conferring at the repair site.

"Call up top," he ordered his deputy. "Tell them to close the floodgates. Then I want the dam cleared of all personnel."

His second in command nodded, but his eyes mirrored Reece's own worry. "If we've got as much water coming at us as they said, this baby won't take the added stress."

"She'll have to."

The engineer threw a wrenching look at the crater blasted out of the curving base. "Not with her core exposed like that."

"We're not going to leave it exposed." He shot an order at the contractor. "I want your crane operator to ram his machine up against the hole. Let it take the force of the water, act as a kind of a plug."

"That piece of equipment cost fifteen million dollars!"

"I'll take full responsibility." His lips stretched in a grim smile. "If this doesn't work and the entire dam comes down on top of the crane, they can deduct the cost of a replacement from my paycheck."

"Dammit, Reece...!"

"You got a better idea?"

The contractor hesitated, shook his head.

"Then do it!" Already on the run, he shouted again for his deputy to clear the dam.

"Where are you going?"

"There are people trapped up canyon. I've got to get to them."

He had to get to Sydney!

Flinging himself inside the tiny elevator, he stabbed at the buttons. Every verse of the Bible his mother had drummed into her five unruly sons ran through his heart during the agonizingly slow ride to the top. The moment he shoved open the elevator door, the sound of a helicopter coming in low and fast assaulted his ears.

The bird set down in the parking lot, its maroon-and-silver logo glistening in the rain. Reece ducked under the whirring blades, yanked open the passenger door and climbed aboard.

"I heard you called for a rescue chopper," Jamie shouted over the scream of the rotor. "I came to help."

"Let's go!"

They lifted off mere seconds later. For the duration of the short ride, Reece listened to the reports from upriver, confirmed that the crane was in place and his men had cleared the dam, and prayed that Sydney had managed to climb up the cliff face.

Rain pelted down, knifing into her flesh. Panting, Sydney shook her hair out of her eyes and tried to gauge the distance to the cliff. Another ten yards. Maybe fifteen.

Her breath stabbed at her lungs. Her knees and back were bent with the strain of dragging Sebastian's dead weight. She had him almost to the foot of the cliff when he groaned.

"Sebastian!" She dropped to her knees, shook his shoulders. "Sebastian, wake up!"

He moaned again and put a shaking hand to his temple.

"You've got to climb up to the ruins! Reece says there's a flash flood…"

His eyes opened. He stared at her dully.

"Listen to me!" She shouted over the screaming wind. "We've got to climb up to the ruins. Reece says there's a flash flood up canyon. It's coming right at us!"

He staggered to his feet and looked around wildly, as if trying to remember where he was. When his glance came back to her, his face twisted.

"I can't let you leave Chalo Canyon alive, you witch. I can't let you take my son."

Still woozy, still off balance from the blow, he lunged for her. Sydney danced away from him easily. Desperate, she tried to think past the fear roaring in her ears of some way to reach him, to make him understand…

Suddenly, she realized that the roar in her ears wasn't fear. She threw a terrified glance up canyon. It sounded like a freight train was tearing right at them.

"Sebastian!"

All around them the roar rose to a deafening pitch.

For a moment she stared into eyes blinded by hate. Then Sebastian lurched away.

"I'll find my gun. I'll end this now. You won't leave. You won't take my son away."

Sobbing, shaking with terror, Sydney stuck her toe into an indentation carved out of the rock. Her scrabbling right hand found a hole just above her head. Her left, another a little higher up. She pulled herself up, scraped her foot across the rock until she found purchase, pulled again.

She didn't dare look up to measure the distance to the cave for fear she'd overbalance and fall backward. Nor could she look down to see if Sebastian was climbing the cliff below her or still searching for his damned gun. Her skin crawled with the fear that he would find it. She could almost feel the bullets slamming into her body.

Sweating, straining, deafened by the howling wind and nerve-shattering roar, she crabbed up the cliff face.

She was halfway to the cave when a wall of muddy water came bursting around the canyon's bend. It crashed toward her, under her, slapping upward, sucking at her feet, her legs. Sydney clung to the wall, her face pressed into stone, her nails clawing at rock.

Then, as fast as it had come, the crest passed. The angry water dropped a foot, a yard, raged on below her. Her fingers numb, her shoulder and calf muscles on fire, she tried to find the strength for the rest of the climb. Only then did she hear Reece's voice amplified a thousand times over, bouncing off the canyon walls.

"Grab the harness! Sydney, behind you! Grab the harness!"

Chapter 16

For the rest of her life, Sydney would remember the day the Chalo raged through the canyon, bringing with it moments of terrifying fear and blinding joy.

One of the worst moments came just after Reece hauled her aboard the chopper. As soon as she caught her breath, she shouted over the noise of the blades to Jamie.

"Your father's down there!"

He took his eyes from the controls long enough for her to see the wrenching anguish in his eyes.

"Reece said he came after you. Tried to shoot you."

She nodded, her throat closing at his pain.

"I did this to him."

The words tore out of Jamie's throat as he stared through the rain-splattered windshield, his arms and legs automatically working the chopper's controls.

"I worried him sick about Arlene and me. I made him think that you, that I—"

"No! It wasn't you." Leaning past Reece, Sydney grabbed his shoulder. "It wasn't you. I'll tell you everything later...when we find him." Her fingers dug into his wet shirt. "He may still be alive. We may find him."

Even as she shouted the encouragement, Reece shook his head. Sebastian's son put what Reece didn't say into flat, hard words.

"He couldn't have survived that." His jaw locked. "And I can't search for his body now. We've got to get back to the dam, see if it's going to hold. If not, my first, my only priority is to evacuate the ranch, make sure Arlene is safe."

The dam! Sydney clutched the edges of the thin, silver solar blanket Reece had wrapped around her. Her frightened eyes sought his.

"Those stress fractures? The ones you were so worried about? They're taking the brunt of the river?"

Incredibly, he flashed her a grin. It was weak and strained around the edges, but it was definitely a grin.

"With the help of a fifteen-million-dollar crane."

Gulping, she sank back on the helo's side seat. Her all-too-vivid imagination kicked into high gear. She could see the dam crumbling, hear the tearing groan of concrete giving way. After her own experience in the canyon, she had no difficulty imagining the terror of the residents of the town when the floodwaters came roaring down on them.

She didn't take a whole breath until the chopper swooped around a bend of the canyon and the Chalo River Dam rose ahead of them. Proud, curved, glistening in the rain, it had caught the floodwaters and thrown them back.

Muddy water churned angrily, slapped up the dam's spine, tearing down what remained of the scaffolding. Only the arm of a massive crane poked out of the swirling mass.

Fascinated, horrified, wishing with all her heart she had a camera to record this awesome spectacle, Sydney jumped out of the helo right behind Reece when they touched down in the parking lot. They joined the cluster of men at the canyon's edge, watching, waiting.

Finally the water found its level. The churning subsided. A profound stillness descended.

After what seemed like a lifetime, Reece broke the silence. "All right. The river's settling. We'll take the spillgates to quarter-open and release the floodwaters at forty cubic feet per second. That should mitigate the impact downriver."

Forty cubic feet sounded like a whole lot to Sydney, but from the grunts of agreement that rose all around her, she suspected it would do the trick. The fierce expression in Reece's eyes when he turned to her confirmed her suspicions.

"We did it! We beat the river."

Smiling, she shook her head. "You did it."

"Stay here, okay? Don't go near the ramparts until we bring the floodwaters down and I give the all clear." A glint of laughter lightened the intensity of his blue eyes. "I don't think my heart could take having to haul you out of any more trees or floods."

"I don't think mine could, either!"

He kissed her, hard and fast and very thoroughly, then strode off to join his men.

Sighing, Sydney watched him disappear into the administration building. She would have preferred to go with him, to get a glimpse of what came next. She needed the visual to flesh out the idea for the documentary that had taken shape in her head.

She'd use stock footage from the thirties and forties. Show the construction of the early dams like Hoover and Hungry Horse up in Montana. Document their repairs over the years. Highlight the efforts of today's engineers to adapt yesterday's structures to new technology, new environmental standards. The theme would be man working with nature, struggling to find that perfect balance between...

The sight of Jamie Chavez standing alone beside his chopper shut down her rush of creative enthusiasm like a fist falling on steel. As she watched, he turned to climb back into the helo.

He was going to look for his father. She saw it in his bleak face and stiff, jerky movements.

Despite the terror Sebastian had put her through, she understood his son's pain. She'd gone through the same, searing loss herself just a few months ago. She didn't move, didn't try to stop him. There'd be time enough later to tell him what happened down at the ruins, tell him as well about his mother.

That time came late that evening.

Haggard and slump-shouldered, Jamie walked into the Lone Eagle Café. Arlene was at his side. She spotted Sydney and Reece first.

Across tables littered with the remains of the steak and beans Reece's ravenous crew had wolfed down, the two women stared at each other. Without saying a word, Arlene left her husband's side and crossed the room.

Reece rose at her approach. He kept silent, recognizing that this was between the two of them.

"I'm sorry," Arlene said hoarsely. "About your videotapes. About—" she lifted a hand so thin the veins stood out, let it drop "—about everything."

Sydney nodded.

"The search-and-rescue crew found Sebastian's body."

"We heard."

Arlene swallowed painfully. "Jamie's devastated, but he has to—He wants to—"

"I have to know," her husband finished, coming to stand behind his wife.

Once more Sydney nodded. "We can go to Reece's room and talk there."

"This is fine," Jamie said with a twist of his lips. "There are no secrets in a small town. You know that."

"Maybe not," Lula put in, huffing out from behind the counter, "but some matters are best left between friends and family."

Plunking mugs of coffee down on the table for Arlene and Jamie, she proceeded to clear the café of everyone but the four people at the table. The door slammed behind her.

With a gesture of weary courtesy, Jamie pulled a chair out for his wife. He sank down in the one next to her.

Sydney had spent most of the afternoon trying to decide how to tell him about his father's desperation. *Whether* to tell him. Sebastian was dead. Would it help his son to know that the father he loved had killed his mother?

Sydney had spent her adult years recording the truth

as seen through a camera. As a documentarian, she knew that truth was never what it seemed. But this story wasn't hers to edit or shape. She knew she had to tell Jamie those harsh, bare facts and let him shape his own truth.

Swallowing, she related the story of the Weeping Woman of Chalo Canyon.

Three days later, Joe Martinez and two other deputies, assisted by a forensics specialist and an archeologist from the University of Arizona uncovered a set of bones buried beneath the rubble in the square tower. The archeologist confirmed that skeletal remains belonged to a female. The forensics specialist identified what looked like a bullet hole in her skull.

Epilogue

Sydney sat bathed in moonlight on a limestone outcropping, her arms wrapped around her knees, her gaze on the ruins across the canyon. A camera mounted on a tripod whirred beside her.

After four long months, the reservoir was slowly rising. After the damage caused by the flood and the extra reinforcement Reece had insisted on, repairs to the dam had taken longer than originally planned. Now they were done, and the water was once again rising up the canyon walls. She couldn't see its movement, couldn't measure its exact progress, but the dark waves lapped at the floor of the cave.

Soon the magical, mystical village she'd first seen as a child would sink into another long sleep. The ruins wouldn't see sunlight for ten years…more than ten years, if Reece's modified repairs proved as cost effective as he predicted.

His job here was done. Hers, too, once the village slipped beneath the waters and disappeared.

Sydney had spent the past three months editing her work, adding structure and definition to the raw footage, inserting titles and graphics, recording narration and music…in effect, sculpting her story. The rough cut had thrilled her. The fine cut would come as soon as she added the ending.

This ending.

Shivering with mingled regret and anticipation, Sydney leaned back against the solid chest behind her. Reece's arms came around her.

"Cold?"

"No. Just…sad that it's almost over. And eager to get on to the next project."

"The next project being our wedding, or your new documentary?"

Laughing, she twisted in his arms. "Our wedding. Definitely our wedding. Your brothers have threatened me with all kinds of dire retribution if I don't make an honest man out of you."

A grin tugged at Reece's lips. "You sure you want to get married on the ranch? We could sneak off for a Vegas quickie."

"No way!"

Sydney had already visited the sprawling spread Reece still thought of as home. It had been a flying trip, one day up and one day back, since she was still rushing to make her deadline. In her nervousness at meeting his mother, four brothers and two sisters-in-law, Sydney hadn't taken a camera with her. She'd regretted the omission as soon as she saw the Bar-H and the men it had bred.

She couldn't wait to go back and capture the grandeur of the San Franciscos against the blue sky...not to mention the grandeur of the *Henderson Hunks,* as the latest addition to the family had privately dubbed them.

Molly Duncan Henderson, recently married to Reece's youngest brother, Sam, had confided to Sydney that the Henderson brothers still overwhelmed her. Individually they could charm the fillings out of a girl's teeth. Collectively, they made for a powerful family. One that had welcomed Sydney with laughter and a readiness to love.

The aching sense of loss she felt at her father's death had eased up there, surrounded by Reece's family. She wanted them all at her wedding. Every one of them.

"You don't know what you're letting yourself in for," her soon-to-be groom warned when she told him so.

"Funny, that's what every one of your brothers said. Marsh, in particular, had some interesting stories to tell about you."

"Ha!" Reece unfolded his long length and rose, then lifted Sydney off the slab of limestone. "Marsh is a cynical cop who thinks every male is a potential criminal. Don't listen to him."

"What does he think about every female?"

The teasing light in Reece's eyes dimmed. "He got hurt a while back. He's still hurting."

Sydney started to ask him how, but it occurred to her that maybe Reece really didn't want to get married at the Bar-H. Maybe he, too, still carried painful memories.

After one long, particularly satisfying bout of lovemaking, they'd lain in each other's arms, talking about where they'd live between their respective travels, about dams and documentaries, about her father…and his.

The story had come out slowly, bit by agonizing bit. In a tight voice, Reece had shared with her what he'd never shared with his brothers. She'd held her breath while he described that awful night he'd listened to his mother sob, walked her up and down the living room, felt his faith in his father crumble into dust.

Maybe…maybe he didn't want to go back to the Bar-H and celebrate their marriage in the shadow of his mother's unhappiness. Rising up on tiptoe, Sydney cupped his face with both hands.

"What about you, Reece? Are you still hurting? Will it pain you to share our vows in the place where your parents' marriage fell apart?"

"No," he said simply. "It's home. It always will be home." A glint of laughter crept into his eyes. "Especially if I end up having to pay for the damage to that crane. We won't be able to afford anything else."

Sydney huffed with indignation, as he'd known she would. She'd been bristling ever since he explained that a report of survey, to document the damage to the crane, had to be processed before he was cleared of all liability.

"*No one* in any bureaucracy in any country in the world would charge you for that. You saved a whole town, for Pete's sake!"

He tried to look humble, but laughter kept tickling the back of his throat. She looked so fierce, so ready to take on all comers.

"Well, I wouldn't go that far."

"I would!" She flung her arms around his neck. "You saved me, too, Reece."

"Several times," he agreed dryly.

He still shuddered every time she drove off in a car, her mind going a thousand miles a minute, her thoughts on the great visuals out the window instead of the road.

"You're still saving me," she murmured, dragging his mouth down to hers. "You save me every time you do this. And this. And—"

"Sydney…"

Groaning, he sank to his knees.

She came down with him, love splintering through her at the magical touch of his hands, his mouth. Whatever came, wherever his work and her films took them, they would always, always have this.

Behind them, the camera whirred. Across the canyon, the ruins sank slowly under the water and settled into sleep once more. A light breeze played across the surface of the water, carrying with it a sound that could have been a soft, gentle, smiling sigh.

* * * * *

The silence on the car ride to the public hearing at the Chicago
Board of Education building on Madison Street was jaw-dropping.
Mingus maneuvered his car through traffic, his expression smug
as he stole occasional glances in her direction. Joanna stared out
the passenger-side window, still lost in the heat of Mingus's touch.
That kiss had left her shaking, her knees quivering and her heart
racing. She couldn't not think about it if she wanted to.

His kiss had been everything she'd imagined and more. It
was summer rain in a blue sky, fudge cake with scoops of praline
ice cream, balloons floating against a backdrop of clouds, small
puppies, bubbles in a spa bath and fireworks over Lake Michigan.
It had left her completely satiated and famished for more. Closing
her eyes and kissing him back had been as natural as breathing.
And there was no denying that she had kissed him back. She hadn't
been able to speak since, no words coming that would explain the
wealth of emotion flowing like a tidal wave through her spirit.

They paused at a red light. Mingus checked his mirrors and
the flow of traffic as he waited for his turn to proceed through

the intersection. Joanna suddenly reached out her hand for his, entwining his fingers between her own.

"I'm still mad at you," Joanna said.

"I know. I'm still mad at myself. I just felt like I was failing you. You need results and I'm not coming up with anything concrete. I want to fix this and suddenly I didn't know if I could. I felt like I was being outwitted. Like someone's playing this game better than I am, but it's not a game. They're playing with your life, and I don't plan to let them beat either one of us."

"From day one you believed me. Most didn't and, to be honest, I don't know that anyone else does. But not once have you looked at me like I'm lying or I'm crazy. This afternoon, you yelling at me felt like doubt, and I couldn't handle you doubting me. It broke my heart."

Mingus squeezed her fingers, still stalled at the light, a line of cars beginning to pull in behind him. "I don't doubt you, baby. But we need to figure this out and, frankly, we're running out of time."

The honking of a car horn yanked his attention back to the road. He pulled into the intersection and turned left. Minutes later he slid into a parking spot and shut down the car engine. Joanna was still staring out the window.

"Are you okay?" he asked.

Joanna nodded and gave him her sweetest smile. "Yeah. I was just thinking that I really like it when you call me 'baby.'"

Don't miss
Tempted by the Badge *by Deborah Fletcher Mello,*
available March 2019 wherever
Harlequin® Romantic Suspense books
and ebooks are sold.

www.Harlequin.com

Looking for more satisfying love stories
with community and family at their core?

Check out **Harlequin® Special Edition**
and **Love Inspired®** books!

New books available every month!

CONNECT WITH US AT:

Facebook.com/groups/HarlequinConnection

Facebook.com/HarlequinBooks

Twitter.com/HarlequinBooks

Instagram.com/HarlequinBooks

Pinterest.com/HarlequinBooks

ReaderService.com

**ROMANCE WHEN
YOU NEED IT**

HFGENRE2018

He knew she was shaken, but he wasn't ready to let her out of his sight. "Melissa, you could have been hurt tonight." Killed, but he couldn't allow himself to voice that awful thought aloud. "I'll see that you get home safely, so don't argue."

Melissa rubbed a hand over her eyes. She was obviously so exhausted she simply nodded and slipped from his SUV. Just as he thought, the beat-up minivan belonged to her.

She jammed her key in the ignition, the engine taking three tries to sputter to life.

Anger that she sacrificed so much for others mingled with worry that she might have died doing just that.

She deserved so much better. To have diamonds and pearls. At least a car that didn't look as if it had been rolled twice.

He glanced back at the shelter before he pulled from the parking lot. Melissa was no doubt worried about the men she'd had to move tonight. But worry for her raged through him.

He knew good and damn well that many of the men who ended up in shelters had simply fallen on hard times and needed a hand. But others…the drug addicts, mentally ill and criminals…

He didn't like the fact that Melissa put herself in danger by trying to help them. Tonight's incident proved the facility wasn't secure.

The thought of losing her bothered him more than he wanted to admit as he followed her through the streets of Austin. His gut tightened when she veered into an area consisting of transitional homes. A couple had been remodeled, but most looked as if they were teardowns. The street was not in the best part of town, either, and was known for shady activities, including drug rings and gangs.

Her house was a tiny bungalow with a sagging little porch and paint-chipped shutters, and sat next to a rotting shanty, where two guys in hoodies hovered by the side porch, heads bent in hushed conversation as if they might be in the middle of a drug deal.

He gritted his teeth as he parked and walked up the graveled path to the front porch. She paused, her key in hand. A handcrafted wreath said Welcome Home, which for some reason twisted his gut even more.

Melissa had never had a real home, while he'd grown up on the ranch with family and brothers and open land.

She offered him a small smile. "Thanks for following me, Dex."

"I'll go in and check the house," he said, itching to make sure that at least her windows and doors were secure. From his vantage point now, it looked as if a stiff wind would blow the house down.

She shook her head. "That's not necessary, but I appreciate it." She ran a shaky hand through her hair. "I'm exhausted. I'm going to bed."

She opened the door and ducked inside without another word and without looking back. An image of her crawling into bed in that lonely old house taunted him.

He wanted to join her. Hold her. Make sure she was all right tonight.

But that would be risky for him.

Still, he couldn't shake the feeling that she was in danger as he walked back to his SUV.

Don't miss
Hostage at Hawk's Landing *by Rita Herron,*
available March 2019 wherever
Harlequin® Intrigue books and ebooks are sold.

www.Harlequin.com

HIEXP0219

Love Harlequin romance?

DISCOVER.

Be the first to find out about promotions, news and exclusive content!

Facebook.com/HarlequinBooks

Twitter.com/HarlequinBooks

Instagram.com/HarlequinBooks

Pinterest.com/HarlequinBooks

ReaderService.com

EXPLORE.

Sign up for the Harlequin e-newsletter and download a free book from any series at **TryHarlequin.com.**

CONNECT.

Join our Harlequin community to share your thoughts and connect with other romance readers!
Facebook.com/groups/HarlequinConnection

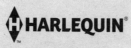

HARLEQUIN®

ROMANCE WHEN
YOU NEED IT

HSOCIAL2018

Reward the book lover in you!

Earn points on your purchase of new Harlequin books from participating retailers.

Turn your points into **FREE BOOKS** of your choice!

Join for FREE today at
www.HarlequinMyRewards.com.

Harlequin My Rewards is a free program (no fees) without any commitments or obligations.

MYR1